TIGER, TIGER

Philip Caveney was born in North Wales in 1951. The son of an RAF officer, he spent much of his childhood travelling the length and breadth of Britain and later lived for several years in Malaysia and Singapore.

His first novel, *The Sins of Rachel Ellis*, was published in 1977. Since then, he has published many novels for adults and since 2007, a series of children's books that have sold all over the world. In 2012, his children's novel *Night on Terror Island* won the Brilliant Books Award.

Find out more on his website:
www.philip-caveney.co.uk

By Philip Caveney

TIGER TIGER

Philip Caveney

HARPER

Harper
An imprint of HarperCollins*Publishers*
1 London Bridge Street
London SE1 9GF

www.harpercollins.co.uk

This paperback edition 2015
1

First published in 1984 by Granada Publishing
Copyright © Philip Caveney 1984
Philip Caveney asserts the moral right to be identified
as the author of this work

A catalogue record for this book is
available from the British Library

ISBN: 9780008138479

MARION BURNS,
ROBBIE ROBINSON.
Good friends both, sadly missed,
This book is for them

ONE

ONE

Chapter 1

The afternoon sun was still fierce. Haji lay stretched out in the shade of a bamboo thicket, his head resting on his great paws. Aligned with the shadows cast through the bamboo screen, the jet-black stripes that crisscrossed his tawny body served to render him virtually invisible. He lay stock-still, but for all that he was not comfortable. There was a dull ache of hunger in the pit of his stomach and his right forepaw throbbed relentlessly where the spines of a *tok landak* had struck him some weeks ago. He had long since chewed the protruding ends away, but the barbed heads had remained buried deep in the flesh of his foot, where they had begun to suppurate. The earlier agonizing pain had given way to a constant nagging ache that was with him every moment of the day and night.

He was an old tiger, and sixteen years of prowling swamps and jungles without serious harm should have taught him more caution. But the hunting had been bad for a long time now and the porcupine's succulent flesh had been a tempting proposition. Perhaps Haji was simply not as fast as he had once been. At any rate, in attempting to flip the spiny creature over onto its back to expose the vulnerable underbelly, something had gone wrong. The *tok landak* had scuttled away to safety, leaving Haji roaring with pain and frustration. Since then, the hunting had not got any easier.

Haji lifted his head slightly and stared through the screen of bushes into the *kampong*, twenty yards to his right. A large group of Upright cubs were playing a noisy game of *Sepak Takraw*, kicking a rattan ball to each other over an improvised net. The cubs were very skilful and the ball rarely touched the ground. The frenzied cries and shouts of their strange squeaky language echoed on the still air. Haji's yellow eyes took in every movement. He watched with curiosity and a little fear; he feared the Uprights as he feared anything which he did not readily understand, but some-

3

thing had called him from the depths of the jungle this day and he had forsaken the constant hunt for food in order to travel out into patches of secondary jungle and scrub. He knew he would not rest easy until it was done. Now, here he lay, closer to the Uprights' lair than he had ever been, and there was nothing for him to do but lie silent and still while he watched.

The Uprights had always mystified him: these strange hairless creatures that walked on two legs, possessed incredible powers, could march around the jungle, seemingly oblivious to the fact that a bigger and stronger creature was lying mere inches from where their tiny feet trod. On the few occasions when Haji had actually made his presence known, the Uprights had all reacted in a variety of extraordinary ways. Some had simply fled, howling and screaming in a most curious fashion, while others had clambered clumsily onto the branches of nearby trees. Most confusing of all, two of these uprights had on separate occasions produced some black sticks that roared fire at Haji, a moving fire that seemed to tear at the bushes and earth, shattering it into abrupt movement. On these two misadventures, it had been Haji who chose to run away, for such things were not then within the range of his experience. He knew now that the black sticks carried death to those animals who did not run quite fast enough, though he could not comprehend how such a thing might be brought about. Once, while Haji had been painstakingly stalking a large *rusa*, an Upright had approached from another direction, pointed his black stick at the beast, and the roaring fire had struck the *rusa* so hard that his whole body shook. Then he had fallen, as dead as a stone.

Haji put out his long rasping tongue and licked absentmindedly at his paw. The action revived fresh spasms of pain from the wound and he growled softly at the discomfort. It hurt his pride to think how clumsy he'd been with the *tok landak*, but it was a pride tempered with healthy respect. He would have to be very hungry indeed before he tackled another of the wretched beasts.

An extra loud yell from the cubs focused his attention, and suddenly something crashed down into the bushes by

4

his side, startling him and almost putting him to flight. But he caught himself as he realized that it was just the rattan ball, which had sailed over the heads of the nearest cubs and come to a halt mere feet from Haji's outstretched paws. He sniffed at it suspiciously, but it lay quite still and harmless and he relaxed again. After a few moments, there was a pounding of naked feet on earth and one of the cubs approached the undergrowth. He snatched up a length of stick and began to poke around in the bushes, probably more wary of snakes than of anything else. He did not see Haji lying in the shade of the bamboo. Haji watched with calm interest. The Upright was small and carried no black stick. He seemed to offer little threat.

The other cubs began to shout and wave. Tired of the game, they were moving on. They beckoned for the lone cub to accompany them, but he pointed into the bushes and jabbered something in his curious high-pitched voice. Evidently the rattan ball belonged to him and he wanted to retrieve it. The others wandered away and it was very quiet now. The Upright turned back and began to employ the stick more aggressively, muttering softly to himself as he searched. He moved a few steps nearer to Haji and looked there, stooping down on one knee and pushing the thick leaves aside with his bare arm. He was so close now that Haji could smell his half-naked little body; the faint odour of sweat drifting from beneath his armpits; the aroma of rice and cooked meat on his breath. Now, the cub's gaze fell on the bamboo thicket. Through the gaps in the upright stalks, he could perceive the shadowy sphere that was his ball. With an exclamation of relief, he moved forward and thrust an arm into the thicket to try and retrieve the ball. It was quite a stretch.

Haji gazed at the little brown hand as it grasped the ball, no more than two feet from his own paws. It was a strange-looking arrangement, more like a soft brown crab with wriggling feet than anything else. But it gripped the ball surely and snatched it out from the cover into sunlight. The cub got to his feet as though to walk away, but then he hesitated, sniffing the air suspiciously. He gazed intently into the thicket, scratching his head in puzzlement. Then he sank down again onto one knee, reached out to push the screen of bamboo aside . . .

'Ché!' A mother's voice from somewhere in the *kampong*. 'Ché!' The cub frowned, half turned, stared off into the jumble of tumbledown dwellings as though reluctant to answer his mother's call. He turned back to the bamboo, reached out his hands again . . .

'Ché!' Again the call, more insistent now. It was time to eat, or wash, or sleep. The cub's tiny fingers, curled around the stems of bamboo, slid gently away. With a sigh, he collected his ball and trudged wearily homewards, forgetting now the unfamiliar odour that had initially roused his curiosity.

Haji watched the cub walk away into the lengthening shadows of late afternoon. Soon, the sun would die bloodily on the horizon and the brief twilight would come and go in silence. In the high-stilted *kampong* houses, oil lamps would be lit and prayers would be muttered to safeguard the villagers from the demons of advancing darkness. And for Haji, the long night's hunt would begin.

He got to his feet and, silent as a ghost, he limped away.

Harry 'Tiger' Sullivan was occupying his favourite table at the Officers' Mess, Kuala Hitam barracks. It was a table like all the others, but it was placed in a strategic position where the sitter could take in every corner of the Mess at a glance. Harry had been using the same table for something like eighteen years now, and it was an unspoken custom in the Mess to leave it free whenever Harry was around. In retirement, he used the table as often as he had when he was a Lieutenant Colonel with the resident regiment, the Fourth Gurkha Rifles. He had now been retired for five years but was as much a central figure at the Mess as he had ever been. Nobody would have dreamed of questioning his presence there.

Trimani, the white-coated Tamil barman, approached the table with the customary chilled glass of 'Tiger' beer. The care and reverence with which Trimani went about the task made it almost a religious ceremony. The glass was wearing a clean towelling band to make it more agreeable to the touch.

'Thank you, Trimani.' Harry put a hand into the breast pocket of his cotton jacket and pulled out a leather wallet containing five cigars. He extracted one, cut the end with a silver gadget he always carried, and placed the cigar between his lips. Trimani was waiting with a match and Harry puffed contentedly, releasing clouds of aromatic smoke.

'The Tuan has had a good day?' ventured Trimani politely. Like every other aspect of the ceremony it was a habitual question.

'Very good, Trimani, thank you very much.' And Harry dropped a fifty-cent coin into the barman's silver tray. With a respectful nod, Trimani retired to his usual place behind the bar.

Harry sighed. The truth of the matter was, of course, that it had been a bloody boring sort of day. Most days for him had been bloody boring since he had left the forces; or more accurately, since he had been obliged to leave the forces. He had always felt bitter about that.

Harry was sixty-seven years old, but few people would have thought it. He was a thin wiry individual with not a pound of excess fat on his body. Though iron grey, his hair was thick (and a shade on the long side by forces standards) and his moustache was immaculately trimmed. He was undoubtedly the most popular officer that the regiment had ever possessed, and he was regarded now by the men with a peculiar kind of affection that elevated him almost to the role of a mascot. His connections with the Fourth went back a long way. He had originally served with them as a junior officer in India during the Burma campaign, where he had steadily risen through the ranks. He had come across to Malaya with them in 1948, where he commanded them during the ten-year 'confrontation' with the Communist terrorists. He had seen the task through admirably, and had expected to move on with them to Sarawak in 1962 to help quell the Brunei Revolt. But a medical examination had discovered a tricky heart problem and he had been promptly – and rather unceremoniously, he thought – dumped in favour of a younger man. Shortly after that, he had been 'bowler-hatted', though he had moved heaven and earth in an attempt to stay in longer. It had been to no avail. He was sixty-three years old and, whatever his views concerning his own health, he must stand aside and give somebody else a chance. And so, reluctantly, he had settled down to enjoy an idyllic, well-pensioned retirement.

And that was where his problems had really begun. A man who had spent his life with energy, authority, and decisiveness did not take very kindly to lazing about on beaches or beside swimming pools, and there was not a great deal more to do in this lonely outpost. Situated in the Dungun district of South Trengganu, on the east coast of the Malay Peninsula, the area was little more than several isolated *kampongs*, the barracks and a few accompanying dwellings, dotted at intervals of a mile or so along the main coast road to Kuala Trengganu, the state capital. All around lay thick and virtually inaccessible jungle. The barracks had been established as a forward grouping point in the campaign against the C.T.s, who had known only too well how to use the jungle to their own advantage. But the emergency had officially ended in 1960, and most of the troops had been dispatched back to the main barracks in Singapore. Now Kuala Hitam was maintained by what amounted to a skeleton crew; worse still, recent rumours of major cutbacks in the Gurkha regiments had become more than just rumours. The numbers were to be whittled down to a mere ten thousand men. For the rest, the prospects were nothing more than a meagre pension or redundancy payment and a one-way ticket back to their homes in India, where they were expected to pick up from where they had left off in 1940. The decision meant inevitable poverty and heartbreak for the majority of men, but, as always, the Gurkhas had accepted their fate with quiet humility. Now it was simply a question of waiting. Harry shared the feelings of regret, but was unable to change anything. His voice, which had once carried so much power in these matters, was now rendered useless; a vague, impotent whimper.

Harry raised the glass of beer to his lips and drank a silent toast to an old adversary, the head of which glowered down at him from above the doorway of the Mess. The taxidermist, as usual, had done a good job, but somehow

8

they were never able to capture that certain look. The tiger's eyes were blind glass, staring vacantly down at the peaceful crowd below. The expression of feral rage was totally contrived. He had died with a look of complete peace on his face; and, in dying, he had gazed up at Harry, seeming to ask, Why?

'Because you're a cattle-killer,' Harry had answered in his mind, knowing in his soul that this was not really the truth. His words had rung hollow, and after some deliberation, he had had to admit that the months of trailing and tracking and sitting up nights over the stinking carcasses of slain cows and goats had all been done in the name of 'sport.' Cattle-killing was merely the excuse, a means to an end. The look in that dying tiger's eyes had shaken him badly. He could not rid his mind of the image for days afterwards, and he had never gone hunting again. That had been back in 1958. He still cleaned and oiled the rifle regularly, more from force of habit than from any conscious intention to use it again. He had impulsively bequeathed the trophy to his regiment, having no desire to put it in his own home. He had realized too late that the beast would always be there in the Mess, staring down at him in silent accusation. Thus, another little ceremony was born. A toast from one tiger to another. After all, it was the death of this cat and many others like him that had earned Harry his nickname; what more fitting celebration than to drink to the creature in 'Tiger' beer, that infamous beverage that was both the delight and the ruin of the armed forces in Malaysia?

The beer was a delicious shock to his dehydrated insides. He set the glass down carefully and tilted back his head a little, allowing the electric fan above him to direct a cooling breeze onto his face and neck. He closed his eyes and gave a small sigh of contentment.

'Bloody hell, Trim, pour me a big one! I've got a mouth like a badger's bum! Oh no, you don't, lads, the first round is mine . . .'

Harry opened his eyes again, the peace and quiet having been rudely shattered by an unfamiliar Australian voice that had all the delicacy of a drum kit falling down a flight of stairs. A small group of young officers had just trooped into

9

the Mess, headed by somebody who was a stranger to Harry. He was a tall athletic fellow, with close-cropped fair hair. Evidently a civilian, judging by his sloppy T-shirt and blue jeans; even out of uniform, military men maintained a certain bearing that was unmistakable.

'Now, alright, Jim, what're you having? What? I should bloody well say so! And how about you? Aw, for chrissakes, have whatever you like! No, no, honestly . . . make that a double, Trim, and make sure it is a bloody double, too! Have one yerself while you're about it . . .'

Harry frowned. There was not a man in the world who could call him a racist. After all, he had worked side by side with the Gurkhas for half his life, and he thought them one of the most agreeable races he had ever encountered. Likewise, he loved and respected the Malays, Indians, and Chinese who peopled the Peninsula; the homely Burmese people he had met in the war. He had even come to honour the Japanese nation against whom he had fought for so long. But try as he might to be fair and totally objective, he could not bring himself to like the Australians. He imagined that, somewhere, there must exist an antipodean male that was not loud, boorish, and obsessed with booze and dirty stories. Unfortunately, he had yet to meet this man.

'Here, this one'll kill ya! There's this bloke, see, goes to the doctor cause he can't get it up anymore. His sheila's goin' berserk with 'im, reckons he don't love her anymore. Anyway, the doctor tells 'im to drop his trousers and when he does, the bloke's got this great big . . .' The rest of the story was obliterated by a burst of raucous laughter from the young officers.

Harry was quietly outraged by this lack of respect. In his day, a certain restraint had always been observed around the Mess; it had been a place where gentlemen congregated. Of course, there had always been room for a certain amount of high-spirits, but the telling of off-colour jokes in a voice loud enough to wake the dead seemed to illustrate just how drastically standards had dropped in the last decade. What seemed most upsetting to Harry was the fact that the young officers were openly encouraging this oaf to do his worst. Well, it was plain that somebody had to draw the line, even

10

if it simply meant removing oneself from the scene of the outrage as quickly as possible. Harry drained his glass, banged it down on the table with just enough force to turn a few heads at the bar. Then he stood up, nodded curtly to Trimani, and strolled out of the room. Trimani smiled apologetically as Harry passed by him. He, at least, understood.

Outside, the night was humid and cacophonous with the chirping of a myriad insects. Some large fat moths flapped vainly around the lantern that overhung the entrance to the Mess. The grizzled old *trishaw* man who had appointed himself Harry's customary driver for this journey eased his creaking vehicle around to the base of the white stone steps. In the glow of his oil lamp, beneath the wide brim of his coolie hat, the man's wizened face looked almost skeletal. He grinned gummily.

'*Selamat petang*, Tuan. You leave early, yes?'

'Yes, we leave now.' Harry smiled warmly at the old Chinese man, whose name he had never enquired after. He could never remember Chinese names anyway. 'Tonight not good for me. Too noisy.'

The driver nodded. He too was a seeker after peace and understood only too well. He waited patiently while Harry climbed into the seat, then gratefully accepted the cigar that was passed to him. He leaned forward as Harry's lighter flared, and inhaled with slow satisfaction. Then he leaned back, removed the cigar, and grinned again.

'Good,' he murmured. 'Good cigar. I thank the Tuan.' He engaged his sandalled feet on the pedals and his skinny legs performed the motion they had been making half his life. The *trishaw* accelerated away from the Mess, crunching on the gravel drive and then turning out onto the deserted road, its lantern blazing a lonely message in the darkness. They began to pick up speed, the wheels making a dry whirring sound as they sped past the black silhouettes of secondary jungle that flanked their path. Riding in this way, smoking with his old travelling companion, Harry felt a peculiar peace settle around him, and he found himself wishing that time could be suspended, and that this long gliding ride through the night might somehow last forever.

Chapter 2

Haji was still patrolling the western end of his extensive home range. It was always necessary to keep on the move, because potential prey soon became alerted to his presence in an area and promptly moved on. It took Haji around ten to twelve days to complete a trip around his territory, which consisted of a rough triangle of fifteen square miles. Right now, he was prowling the secondary jungle that ran beside the coast road, for he had long ago learned that troops of monkeys often chose to congregate there, thinking themselves safe so near to the wandering grounds of the Uprights. When they thought themselves to be beyond danger, they sometimes got careless and were slow to react to an unexpected attack . . . but tonight, Haji was out of luck. Somehow the monkeys had got wind of his notion and stayed safely in the topmost limbs of the Meranti trees.

Haji was unhappy, but quite used to such hard times. Even when the hunting was good, he could expect eighteen unsuccessful stalks for each triumph. The rest of the jungle creatures conspired against him. The monkeys gibbered his presence from the tall trees and the birds, hearing this, quickly took up the cry. The *rusa* uttered their distinctive 'pooking' sound to alert their brothers, whenever their sharp noses picked up the merest trace of that distinctive, musky, tiger smell. Hampered as he was by his wound and his advancing years, Haji was doing well to bring down one kill in thirty, and in between he could expect nothing but long bouts of frantic hunger. When at last he did succeed in killing something, a *rusa*, a wild pig, sometimes even a fat *seladang* calf (provided he could snatch the creature away from its massive, highly aggressive parents) then he would gorge himself until his stomach was a bloated obscenity, consuming maybe eighty pounds of meat in one sitting. It had been three days since he had devoured what remained of his last kill, an insubstantial mouse deer that hardly warranted the effort it had taken to stalk it. But hunger

12

dictated its own rules and the instinct for survival kept him moving.

He paused for a moment to listen. Far away to his right, deep in jungle sanctuary, the lonely sound of an argus pheasant calling to his mate. Silence for a moment and then a barking deer sounded an alarm as the wind carried a familiar odour to his nostrils. Haji growled softly to himself and was about to move on when a new sound came to his sensitive ears. He froze in his tracks, snapped his gaze to the roadside at his left. The sound was not made by any kind of animal that he knew of. It was a rapid whirring noise, much too loud to be produced by the wings of any insect. Haji slunk beneath the cover of some large ferns as a light came soaring out of the darkness. He twisted around, holding himself ready to run if need be. For an instant, the twin orbs of his eyes mirrored the bouncing reflection of the light.

A curious vehicle sped into view, a gleaming, clattering, froglike thing in which two Uprights were riding. Haji could see them quite clearly for an instant in the glow of the light, which swung from side to side in front of their heads, like a dangerous firefly. Haji could see the naked wrinkled sternness of their faces, as they gazed unswervingly at the road ahead of them. How foolish to travel in such an unthinking manner, always looking forward when danger might lie in the shadows at either side of them; or was it simply that the Uprights were so powerful, they did not fear the beasts of the jungle? They did not *look* very powerful, that was for sure.

The Uprights left a curious smell behind them on the wind, a fragrant burning-leaf smell that lingered on the warm air for some moments. Haji sniffed, grimaced, watched as the Uprights sped away into blackness, taking their light with them. For some time, he was still aware of the constant whirring noise, fading gradually into distance. Then his thoughts returned to the sound of the barking deer he had heard before the interruption. He emerged from the bushes and moved right of his original path, heading deeper into jungle, his head down, his mind intent on the long hunt ahead of him.

The barking deer sounded again and Haji homed in on

the noise, moving with the calm, silent intent of one who had been hungry for far too long.

The *trishaw* driver came to a halt outside Harry's bungalow, part of a small estate just off the coast road, a mile south of the nearest village, Kampong Panjang, which they had passed on the two-mile journey from Kuala Hitam barracks. Harry alighted and pressed a dollar into the driver's arthritic hand. The fare was always the same, whatever the distance, and the old man would probably have been insulted if Harry tried to give him more than that.

'Safe journey back,' he told the Chinaman.

'Of course, Tuan!' The old man grinned, waved briefly, and pedalled gamely away, hoping to reach his own home safely. Few *trishaw* owners ventured to drive at night, preferring to leave it to the taxicab drivers, but this engaging fellow had somehow discovered Harry's regular Mess nights and would not have dreamed of missing a single one of them. Neither, for that matter, would Harry have dreamed of using another driver.

'You get to a certain age,' thought Harry, 'and all your life becomes a ritual. Has to. The only way you can make any bloody sense of it.'

He unlatched the metal gate and strolled into the large, neatly ordered garden. The path was wide enough to take a car but curiously, in all his years in the army, he had never learned to drive. There had always been somebody to ferry him about and that was the way he preferred to keep things now. He strolled up the path, past banana and papaya trees, whistling tunelessly to himself. The bungalow was like many others, purposely built for British tenants. A long, low, white-painted building with a green slate roof and an adjoining verandah; it was compact, practical and possessed no particular style. The windows were comprised of slatted bars of frosted glass that could be levered open, like venetian blinds, to admit fresh air. These were reinforced by metal bars that had been disguised as wrought-iron decorations in an attempt to make them look more attractive. In fact, they looked quite hideous. Harry, who believed in calling a spade a spade, would have preferred

14

plain upright bars. A more acceptable feature were the sliding metal grills that could be padlocked across the front and back doors of the house. A legacy of more Communist-threatened times, they were still very useful weapons in the constant war against house-thieves that had been going on for many years and showed no signs of letting up yet.

No sooner had Harry inserted his key in the front door and stepped into the house, than Pawn, Harry's aged *amah*, came bustling up to greet him. There was a toothy smile of welcome on her wizened little monkey-face and she still held a straw broom with which she had presumably been dusting somewhere. Pawn never stopped work while she was in the house and when there was no work, she quite simply invented some. She lived at Kampong Panjang and usually went home to her own family at five o'clock. But on the nights that Harry went to the Mess, she insisted on staying the night in the *amah*'s room at the back of the house, to ensure that the 'Tuan' was properly looked after when he came in. Harry would quite happily have looked after himself, but once Pawn had an idea fixed firmly in her mind, it was impossible to shake it.

'Tuan have good time soldiers' Mess?' she inquired; and before waiting for a reply, she was hurrying off to the kitchen to prepare the cocoa and biscuits that Harry always had before retiring for the night.

He shook his head ruefully, wondering just exactly how it was that he had managed to get himself saddled with a cranky old creature like Pawn. Most of his acquaintances had pretty young Chinese *amahs* to care for their needs. It was easy enough to organize: there were countless agencies in Kuala Trengganu that specialized in providing the girls. You simply had to tell them what your preferences were and if the girl turned out to be lazy or inefficient, you simply sent her away and ordered another one. But Pawn now, she'd been a legacy of sorts. She'd worked for the previous occupant of the house, a mining engineer, and the day Harry had moved in she'd just arrived on his doorstep, walked past him into the house, and commenced work. Mind you, it was not as if Harry had any cause for complaint. She was an excellent worker, worth every cent of the one hundred and twenty dollars a month wage she received. This worked out at about fifteen pounds and was considered a decent wage by Malay standards. She was far too proud to accept anything more than her basic salary, but Harry had found that she was not averse to accepting little gifts from time to time, particularly if they were intended for her grandson, Ché, of whom she was very proud. The boy was a bright, articulate twelve-year-old, who sometimes accompanied his grandmother to the 'Tuan's' house and had, as a result, become a great friend of Harry's. In fact, if the truth were known, Harry doted on the boy, reserving for him the kind of affection that he would have given to his own son, if he had ever sired one.

A photograph of his late wife, Meg, stood on the sideboard. Harry walked over to it now, as he often did, picked it up, and stared thoughtfully at the face he had loved for so many years. She had always been a rather frail sort of creature and it was a wonder that she had ever taken to a life in the tropics as well as she had. She had died quite suddenly, in 1950, a cerebral haemorrhage. They had tried for children most of their married life, but something was evidently wrong with one of them. Ironically enough, the night before Meg had died, the two of them had discussed the possibility of adopting a Malaysian child. They had both been strongly in favour of the idea. Later, that same evening, Meg had awoken from sleep complaining of a terrible headache. She got up to go to the bathroom and fetch some aspirins, but halfway to the door, she had spun around to look at Harry, her face suddenly drained of colour and she had spoken his name once, softly, in a tiny, frightened tone. In that instant, he had somehow known that it was all over for her, that he would never hear her voice again. She had crumpled lifelessly to the floor before Harry could reach her and there was not a thing in the world he could have done to save her. Then, his grief and torment had been indescribable; but now, looking back with the advantage of hindsight, he knew that when his time came, this is how he would want it to be. Quick, clean, a minimum of fuss and pain; far better than lingering on in some hospital ward, a useless, incontinent old fossil. His own father had died that way, during the war. Harry had only been allowed leave to visit him once and he vividly remembered leaving the hospital room for the silence of the corridor outside, where he had proceeded to cry like a baby for several minutes, unable to stop himself. It was not the grief of losing his father that had affected him so; it was more a horror at the appalling loss of dignity the old man was suffering. He had been incapable of doing anything for himself by this time. In Harry's opinion, all a man had was his dignity. Lose that and you had lost the reason for living. But his father *had* lived on, a horrifying eighteen months longer in that tiny cheerless hospital room. It was Harry's personal nightmare to find himself with a similar prospect at the end of his life.

Pawn came bustling in with a silver tray holding the mug of cocoa and two digestive biscuits that constituted Harry's usual bedtime snack. He sat himself down in his favourite armchair, the tray placed on the table beside him. He glanced through the day's news in the *Straits Times*, but there was little that took his interest. Pawn excused herself and retired to her little room. Harry sipped at his cocoa and watched the antics of a couple of *chit-chats* on the ceiling above his head. The smaller of the two, presumably the male, was chasing his somewhat larger mate around the room, but she seemed to resent his advances, and consequently their antics took in every square inch of the wall and ceiling. Harry soon tired of them and, after locking doors and windows and switching off the lights, he retired to his bedroom. He changed into a pair of silk pyjamas, climbed into bed, and let the mosquito net down around him. He lay down for a few moments with the bedside light on, staring blankly up at the ceiling above his head. A varied collection of moths and other flying insects had congregated in the pool of light reflected on it, but Harry was hardly aware of them. He was thinking of the boorish Australian he had seen in the Mess earlier. For some reason he was not entirely sure of, he felt vaguely threatened by the man's presence. Perhaps he felt that this man represented the new order here on the archipelago, and perhaps he also realized that his kind was disappearing fast from these parts.

He smiled wryly.

'I'm an endangered species,' he murmured, and reaching out he switched out the light. He slept and dreamed he was riding in a *trishaw*.

Chapter 3

Haji woke from a fitful doze and the world snapped into focus as he opened his large yellow eyes. The first flame of dawn was still an unfulfilled promise on the far horizon and it was cool. The damp, shivering land awaited the first rays of warmth to ignite the spark of life. Haji stretched and yawned, throwing out a long rumbling growl that would have sounded more content had it been fuelled by a full belly. Wasting little time, he struck out along a well-worn cattle track into deep jungle, his eyes and ears alert to anything they might encounter. They were his greatest aids, much more developed than his comparatively poor sense of smell, and the day that they began to fail him would be the day that Haji would admit defeat. But now, there was a terrible hunger, knotting and coiling in his belly, and while his legs still possessed the strength to carry him he would hunt to the best of his ability, and somehow stay alive.

The jungle was beginning to come awake. There was a distant whooping of gibbons in the forest canopy, interspersed with the distinctive 'Kuang! Kuang!' cry of an argus pheasant. Black and yellow hornbills fluttered amongst the foliage and there was the familiar weeping tones of the bird that the Malays had named, *Burung Anak Mati* or 'bird whose child has died.' But none of that distracted Haji from his quest for what was good to eat and within his reach. Presently, his ears were rewarded by a rustling in the undergrowth some eighty yards ahead of him. He stopped in his tracks and listened intently. He could hear quite clearly the crunching of a deer's wide jaws on a bunch of leaves. Haji flattened himself down against the ground and began to move around to his right, keeping himself downwind of his intended prey, hoping to get it in sight. He moved with infinite care and precision, knowing that one telltale rustle in the grass would be enough to frighten the creature away. Slowly, slowly, setting down each foot in a carefully considered spot, he began to shorten the distance between himself and the deer. After twenty minutes, he had worked himself close enough to see it. A *rusa*, he could glimpse the rust-red hide, dappled by the rising sun. The *rusa* was nervous. He kept lifting his head between mouthfuls, staring skittishly this way and that. On such occasions, Haji remained still, not moving so much as a muscle. Each time that the deer returned to its meal, he inched forward again, his eyes never leaving the creature for an instant. In this way, another half-hour passed and now Haji was within twenty yards of the *rusa*; but here, the cover ended. There was a clearing now, over which he could not pass undetected. His only hope was to rush the beast and trust that the resulting panic would confuse his prey long enough for Haji to leap upon it. He flexed his muscles, craned forward, ready to rush upon the deer like a bow from an arrow; and in that instant, another deer further upwind caught the familiar smell of tiger and gave a loud cry of warning.

The *rusa* wheeled about with a snort, and with a bellow of rage Haji broke from cover, propelling his four hundred pounds of body weight along with tremendous bursts of power from his heavily muscled legs. For an instant, the *rusa* seemed frozen to the spot with fear, but abruptly the instinct for survival maintained itself and the deer turned and bolted across the clearing with Haji mere inches from his flying heels. But where Haji was already at top speed, the *rusa* was just approaching his. He lengthened his stride, sailed effortlessly across a fallen tree stump and was off, gathering speed all the time. Haji followed for just a few yards, knowing only too well when he was beaten. He dropped down onto the grass, panting for breath while he watched the *rusa* recede into distance, tail flashing impertinently at his would-be killer.

Haji fashioned his rage and frustration into a great blasting roar that seemed to shake the ground on which he stood. The noise disturbed a troop of pig-tailed monkeys

19

resting in the top limbs of a nearby Kapok tree. Safe in their leafy sanctuary, they began to chatter and shriek abuse at him, and Haji, blind to everything but his own anger, flung himself at the base of the tree and began to tear at the wood in a frenzy, his great claws rending the soft wood to shreds and scattering bits of tree bark in every direction. The monkeys quietened for a moment, but then, seeing that they were safe, began their impudent mockery again, leaping up and down on the branches and grimacing, while Haji raged vainly, far below them.

At last, his anger ran its course and he drew back from the tree, still growling bitterly beneath his breath. He paced up and down for a moment, ignoring the monkeys, his head low, his eyes fixed to the ground while he waited for the great calm to come to him again. At last it did. He stared once along the track the *rusa* had taken. No sense in going that way now, the deer's panic would have alerted every creature for miles in that direction. Haji gave one last roar, but this time it was controlled, decisive. He struck out along a path to his left which led to secondary jungle and, eventually, Kampong Panjang.

The monkeys watched him stalk away and they fell silent again. A couple of the braver ones stood tall and made threatening gestures with their arms in the direction he had gone; even so, it was some considerable time before they ventured to leave the safety of their tall Kapok tree.

Harry strolled in through the open glass doors of the Kuala Hitam Sports Club, nodding to the pretty Chinese receptionist, who rewarded him with a radiant smile. He passed through another open doorway and was outside again. He turned right, past the forest of white-painted chairs and tables that ran alongside the long open-air bar, which in turn overlooked the three well-maintained tennis courts belonging to the club. Harry had come for his regular game with Captain Dennis Tremayne, a long-standing friend who still served with the Fourth and was therefore a useful source of gossip where they were concerned. He was considerably younger than Harry, but that hardly seemed to matter. Tennis was the one sport that Harry really enjoyed

20

and he was thankful that he had never put on any weight in his advancing years. Nothing looked more ludicrous than a fat man in shorts attempting to play a game that was quite beyond his capabilities. But it was probably quite true to say that Harry cut a more imposing figure in shorts than Dennis, who, at the age of forty-four, was already a little on the stout side.

Harry spotted Dennis sitting at one of the small tables.

'Hello old chap!' chuckled Dennis. 'It seems we're a bit early for our game today. Let me get you a drink.'

'Fresh orange juice, please.' Harry settled into a chair as Dennis signalled to the barman.

'Two fresh oranges, please. Plenty of ice,' Dennis grinned and turned his attention to the game in progress. 'All action out there today,' he observed. 'Hope they don't expect that sort of routine from us.' He had a plump, ruddy-complexioned face that always wore a happy expression. His cornflower blue eyes were hidden today behind a pair of mirrored sunglasses. 'Strewth,' he exclaimed. 'Is it just me or does it get hotter here all the time?' He motioned to Harry's sweater. 'Beats me how you can wear that thing.'

'Well, don't forget Dennis, I've been living in this climate for most of my adult life. India, Burma, Malaya, all got one thing in common – they're bloody hot. Couldn't stand it any other way now.'

Dennis nodded.

'You er . . . wouldn't fancy going back to Blighty ever?'

'I should say not! I'd freeze to death.' He narrowed his eyes suspiciously. 'Why did you ask that?'

'Oh, no reason, really . . .'

'No reason, my hat! What's up? C'mon Dennis, spill the beans, you know you never could hide anything from me.'

Dennis raised his hands in capitulation.

'Alright, alright, I surrender!' He leaned forward, lowered his voice slightly. 'It's just that word came through today about some more cuts and –'

'*More* cuts!' Harry shook his head. 'Don't see how they can do it, frankly. Surely they've cut the Gurkhas down as much as they possibly can. Trimming the force to ten thousand men, it's butchery! '

Dennis nodded sympathetically.

'Well, you know my views on that one Harry, I couldn't agree with you more. But the particular news I'm referring to concerns Kuala Hitam in particular. Seems the top brass have got it into their heads that it's unnecessary. It's got to go, old son. Complete demobilization by 1969. Fact. Heard it myself, just this morning.'

'What . . . you mean . . . *everything*?'

'The works. Lock, stock, and barrel. What troops we leave in Malaya will be based at the barracks in Singapore. As for this lot – ' He gestured briefly around him and then made a sawing motion across his throat with his index finger. 'Which is why I asked you if you ever thought of going home,' he concluded.

Harry stared at the grey Formica top of the table.

'Dammit Dennis, this *is* my home. What the hell would there be for me over there, anyway? My relatives are all dead – '

'You've a nephew, haven't you?'

'Oh yes, and very pleased he'd be to have a crotchety old devil like me descending on his household from the far-off tropics, I'm sure.'

Dennis smiled. 'I wouldn't call you crotchety,' he said.

'Well, thank you for that anyway. But let's face it, Dennis, here I be and here I stay, until the Lord in all his infinite wisdom sees fit to reorganize my accommodation. What will you be doing?'

'Oh, I'll be going back home. Expecting confirmation any day now. Suffolk, I hope. Where my roots are. The fact is, I'm quite looking forward to it. I keep imagining snow at Christmas, all that sort of thing. I'm a romantic old devil at heart, you know. And Kate's thrilled to bits. There're lots of things she misses. Good shops, fashions, family . . . Well, she's all but got the bags packed.'

Harry nodded.

'And what about that pretty young daughter of yours?'

'I think Melissa is pleased too. Things are a bit too quiet around these parts for her liking.'

The barman arrived with the drinks, tall glasses filled with freshly blended orange juice and topped with crushed ice.

He set them down on the table and left.

'I'll miss you,' observed Harry, after a few moments' silence. 'I'll miss you all.'

'Yes . . . well, look here, old chap. If you ever want to come and visit us, there'll always be a place for you. I hope you realize that.'

Harry sipped his drink thoughtfully, and stared impatiently at the couple sweating it out on the tennis court. 'Are they never going to finish?' he muttered. 'In the old days, these games always finished bang on time . . .' His voice trailed off as he recognized one of the players. It was the loudmouthed Australian from the night before. 'I say Dennis, who *is* that fellow on the court?'

Dennis lifted his sunglasses, peered in the direction that Harry was indicating.

'It's Corporal Barnes, isn't it?'

'No, not him! The other one.'

'Oh! You mean Bob Beresford.'

'Do I indeed? And who, may I ask, is Bob Beresford? He's not an enlisted man, surely to God?'

'No, a civvy. He's working at Kuala Hitam on the Gurkha repatriation scheme though, so he's been given the run of the place.'

'Yes. He was at the Mess last night. Just what exactly is he supposed to be teaching the Gurkhas? How to tell dirty stories?'

'I don't think so. Farming techniques, I believe. You know . . . irrigation, animal husbandry, that sort of thing. How to make the most out of very limited resources, basically. I can't help thinking that these repatriation schemes are more an attempt to salve the British government's conscience than anything else. But Beresford seems to be making the best of it. He's certainly well-liked by the men.' Dennis smiled warily at Harry. 'I get the impression he hasn't made an instant hit with you though,' he observed.

Harry grimaced and shrugged.

'Well . . . you know how I feel about the Aussies, Dennis. I mean, good God, they've all descended from convicts anyway! And that one was in the Mess last night, shouting his mouth off to all and sundry, telling some filthy story . . . it . . . shows a lack of respect, that's all.'

Dennis chuckled.

'Oh come on, Harry. None of us are above telling a dirty story now and then. The British tell it in a whisper and the Aussies tell it to the world. I'm not so sure that they haven't got the healthier attitude. It just comes down to what you're used to really. Beresford isn't so bad; and I tell you what, you've got something in common with him.'

Harry fixed his friend with a suspicious look.

'Really? And what might that be?'

'By all accounts, he fancies himself a bit of a crack-shot. Done some hunting in his time, or so he tells me.'

Harry shook his head.

'I haven't hunted for years, as well you know. If this Beresford chap still does, it just confirms that he's got some growing up to do.'

Dennis laughed out loud.

'Good heavens, Harry, give the poor lad a break, will you! It seems you've really got it in for him.'

'Not at all, not at all! I just think people should show a little bit of resp – Ah, looks as though they've finally called it a day!'

Beresford and his partner were leaving the court. The Australian was pumping his partner's hand in what looked like an exaggerated display of good sportsmanship.

'Great game, Ron! Let me buy you a drink. . .'

Dennis and Harry collected their kit and walked out towards the court. Beresford eyed the two of them with a mocking glint in his eye. As he walked past, Harry distinctly heard the Australian say to Corporal Barnes, 'Strewth, look at these two old buggers goin' out for a bash!' Barnes smothered a laugh, but Harry pretended he had heard nothing. He wasn't going to let the observations of some jumped-up sheep-farmer from the outback make any impression on him. He followed Dennis into the court and closed the metal gate behind him.

Dennis had heard nothing of the brief exchange.

'Let's have a quick warm-up,' he suggested. Then he laughed. 'I say, that's a bit of a joke. I'm sweating like a pig *now*.' He trotted over to the far side of the court and Harry

24

served a lazy ball over to him. They played for some time in silence. They rarely bothered to score the games; it was playing that they relished, not winning.

The white surface of the court reflected the fierce sun up at them and it was somewhat like playing tennis on a vast electric hot plate. After a few moments their clothes were sticking to them. Harry played mechanically, his thoughts not really on the game.

For some reason, his mind had slipped back to a much earlier memory, a memory of Britain before the last war. He was unsure of the actual year, but it had been a fine summer and there was a tennis court not far from the family home in Sussex. He had been a young man in his twenties then, with no thought of enlisting in the army, no thought of doing anything in particular. His family was rich and landed and though he would never have admitted it at the time, he was a wealthy layabout. Life at his parents' home seemed to comprise an endless succession of parties, dances, frivolous social functions; and as the potential inheritor of his father's land and wealth, he was considered very eligible by the young ladies in the neighbourhood and did not go short of female companionship.

But marriage had been the last thing on his mind; at least, until that particular day, the day when they had all gone to play tennis and Harry had spotted an exquisite young female on the court, a frail little thing, dressed in white, who played tennis like nobody's business. Harry had watched her for ages as she dashed about the court, a look of grim determination on her pretty face. He had fallen in love with here then and there; and when his mother had wandered over to him to enquire what it was he was looking at, he had smiled at her and replied, 'My future wife, I think.'

Meg. Sometimes in the night, he lay alone in the darkness trying to conjure into his mind, a vision of her face. He could not do it. Her features were soft wax blurred by time. In the end, he would have to switch on the light and fetch her photograph, just to reassure himself that she *had* existed. It frightened him, this loss of definition. It made him wonder if the past was not just a series of hazy ghosts set to haunt him for eternity. . .

'Come on, Harry, wake up! You missed that by a mile.'

'Hmm?' The present came abruptly back into focus. Dennis was peering at him over the net.

'Do you want to rest for a moment?'

'Certainly not!' Harry retrieved the ball and stepped up to the serving line. He flung the ball skywards, whipped back his arm to serve. An unexpected pain lanced through his chest, making his breath escape in an involuntary exclamation of surpise.

The ball dropped untouched beside him and he stood where he was for a moment, swaying slightly. He could not seem to get his breath and his heart was thudding like a great hammer in his chest.

'Harry? Are you alright, old chap? You've gone white as a sheet.'

'Yes, yes! I'm fine . . .' Harry stooped to retrieve the ball but as he stood up, the court seemed to seesaw crazily from left to right. His racquet clattered to the ground and he flung out his arms to try to maintain his balance. Suddenly Dennis was at his side, supporting his arm.

'Here, here, old chap. You've been in the sun too long, I think.'

'Don't be ridiculous,' protested Harry feebly. 'I'll be fine in a moment. Let's play on.'

'I don't think we better had.' Dennis was easing him towards the exit. 'Come and sit down for a while, at least till the feeling passes.'

'This is really quite silly . . . I'm alright I tell you.' Harry was aware of anxious faces peering at him from the press of tables. He felt totally humiliated, an object of ridicule. He tried to detach his arm from Dennis's grasp, so that he might walk under his own steam, but when he exerted any effort, the dizziness seemed to get worse, filling his head with a powerful red hum. He felt vaguely nauseous.

'Here old chap, this way. Our table's just a few more feet . . .'

Out of the corner of his eye, Harry could see Beresford and his companion watching the scene with expressions of amusement on their faces. The Australian turned to mutter something to his companion and the two of them collapsed into fits of laughter. Harry wanted to die of shame. He was lowered into a seat and a cold drink was thrust into his hand.

'How do you feel Harry?' It was Dennis's voice, but it seemed terribly distant.

Harry forced a smile.

'I'll survive,' he muttered. 'Just a dizzy spell, that's all.'

'Alright . . .' Dennis sounded far from being reassured. 'I'll go and fetch your stuff.'

'But . . . aren't we going to play on again, in a minute or two?'

Dennis didn't answer, he just walked away, leaving Harry to brave the glare of two hundred sympathetic eyes. Harry could imagine what they were thinking.

'Poor old man. Poor old man. Poor *old* man . . .'

And he knew in his heart that he would never have the courage to come to this place again.

Bob Beresford threw his kit bag carelessly into the back of his beaten-up old Land Rover, climbed into the seat, kicked the engine into life and drove away from the sports club, chuckling to himself. Honestly, these bloody old majors who thought they were still fighting a bloody war! Malaya seemed to be full of them. Bob still wasn't quite sure what to think about Malaya. He missed the social life he had back in Oz, but it was plain that he'd landed himself a cushy number here with the repatriation scheme. The pay was excellent, considering that he only actually worked three mornings a week. The rest of the time was his own and though there wasn't a great deal to do, he certainly couldn't complain that he was overworked. The Gurkhas were a likable bunch of blokes who followed their various courses with quiet dedication. They never complained, though, of course, they had every reason to. After fighting Britain's wars for the last twenty years, they were being surreptitiously swept under the carpet. In similar circumstances, Bob would have been fighting and yelling every inch of the way, but in this instance it was simply none of his business.

As he drove, his eyes kept scanning the screens of secondary jungle on either side for signs of life. It was his old man's influence that had turned Bob into a keen amateur hunter; Roy Beresford had been an obsessive animal hunter most of his life. He was forever undertaking extensive hunting trips to New Zealand, after deer and boar mostly. Bob had never been old enough to accompany his father, but his earliest memories were of being in Roy's trophy room, standing beneath the gigantic spread of antlers belonging to a fine stag. Roy had told him the story of that particular hunt a hundred times. Where most children got fairy stories last thing at night, Bob got true-life adventures from his dad and thus, it was easy to see how the hunting bug had bitten him. Bob's greatest regret was that his father had died of cancer, long before he was big enough to accompany him on an expedition. Since then, Bob had been doing his utmost to wear his father's boots and the need to do so had become a singular obsession with him. As yet, he had not organized himself into hunting in Malaya. For one thing, the territory was completely new to him and he felt that he would first have to find himself a good guide, someone who knew how to track in such a difficult environment. The land here was, for the most part, covered in thick inaccessible jungle and Bob didn't much fancy the idea of wandering in there unaccompanied. But most of the locals he had talked to had displayed an astonishing ignorance of their native wildlife. Oh indeed, the Tuan was quite correct. There *were* tigers and *rusa* and wild pigs and even the occasional elephant out there somewhere, but why any man should be interested in going after the creatures was quite beyond them. It was part of the Malays' simple, happy-go-lucky policy to get on with their own lives and leave the beasts of the jungle to do likewise. Bob lived in hope of finding a Malay with a more adventurous policy.

He turned left off the coast road and entered the small estate of houses where the army had allotted him a bungalow. He lurched the Land Rover unceremoniously into the drive, clambered out, grabbed his kit, and entered the house through the open door. Lim hurried into the room at the sound of his arrival.

Lim. Now there was one of the benefits of living in Malaya. Lim was his *amah*, slim, pretty, eighteen years old

28

and Chinese. Bob had been quite particular in his instructions to the agency. In the few weeks that he had been at Kuala Hitam, his relationship with Lim had developed beyond that of mere servant and master. She lived in full time, and when the nights were long and lonely, which they invariably were, it was not *her* tiny room to which she retired, but the Tuan's. Bob was careful to keep the situation well under control, showing little outward emotion for her. He was well aware that a large percentage of Chinese girls aspired to nothing more than marriage to a white man, shortly followed by a oneway trip out of the country of their birth, preferably to Britain or best of all, America. It was a part of the Chinese preoccupation with all things Western. Lim's full name was Pik Sen Lim, but for reasons best known to herself she preferred to be called Suzy Lim. Most young Chinese girls had Western versions of their names and were anxious that they should be used in place of their existing ones. Lim knew too that once his work was finished, the Tuan would be heading home, not to Britain or the United States, but to Australia. Even so, she seemed to have resolved in her mind that anywhere would be preferable to her current home and never lost an opportunity of telling him how much she would love to see the Sydney Harbour Bridge or a kangaroo or an aborigine. But unfortunately for her, Bob was planning to remain a bachelor for many years to come.

She stood now, a smile of welcome on her face, attentive to any needs he might have.

'Bob want drink now?' She insisted on calling him by his first name, which had proved embarrassing on the few occasions when he had had company.

'No thanks.'

'You take these clothes off,' she advised him. 'I wash.'

'Alright.' He stripped off his tennis gear without further ado, ignoring Lim's giggles as he strode naked to his bedroom. 'I'm going to have a shower,' he announced.

'There is letter for you in bedroom,' Lim called after him.

It was lying on the bedside table, airmail from Australia. He recognized his mother's laborious handwriting. He picked it up, looked at it blankly for a moment, and then turned to gaze thoughtfully out of the slatted window. He could see next door's *amah*, dressed in a brightly coloured *san fu*, pinning out ranks of billowing washing on the line. Above the rooftops behind her, a lushly forested hillside was framed against a sky that was cloudless turquoise. Bob looked back at the envelope and frowned. He pulled open the drawer of the bedside table, slipped the letter inside with four others, none of which had been read. Then he closed the drawer again and, turning, he went to the bathroom to take his shower.

Chapter 4

Harry prepared himself for bed. He felt fine now, as good as ever. He regretted all the fuss he'd caused at the tennis court earlier that day. The trouble was that the grapevine was so efficient here. Word would soon get around that old 'Tiger' Sullivan had had a bit of a turn. Well . . . let them talk! Why should he let it bother him?

Dennis hadn't helped matters much, he'd fussed around like an old hen, trying to get Harry to promise him that he'd see a doctor. The very idea! Harry had never bothered with doctors in his life and he didn't intend to start now. Leeches, the lot of them! Eventually he'd managed to persuade Dennis to push off home and leave him in peace. He felt sad, for he realized that the games of tennis would have to be crossed off his agenda and he did so look forward to them. But pride was a fearsome thing and it would never allow him to revisit the scene of such a humiliation. At any rate, Dennis would be far from keen to get him out on a court again, so there was little to be done in that direction. He would have to take up chess, something a bit more suitable for his declining years.

After all, that was the general belief, wasn't it? That anyone over the age of fifty was ready for the scrap heap, obsolete, of no use to anybody; what did it matter how much they had achieved in their lives? Let them retire to a grim silent home somewhere and eke out their lives playing chess and doing crossword puzzles.

Harry frowned. My God, he *was* feeling bitter! Everybody went through it eventually, why should he be any exception? He undressed slowly, hanging his clothes in neat ranks over the back of a chair. Then turning to look for his pyjamas, he caught sight of his naked reflection in the wardrobe mirror. He froze, momentarily horrified by this vision of stark skinny manhood. Lord, the ravages that time made upon flesh and bone! It turned muscle to folds of saggy flesh, etched itself deep into hollows and crevices, stretched dry parchment skin tight across sharp bone ridges; and worst of all, it *shrank* you, turned your atoms in upon themselves, until you were literally a flimsy parody of your former self. Harry's gaze moved quickly over his own reflection, from head to toe, pausing only over some particularly harrowing feature. The rib cage, over which the flesh was as thin as an excuse; the forearms, two lengths of knotted sinew from which the hands dangled like ungainly flippers. He glanced sideways to the dressing table, where a photograph of himself stood. It had been taken during the war, shortly after his arrival in Burma. It showed a tall, suntanned individual in khaki battle-dress, his muscular arms crossed over his chest, a mischievous grin on his handsome face. His hair was a series of thick black curls that had yet to be taken in hand by the regimental barber and he had not yet decided to grow the moustache that would later become a permanent feature. He moved over to the photograph, picked it up, examined it more closely. A dark rage flared up in his heart. Why, he was unrecognizable! His *mother*, were she still alive, would not recognize the hideous, shrunken wretch that he had become. With an abrupt movement, he snatched the picture up, with the intention of flinging it across the room; but in that same instant, his rage died, he felt vaguely ridiculous.

'Bloody old fool,' he murmured softly. He replaced the photograph carefully on the dressing table. After a moment's thought, he laid the picture face down on the polished wood, reasoning to himself that if he did not look at it again, it could not antagonize him.

He moved back to his bed, found the pyjamas he had

31

been looking for, and dressed himself in them. He did not look in the wardrobe mirror again that night.

The hunger that Haji felt in his belly was now a scream, a wide gaping scream that begged to be crammed tight-shut with a plug of raw, bloody meat; yet even in the midst of his hunger, he kept control. As he crept through the darkness, every sense stayed alert. His pupils had dilated to their fullest extent, enabling him to see quite clearly. He was patrolling the road just below Kampong Panjang, for into his head had come the idea that here his luck might change. His usual fear of the Uprights had been made more flexible by the current predicament in which he found himself. He worked his way along a monsoon ditch at the base of a short decline which led down from the road. The night was fine and clear and, for the moment, silent save for the steady background of insect noise. Patches of vividly coloured wild orchids perfumed the air. Haji began to think that he had made a mistake coming here. There was no movement amongst the trees and bushes, only the soft sighing of a night breeze. He paused for a moment to listen, his head tilted to one side. Now, he could faintly discern another sound, rising gently above the noise of the wind. Distant, mournful, it rose and fell in a cadence. Haji waited. The sound gradually became clearer. It was an Upright, coming along the road, singing. Haji dropped low on his belly and crept silently up the slope to peer over the rise.

An Upright cub was strolling towards him. More interestingly, the boy was leading a skinny white cow on a piece of rope. All this Haji saw in an instant and then he dropped down again, to glide along the ditch, so as to come up again behind the cow. The nearness of the Upright cub made him nervous, but the prospect of the cow's red flesh was too tempting a proposition for him. He stole along for twenty yards or so, then waited for a few moments, his ears alert to the sound of bare feet and hard hooves on the dry dirt surface of the road. At last, he turned and moved swiftly up the bank, until he was crouched on the edge of it, some ten yards behind the Upright and his cow. The beast's flanks waddled in invitation. Haji began to inch forward.

The cow became abruptly nervous. She snorted, pulled back on the rope. The cub stopped singing, and turning he yelled something at the frightened creature. He began to tug at the rope, but the cow would not go along. She began to low in a deep, distressed tone, wrenching her head from side to side. Haji, afraid of the sounds attracting more Uprights, launched his attack, taking the intervening gap at a steady run. Glancing up, the cub saw Haji and gave a scream of terror. He stood transfixed, still clutching the rope.

Haji launched himself onto the cow's back, his claws extended to grip the animal's shoulders. At the same time, he bit down into the nape of the cow's skinny neck with all his force, his great yellowed canine teeth crushing nerves and blood vessels. The combined weight and impetus of his leap bore the cow, bawling and squealing, to her knees. Haji swung his weight sideways, twisting his prey around, while his jaws took a firmer hold on the creature's throat.

At last, the cub had the presence of mind to relinquish his grip on the rope. Half-deafened by Haji's bellowing roars, he stumbled backwards, away from the nightmare that had suddenly engulfed his most precious possession. The cow was kicking feebly, her eyes bulging as the tiger's jaws throttled the life from her. The cub tripped, sprawled on the road, and the shock of the fall finally returned his voice to him. Screaming with terror, he staggered upright and began to run in the direction of the *kampong*.

Haji was intent on his kill. The cow's struggles were becoming weaker and Haji's mouth was filling up with the delicious taste of hot blood. He gave a couple of powerful wrenches from side to side, in order to hasten the end. At last, the cow gave a final convulsive shudder and was still. Anxious to waste as little time as possible, Haji swung the creature around and began to drag it, in a series of violent jerks, towards the bank. In doing so, he displayed the awesome power that tigers have at their disposal. It would have taken six strong Uprights to even move the cow three inches to left or right, but within a few moments, Haji had dragged the white carcass across the road and had dropped it over the steep bank. Once there, he leaped down beside it and began to jerk it along, deeper into the jungle, pulling it between bushes and over rocks, an incredible task. The cow's long horns were jamming in roots and behind tree trunks and Haji had to keep backtracking, in order to release them. He went on, though, covering an amazing distance over such difficult terrain. In this matter, Haji displayed the characteristic guilt that tigers always felt when they had killed a domestic animal or, for that matter, an Upright. He dragged the kill much further than he would have had the beast been his natural prey, a wild pig or a *rusa*. Despite his awful hunger, he rejected two perfectly good feeding spots and did not call a halt until he was a mile and a half from the scene of the kill. At last, he dropped the cow in a sheltered hollow, where there was a flowing stream in which he could slake his thirst. He then settled down to eat.

As was always his habit, Haji began with the rump, tearing ravenously at the soft flesh and ripping it away in huge mouthfuls, which he virtually swallowed whole, such was his haste. His feasting was accompanied by a series of hideous noises, slurps, grunts, the dull crunching of brittle bones. As his hunger diminished, he began to take more time over the meal, savouring the raw meat and chewing it more thoroughly. From the rump, he moved to the thick flesh between the cow's thighs and then he tore open the stomach, spilling the entrails onto the ground. These he also devoured, but then he paused in his eating to drag the cow forward a few yards, thus leaving the foul-tasting rumen pouch safely out of the way. By the time his appetite was truly fulfilled, he had eaten almost half of the carcass. He crept over to the stream and drank deeply, lapping up the water with his great, rasping tongue until his stomach was bloated. Then with a deep rumble of satisfaction, he strolled back to the carcass, walked proudly around it a few times, then backed up to it and with his slender rear legs, he began to kick dry grass over the remains. He did this for several minutes, but turning he saw that the white hide was still clearly visible. He went over to a thick clump of ferns, tore them from the ground with his mouth and turning back, deposited the whole clump on top of the dead cow. He paraded around the slain beast again, critically surveying his

34

handiwork. He paused a couple of times, to kick more grass over it from different angles. At last, satisfied with his efforts, he moved away from the kill and sat, licking contentedly at his bloody paws for a while. For the first time in days, he felt content, and he shaped the feeling of well-being into a loud blasting roar of triumph, which echoed in the silence of the night and sent flocks of slumbering birds flapping from the treetops in alarm. The sound of his own voice pleased him, and he sent another roar close on the heels of its predecessor, then another, and another, great sonorous exhalations that could be heard for miles in every direction.

Then, well pleased with himself and his night's hunting, he sauntered away to find a secure place to sleep for the night.

A distant sound woke Bob Beresford from a shallow, dreamless sleep. He lay for a moment, staring up at the darkened ceiling and wondering where he was. For a few seconds, he had the fleeting impression that he was aboard an aeroplane; but then he realized it was just the noise and the cool breeze from the large electric fan above his head. It had not been that noise that woke him though. He lay still, listening intently, and after a couple of minutes he could discern the sound again – a long, mournful wail, distorted by distance. It might have been anything. A locomotive horn, perhaps, from the iron mine over at Padang Pulst . . .

Lim stirred in her sleep beside him and became aware of his wakefulness.

'Bob not sleep?' she murmured, her own voice a dreamy slur. 'You want me fetch drink . . . you want . . .?' But then she was gone again, submerged in the pool of slumber from which she had but briefly surfaced. Bob smiled. He closed his own eyes, tried to settle back down, but then the noise came again, long, constant, not a mechanical sound at all. It went on for some considerable time, repeating at regular intervals, and then at last it stopped abruptly, as though the animal responsible had called it a night and had drifted away in search of sleep.

'Wish I could bloody well find some,' thought Bob, but he

35

knew only too well that once disturbed in this way, he would lie awake till dawn, thinking bad thoughts. Thoughts of his father who lay dead in the cold earth and of his mother, whom he had abandoned because she had remarried. Bob had worshipped his father. He could never bring himself to understand how she could have forgotten him so readily; worse still, how she could have chosen a no-account bank clerk to take his place. Well, Bob had fixed her wagon, right enough. It didn't matter how many letters she wrote him, he was just going to let her stew in her own juice along with the bloody little twerp she called her husband. Some people might think of it as rough justice, but then, they hadn't known Roy Beresford. They hadn't known the sort of man he was.

Bob fumbled around on the bedside cabinet until he found his cigarettes and matches. The brief flare of light as he struck a match lit the room with a strange glow. He lay, staring up at the ceiling, smoking his cigarette and occasionally glancing at the red glowing tip of hot ash as it burned steadily downwards in the darkness.

Chapter 5

Haji woke with new spirit. His hunger was satisfied, his pride restored. He was once again a killer of flesh. He emerged from the thicket where he had been resting and stretched himself luxuriously for a few minutes, aimless for the time being, for he knew that there was another dinner stored safely away which he could go to whenever his hunger returned. Some monkeys in a nearby tree shrieked an alarm, and he noted with satisfaction that there was a new respect in their manner.

He strolled off along a well-worn cattle track, moving gracefully and stopping from time to time to spray the trees and bushes with the aid of a scent gland beneath his tail. This was simply a way of marking out his territory. The secretion, mixed liberally with urine, possessed a powerful stink that could linger for weeks, provided it did not rain.

Now that the urgency of his hunting had, for the time being, been dispelled, he travelled with the air of a sophisticated landowner surveying his property. Even the dull pain in his injured leg was temporarily forgotten. The sun was rapidly gaining in heat and Haji could hear the curious maddening song of a brain-fever bird in the treetops to his left. The track led down a slope to where a sluggish yellow river wound its way between sandbanks and boulders. Without hesitation, Haji plunged into the water, glad of the chance to cool off. He submerged his body completely, leaving just his head sticking above the surface. The water was wonderfully cooling, especially to the wound on his leg and he would have been content to remain there for the rest of the day; but after an hour or so of lounging, his keen eyes caught sight of a telltale swirl in the water that spoke of a large crocodile nosing his way. Haji had no real enemies in nature, unless of course one counted the Uprights, who could be dangerous when roused; but he knew well enough that the only other beast likely to try and attack him would be a crocodile. Stupid and brutish creatures, they tended to go for anything that moved and in their natural element, water, they were unbeatable. Haji, perhaps wisely, decided to curtail his bathing session and move on to new pastures. But he waded out with dignity, refusing to hurry himself, even though the crocodile's snout was no more than a few feet away from him when he finally clambered back onto dry land. He half turned, directed a threatening roar at the pair of beady eyes surveying him from the surface of the water, and the crocodile, thinking better of his own motives, dropped from sight and looked elsewhere for a meal. Haji growled and shook himself to remove the water from his fur. Then he went on his way, moving along beside the river for some distance. He could see the brilliant blue flash of kingfishers as they skimmed down to touch the surface of the water and occasionally, there would be the curious wriggling wake of a long sea snake that had journeyed in from the coast.

After a while, Haji moved right, along another track into deeper jungle. He was astonished to find the powerful scent of a male tiger, sprayed on the bushes and trees. He came to a halt, sniffing and grimacing. It was rare for one male tiger to invade another one's territory. It was true, certainly, that young tigers who did not possess their own home ranges sometimes crossed an established run, but such creatures were merely transients. They killed game on their travels but were rarely opposed by the resident animal, for they were only en route to another place. They certainly didn't go around marking out territory in such a brazen way, and Haji was very angry that his authority should be challenged in this manner. He paced up and down for a moment, growling to himself, not sure how to resolve the matter. After some moments of indecision, he simply lifted his tail and blanketed the area with his own scent, so that if the intruder should return this way he would be left in no doubt about Haji's feelings over the outrage. This accomplished, Haji moved to the centre of the track and made two distinct scrape marks in the dirt with his hind feet, a further indication that the territory was his. He made as though to move off again, but returned after a few steps, still not satisfied with his efforts. He squatted down near the bushes and defecated, leaving a large pile of steaming dung as a calling card. There could be no mistaking a move like that.

Content at last that he had made his intentions clear, he moved on again, stopping to spray at regular intervals. The scent of the other cat kept recurring along the track for some considerable distance until Haji reached a place where the intruder had veered off towards the river, leaving two scrape marks to indicate his change of direction. Haji growled, sniffed at the ground and gave out one last obliterating spray as a parting gesture. Then he moved along his way, trotting briskly, his head down. His aim was to make a wide rambling circle within the confines of his territory and arrive back for a second feed on his kill, around dusk. The rather vague intentions he had were soon channelled into more positive notions, when a mile or two along the track, he came across another scent. This one, however, did not antagonize him, for it belonged to Timah, one of the two resident tigresses that shared Haji's range. Haji had not yet mated with Timah for she was only just coming to maturity and would be expecting her first 'heat'

38

any time now. The older tigress, Seti, was already heavily pregnant after a brief encounter with Haji some four months back and could expect to drop her litter in a day or so.

As is the accustomed way with tigers, Haji lived a solitary existence, as did his two mates. They would only meet up to copulate and then after a few hours together would go their separate ways. It was true that sometimes, when chance brought them within range of each other, they would meet up briefly and possibly even share a kill. Such was Haji's intention now. Timah's scent was still fresh and he was soon able to locate her, by a series of calls which she promptly answered. A short while later, he found her waiting on the track ahead of him and hurried forward to join her. They made the familiar coughing greeting to each other that tigers invariably used and they rubbed against each other, flank to flank, purring contentedly like overgrown domestic tabbies. Timah was a particularly handsome creature. Some three years old, in the first flush of maturity, she was considerably smaller than Haji and shorter in total length by over a foot; but her fine dark coat was smooth and glossy and her green eyes glittered with quick intelligence. In old age, Haji's coat had grown tattered and pale, and there were many grey hairs about his face and throat. But for all that, Timah was still his mate. In many ways, Haji preferred Timah to good dependable old Seti, who had borne him four litters over the years. Raising cubs was an arduous business for any tigress, for she was obliged to keep them with her for two years until they were deemed adept enough to look after themselves. Then, they either left of their own accord or were physically driven away, so they might search for territories of their own. More often than not, there would not be one available and they would have to content themselves with being transients for a year or so, until a resident cat died or moved away, leaving a range free. The cruel laws of nature usually maintained the balance and it was rare to have a waiting list. But there were instances of a maturing cat fighting an old male for possession of his territory, and it was such a circumstance that Haji feared.

But all that was quickly put out of his mind by the

39

playful, mischievous Timah. In some ways still a cub at heart, she had obviously decided that she wanted to romp and she began to leap around Haji, pawing at him in a display of mock-fighting and then, when he reciprocated, gambolling off into the bushes for a game of hide-and-seek. Dour old Haji felt this to be a little beneath his dignity and after going along with it for a short while, be brought matters to a head by gripping Timah firmly by the nape of the neck and biting her just a little bit harder than qualified as mere play. She quietened down considerably after that and contented herself with trotting obediently along behind him, especially when he intimated to her that a splendid meal was waiting at the end of the journey.

They set off, with keen appetites and high expectations, into the dappled green depths of the jungle.

It was late afternoon and Harry was seated at the little table on the verandah, drinking Darjeeling tea and enjoying the last few peaceful hours before dusk. Behind him, Pawn worked tirelessly, flitting about the various rooms of the house like a restless fly. It was once again Mess night, and she was anxious to have everything spick and span for the Tuan before he left.

The stillness of the day was abruptly shattered by the bronchial wheezing of a battered old Ford saloon as it came clattering into view around the corner. The car had an overall background colour of dark grey, but was liberally splattered with patches of other colours where rusty abrasions had been plastered over with metal filler. All in all, it was surprising that Doctor Kalim's car had not fallen apart long ago. It showered flakes of rust onto the drive as it eased in through the open gateway and came to a shuddering, sorrowful halt. Harry raised his eyes heavenwards, for he had half expected this visit. Nonetheless, he called through into the house.

'Pawn! Bring out an extra cup and saucer, please!'

Doctor Kalim emerged from his car and, as always, Harry was struck by the incongruity of it all. Kalim was a neat and dapper little Muslim, who always insisted on wearing an immaculate white shirt, his English university tie and a sombre black suit, which must have been hellishly uncomfortable in such heat. The whole effect was topped by a wide-brimmed black fedora, which added another six inches to his unimposing stature. He leaned into the back of the car, retrieved his leather briefcase, and came striding purposefully up the driveway, peering at Harry through a pair of pebble-lensed spectacles.

He stepped onto the verandah just as Pawn emerged from the house carrying the spare crockery.

'Doctor Kalim!' announced Harry graciously. 'This *is* an unexpected pleasure. Won't you sit down and take a cup of tea?'

Kalim gave a stiff little bow of assent.

'Thank you, Mr Sullivan, I'd love some.' He sat himself in the spare chair, removed his hat, and placed it carefully on the table. Pawn set the cup down in front of him and withdrew into the house, trying hard not to smile.

'Allow me to fill your cup,' said Harry. 'It's only just been made.' He leaned over and filled Kalim's cup to the brim. 'There now. It's such a pleasure to sit out here in the afternoon and drink a good tea, don't you think?'

Kalim said nothing.

'I er . . . take it this is just a social call?' ventured Harry, knowing in his heart that such was surely not the case. Kalim had been his doctor for six years now, and though in that time Harry had never called on the fellow *once*, Kalim had often taken the initiative himself. The plain fact was that Harry didn't like doctors or surgeries or hospitals and would have had to be taken forcibly, even after a major accident.

'Indeed, this is not a social call, Mr Sullivan, as I am thinking you must be most aware.' Kalim talked slowly and emphatically, for despite his years at university he still had problems with his English. 'Your very good chum, Mr Tremayne, is asking me to be calling on you. He is telling me that you are having a very bad *do* at the tennis courts, yesterday.'

Harry smiled, spread his arms.

'Well, here I am, Doctor,' he exclaimed. 'How do I look?'

Kalim clenched his teeth and lifted the corners of his

41

mouth, a device that was supposed to pass for smiling.

'Come, come, Mr Sullivan. As I am sure you are aware, how you *look* has very little to do with it. Tell me, when did you have last a major physical checkup?'

'Oh, let me see now . . . that would have been in '62, when we had the trouble in Brunei. Told me then I had a dodgy ticker, but that if I looked after it, there'd be no problem . . .'

A look of supreme annoyance came over Kalim's usually placid face.

'Oh really, Mr Sullivan! Would you be saying that playing tennis is a particularly good way of looking after this . . . dodgy ticker, as you call it? Sometimes, I despair of the British mentality, I really do. Mr Tremayne was telling me that you had a very nasty turn. It's a wonder you didn't kill yourself.'

Harry gave a gesture of dismissal.

'Dennis Tremayne is a natural-born exaggerater. Always has been. The fact is, it was hot. I had a bit of a dizzy spell, that's all.'

'A dizzy spell. Do you not think that I am being better qualified to judge the severity of what was happening to you?'

'My dear Doctor Kalim! You weren't even *there*, old man, so how can you be expected to know what was wrong with me? I say, do drink up your tea before it goes cold.'

Kalim muttered something beneath his breath, but obediently, he picked up his cup and sipped at it a few times. He watched, horrified, as Harry took a cigar case from his shirt pocket. He extracted one, put it into his mouth, and then offered the case to Kalim.

'No, thank you very much, I don't. And neither should you, if you are not minding me saying so.'

'Say what you like,' muttered Harry gruffly. He struck a match and lit the cigar. 'It's your loss. These are very fine Havanas.'

Kalim shook his head in mute exasperation. He thought for a moment, then leaned down, opened his briefcase and took out a stethoscope.

'Well you can put that away for a start,' warned Harry.

'Mr Sullivan . . . now, it would not be taking me more than two minutes to be having a quick listen to your dodgy old ticker. We could be doing it right here, you will not even have to get out of your chair . . .'

'Certainly not. I'm not having you listen to my insides, some things *are* sacred you know!'

'But really, this is being most childish . . .'

'You can say what you like, I know my rights. If I don't want to be looked at, then there's nothing you can do to make me. Now please, Doctor Kalim, stop being a confounded nuisance, sit still, and drink your bloody tea!'

'Well, really!' Kalim was outraged. He thrust the stethoscope back into his briefcase and sat where he was for a moment, staring out across the garden, a look of dark, impotent fury on his face. 'When I think of the poor people around here who would give anything to secure a doctor's help,' he muttered. 'And then I am encountering people like you, Mr Sullivan . . . people who are refusing to help themselves. It is making me most annoyed.' He sipped again at his tea. 'Let me tell you the symptoms I think you were experiencing yesterday. You have already spoken of dizziness. I think also there would have been a sharp pain in the chest, a pounding of the heart, an inability to control one's breathing . . . shall I go on, Mr Sullivan? Possibly, you were feeling nauseous and could not maintain your balance; Mr Tremayne is already confirming that point with me. He is saying he had to be holding you upright . . .' He glanced accusingly at Harry. 'Well? Are these the symptoms you were having?'

Harry shrugged expressively.

'Perhaps,' he said, noncommittally.

'Well then, Mr Sullivan, it is hardly needing a doctor to be telling you that it was most probably a heart attack you were suffering yesterday.'

'A . . .?' Harry laughed unconvincingly.

'Oh, so it is a matter for merriment is it?' cried Kalim. He was getting more and more annoyed and his voice was sliding rapidly higher and higher up the vocal scale.

'Not at all, not at all. But really, Doctor, a heart attack! Why, I'm as strong as a mule. I hardly think I'd be wandering about today, if I'd really had a heart attack yesterday.'

'There are being all different kinds of heart seizures,' shrieked Kalim. 'There are earth tremors and earthquakes, but all of them are starting in the same place. That is exactly why I am wanting to examine you, you silly old man! Now I am asking you for the last time, Mr Sullivan. Will you submit yourself to me for a thorough physical examination?'

'I will not,' replied Harry coolly.

Kalim stood up, crammed his hat down on his head, and snatched up his briefcase.

'Then I am clearly wasting my time here,' he announced.

'I could have told you that before you sat down,' said Harry.

Kalim gave an involuntary cry of exasperation. 'You are without doubt the most cantankerous, impossible old fool,' he concluded, and began to walk away.

'And you, my dear Doctor Kalim, are without doubt the most insufferable quack!' retorted Harry.

Kalim stopped in his tracks for a moment. He gazed back at Harry with a look that would have scorched the varnish of a grand piano. Then he strode away, clambered back into his ramshackle car, and reversed carelessly out of the drive, catching the left rear wing on a gatepost and scraping a new area free of grey paint.

Harry winced, then chuckled. The car lurched around in a ragged circle and accelerated away down the road, making a noise like an electric mixer filled with chestnuts. Pawn came to the door, gazed out in surprise.

'Doctor man not stay very long,' she observed drily.

'No,' chuckled Harry, puffing on his cigar. 'I don't think he was feeling very well.'

Chapter 6

The tiger's head above the doorway seemed to have acquired a grin. Harry settled into his familiar seat with a decided feeling of well-being for the world in general, even for Doctor Kalim. Harry was hatching a wicked little plan which involved sending the good doctor a box of Havana cigars. Trimani must have caught on to the Tuan's feeling of contentment, for he brought the glass of beer with a huge dazzling grin stretched across his dark face. He lit Harry's cigar for him and received a Havana for himself, along with the more usual fifty-cent tip.

After a little while, Dennis came in, with his lovely young daughter, Melissa, in tow. She hurried over to Harry's table while her father sorted out some business at the bar.

'Hello, Uncle Harry!' She kissed him energetically on the cheek. She always had called him 'uncle,' though, of course, they were really not related.

He beamed at her.

'And how are you?' he enquired. 'Found anything to occupy yourself yet?'

'I'm afraid not. Everything's so quiet around here!' Melissa had recently finished school in Singapore and was anxious now to do a little living. Harry sympathized with her. There really wasn't that much for an eighteen-year-old to get involved in here, the most energetic preoccupation being the acquisition of a suntan. That was a novelty that wore off after a few days.

'I expect you're itching to get back to England, aren't you?'

'I should say so!'

'Will you go to university or something?'

She shook her head.

'No thanks. I've had enough schooling to last a lifetime. What I want is a career and a lot of fun, but not necessarily in that order . . . Oh, but Uncle Harry, I wish you were coming back with us. Writing letters just won't be the same somehow.'

'Yes, well, I think I've already had this conversation with Dennis . . .'

'Somebody mention my name?' Dennis arrived carrying drinks, one of which he passed to Melissa.

'Good heavens, what is she drinking now?' cried Harry, in mock horror.

'Gin fizz,' announced Melissa. 'And don't forget, it's legal now. I was eighteen last week, in case you've forgotten.' She winked slyly. 'Age of consent,' she murmured.

Harry laughed. He was extremely fond of Melissa and would accept things from her that he would not have tolerated in others. She was a lean, very attractive girl, with thick dark hair and enchanting hazel eyes; very like her mother in looks, but infinitely more outgoing in her personality. Harry's affection for her was, of course, purely platonic, almost paternal. In many ways it was similar to the relationship that he had with Pawn's grandson, Ché.

'You're a lucky fellow,' he told Dennis. 'Lovely wife, lovely daughter. Where is Kate, by the way?'

'Oh, you know her. More content to sit at home with a good book. Can't say I blame her really. There's not much here if you don't enjoy a drink.'

Harry nodded.

'I've a bone to pick with you,' he said.

'Oh?' Dennis looked wary. 'Why, what's up?'

'You know very well what's up, so don't give me the wide-eyed innocent look. There was a certain Muslim doctor round at my place today . . .'

'Ah.'

'You may know him. Drives about in a battered old Ford.'

'Ah. Yes, well . . .'

'What on earth are you both on about?' demanded Melissa.

Dennis smiled sheepishly.

'I think your Uncle Harry is referring to ah . . . Doctor Kalim . . . who I just happened to bump into this morning . . . and I may have, inadvertently of course . . . happened to mention Harry's little upset at the courts yesterday. I mean, not even *thinking* that Kalim, as a doctor, might want to ah, investigate the situation . . .'

'Oh really, Daddy! Have you been spreading nasty rumours about poor Uncle Harry? Anyone can see he's fitter than you are.'

'Well that's not saying very much,' observed Dennis drily.

'You must remember that Uncle Harry is sixty-eight years old.'

46

'Sixty-seven,' corrected Harry.

'Exactly! And if *I'm* as healthy and downright good-looking as he is when I'm sixty-eight . . .'

'Sixty-seven!'

'. . . then I'll feel very pleased with myself.'

'Hear, hear,' enthused Harry. 'For that, I think you deserve another gin fizz. Dennis, will you have another drink?'

'Me? Thought I was in the doghouse.'

'Well, we all make mistakes from time to time. Actually, I rather enjoyed Kalim's little visit. Haven't had a good row in ages. So, what'll it be?'

'Well, nothing for the moment, old chap. I've got to pop over to my office and pick up some papers. But I'll certainly take you up on it when I get back. Meanwhile, perhaps you wouldn't mind keeping this young lady out of mischief.'

'Delighted. Can't you let the papers ride for a while, though?'

'Afraid not. Some of us have to work around here, you know. See you in a bit.'

He went out of the room.

'Poor Daddy,' observed Melissa thoughtfully. 'He's had rather a lot on his plate lately. I expect he'll be glad to get back to England for a rest.'

Harry motioned to Trimani, who came hurrying over from the bar.

'One Tiger beer. One . . . gin fizz, please.'

'Right away, Tuan!' And he was gone.

Melissa shook her head.

'Look at the way they run around for you, Uncle Harry. But if anybody else tried to get that kind of service, they'd just be ignored. Why is that?'

'Because I'm a relic, I suppose.' He shrugged. 'In my day, that's how it was always done, nobody thought anything of it. Trimani there, he's served at this Mess a long time. I expect he remembers the old ways too, but lately he's been told by a lot of people that he doesn't have to bow and scrape to the white sahibs anymore, that he's equal to them, and should they require a drink well, let them jolly well come and ask for one. I don't suppose any of them bothered

47

to ask him what he'd *like* to do, but that's neither here nor there. Still, for all his new freedom, he chooses to keep one memory of the old days alive and that memory is me. Oh, you're absolutely right, Melissa. Nobody else here gets the same treatment I do; but then, nobody else here goes as far back as me and Trimani. We're the only two dinosaurs left in this particular patch of swamp.'

'You're not a dinosaur,' cried Melissa emphatically. 'And neither is Trimani.'

'Pardon, Missy?' inquired the barman, who had just arrived with the drinks.

She stared at him, flustered.

'Oh . . . ah . . . I was just saying, Trimani . . . you're not a . . . dinosaur.'

Trimani shook his head gravely.

'No, Missy, that is right. I am a Buddhist.' He set down the drinks, smiled proudly, and walked away. Harry and Melissa managed to hold back their laughter until he was out of earshot.

'You see, I told you,' giggled Melissa. 'He's *not* a dinosaur.'

She sipped at her gin fizz. It was deliciously cold and she found herself musing that she was rarely happier than when she was in Uncle Harry's company. She had really meant what she said about missing him. There was nothing strange about it either; it was simply that Harry Sullivan had always represented a kind of reassuring steadfastness that she had come to rely on. Even when she was a little girl, she had relished the visits to Uncle Harry's house. She would sit on his lap, inhaling the familiar cigar-smoke smell of him, while she listened enthralled to his wonderful stories of adventure in far away places.

Even then he'd been alone, of course. The Tremaynes had not come to live in Malaya until 1956, when Melissa was eight years old. Harry had already been a widower for six years and he was then, what he was now, an extremely nice, but very lonely old man. As far as Melissa knew, he had not had a relationship with another woman since his wife died; at least, not one that was anything more than platonic, though lord knows, he must have had some opportunities along the way.

'Do you remember much of England?' he asked her now.

'Not really. Little things.' She smiled. 'I remember building a snowman one Christmas and I remember a field, I think, that must have been outside our back garden . . . There's nothing definite, you know, just very abstract images. Oh, I remember a dog too, a big black thing. Must have been ours I suppose, goodness knows what must have happened to him.' She shook her head. 'Not much to go on, is it? Everyone keeps telling me how very cold it is over there and . . .'

Her voice trailed away as her attention was distracted by the entrance of a stranger, a tall, blond-haired man, wearing jeans and a white T-shirt. He was walking slowly, rather dejectedly, she thought, his hands in his pockets and a rather glum expression on his handsome, tanned face. He moved over to the bar and began chatting to Trimani.

'Is something wrong?' enquired Harry, who had not noticed the focus of her attention.

'I was just wondering who the dish was.'

'The what?'

She smiled apologetically.

'It's just an expression I picked up from a magazine. It means good-looking, that's all . . . and I wondered who he was. I haven't seen him before.'

'Who?' cried Harry in exasperation.

Melissa leaned closer in order to whisper. 'I'm talking about the chap by the bar. There . . . wearing blue jeans . . .'

Harry looked in the direction she was indicating.

'Him?' he cried.

'Shush! Yes, him. Why, what's wrong?'

'That's Beresford!'

'Oh. Well, he's very handsome.'

'But . . . he's Australian!'

Melissa giggled. 'Well alright then. He's a handsome Australian. I say . . . why is Trimani pointing at us like that?'

'I can't imagine!' muttered Harry. He was somewhat taken aback. He had always thought that Melissa had some degree of discernment.

'He *is* though, Uncle Harry. Look.'

Harry looked. Sure enough, Beresford was chatting to Trimani, and Trimani *did* seem to be pointing at the table where Harry and Melissa were sitting.

'Do you know him very well?' asked Melissa.

'Hardly at all. Never even passed the time of day with him.'

'Well, he seems to think he knows you. He's coming over.'

'What?' Harry glanced up in alarm. The Australian was sailing towards him with a disarming grin on his face. A few steps brought him right to the side of the table.

'Hello there. Hope you don't mind me introducing myself. I'm Bob Beresford. You must be Harry Sullivan.' He thrust out a hand that was doubtless intended as a shaking device, but Harry just sat there staring at him; so he swivelled slightly to the left and offered the hand to Melissa, who took it more readily. 'I'm afraid I don't know your name, miss.'

'Melissa. Melissa Tremayne. Pleased to meet you Mr Beresford.'

'Tremayne. That wouldn't be anything to do with Captain Tremayne, by any chance?'

'His daughter.'

'Well now . . . fancy that!' There was a brief, rather uncomfortable silence. Bob turned back to Harry. 'Well, I hope you don't mind me coming forward like this, but I had to come over and offer to buy you a drink, the moment I learned it was you what bagged the big stripey over there.'

'Bagged the . . .?' Harry was beginning to suspect that the rest of the local population had decided to switch to new language overnight, without informing him. He glanced at Melissa for some support.

'I think he means the tiger,' she said cautiously.

'Yeah, sure, the big old bugger stuck on the wall there . . .'

Harry raised his eyebrows.

'May I remind you that there is a lady present?' he asked icily.

'Oh, that's alright, Uncle Harry. I've heard worse at school! Won't you sit down with us, Mr Beresford?'

50

'Ah, thanks very much, Miss Tremayne.'

'Melissa.'

'Right, Melissa.' Bob pulled up a chair and sat himself down at the table. 'And you must both call me Bob. Now, I took the liberty of asking Trim to bring over another round of drinks; you see, Mr Sullivan, we're birds of the same feather. I do a bit of hunting meself and I was thinking . . .'

Harry took a deep breath.

'Mr Beresford . . .'

'Bob. My friends call me Bob.'

'Mr Beresford. I can assure you that . . .'

''Course, I've never actually gone after tigers before. That's where you come in. See, I've heard that a bloody big tiger killed a cow last night, on the coast road just outside of Kampong Panjang . . . and I was thinkin' that you and me, the two of us together, so to speak, could team up and have a crack at him . . .'

'*Mister* Beresford!' Harry's voice was harsh. Even the impetuous Australian stopped to listen this time.

'First, let me assure you that I have not gone hunting tiger, nor anything else for that matter, for something like eight years. I am a retired man, Mr Beresford, I am sixty-seven years old and, frankly, I do not feel in the least bit interested in renewing the hobby. I hope I have made myself clear.'

It became very quiet again. Trimani arrived with the tray of drinks, sensed the uncomfortable atmosphere, set down his load and departed as rapidly as possible. Bob took a packet of cigarettes from his back pocket, extracted one, offered the pack to Melissa who shook her head dumbly. He lit his own smoke and then tried another angle.

'Of course, Mr Sullivan, you wouldn't actually have to join in the hunt. See, what I'm really lookin' for is a good guide, a tracker, someone who knows the ropes. I'd be willin' to pay . . .' He saw from the outraged expression on Harry's face that he had put his foot in it again and he glanced wildly at Melissa, hoping that she might bail him out.

'What er . . . part of Australia are you from . . . ah . . . Bob?' she ventured.

'From New South Wales. Do you know it at all?'

'I'm afraid not.'

'Oh, well you must go there sometime, it's very beautiful.'

'Anywhere near Botany Bay?' enquired Harry unexpectedly.

'Why do you ask that Mr Sullivan?' asked Bob, brightening a little.

'That's where all the convicts landed, isn't it?'

The two men glowered at each other across the table for a moment.

'You know,' exclaimed Melissa, with exaggerated jollity. 'I was only saying to Daddy the other day. I wouldn't mind learning to shoot, myself.'

'Oh well, Miss Tremayne . . . Melissa . . . I'd be only too glad to give you some lessons, anytime you like . . .'

'If Miss Tremayne decides she wants shooting lessons, I think she knows only too well that *I* can provide them,' said Harry tonelessly. He turned to gaze at Melissa. 'Strange you've never mentioned it before.'

'Oh, well I . . .'

'You *can* still shoot then?' murmured Bob.

'I beg your pardon?'

'You can still shoot, Mr Sullivan. Only, I thought perhaps the reason you didn't hunt anymore was because your eyes had gone . . . something like that.'

'My eyesight is perfect, thank you.'

'Well, it's interesting this, but me and some of the junior officers have got together and organized a little target-shooting event for Saturday. They've got permission to use the rifle range at the barracks. Officially, the prize is just a crate of beer . . . but we're going to put up a little money between ourselves, just to make it more fun. Everybody puts in fifty dollars and the winner takes the lot . . .'

'Gambling.' Harry said the one word in a measured, icy tone that seemed to transform it into something quite filthy.

'Yeah . . . well, I appreciate not everybody approves of it . . . but you've got to do something to pass the hours away, haven't you?'

'Oh, Uncle Harry! It sounds like terrific fun,' enthused Melissa. 'Why don't you go in for it? Then I could come

52

along and cheer you on.' She turned back to Bob. 'Are members of the public allowed to come?'

'Sure. The more the merrier, that's what I reckon. But maybe Mr Sullivan doesn't feel up to it...' He glanced slyly at Harry. 'After all, some of those young officers are crack shots; could be he doesn't want to risk his fifty dollars.'

'What time *is* this competition?' snapped Harry defensively.

'We're starting off at ten in the morning before the sun gets too strong.'

'I'll be there,' announced Harry calmly.

'Fantastic!' Melissa clapped her hands in anticipation. 'I can hardly wait. I've always wanted to see you in action, Uncle Harry!' She lifted her gin fizz and took a generous swallow of it. 'Here's to Saturday,' she said.

'Cheers.' Bob raised his glass of beer and drank. Then the two of them glanced at Harry, but he remained motionless, his face impassive. The awkward silence returned.

'About this tiger, Mr Sullivan,' ventured Bob warily. 'Couldn't you give me some advice, at least? I don't know the first thing about tiger hunting. I've been asking around the *kampongs* for guides, but nobody seems to have much idea. I suppose the obvious thing to do is to find the carcass of the cow he killed and then try tracking him into the jungle from there...'

Harry let out an exclamation of contempt.

'Mr Beresford, that is the last thing you do! I only once ever resorted to trailing a tiger through its home ground and that time I was lucky to escape with my life. The tiger was wounded. The only possible reason for following a cat into the jungle is to put it out of its misery after your first shot has failed to finish it off.'

Bob shrugged.

'Fair enough. But... how do you get the shot in, in the first place?'

Harry gazed at Bob contemptuously, almost wearily, like an aged schoolmaster regarding a particularly troublesome pupil.

'You build a *machan*, Mr Beresford.'

'A what?'

'A tree platform. You place it in a tree overlooking the half-eaten kill. A tiger will return every night to feed on it. You fix a flashlight to the barrel of your gun and when you hear the cat eating, you aim, switch on the light, and shoot.' He spread his hands in a gesture of finality. 'One dead tiger,' he said calmly. 'Or possibly, one wounded tiger, which is when you come down the tree and follow him up.'

'Ah. That sound a bit more sporting!'

Harry stared at Bob for a moment in silence.

'Excuse me,' he said at last. 'I didn't realize we were discussing sport. I thought we were talking about killing tigers.'

Bob frowned. 'Is there a difference?' he enquired.

'Oh yes. I wasn't aware of it myself for a very long time. But now I can tell you with authority, that there *is* a difference; and one day, you'll learn that for yourself.' He picked up his drink and sipped at it thoughtfully.

'So . . . er . . . how do I go about making this . . . *machan*?'

'There will be someone in the *kampongs* who remembers. Ask the older men to help you. It's a long time since I heard of a tiger venturing out of the jungle. It may just kill once and go back, in which case there's no reason to try and shoot it.'

'Reason?' Bob chuckled. ''Course there's a reason!' He jerked a thumb over his shoulder at the tiger's head trophy on the wall. 'I want to put another head on the wall beside that one.' He leaned forward as though confiding a secret. 'I don't want to worry you, Harry, but from what I've heard, this new tiger is a lot bigger than the one you've got there . . .'

'Oh, I don't doubt it! It was one of the villagers who told you about it, was it?'

'Well, yes . . .'

'The Malays have a marvellous capacity for exaggeration.' Harry pointed to the trophy. 'That fellow there now. On several occasions, he was described to me as being over twelve feet long. A beast as big as a horse, with jaws like a crocodile, and as tall as a grown man. I measured him when

54

I'd finished him off. He went exactly eight feet, six inches, between pegs. Not small by Malayan standards, but not exactly a monster either.'

Bob looked puzzled. 'Between pegs?' he echoed.

'There are two ways of measuring tigers, Mr Beresford. The honest way is to drive a wooden peg into the ground by the tip of his nose and at the tip of his tail, then measure a straight line between. *Some* hunters prefer to measure over curves . . . laying the tape along all the contours of the body. That can add on another four or five inches. Very good for the ego, no doubt. Of course, it was the rajas in India who had the most ingenious method. They had special tape measures constructed that had a couple of inches taken out of every foot. Hence all those records of eleven- and twelve-foot cats, shot from the backs of elephants. It's true that the Indian tiger does tend to be a little larger than its Malayan counterpart, but even so . . .' He went into a silent muse for a few moments, his eyes narrowing as though he were squinting into some misty world that his companions could not see. Then he said, 'I really wish you would leave that tiger alone, Mr Beresford.'

'Why?' The other man stared back at him defiantly.

'How many tigers do you suppose are out in that jungle now, Mr Beresford? Do you think you could put a figure on it?'

Bob shrugged. 'Wouldn't have a clue,' he admitted. 'Hey, but look here. You're a fine one to talk, I must say! You've hunted them before, what makes it right for you and wrong for me?'

'I didn't say that it was right for me.'

'Yeah . . . well, anyway, this one's a cattle-killer.'

Harry smiled sardonically but he kept gazing intently into the other man's eyes.

'Ah, yes,' he murmured. 'Of course he is. I'd forgotten about that.'

Melissa had been listening quietly to the two men's conversation for some time but now she saw the need to move in and referee again. The atmosphere of antagonism between the two of them was extraordinary, though it did seem to stem more from Harry than from the young

Australian.

Harry said nothing further, but simply sat regarding the two of them with an expression of open resentment on his face. For Melissa's part, she was quite happy to chat with Bob Beresford, who was the most interesting proposition that had come her way in a long time. Not only was he strikingly handsome, but he was cheerful and easy to talk to. Still, Harry's presence made the whole thing rather uncomfortable and Melissa was relieved when she saw her father returning with a bundle of papers under his arm. The relief was short-lived, though, for Harry immediately excused himself, mumbling something about some work he had to do.

'What on earth's wrong with Harry?' asked Dennis, as the old man swept out of the room. 'He's got a face like thunder.'

There was a brief silence.

'Anybody fancy a drink?' asked Bob awkwardly.

Haji was just about at his wits' end with Timah. His repeated cuffings and bites served only to discipline her for a very short time. Then her spirits would rise again and she would resume her childish antics, hiding among the bushes, pouncing out at him unexpectedly, pursuing him along the cattle trails like some overgrown cub. It was more than his dignity could bear, and in the end he was moved to indicate to her, by a series of movements and growls, that if she did not curb her frivolity, he would refuse to take her to the kill. This did the trick, for she was every bit as hungry as he was and now she trotted obediently along in his wake.

After some time, they neared the place where Haji had made the kill and they could smell quite clearly the stink of rotten meat that had lain in the hot sun all day. This was tantalizing and Timah would have gone straight to the feast, but Haji directed a low growl of warning at her and she flopped down in the grass to wait with quiet reluctance. Haji did likewise, listening intently and peering into the darkness. He could see the mound of vegetation where the carcass lay and the rustling sounds of movement that reached him from the spot were quickly identified. A pair of large monitor lizards had found the kill and were snapping eagerly at the exposed viscera. Always suspicious, Haji took a long, slow stroll around the area, viewing it from every angle until he was sure that everything was as he had left it. Then, circling back to Timah, he indicated that all was well. The lizards skittered madly away as the big cats approached.

Haji flopped down again, waiting politely while Timah ate her fill. This she did quite eagerly, throwing herself upon the carcass and tearing at the putrefying flesh in a frenzy. She consumed over half the meat that was left on the carcass and at last, satisfied, she moved off to the river to quench her thirst. Now it was Haji's turn. His appetite was less keen, for he had dined well the previous night. Even so, he had little trouble in stripping the cow down to a poor collection of bare bones. Then he too moved to the river to drink. They lay stretched out beside the kill for a while, listening to the steady vibrant hum of the insects in the night. But Haji was always restless in the vicinity of an eating place and after a short while he got up and led the way along a familiar cattle trail. Timah followed him for a distance of several miles but then they came to a place where the trail forked left and right. Haji started along the right fork, but after he had gone a little way, he realized that Timah was no longer following him. He turned to gaze back at her. She was standing, looking at him, and everything about her stance and expression told him that she wished to take the lefthand path. He growled once, a half-hearted command for her to follow him, but he knew before he had uttered the sound that she would not heed him. In many ways, after the wild behaviour she had exhibited earlier, he was relieved. Without further comment, he continued on his way and when he glanced back a second time the trail behind him was quite empty. He was not surprised to see this. The solitary life was the way of the tiger.

He moved on along the path and vanished into darkness.

The car sped recklessly along the jungle road. Melissa glanced at her father's face. In the green glow of the dashboard it looked alien, unfamiliar. The two of them had just been discussing Uncle Harry's mysterious mood earlier that evening.

'The long and the short of it,' concluded Dennis, 'is that he just doesn't like Bob Beresford.'

'Why ever not?'

'Oh, search me. But it's a fact. Harry always says it's because the poor fellow's Australian, but somehow that isn't reason enough. Do you sense an . . . antagonism between them? Almost a rivalry?'

'Yes, but from Uncle Harry more than from Bob.'

Dennis glanced at her slyly. 'Oh, so it's Bob already, is it?'

She smiled. 'Yes, why not? I'm eighteen now, Daddy, you must bear that in mind!'

'Melissa, I stopped trying to keep you in order years ago. I've got nothing against the Aussies, anyway.'

'He's not like most Aussies.'

'Hmm.' Dennis frowned. 'Just the same, I'd watch what you say to Harry. He might get jealous.'

Melissa chuckled. 'Oh really, you have to laugh. Anyone would think Harry and I are engaged, the way you're going on.'

'Yes, but you know how fond he is of you, Melissa. God knows what he'll do when we shove off back to England. Poor old fellow . . .'

'We've done everything we can to get him to go with us.'

'Yes . . .' Dennis sighed. 'But let's face it, he wouldn't be happy anyplace but here. He *belongs*.'

The car sped onwards in the comforting direction of home.

Chapter 7

It was early morning and Haji was prowling amongst familiar mangrove swamps, where the silted yellow sluggishness of a river collapsed into a misery of pools and muddy sandbanks. A couple of fat frogs leapt away from his approach and slapped into water. He was, as yet, not hungry enough to bother with them, but when times were particularly hard, there was very little that he considered beneath his dignity. Before now he had eaten many frogs, also snakes, crabs, turtles, and even fish when the opportunity had presented itself. Wild pigs were generally the mainstay of his diet, but lately there seemed to be a bewildering shortage of the creatures and the only signs of them he had encountered all day had been months old.

He came to a place now where a great outcrop of rock jutted up from the surrounding trees and undergrowth and he recalled that here was an old favourite sleeping place of his, a small cave at the base of the rock. But as he neared it, he was perturbed by a powerful smell that seemed to be issuing from within. It was in a strange way familiar and at the same time it incorporated another smell that did not belong with the first odour. He came to a halt for a moment, sniffing and grimacing, unsure of what to do. At last, he ventured a little nearer and issued a loud roar of enquiry; whereupon several large black shapes came squawking and flapping out of the darkness, almost blundering right into him. Haji was so startled, he almost turned tail and ran. But then he realized that the creatures had been just a flock of scavenging magpies who had clearly not noticed his approach. Still, the shock had unnerved him a little and he paced backwards and forwards for several minutes, his head down, while he made low rumbling growls deep in his throat. He began to move away from the cave, but the smell antagonized him with its nagging familiarity and at the back of his mind was the thought that the cave must hold some kind of food if the magpies had been there. So he approached again, slowly, cautiously, craning his head forward to peer into the dark interior. The smell became more powerful by the moment.

He slipped into the cool shade, setting down his feet on the chill rocks with great precision. Now, he realized why the smell had seemed so familiar to him. Against the back wall of the cave, where the ceiling curved down low to meet the ground, he could discern the long striped back of a tigress lying on her side. It was his other, older mate, Seti.

Haji uttered the habitual coughing growl of welcome that tigers use, but she made no reply. She was lying with her

59

head turned away from him and seemed to be resting, though she should surely have woken at the sound of his voice. Haji was unsettled by the strangeness of her behaviour and nervously he called her again, but she remained silent. He stood for several long moments, debating what to do. The unfamiliar smell was frightening him. In it, he thought he detected something that spoke of birth and his suspicions were confirmed when he spotted a tiny cub stretched on the ground beside Seti. He stepped forward and nuzzled it, but it did not move or make a sound. Now he crept fearfully up to Seti and saw that a second cub lay nearby, but that too was strangely still and silent. Then he saw that a third cub lay half in, half out of Seti's body, the tiny wrinkled face and paws immersed in a sea of congealed blood. A thick mantle of flies buzzed greedily over the area, settling, flying up, resettling.

With an angry growl, Haji moved forward so he could nuzzle at Seti's face. She was lying stretched out, her dry tongue lolling from her open mouth, which seemed to hold an expression of pain. At first, Haji thought that her eyes were closed for he could see no glimmer of light from them. But then he realized that she had no eyes, for the thieving magpies had stolen them and that was why she was so still and quiet. He knew now that the third smell was the awful stench of death, and he shrank back from it in fear, hugging the wall of the cave as he crept away. He turned back once or twice and cried fearfully for the cubs to follow him but then he realized that the death-smell was on them too and anyway, they had been so young they could barely crawl to their mother's milk. As she was blind in death, so had they been in life, however brief that was.

Haji reeled out into the sunlight, frightened, bewildered. He knew now that Seti and the cubs could never emerge from the cave, that the death-smell had bound them there forever. He would never encounter them on the trail again and though he could not really understand grief, there was an anxiety in him at the loss of his old companion and his inability to fully comprehend what had happened to her. He paced up and down, walking faster and faster, and working himself into a kind of frenzy, for he could still feel the

60

stench of the death-smell in his nostrils and he was torn between a natural impulse to run away and a powerful desire to stay with his mate. But the image of her blind eyes kept coming back to him, telling him that it was useless to stay and risk the death-smell, for she could never find him now.

At last he articulated the frenzy of conflicting emotions within him into a great shattering roar, which he flung to the wind. It echoed from the crags of rock, seeming to multiply in volume and duration until the entire jungle for miles around throbbed to the sound of his confusion. Flocks of birds scattered skywards, deer raced into jungle, milling in confusion, troops of monkeys shrieked feeble insults in return. But the roaring continued, all through the long morning and late into the afternoon.

Harry stepped out of the taxicab onto the crowded pavement of one of the main streets of Kuala Trengganu, the state capital. He handed the driver a five-dollar bill and waved away the change. The taxi accelerated off into a melee of cars and bicycles all reassuringly ploughing a path down the *left*-hand side of the road. Harry glanced quickly about. Kuala Trengganu, like most sizeable Malay towns, was a riot of sounds, smells, and visual peculiarities. Harry didn't make the trip very often, but the only real shops were here and he had something special in mind. He noticed a couple of bedraggled beggars advancing towards him with their arms outstretched, and he wisely took to his heels, striding purposely past the ranks of Chinese emporiums and eating places, each with their own garish advertisements for drink and cigarettes displayed on tin boards outside. It was not that he begrudged the beggars a few cents, but he had learned from experience that news of a generous Englishman could spread amongst the begging community like wildfire and then the wretched creatures would appear as if by magic, crawling out of every nook and cranny. In such instances, it was simply impossible to give everybody something, there were just too many of them; and so, one played a kind of cat-and-mouse game with them, only rewarding those who showed uncanny persistence in staying the distance.

Harry headed for a certain area, where a row of Chinese merchants operated stores that specialized in watches, cameras, and radios. As he struggled through a crowded market, he felt a sharp tugging at his sleeve and glancing down he saw that a Tamil beggar was standing beside him. At first, he thought the man was very short, because he stood no higher than Harry's elbow.

'Please, Tuan, please!' He gazed imploringly up, one hand extended for coins.

'No, I'm sorry, I haven't any . . .' The excuse died in Harry's throat, for, glancing down, he saw that the man was suffering from elephantiasis. His body was perfectly normal but his legs had degenerated into two vividly coloured stumps of bloated, clublike flesh, spreading out at the base into wide formless trunks from each of which a single yellow toenail protruded. Harry felt nauseated, humbled. He glanced back at the man's face which was a portrait of suffering.

'Please, Tuan . . .'

'Yes . . . yes, of course.' Harry fumbled in his pocket and pulled out what change there was, and thrust it into the man's hand. Then he moved on, not wanting to see those hideous legs again. From behind him came the man's profuse thanks.

'*Terima kasih, Tuan! Terima kasih* . . .'

His head down, Harry hurried onwards. Lord, this country of mixed experiences. Just when a man was beginning to think that he was inured to shock, along came something like that to put him firmly in his place again. Sometimes he wondered if the white man really had any place out here. Perhaps it was a good thing that the colonial system was finally falling apart . . . and yet, from his middle youth onwards, it was the only life that Harry had known. He would stay on now. He would have to.

He climbed up the steps by the monsoon drain and onto a raised pavement. This was the area he had been heading for. After a few moments, he came to the particular shop he wanted. He had long ago learned that it was good policy to frequent one particular shop. After a while, the trader got to know you and recognizing that regular trade was a good thing, he would start his bartering at a much more realistic level than he would with the average passing tourist. The shop was packed tight with electrical goods and ranks of glittering watches were displayed beneath glass counters. It was on this selection that Harry fixed his gaze.

In an instant, the proprietor, a tubby bespectacled little Chinese man called Hong, had bustled over to greet him.

'Hello sir! You look for something special?' He indicated the watches. 'Good watches, sir. Best in Trengganu. Best in Malaya!'

Harry smiled. The man was evidently very proud of his shop.

'Well, let me see now . . .' Harry knew that it was best to make the transaction slow. A man who bought on impulse was likely to end up with a bad deal. 'I *am* looking for a watch. A *good* watch, you understand. A gift for a very good friend.'

'Ah! You want special watch! I show!' He indicated some beautiful Japanese chronometers. 'These best in world,' he announced. 'Fine made, got two-year guarantee . . .' He was already removing them from the glass case, but Harry shook his head.

'These are, indeed, very good watches. But not what I'm looking for.'

'No?' The man looked quite amazed by this revelation. 'Ah! You want good Swiss watch?'

'How about an English watch?' ventured Harry.

Hong grimaced. 'The English not make good watch,' he said sorrowfully. 'Go wrong all time. I not sell English watch. But Swiss very good! See here, twenty-one jewel, shock-proof, water-proof, anti-magnetic . . .'

'Hmm.' Harry rubbed his chin, scanned the ranks of glittering merchandise. 'It's still not right. I want something simple, easy to understand. It's for a young boy, you see . . .'

'Ah! Young boy! I got good watch for young boy. This one! Shock-proof, dust-proof, water-proof, anti-magnetic, one-year guarantee . . .'

'No. It's still not quite . . . ah, now *that* looks the sort of thing!' He pointed to a simple silver pocket-watch on a leather fob. 'Let me see that one,' he said.

'This watch, sir?' Hong could scarcely believe his eyes. 'You want this one? But this one not show date! This one not carry guarantee, not dust-proof, water-proof . . .'

'Yes, well, I'd like to see it anyway.'

'OK, sir.' Hong bobbed down behind the counter, extracted the watch, and, as Harry had expected, reemerged with a whole new point of view. 'Here you are, sir. This very fine watch, very rare. Swiss mechanism. Twenty-one jewel, shock-proof, water-proof, two-year guarantee . . .'

Harry suppressed a smile.

'I thought you just said it didn't have any of those things.'

Hong spread his hands and smiled sheepishly. 'But sir, that was when I didn't want you to buy this watch.'

In spite of himself, Harry had to laugh. It was an outlandish explanation, but it held good for all the merchants in this town. He picked up the watch and examined it critically. It looked robust enough, a simple silver pocket-watch that showed the time clearly and looked like it could take some rough handling. 'Alright,' murmured Harry. 'How much?'

Hong gazed at him for a moment with an inscrutable smile on his face.

'This watch, sir. I sell you for . . . twenty-five dollars.'

'Twenty-five!' Harry registered disgust and made as if to walk off. 'Hong, it's time I started going to some of the other shops,' he said.

'Just a minute, just a minute!' Hong smiled again, broader than before. 'You good man . . . I good man. I make you special price. Twenty dollars.'

'Twenty? That's still robbery. I'll give you . . . six dollars for it.'

Now it was Hong's turn to be outraged.

'Six? You want watch for six? If I sell for that much, I go out of business. Six . . . you give me fifteen dollars, I can not go less.'

'Eight dollars!'

'Twelve!'

'Well . . . alright, ten dollars, my last offer.'

'Ten dollars! Madness! Twelve my lowest price!'

'You said that about fifteen. I'll give you ten.'

Hong shook his head adamantly.

'Sorry, sir. Twelve. Cannot go lower.'

'Then I don't want the watch.' Again, he made as if to walk away.

'Alright, alright, alright!' Hong was tearing at his hair. 'I give you for ten.'

'Eight?' ventured Harry with a grin, but Hong's look of horror told him that this was clearly not playing the game. 'Alright, only joking.' He counted out the notes and put the watch into his pocket.

'Now sir, you want anything else? Binocular? Got very nice, very cheap. Radio, pick up all English station? Record player, new from Japan? Good. Identity bracelet? Cassette recorder . . .?'

Harry retreated from the onslaught with a brief wave and set out again into the crowds. News of his kindness to the deformed cripple had evidently got around, for suddenly there seemed to be an awful lot of beggars in evidence – lame men, people missing limbs, women with tiny howling babies. Harry slipped smartly around the corner and strode quickly away in the other direction. When he was in Kuala Trengganu, he usually sought one little luxury that was not readily available at home. He went to a small barber shop where he had a haircut and a beautifully close shave that was administered with a horrifying looking cutthroat razor. As he sat back in his chair, he brought out the silver watch and examined it carefully.

'Nice watch,' observed the barber. 'How much you pay?'

'Ten dollars.'

'I can get watch like that for six dollar.'

Harry nodded.

'This shave is costing me one dollar,' he said. 'If I were a Malay, I could get it for twenty-five cents.'

And the barber threw back his head and laughed merrily, his dark eyes twinkling. Harry laughed along with him. No further explanation was necessary.

The afternoon sun was still fierce. Bob Beresford felt the

heat of it on his neck as he brought the Land Rover to an abrupt, squealing halt on the stretch of road that ran alongside Kampong Panjang. He clambered out of the vehicle, collected his rifle from the back seat, and slinging the weapon carelessly over his shoulder he headed into the village. The *kampong* was a jumble of rattan and corrugated iron dwellings, all of them supported three or four feet above the ground on a series of stout posts, a practical necessity in a land that swarmed with venomous snakes, scorpions, and centipedes. The village seemed to have been constructed with no particular sense of order, one building encroaching close upon the next, with just a well-trampled muddy walkway in between. As Bob approached, he was quickly spotted by groups of children who flocked around him excitedly, pointing to his gun, and jabbering in Malay. As soon as they divined that he had some purpose in coming here, they fell in behind him like a platoon of miniature troops. Bob could barely speak their language and could only gaze at them enquiringly and repeat over and over, '*Penghulu?*' Somebody had told him that this was the Malay word for the village headman. Perhaps his pronunciation was bad, because it took some considerable time to make his wishes known. At last, with wild exclamations, the laughing children took the lead and drew him deeper and deeper into the village. Finally, they deposited him outside a dwelling that looked no grander than the others and the children began to shout and yell, until a little, wizened monkey of a man, dressed in a red sarong, emerged from the interior of the house and clambered down the stairs. He growled something at the children and their noise subsided abruptly. Then the *penghulu* smiled apologetically at Bob and lowered his head in a polite bow.

'Good day, Tuan. Can I be a help?' His English was surprisingly fluent. The children began to giggle. The *penghulu* gave a shout and stepped menacingly towards them, at which point the children scattered in every direction, leaving the two men to their own devices. The *penghulu* turned back and raised his eyes briefly heavenwards, an expression that said, 'Ah, these children! What can a man do with them?' Then he enquired politely, 'Will the Tuan take some tea?'

'Ah . . . no, thanks very much. But I could use some help. I came about the tiger . . .'

The *penghulu* looked puzzled. Evidently, he had not come across the word before.

'*Harimau*,' prompted Bob, who had taken the trouble of finding out a few easy terms from some of his pupils.

'Ah!' The *penghulu* nodded gravely. He eyed Bob's rifle curiously. 'You want shoot him?' he murmured.

'If I can. Can you show me the place where he took the cow?'

The *penghulu* smiled, nodded. He turned back to the house and shouted something in his native tongue. After a moment's silence, the sound of a scolding woman's voice emerged from within, a long stream of words that seemed to contain not one pause for breath. The *penghulu* grimaced, winked slyly at Bob, and then chuckled.

'Women,' he murmured. 'Why do we marry them? Come!' He led Bob away from the house, ignoring the barrage of invective that was still emerging from there. They could hear the woman's complaining voice for some distance.

Bob took out a packet of English cigarettes, offered one to the old man, who accepted it gratefully, and then put one between his own lips. He lit both cigarettes with his silver Ronson. The *penghulu* gazed at this admiringly and then strolled happily beside the Australian, puffing ostentatiously on his cigarette, aware that people in the surrounding houses were observing him. He was a curious-looking fellow. No more than five feet, three inches high, his legs were quite short in proportion to his body and rather bandy, emphasizing the apishness of his appearance. As well as the sarong, he was wearing a grubby white short-sleeved shirt and a pair of blue rubber flip-flops. His large, rather discoloured teeth were liberally dotted with bright gold fillings that tended to reflect the sunlight whenever he grinned. It was impossible to guess at his age. His tiny, excessively lined face suggested an octogenarian but he was as agile and wiry as a gibbon as he trotted along through the village.

'Is it far away?' enquired Bob.

'Not far, Tuan. *Si-Pudong* take cow on road, out by *kampong*. Then he carry 'way. No man know where to. Herd-boy very frighted, but *Si-Pudong* not touch him. He read words on boy here!' The *penghulu* tapped his own forehead and smiled. 'So, *Si-Pudong* 'fraid to eat boy. Take cow 'stead.'

Bob did not understand this at all and resolved to ask somebody else to explain it to him in the near future. The two of them moved out of the outskirts of the village and onto the road. Several children ventured to follow them, but the *penghulu* shouted for them to stay put, which they did, rather reluctantly, staring glumly after the two men as they strode away.

They walked for some distance in silence, glancing occasionally into the thick jungle that flanked the road. It was oppressively hot at the moment, and Bob felt the tickle of sweat as it ran down his neck, beneath his khaki shirt. After a surprisingly short distance, the *penghulu* announced, 'Cow killed here!' He pointed to some scrape-marks in the hard dirt surface of the road and, peering closer, Bob could see some patches of dried blood. Now the *penghulu* pointed to the right, where behind a screen of ferns and scrub, the ground declined sharply into a monsoon ditch. '*Ha − Si-Pudong*, he come up out of ditch, attack from behind,' explained the *penghulu*. Bob glanced at him suspiciously. He had the distinct impression that the old man had been about to say *harimau*, the normal Malay word for tiger, but he had stopped himself, almost as though he was afraid to say it. Just exactly what *Si-Pudong* meant, he would have to check up later. Bob moved over to the ditch and slid down into it, closely followed by the *penghulu*. The ground was comparatively moist here, and after some searching about they found a series of pugmarks.

'Ai!' exclaimed the *penghulu*, pointing. 'There were two of them! See, Tuan.' He indicated a pair of large, squarish prints. 'Man-cat stand here. Go up bank to kill.' Now he pointed out some smaller tracks, a little distance back. 'His woman wait here, while he do all work.' He thought to himself for a moment, then added, 'Just like my wife.'

68

Bob smiled, scratched his head. He certainly hadn't expected two tigers. He moved along the ditch a little way until he reached the place where the cow had been dropped down the bank. The grass was visibly crushed and flattened and there was a long deep furrow, presumably where one of the creature's horns had gouged deep into the soil. There was a little dried blood matted into some tufts of grass, and from here a distinct trail led off through the undergrowth. Bob gazed after it for a moment, then turned to the *penghulu* and indicated that he intended to follow. The old man looked far from eager, so Bob took out his cigarettes and lighter, handed them to the *penghulu* and suggested that he should wait up on the road. With a grateful nod, the *penghulu* scrambled up over the bank and Bob set off into the jungle.

It was as though somebody had switched off the sun.

The instant he passed into the shadow of the trees, it seemed that the heat had simply evaporated, and he was immersed in a chilly world of green-dappled mystery. As he moved further onwards, the trees high above his head formed a thick dark canopy through which the rays of sunlight could only occasionally stab. But the trail he was following was easy enough to find. The drag marks led through the midst of lush ferns and tangled vines, around the gnarled roots of balau trees, along winding cattle trails, and deep through the heart of seemingly impenetrable bamboo thickets. Bob followed silently, glancing nervously this way and that. It was his first experience of entering real jungle and the dank humidity of it made him feel very claustrophobic. He started once when a pig-tailed monkey scuttled away from his advance with a shrill shriek of alarm, but he kept doggedly onwards, even when the trail stretched on much further than he would have believed possible. He marvelled at the sheer brute strength of the tiger. From time to time, he came across the chafed roots of trees and bushes, where the horns of the cow had evidently lodged for a time. The torn shredded bark suggested that the cat had exercised prodigious power in pulling the carcass free, and Bob began to wonder if the *penghulu* had been right about the second tiger. Surely it must have taken two strong animals to move the body this far.

Bob had no impression of time. He had forgotten to put on his wristwatch that morning and now it seemed like hours that he had been walking in this way. The trail led on through green shadow. Bob's nerves began to get the better of him. On two distinct occasions, he had the vivid impression that something was gliding intently along behind him. Each time, he snapped fearfully around, his rifle ready to fire, only to find nothing but the empty jungle mocking him. He was on the verge of giving up and retracing his steps, when unexpectedly, the trail culminated at the edge of a sluggish-looking stream of water. It was a disappointing end to his search, for there was nothing here but a sorry-looking pile of bones and offal. It was obvious that no tiger would bother to return to this particular meal.

Bob came to a halt, mopped at his brow, which was sweating profusely despite the comparative cool of the jungle. Instinctively, he reached into his pocket for cigarettes and then remembered that he had given them to the *penghulu*. He swore vividly, shrugged his broad shoulders and turned back, retracing his steps.

If it had taken him a long time to come this far, the return journey seemed to take twice the time. He saw not a living thing on the way back, save for a brilliantly coloured tree snake hanging from an overhead limb. It had a glossy black body marked with a series of green and red spots, and he gave the creature a wide berth, not being sure whether it was poisonous or not. After what seemed like an uneventful eternity of trekking, he emerged into sunlight again.

The *penghulu* was sitting beside the road, smoking a cigarette and humming happily to himself. He glanced up in surprise as the Australian's head appeared above the bank. Then he smiled, his gold teeth throwing out a dazzling welcome.

'Ah, Tuan! You find *Si-Pudong*, yes?'

'No.' Bob clambered up onto the road and flopped down to rest for a moment. He accepted his lighter and cigarettes gratefully. Opening them, he found that there were only three left. He glanced disapprovingly at the *penghulu*, who smiled sheepishly and spread his arms in a gesture of regret.

'You gone long time, Tuan,' he said defensively.

'Aww, that's alright.' Bob lit himself a smoke and inhaled deeply. 'The cow was all eaten up,' he announced. 'If I'm going to shoot that tiger, I need to be onto the kill much quicker than this.' He thought for a moment and then reached into his pocket and pulled out a notebook and pencil. 'I tell you what,' he said. 'I'm going to write the address of my house down here. Can you read some English? It's only a mile or so away from here on the Kuala Trengganu road. Now, this is what I'm going to do. I'm going to give you twenty dollars . . .'

The *penghulu*'s eyes lit up.

'Now, the next time you or any of your people hear of a tiger killing a cow *anywhere* in Trengganu, you come and let me know, understand? So you see, it's in your interest to help me out.' He reached into his pocket, drew out his wallet and handed a twenty-dollar bill to the *penghulu*, who accepted it eagerly. 'Another thing, you got any friends who can work with wood? Savvy? A carpenter, you know . . .?' He mimed the action of sawing and hammering wood, and the *penghulu* nodded.

'My cousin,' he said with conviction.

'Alright, let's go and see your cousin. I want him to make me a special seat that I can rope up into the trees, a seat I can shoot from, you understand? I'll meet his price, whatever it is! And look, I'm going to need men to help me later on, and they all get paid too. You'll be able to buy a lot of cigarettes before we're through. I'm a good man, chief, I always look after my friends. What do you say, are you going to help me out?'

The *penghulu* crumpled the twenty-dollar bill in his hand.

'I good man too, Tuan! You not worry, I keep ears open, all over. I hear something, I send word, never fear!' And he grinned, a wide golden grin. 'Now, you come talk my cousin. He best woodman in all *kampong*. He make you good shooting seat, you will see.' And he led Bob back in the direction of the village.

On the way back, to seal the bargain, they smoked the last two cigarettes.

Chapter 8

It was a little after eight o'clock and Harry had already been up for something like three hours. He sat in his favourite rattan chair on the verandah remembering how, when he was younger, he had possessed the ability to sleep like a proverbial log. But as a man got older, his capacity for sleep seemed to dwindle. Now, the advent of the night was no longer a pleasure to him, but an irksome task that had to be endured in a seemingly endless fit of tossing and turning. More often than not, he would arise with the dawn and pace about his home, searching for little jobs to occupy himself while the hours slowly creaked past.

It was with a feeling of elation that he heard the metal garden gate clang open, telling him that Pawn had arrived to make the breakfast and, what was more important, today was the day she always brought Ché with her. They advanced slowly up the drive, an incongruous couple, she small and creaking in her sarong, he, a spindly hyperactive twelve-year-old, dressed in shorts and a torn T-shirt. He bounded up onto the porch ahead of his grandmother, his dark eyes flashing in merry greeting.

'Good morning, Tuan!' Like most young Malay boys, his English was excellent, and he had long ago lost any bashfulness that he might originally have possessed.

'Good morning, Ché . . . Pawn . . .' The old woman clambered up the stairs, grinning as always.

'I am late, Tuan?' she enquired fearfully.

'Oh, I hardly think so! Anyway, I think we'll leave breakfast for an hour or so. I haven't much of an appetite yet.'

'Yes, Tuan.' She bowed very slightly and moved on into the house.

'Ché, come and sit with me,' suggested Harry. 'Tell me all the news!'

Ché pulled up the spare seat and sat himself down on it, lifting his bare legs up so that he could rest his chin on his knees. Then he sat regarding Harry with a good-natured grin on his face.

'The Tuan is well today?' he enquired.

'Oh, well enough, Ché, well enough. A little old, but there's not much I can do about that is there? Now then, what's been happening over in Kampong Panjang?

Ché's face became very animated.

'Well, Tuan, such excitement in the *kampong* two nights ago! A great *tok belang* killed a cow on the road just beyond the village. The cow belonged to my best friend, Majid, and he stood as close to the beast as I am to you!'

Harry smiled. He noted that like many Malays, Ché had a terrible reluctance to say the word 'tiger.' This stemmed from the old superstition that the very mention of the creature's name was enough to bring its wrath down on one's head. In most areas of Malaya, the superstition had faded except amongst the very old, but here in Trengganu it persisted amongst many of the inhabitants and may well have been passed on to Ché by his parents or grandparents.

'A big tiger, you say? How big?'

'Majid described him to me. He was fifteen feet long and stood as high as a fully grown deer. His eyes blazed like hot coals and his teeth were like great white daggers, this long!' Ché held the palms of his hands six inches apart. 'A truly terrible beast, Tuan. Poor Majid was fixed to the spot for a moment, but of course the beast did not attack him, for he was facing it.'

Harry nodded. He knew all about the fervent Malay belief that every good man had a verse from the Koran written on his forehead that proclaimed mankind's superiority over the beasts of the jungle. Whenever confronted with this, a tiger is incapable of attacking its intended victim; and that was why, of course, nine times out of ten, a tiger would attack a man from behind. Beliefs like this were indelibly printed in the Malay consciousness and no amount of reasoning could shake that kind of faith. Harry could quite easily explain that Majid had probably been in no danger whatsoever; that a tiger only ever attacks a human being if it is very old or badly wounded, unable to catch its usual prey; moreover, that it would be quite natural for a tiger to attack from the rear, simply to maintain an element of surprise, but none of these arguments would make Ché cast off his own beliefs. So Harry simply asked, 'Where do you think this tiger came from?'

The question was more complicated than it might seem to Western ears. To a Malay's way of thinking, no tiger could just be *there*, a native cat wandering out of its jungle home. Ché thought for a moment before replying.

'Some people in the village say that it might be a weretiger. There is an old *bomoh* who lives along near Kampong Machis and he claims to have the power of turning into a *h – tok belang*. But more likely, it goes the other way about. A beast from Kandong Balok has been living amongst us for some time and now is seeking his old ways.'

Harry nodded, knowing better than to laugh and cause offence. He knew all about Kandong Balok, the mythical kingdom of tigers that lay far beneath the earth in a secret place. There ruled Dato Uban, the king of all tigers, in a home made of human bones and thatched with human hair. From time to time, one of Dato's subjects would yearn to live as a human and then this particular tiger would leave Kandong Balok by means of a secret tunnel. En route, a mysterious transformation would occur, the tiger would take human form and would go to live in some *kampong*, the other inhabitants never dreaming that such a creature dwelled amongst them. Sometimes, the changeling would become homesick and would visit Kandong Balock occasionally, reverting to its original form as it moved through the tunnel. Other times, the beast would simply hunger for raw flesh and, like the troublesome weretigers, would change its shape and kill cattle or even human beings.

The *kampongs* were rife with stories about weretigers, which were usually told to a huddled family audience late at night, in the glow of a solitary oil lamp. Details varied, but the basis was always more or less the same. A woman would be married happily for years to a man who was a good provider, a gentle sensitive husband. A tiger would start to prey on luckless villagers at night and the poor woman would never suspect a thing, until she awoke early one morning to see her husband's head coming up the short

74

ladder into the house, a head that was supported by the crouching body of a tiger! This was her husband, caught in mid-transformation. What happened to the marriage at this point was generally left as a matter of conjecture. Another popular story involved a brave man, lying beneath the slain body of his wife with a *kris* in each hand and stabbing the tiger when it came to eat. In the morning, a well-respected villager would be found with two daggers stuck in his ribs. There were countless other stories of course, all so similar that it was a wonder the Malays believed in them as faithfully as they did. Harry had his own particular favourite and he now asked Ché to recount it for him, for he loved to observe the boy's excitement whenever he told such a tale.

'Well Tuan, since you like the story so much, I will tell you it again. In the days before the *tok belang* looked as he does now, he was nothing more than a wild little boy, wandering in the jungle. One day, he was befriended by a strange old man who lived in a hut alone. The old man was very kind to the boy and taught him the ways of man, how to eat properly, how to speak and wear clothes, for, of course, up to this time, the boy had been quite naked. Well, the people in the nearest *kampong* soon came to hear about all this and they sent a man to insist that the wild boy must go to school. The old man was sad to lose his friend, but at last he agreed and the boy was sent to the *kampong* school. Now, the teacher there was a very stern man and he quickly lost patience with the wild boy, for he was always fighting with the others, biting, and scratching them most cruelly. The teacher had a strong cane which he used to punish bad boys, and he warned the wild one that he must be quiet or he would suffer. But after a little while, the wild boy began to fight again and the teacher snatched up the cane, shouting, "Now I shall beat you, for you are truly nothing but a wild animal!" And he hit the boy very hard with the cane. At this instant, the boy dropped onto his hands and knees. The teacher hit him again and the boy growled. He hit him a third time and whiskers grew from his cheeks. A fourth time and a tail grew between his legs. The teacher was in a rage and he kept striking the boy, so hard that the

75

cane scarred his body with black stripes and then, suddenly, the creature leapt to the door and ran away to the jungle, where it has remained ever since. And to this day, he carries the stripes on his back to remind him of that terrible beating.'

Ché sat back with a smile of satisfaction, for he felt that he had told the story well. Harry applauded him gently and thought to himself, 'Lord, how I'd miss this boy if I ever decided to go back to England.' He sighed gently.

'You are sad, Tuan?' asked Ché, ever sensitive to the old man's moods.

'Why do you ask that?'

'Oh . . . suddenly your face changed, as though a cloud had passed over the sun.'

Harry chuckled. 'You don't miss much,' he observed. 'I was just thinking that many of my friends . . . will be going away soon.'

Ché looked alarmed.

'You will go with them?' he cried.

'No. I don't think so.'

'Good. There are many of your friends here, too. You belong here.' Ché said this with conviction and seemed to dismiss the idea completely. Of course, the Tuan would stay. The thought of him going anywhere else was unthinkable.

'I . . . went into Kuala Trengganu yesterday,' announced Harry slyly.

'Oh . . .?' Ché tried to sound casual, but he knew that the Tuan was leading up to something. 'It is a fine place. I have been there myself, twice.'

'Yes indeed. Many fine shops . . .'

Harry took a small leather box out of his pocket. Ché's eyes lit up.

'What have you there, Tuan?' he enquired.

'Oh . . . just something I bought.'

'For yourself?'

'No. For a friend of mine. I wonder if he'll like it.' He opened the box, removed the watch, and let it dangle on its leather fob before Ché's eyes.

'Oh, Tuan! It shines like the sun! I think your friend will

76

like it very much.' He gazed at Harry suspiciously for a moment. 'Who is this friend you speak of?' he demanded.

'A very special friend of mine. A friend who tells me marvellous stories.'

'Me? It is for me, Tuan? Oh, thank you!' Ché stretched out his hand for the gift, but a sudden rush of perversity took Harry and he moved it away a little. 'But I cannot give it to my friend yet,' he continued.

'Why not?'

'First, he would have to say something else for me.'

Ché laughed merrily. 'What must I say, Tuan? Another story?'

Harry shook his head.

'Just one word. Just to prove to me that he has his wits about him. I want him to say "tiger."'

Ché's face fell.

'But Tuan, I cannot! It is unlucky...'

'Oh well.' Harry feigned disappointment. 'If you can't say that one word...'

'But Tuan...' Ché glanced at his feet. 'You don't understand. It is an unlucky word. It brings down the t – the creature's curse onto your head. Of course, I don't *really* believe the old stories, but...'

'You mean... I'll have to take this marvellous watch back to the shop?'

'No, I... uh... I...' Ché fixed his gaze stubbornly to the floor, then glanced up at the glittering silver watch in Harry's grasp. 'Tiger...' he mumbled, in a voice that was barely a whisper.

'Oh, you'll have to say it louder than that,' chided Harry.

'Tiger! There, Tuan, I've said it.'

'So you have,' admitted Harry. And he gave the watch to the boy. Ché's misgivings were swept aside by the rush of his delight as he held the watch to his ear and listened to its ticking.

'Oh, Tuan, it is a beautiful watch, the most wonderful watch ever! I can hear it ticking so loudly! Thank you, Tuan, thank you!' He rushed to hug Harry, tears of gratitude in his eyes. 'May I take it to show my grandmother?'

'Of course!' Harry was every bit as delighted as the boy was. Perhaps more so. Ché rushed into the house, yelling for Pawn to come and witness for herself the incredible watch. But once he was gone, Harry felt vaguely annoyed with himself. Why had he taxed the poor little devil so cruelly? Surely, in all the years he'd lived here, he'd learned that the one thing you shouldn't fool around with were the beliefs that people held dear, no matter how ridiculous they might seem. He had enjoyed giving the present and he had simply wanted to prolong the enjoyment, but it had been a rather thoughtless method of doing so. Still, there was no harm done, he was sure of that. He settled back in his chair and closed his eyes, feeling a deep contentment settle over him. Perhaps he might manage a little nap before breakfast. Yes, why ever not? It had been a good day, so far.

He slept and dreamed of tigers.

Melissa gazed critically at her reflection in the hand mirror, as she methodically ran a brush through her long dark hair. She had been sunbathing on the lawn with her mother for most of the morning and had become bored to distraction. Nothing ever happened here. Sometimes she felt moved to screaming, such was her dissatisfaction. It was ridiculous, here she was, a free agent, able to do just whatever took her fancy; yet what use was such freedom when life consisted of nothing but interminable bouts of boredom? Social life in Malaya tended to consist of long periods of *lounging*. Of course, the background varied from time to time. One could lounge on an idyllic beach, or beside the glittering waters of the local swimming pool . . . well, for that matter, one could simply lounge in the back garden and have done with it.

For the more athletically inclined, there was always tennis or squash . . . good wholesome exercise, nobody could argue with that, but offering little in the way of frivolity. There was really no 'action' here. Melissa glanced thoughtfully at a couple of newspaper articles pinned to the wall beside her desk, both of them torn from British periodicals, which were widely available here, but typically several weeks out-of-date. The first cutting showed a photograph of a hippie girl dancing stark naked at an English pop festival.

THE GIRL WHO LET IT ALL HANG OUT! blared the headline, while the editorial ran on to describe an orgy of rock music and hallucinogenic drugs outraging the inhabitants of a little village near Glastonbury. The other cutting had a similar theme: TOP POP GROUP IN DRUG ORGY ARREST! and a couple of very familiar faces were pictured being escorted from the doorway of a country house by a pair of burly policemen. Melissa sighed. Britain sounded like a much more interesting place than Malaya and she could hardly wait to experience it for herself. She put down the hand mirror, got up, and strolled to the slatted bedroom window. Peering out, she could see her mother stretched out on a sun-bed, apparently asleep. She lay in the midst of a large empty garden and beyond that lay the silent, sun-baked street and not a soul moved along it in the heat of the afternoon.

Melissa felt a great silent wave of emotion welling up inside her, but as she had on numerous occasions before, she willed herself to take control of it. There was at least one area of hope on the horizon: the shooting contest in two days' time. Of course, she had not the remotest interest in shooting, but Bob Beresford would be there, and that particular young man was beginning to receive more and more of her attention as time went by. She constantly found herself thinking about him; worse still, in bed during the long hot sleepless nights, her thoughts turned into the most torrid fantasies, in which he figured prominently. She began to wonder if she was not becoming a little obsessed with him. Her concept of men was still surprisingly girlish, nurtured by the overprotective lifestyle she had experienced in the girls' boarding school in which she had but lately resided. The fact that she was still a virgin at eighteen was frankly not from choice. She had simply not been given the opportunity of being with boys, right from the age when she was first interested in them, and now that she had 'done her time,' that was one matter she intended putting right at the earliest opportunity. At boarding school, nobody would ever admit to being a virgin so great was the shame of it. Free time was often spent recounting lewd adventures with the opposite sex, and though eighty percent of them were undoubtedly pure fiction it was not done to accuse the author of being a liar.

As a consequence of all this, sex, to Melissa, had taken on the form of a terrifying hurdle over which she must scramble before she could ever hope to enjoy herself. She was not so hardened that sex with just anybody would suffice; but Bob Beresford was lean, attractive, and very manly. She could quite easily visualize herself going to bed with him.

She felt suddenly ashamed by the openness of her own thoughts and she blushed, glancing around nervously, as though afraid that somebody might be observing her. She moved back to her desk, sat down again, and picked up the hand mirror. She *was* pretty, there was no doubt of that . . . but Bob did not seem to be very forthright. It might be up to her to make the first move . . .

'Melissa? Aren't you coming out again? It's beautiful out here.' Her mother's voice shrilled from the garden.

'Coming,' she replied wearily. She put the mirror down on the desk and stood up; but the mirror, dangerously close to the edge of the wood, overbalanced, and fell with a crash onto the tiled floor. With an exclamation of anger, Melissa stooped and retrieved it. There was a wide diagonal crack running across its surface. When Melissa examined her reflection, the two halves of her face did not fit together properly, giving the impression that she was horribly deformed.

'Just what I needed,' she muttered darkly. 'Seven years' bad luck.'

She dropped the mirror into the litter bin on her way out of the room.

Haji hugged the darkness to him like a second skin as he advanced cautiously on the sleeping *kampong*. He was wise enough to know that what had worked before would work again. He was also clever enough to realize that he must not strike in the same place. So, through the early evening, he had haunted the roads and secondary jungle nearer to Kampong Wau, and as the hours passed by he had moved progressively nearer to the buildings, taking breaks to listen and watch. Now, the very last lamps had been extinguished for over an hour and the only movements came from within a flimsy wooden stockade, where several skinny cows had been herded for the night. They were quite settled at the moment, but occasionally one would stamp a foot or rub an irritating itch against the stockade, and at such times Haji would freeze, hugging the ground and gazing all around to ensure that no Upright had come out of his home to investigate.

The moon was full and he could see quite plainly every detail of the village before him. Somewhere, hidden from his view, a dog yapped briefly and Haji licked his lips, for he had eaten dogs on several occasions and knew what tender morsels they were. But tonight he had fixed his sights on one of the occupants of the stockade, and nothing would dissuade him from his choice at this late stage. He crept nearer, placing his feet with delicate precision. His wounded forepaw had passed the point of pain and had lapsed into a semi-numbness, which he found even more irritating because it might cause him to act clumsily at a critical moment. Earlier that same day, it had caused him to stumble as he began to run at an unsuspecting wild pig. Haji had recovered quickly, but the mistake cost him precious moments and the pig had escaped by a hair's breadth, plunging into the jungle with nothing more than a few claw marks across its rump.

It was necessary now to cross a stretch of open ground flanked by houses, and he moved over it as fleet and silent as a shadow, until he was no more than a few yards from the stockade. Abruptly, the cows became aware that something was wrong. They snorted, began to mill around uncertainly in the centre of the small pen. There was little room for them to move and certainly nowhere for them to run to. Haji closed the final distance and took the five-foot fence in a single bound, coming over the top of it like a terrible striped shadow. He came down in the midst of the cattle and then all hell broke loose. Their eyes bulging in fear and lowing at the tops of their voices, the cows reeled away from him, their combined weight connecting with the flimsy fencing and shattering the roughly nailed wood. In the same instant, Haji selected his kill, a large leggy calf that was

81

bawling frantically for its mother, and with one, well-aimed spring he had dragged the luckless infant into the dirt and was tearing at its throat. In a confusion of dust and legs and noise, the calf was slaughtered and then Haji was dragging it to the breach in the wall that the other cows were now spilling out of. In the *kampong*, oil lamps were being lit and the voices of nearby Uprights were shouting out in anger and surprise. For some reason, the cows' panicked senses made them whirl around and come thundering back at Haji, whereupon he relinquished his hold on the calf's throat and let out a blood-chilling roar that halted them in their tracks. They milled about again and lit out in another direction. Haji grabbed the still-quivering calf, jerked it around the edge of the stockade, but its legs became entangled in some lengths of fallen wood and wire and he was stuck for the moment. He became aware of Uprights emerging into the night, jabbering excitedly. With a snarl of rage, he took a firmer grip on the calf and heaved it with all his strength, tearing the carcass away and leaving one of its rear legs behind, neatly torn off at the knee. Then with a prodigious effort, he hefted the creature just clear of the ground and raced across the clearing.

The *kampong* was now in pandemonium, shouts and curses spilling from every house. But to the bleary eyes of people stumbling from their beds, Haji was little more than a shadow, disappearing into the secondary jungle that bordered the village. The man who owned the calf quickly discovered his loss and began to exhort his friends into forming a rescue party. Hardly surprisingly, nobody seemed very keen on the idea of following the tiger into the jungle and anyway, they were more concerned with rounding up the other cattle and repairing the stockade. By the time anybody was organized enough to think of doing anything, Haji was half a mile away in the deepest jungle, enjoying a late but very satisfactory supper.

Chapter 9

On Wednesdays, it was Harry's custom to meet up with Dennis at the Officers' Mess for a lunchtime drink. The ever-faithful *trishaw* driver would turn up at Harry's doorstep around twelve o'clock and whisk him over to the barracks. No spoken agreement had ever been made about this. Harry was just grateful that he was saved the inconvenience of arranging transport on a weekly basis and he was careful to ensure that the old man was kept in a steady supply of cigars, which he evidently prized much more than extra money.

On this particular morning, however, the *trishaw* was uncharacteristically late. It was twelve-thirty, and Harry was just beginning to think about walking out in search of a cab when he saw the old man pedalling wearily up to the garden gate. Harry hurried out of the house and was concerned to see that the driver looked rather ill. His thin face was more haggard than ever, his eyes were ringed with redness, and there was an overall weariness about him that suggested he was far from healthy.

'Sorry for lateness, Tuan,' he croaked.

'Sorry nothing! You look terrible. Are you ill?'

The old man shrugged. 'It is nothing, Tuan . . . come, climb in. You are late . . .'

Harry shook his head.

'Don't be ridiculous!' he retorted. 'You can't drive me anywhere in that condition.' He stepped forward and put his hand on the old man's forehead. 'Good lord, you've got a fever. You should be in bed.'

'No, Tuan, I must work. Please, we go now, yes?'

Harry frowned, thought for a moment. Then a solution occurred to him.

'Here, come along, off the bike.' He grasped the driver by the elbow and helped him down. 'Now, *you* climb in,' he insisted.

'But Tuan . . . what . . .? Surely, you cannot . . .?' Harry pushed him firmly but gently into the passenger seat and then climbed astride the bicycle.

'Let me see now,' he murmured. 'There can't be all that much to it . . .'

'Tuan, you cannot do this! It is not proper,' protested the driver, but Harry waved him to silence.

'Nonsense,' he replied. 'You go pedalling this thing in your condition and you're liable to collapse. Now then . . .' He applied his own feet to the pedals and the *trishaw* began to move slowly along the road. 'There, nothing to it. We'll soon have you home. Your *kampong* is near the Mess anyway, isn't it? I can walk from there.'

'But how you get home?'

'I'll take a cab. And I don't expect to see you again until you're recovered, understand?'

The driver was clearly not happy, but it was plain that protesting would do no good. He slumped back in his seat, trying to keep as much out of sight as possible. Meanwhile, Harry was really rather enjoying the experience. The weight of the *trishaw* was considerable and it was harder going than he would have imagined, but for all that there was a certain exhilaration involved and he soon had the vehicle speeding along the coast road. He overtook a couple of coolies strolling along the verge who became quite excited when they saw what was going on. They shouted and gesticulated loudly and Harry gave them a brief, but dignified wave as he sped by.

'You know,' he observed to his old companion, 'I could see myself doing this for a living. Here . . .' He handed the old man a couple of cigars and his lighter.

'Thank you, Tuan.' He took them, lit both and handed one back to Harry. 'You are very good man. Very kind.'

Harry shrugged. 'I don't know about that, but I'm beginning to think I'd make a damned good *trishaw* driver.' Harry noticed a familiar grey Ford saloon heading towards him from the other direction and he waved gaily. For an instant, he had a most satisfying vision of Doctor Kalim's staring face, looking as though the owner of it were about to have a coronary of his own and then the car was gone. Harry laughed uproariously.

'Something is funny, Tuan?'

'Oh, yes, perfect, absolutely perfect! I *am* enjoying myself today!'

They travelled onwards at a good rate and had reached the old driver's village within quarter of an hour. Once there, Harry pressed a twenty-dollar bill into his hand, presented him with a couple more cigars, and insisted that he go straight home to bed. 'If you call for me in such a state again,' he warned, 'I shall be very angry.' And with that, he bundled the poor fellow in the direction of his home, ignoring the barrage of profuse thanks which were directed at him. Without further hesitation, he set off at a brisk pace to walk the remaining half-mile to the Mess.

He arrived there a little after one o'clock and found Dennis waiting for him at the bar.

'Hello old chap. Thought you'd deserted me!'

'Had a bit of trouble on the way in.' Harry recounted what happened, much to Dennis's delight.

'God, I'd have given anything to see that,' he laughed. 'I bet Kalim's face was a picture.' He ordered drinks. The Tiger beer was very refreshing to Harry's somewhat parched throat and he drained the first one almost in one swallow, ordered up another round. 'Steady on,' murmured Dennis. 'What's the hurry?'

'Well, we *trishaw* drivers can work up a big thirst, you know. What's new at the barracks?'

'Same old thing. Mind you, I've had my marching orders.'

'Oh? When?'

'Three months time. Little camp in Suffolk. Curiously enough, it's actually the place I requested . . . I don't mind telling you, I'm looking forward to it. The girls are over the moon, too. Well, you can't blame 'em, there's nothing for them here . . .'

Harry sipped thoughtfully at his beer.

'So that's it then. I kept hoping for a change of plan . . .' It was said with such heartfelt sadness that Dennis felt momentarily at a loss to reply. There was a brief silence, before he came back with the usual reassurances.

'Well, look here old man, we'll be able to write to each

other . . . and you know, don't you, that if you should ever fancy a holiday over there– Well, I don't have to tell you, I'm sure. Here, Trimani! Another round, please!'

'We haven't finished this one yet,' observed Harry.

'Ah well, who's counting?' Dennis made an attempt to swing the conversation around to something else. 'I hear there was another cow killed last night, over in Kampong Wau. Apparently, the cattle were all penned up in the middle of the village and the tiger came in and took a calf just the same. I . . . uh . . . also hear that your friend, Bob Beresford, has appointed himself Great White Sahib for the area. He's been riding round in his Land Rover all day, mobilizing the villagers into action. He's intending to finish off that tiger's career very shortly.'

Harry grunted. 'When does he find the time to fulfil his duties?' he muttered sarcastically.

Dennis shrugged.

'Like a lot of other people around here. Mr Beresford finds himself with a lot of free time on his hands. At least he's putting it to some use. . .'

'Use? Shooting some poor old bugger who's become so desperate for food, he has to pilfer from the *kampongs*? Listen Dennis, Beresford told me exactly why he wanted that tiger. A trophy to display to the world, nothing more.'

'Melissa told me that he was asking you for some help the other night.'

Harry sneered. 'As I recall, he *did* offer me the chance of being his tracker, or some such thing. Doubtless a great honour, but one that I felt obliged to refuse.'

'You know, Harry, nobody knows more about hunting tigers around here than you. Don't you feel you could give him a little help?'

'For God's sake, Dennis! I refuse to get drawn into this business. For one thing, I fail to see what real harm the poor brute has done. The death of a couple of skinny cows doesn't constitute a crisis, surely?'

'But once a cat starts killing . . .'

'Not necessarily, Dennis. Perhaps, if he's old or injured, he might begin to make a regular nuisance of himself, in which case I'd be more willing to accept the necessity of

86

killing him. But let's face it, Dennis, there are plenty of cussed old devils around here who haven't changed their habits in years.' He concluded this sentence with a sly wink, leaving Dennis in no doubt as to which particular tiger Harry was referring.

In the late afternoon, Haji returned to the place where he had left the carcass of the calf; but as he neared the area, his keen ears picked up the sound of Upright voices and he went into cover, creeping slowly forward through the undergrowth, until he could observe what was going on. A short distance to the right of the kill, a couple of dusky Uprights were standing at the base of a tall Kapok tree, staring up into its branches as they hauled a curious wooden thing into position. Meanwhile, a third Upright, paler than his two companions, strutted about barking authoritatively and pointing up into the foliage. Everything about their actions suggested that they were in a hurry, and Haji, curious about their presence, settled down to wait.

After a little while, the pale Upright clambered awkwardly up the tree and a black stick was handed up to him. He seated himself precariously on the wooden contraption that had previously been hoisted skyward and remained there, looking most out of place, his long thin legs dangling some eight feet from the ground. At this point, the two dusky Uprights shouted their farewells and hurried away into the jungle.

Haji was puzzled. He could smell the appetizing aroma of decaying meat wafting across the clearing, but he certainly wasn't foolish enough to go and eat while an Upright kept watch over the proceedings, especially one that was armed with a black stick. Still, it was early yet and the brief tropical twilight was less than half an hour away. Perhaps if Haji waited long enough, the Upright would abandon his mysterious game. So Haji simply stretched out in the soft grass and had a catnap, waking every so often to assure himself that the Upright was still in position. The twilight came and went, with a hypnotic chirping of insects and then the night sky deepened and filled with stars, but the Upright did not budge, although he had begun to fidget on his uncomfortable seat. Haji stretched himself lazily and then took a long slow stroll around the area, moving silently amidst the trees and ferns. At one point, he came very close to the kill. The smell was overpoweringly delicious and for a moment, his willpower weakened, he was on the verge of attempting to sneak out to it; but then the memory of the black stick returned. He thought of the terrible power he himself had seen unleashed and he backed away again, into cover. Now he circled back behind the tree in which the Upright sat, and going down flat against the ground, he cautiously crept up to it. Gazing up, he could see the Upright's strange leathery feet dangling enticingly six feet above his head. What a simple matter it would have been to rear up and snatch the silly fellow off his perch! But Haji's old fear of the Uprights still persisted and instead he lay where he was, listening intently. From time to time, there would be a sharp slapping noise and a muttered curse, which suggested that this particular Upright was having problems with the mosquitos that swarmed amongst the trees at night. Moreover, the wooden seat creaked loudly every time he shifted position. His presence must have been known to every inhabitant of the jungle who passed nearby.

Haji was curious about the Upright's presence here in a tree, a place where that particular species rarely visited. Why had he forsaken the safety and comfort of his more familiar home? The black stick was a clue, of course. The black sticks roared death at other creatures with their moving fire and perhaps it was the Upright's intention to fling death at something he thought might stray here. But what? Surely not the calf, the Upright could not be so stupid as to think that was still alive ... Haji was quite unable to equate himself as being a likely target and so he lay beneath the tree for some time, watching eagerly to see if any action might occur. But the hours passed relentlessly and nothing happened. Once there was a brief flare of fire up in the tree and Haji was about to run when just as suddenly it went out again. Then there was the vaguely familiar smoke-smell that the Uprights sometimes

88

carried with them. A little later, a small white thing fell from the tree and lay smoking in the grass. Haji was tiring of the whole affair and was on the point of taking himself elsewhere in search of other prey when he became aware of soft rhythmic sounds coming from the tree-seat, sounds that seemed to suggest sleep. Haji tilted his head to one side and listened. Sure enough, it did seem like the Upright had gone to sleep, but just to be sure Haji waited for several more minutes before moving off in another wide circle, which brought him slowly, cautiously, up to the kill.

His first thought was to drag it away and consume it elsewhere. The Upright might wake and see him . . . and now, for the first time, it occurred to Haji that the Upright could just as easily direct the power of the black stick against a lone tiger as anything else. And who else might be expected to come to this area but the one who had killed the meat in the first place? It was he, Haji, and no other who the Upright sought! This conclusion caused a kind of anger to well up in Haji and he would have roared his defiance, but good sense warned him that, first, he should secure the meat that belonged to him. He took the half-consumed carcass in his great jaws, lifted it clear off the ground and began to carry it away; but abruptly, he came to a halt. The carcass would not move! Setting it down again, Haji examined a thick piece of rope that was fastened around the calf's middle. The other end was attached to a stout stake that had been hammered deep into the ground. Haji sniffed the attachment suspiciously. Then, glancing back nervously at the tree, he lifted the carcass up again and began to pull with all his might. At first, his efforts seemed fruitless, but then the head of the stake began to slowly pull free of the earth that held it. Haji spread his forepaws wide, braced himself, and gave one enormous heave that wrenched the wood completely out of the ground. Then, with the rope and stake trailing behind him, he carried the food triumphantly away into the jungle. Behind him, slumped on the *machan*, a lone Upright slept, dreaming of success.

Chapter 10

The constant hunt for food was disrupted by the long wailing cries of a tigress whose time for mating was at hand. Haji recognized the voice of Timah, and instantly all thought of food was forgotten. It was early morning and the sounds of Timah's distress echoed eerily through the jungle clearings, a loud prolonged caterwauling impossible to ignore. Haji began to answer with calls of his own, and moving quickly along cattle trails he soon reached an area where she had recently passed, the ferns and bushes reeking with the musky scent that she had copiously sprayed. Her moaning was nearer now, but Haji was alarmed to hear a third voice, calling off to the east, one he didn't recognize. This voice too was answering Timah and it was unmistakably male. Haji thought of the unfamiliar sprayings and scrape marks he had recently found and he bristled with anger. Pausing for a moment, he threw back his head and roared shatteringly, but this time he introduced an edge of warning into the cry that demanded the stranger keep his distance. The third voice kept up its arrogant barrage and gradually the three cats converged on each other.

At last, Haji emerged into a small clearing, to find Timah awaiting him. She moved towards him flirtatiously, prowling with a slow sensuous grace that she had newly discovered. When she reached him, she moved her soft flank invitingly against his and curled the end of her tail over to trail along the length of Haji's spine. But he was still aware of the stranger's voice calling, very close now. Timah halted her caresses and stared off, puzzled, in the direction from which the voice was issuing. She was clearly as surprised by this manifestation as Haji was. After a few moments, she returned to her shameless advances with renewed urgency, but Haji could not settle. He prowled backwards and forwards, growling deep in his throat, while he anticipated the confrontation that must

90

inevitably come.

Suddenly, the newcomer burst impetuously into the clearing and stood confronting the two of them. He was a handsome young male, just reaching maturity. He could not have been much over four summers old and, while he lacked Haji's dimensions, he was clearly healthy and at the peak of his strength. He stood with his legs braced, snarling arrogant defiance at Haji across the clearing. Haji responded with a roar that would have scared most competitors away, such was its force, but the newcomer stood his ground, his ears raised to show the white spots on the back of them, a symbol of aggression. Haji moved away from Timah and paced silently toward the youngster, until they stood about ten feet apart. Meanwhile, Timah, with an air of silent resignation, plumped herself down in the grass to await the outcome of the contest. To the victor would go the spoils of war.

Now began a long and noisy show of power as the two males paced restlessly up and down, bellowing and raging, bristling the white ruffs around their necks and making short ritual dashes at each other, then pulling away at the last instant. The clearing echoed to the noise of them and the display went on for some considerable time before they tired of it and decided to get down to some real fighting. It was the young male who made the first attack. He took a sudden lunging run at Haji, his great clawed feet making slashing attacks at the older cat's eyes, but Haji twisted aside, turned in against his adversary's flank and sank his claws and teeth into the thick neck as it dashed by him. The youngster roared in pain and whirled about in a flurry, striking back with a series of blows that thrust Haji bodily away from him. He followed straight after, lunging full length onto Haji, his jaws seeking the older cat's throat. But Haji's legs raked savagely against his opponent's chest, flinging him aside, and the young tiger was persuaded not to try that line of attack again.

The two of them drew back from each other and fell silent, each of them intent upon the other. They prowled cautiously around, each of them seeking an opening, like two wrestlers weighing each other's weaknesses. The younger cat now became aware of Haji's injured leg and instinctively directed his next attack in that area. He leapt abruptly in, trying to sink his teeth into the swollen flesh; but he received such a devastating flurry of blows about the head for his troubles that he turned away again, and then Haji's claws sank into his flank and the two of them locked together. Their struggles took them over the edge of a steep slope and they tumbled headlong, a bundle of kicking legs and foaming jaws. At the base of the hill they struck a tree trunk and sprawled heavily apart. The youngster was up first. He crept up to the base of the tree while Haji was still recovering from his daze; then dashing around it, he struck Haji head on, three hundred and fifty pounds of ferocious power, driving the older cat backwards with a series of relentless, crushing blows. Haji felt one of his ears rip into bloody tatters and this served to release a rage in him that was extraordinary. With a howl of hatred, he burst back at his tormentor, blind to everything but his own fury. The tables were abruptly turned and now it was the young cat who retreated from the onslaught. He was backed up against the tree trunk again and he was caught there for an instant like a heavy-weight boxer slumped against the ropes, while Haji delivered some fearful damage, his great claws ripping deep into the other's head and neck. But then the youngster had the sense to slip around the trunk of the tree and he kept it between him and Haji for a moment while he struggled to regain his breath. The two of them circled warily around the base of the tree now. The youngster could see that Haji had expended much of his last reserves of strength in that recent outburst. Now he was weakening rapidly, hampered by his injured leg. A decisive attack now could just turn the tables . . .

The youngster backed abruptly away from the tree into open ground and Haji followed closely, realizing only too well that his adversary was rallying for an all-out assault. In this next confrontation, the outcome of the fight would be resolved. There was a moment of silence, while two pairs of yellow eyes flashed dumb hatred at each other. Then, as if at some prearranged signal, the two great cats ran at each other and collided in a fury of claw and fang. Haji struck badly, twisting his injured foot inwards against the other cat's chest. He howled in pain and, sensing an advantage, the youngster struck home with his heavy paws, pounding and tearing at Haji with incredible force. Haji was virtually blinded by the barrage and could do nothing but retreat before it. In that instant, he knew that he had lost the fight. The triumphant roar of the youngster mocked him as he turned tail and ran away into the jungle, for to stay longer was to die, and Haji had always been a survivor.

But his own shame weighed terribly on him as he plunged away into the undergrowth with his tormentor still hard on his heels. He raced into a bamboo thicket and buried himself deep in the cool leafy sanctuary. Thankfully, the younger cat gave up the chase now, contenting himself with parading up and down outside the thicket, roaring triumphantly and telling the jungle at large about his magnificent victory.

Haji slumped down in exhaustion and began to lick his wounds in humiliation. He was an exile now. Not only would the victor take his mate, but he would lay claim to his territory as well and would waste no time in chasing Haji off it. Then the old cat would be nothing but a transient, a tiger without a range to prowl. He would be allowed to linger no more than a day or so in any one place, and all the creatures of the jungle would know of his shame. In such a condition, he could not hope to live for very much longer.

He lapped weakly at his injured paw. The fight had unsettled the quills in their fleshy beds and new pain rivered spasmodically through it. His head, neck, and flanks were scarred deeply and fresh blood dripped from the wounds. He had meant to move on, but now found he had scarcely the strength to rise. Peering back, he saw the youngster strutting away in the direction of Timah and knew that, for the moment, the bamboo thicket was as secure a place as any other. He let his head drop into his forepaws and he gave a long low moan, deep in his throat, to articulate the misery that he felt. And he lay slumped and unmoving in the midst of the thicket all through the rest of that day and far into the night.

Harry emerged from a taxicab outside the gates of Kuala Hitam barracks. He reached in and took out the rifle in its leather carrying case and slung this carelessly over his shoulder. He paid the driver and then walked towards the gates.

Everywhere seemed horribly quiet, there was the distinct air of 'nothing happening.' The few huts and buildings he passed seemed devoid of any life. Once this place had fairly bustled with activity. Of course, Harry had no wish to go back to the dark days of the confrontation, but it was sad that a place like Kuala Hitam couldn't function without some kind of war to support it . . .

When he reached the shooting range, it quickly became apparent why there was nobody at the camp; they were all here. A large crowd had assembled by the firing line and it was quite obvious that everybody who had a dollar or two to spare was going to have a bet. A couple of young Gurkha officers were sliding in and out of the crowd taking odds and a lot of money appeared to be changing hands. Of course, it was against all the laws of protocol, but Harry could hardly blame anybody for their actions. If such a silly little event was the high spot of everybody's month, then there was something very wrong with the way things were around here.

He moved into the crowd and instantly people started recognizing him. Harry had long since earned the dubious status of a local celebrity, and at social gatherings he tended to find himself being greeted by people whom he scarcely knew or, for that matter, *wanted* to know. He moved towards the shooting line, nodding and keeping his best 'professional' smile glued to his face, but the smile faded somewhat as he noticed Melissa talking earnestly with Bob Beresford. She glanced up as he approached.

'Oh, Uncle Harry, there you are! We were beginning to think you'd changed your mind!' Harry winced at the way she said the word 'we' as if she and Beresford had already formed some kind of partnership. Well, it was probably just a matter of time anyway, he realized that now. He tried not to feel resentment towards the Australian, but he felt it rising again the moment he heard the man's droning accent.

'Great to see you, Harry! I hope you don't mind me callin' you that . . .' Bob paused briefly for a reply, didn't get one and hurried on again. 'Now, if I can just explain what's going to happen here. First off, you give your fifty dollars to Harun over there . . .' He indicated one of the young officers. 'It works out that there's eight of us all together, so what happens is we all pair off see, we have a sort of elimination series. Whoever wins out of the first pair goes on to meet the winner of the next pair and so on. The eventual winner takes the pot.'

Harry nodded. 'What are the targets?'

'Just standard bulls. You get six shots each and the highest number of inner rings gets it. They aren't too big, think you'll be able to see them okay?'

'I think I'll manage,' snapped Harry, curtly.

'Yeah, well . . . we've drawn lots for partners already. You're paired against me, as it happens.'

'What a surprise,' said Harry drily.

'You'd better be good,' announced Melissa brightly. 'I've put down five dollars on you, Uncle Harry.'

He glared at her. 'You've bet?' he enquired. 'But I thought only the competitors could . . .?'

Bob coughed. 'Oh no, Mr Sullivan. We've organized a tote for the spectators as well. Shame if they can't get in on the fun too, eh? There's no profit in that part of it for us. The winners share the pot.' He grinned, spread his hands in a gesture of benevolence. 'It's a bit of a laugh!' he concluded. 'Anyway, I told Melissa she should put her money on me. I'm going to win this.'

Harry gazed at him for a moment. 'Are you always so sure of yourself, Mr Beresford?' he asked.

'Only where shootin's concerned. I never miss.' He said the last three words with slow steady pride.

'Well, Uncle Harry's no slouch either,' chuckled Melissa. 'I tell you what! This will be a good way to settle that little dispute the other night . . . about the shooting lessons! Whoever wins out of the pair of you is hired. How about that?' The two men gazed at each other in silence. Melissa instantly wished she hadn't said it.

'Here no, look, that's a silly idea . . .' she began, but Bob waved her to silence.

'Sounds fine to me! What do you say Mr Sullivan?'

'Just as you wish,' he murmured. He turned to Melissa. 'Where's your father today?' he enquired.

'He had to work I'm afraid. Poor Daddy, he misses all the fun.'

'Does he know you're here?'

'Yes, of course! Anyway, what does it matter? I'm old enough to do as I like.'

Harry noticed that, as she said this, her eyes slid sideways to observe Beresford's reaction, as though she was constantly seeking his approval.

'Yes, of course . . .' He turned abruptly away and went to find a seat, where he could await his turn. When the young officer approached him, he dutifully handed over his fifty dollars.

'What has the silly old bugger got against me?' murmured Bob irritably.

'He's not a silly old bugger,' retorted Melissa and was vaguely surprised by her own defensiveness. 'When you get to know him, you'll realize that. But it's true, you do rub him up the wrong way . . .'

'I try to be nice,' said Bob. 'I certainly don't bear *him* any grudge. But you saw what happened just then. I asked if I could call him Harry, he didn't say a bloody word. I ended up calling him Mr Sullivan, the same as ever. I mean, how am I expected to make friends with somebody like that?'

'I don't know,' she admitted. 'But I'd hate to think of the two of you as enemies. Why don't you — Why don't you let him win?'

'What?'

'It would mean a lot to him.'

'I'm sure it bloody would, but I couldn't do that!'

'Why not?'

96

He stared at her. 'Well . . . because . . . because it wouldn't be the truth. And anyway, I always shoot to win.'

Melissa sighed. 'I had a feeling you'd say something like that,' she said.

The contest got under way and the two Gurkha officers who had drawn first shot got out their rifles and took their place on the shooting line. They tossed a coin to see who would go first. The crowd drew back and went quiet. The first man scored three bulls and three outers; the second four bulls and two outers. Amidst applause, he went to await the next round, while his opponent consoled himself with a can of beer. Another two men shot next. Then it was Harry and Bob's turn.

Harry took out his rifle from its case and approached the shooting line. Bob let out a low whistle of admiration when he saw the weapon.

'Here, that's a beaut. It's an old Martini-Henry isn't it?'

'That's right. A 450/400.'

'Like to sell it?'

'No thank you.'

'Well, it's a nice old gun, but not the sort I'd choose for a competition like this. Bit old-fashioned, if you ask me.' He hefted his own rifle. 'Now you take my gun here. Had it custom-made in Oz. It's got a . . .'

'Mr Beresford, this is the only rifle I possess and, furthermore, the only weapon I'd ever feel truly happy with.' Harry reached into his pocket and took out a coin, which he flipped in the air. 'Heads or tails?' he demanded.

'Heads!'

Harry unclenched his fist.

'It's tails. After you Mr Beresford.'

'Suit y'self.' Bob took his position on the line in the designated kneeling position and sighted on the fresh target, some thirty feet away. He began to fire, rapidly, methodically, loading a fresh cartridge into the chamber after each shot. After the sixth, he stood up confidently with a smile on his face, as the shouter raced over to check the score. The man waved his arms excitedly.

'Six bulls!' he cried joyfully. The crowd broke into spontaneous applause. Bob leaned towards Harry with a triumphant smile on his face.

'Good luck,' he said, and he made no attempt to hide the sarcasm in his voice.

With a frown, Harry approached the firing line, knowing that the very best he could hope for was a draw. He waved to the shouter and called out. 'Announce them one at a time! I don't want to waste any bullets!' This brought some laughter from the crowd, who were obviously rooting for him.

'Go on, Tiger!' yelled a couple of voices, though what they expected him to do in the face of such competition was anybody's guess. He kneeled down on the line and slid the wooden stock of the rifle against his right shoulder. It had been a long time since he felt it there and it was oddly reassuring. He loaded a cartridge into the chamber and took a long careful aim. His eyes were not as good as they once were and he had to stare very hard at the small white target before it came into focus. He steadied himself, squeezed the trigger, felt the abrupt jolting kick of the old rifle as it fired. The crowd held its breath as the shouter hurried over to the target.

'One bull!' he yelled and scuttled back to safety.

Harry took his time with the reloading, knowing that hurrying made a man clumsy. Again he took a long aim, wanting to be absolutely sure before firing. He squeezed the trigger.

'Two bulls!' A murmur of anticipation ran through the crowd. The old man still knew how to do it. Maybe the first shot had been a fluke, but two in a row, that wasn't bad at all. Over in the crowd, Melissa glanced at Bob. 'You could have missed just one shot,' she whispered.

'I told you,' he hissed. 'I never miss.'

Harry squared up for his third shot and got another bull. Likewise, with his fourth. The crowd was growing tense with excitement. In the silence, the slightest movement was unbearably loud. Taking aim for his fifth shot, Harry paused for a moment to mop at his brow. Sweat was running down into his eyes and he muttered to himself for a moment, before resighting. A nervous cough in the crowd made him hesitate and he let the barrel of the gun drop again before realigning his aim. He took a deep breath, squeezed the trigger.

'Five bulls!' The crowd broke into spontaneous applause then corrected themselves, remembering that there was one more shot to go.

Harry took a cartridge from his belt, fumbled it, picked it up again. His eyes were watering from the effort of peering with such intense concentration. He wished he'd thought to bring a hat. He considered asking if anybody had one he could borrow, but thought better of it. One more shot and he was home. Then, of course, there would be another shoot-off, because a draw was no use to anybody in this contest. He wilted at the thought of it. He wasn't sure if his eyes, or for that matter his nerves, could take another round of this kind of punishment. He shook his head, wiped the sweat from his forehead. Then he realized that everybody else was waiting patiently for him to shoot and he lifted the rifle, aimed it. His hands were clammy, they seemed to stick to the wood of the gun. In front of him, the target seemed to fade to a white fuzzy blob, then redefine itself, dissolve, sharpen, dissolve . . .

The trick was to fire when it came into focus.

He stroked the trigger with his finger. The gun recoiled, the shot felt good but he had doubts about it. He waited in the silence while the shouter raced eagerly to the target. The man came to a halt, gazing at the holes in the rings as though they foretold his own destiny. Then his shoulders sagged, he gazed up at the crowd.

'One outer,' he said flatly.

A great collective groan spilled from the crowd. Harry's loss was now their loss. They had so much wanted the old man to win. He took it with all the good grace he could muster, turning away with a shrug and a smile and they loved him for it. He strolled back to much applause and a consoling hug from Melissa. Ironically, for the moment at least, he was the winner.

'Oh, Uncle Harry, you were magnificent. That was *so* close . . .'

'Yeah, great shootin' Mr Sullivan. You're a tough man to

beat.' Bob cranked Harry's hand enthusiastically but his eyes suggested that he resented losing the adoration of the crowd, even if it was only for a short time. 'But look here, now that you've proved what a good shot you are, surely you'll help me tackle this tiger?'

Harry raised his eyebrows ever so slightly. 'You mean to say you haven't bagged him yet?'

Bob was quite unaware of the sarcasm in Harry's voice.

'Sat up all last night over his kill. Didn't see hide nor hair of the bugger. But when I fell asleep, he managed to make off with the carcass without waking me ... I mean, strewth, Mr Sullivan, the calf was roped to the ground! Have you ever heard tell of such a thing?'

'Oh yes, indeed. Nothing a tiger does is straightforward, especially when he gets old and wily ... Is *your* tiger old and wily, Mr Beresford?'

'Well, how would I know that?'

'By looking at the *signs*, man!'

Bob frowned. 'This is exactly what I've been telling you. What I know about tracking, you could print on the back of a matchbox. Oh, Mr Sullivan, if you'd only come out to the place I was last night ... have a look at the tracks, see if you could give me a bit of advice. What do you say?'

Harry glanced not at Bob, but at Melissa. She was gazing at him hopefully, the same expression she used to use when she was younger and the pair of them were walking past the ice-cream parlour in Kuala Trengganu. He had never been able to resist the look then and time had in no way hardened him.

'Well ...' he murmured, 'I appear to be fifty dollars down today ... and as a professional tracker I suppose I should ask a fee. After all, it'll be nothing to you if you're so certain of winning the contest here ... so if you're prepared to pay me fifty dollars for my work, I suppose it's alright.'

'Done! We could drive out there tomorrow afternoon, after my lessons. I'll pick you up in my Land Rover around three o'clock, alright?'

'Just as you wish.'

At this moment, Bob was called away for the next round

100

of the shoot-off, so Harry and Melissa found a couple of cane chairs and settled down to watch the remainder of the contest. People kept wandering over to Harry to slap him on the back and say what a close thing it had been. Harry bore this with quiet humility and Melissa had to stifle a laugh when she saw the look of silent desperation on his face.

'They *are* right, you know,' she observed. 'It's marvellous considering it must be years since you've even fired a gun. Doesn't it make you want to take it up again?'

'It depends what you mean by *it*,' he replied. 'Shooting at paper targets is fine. I've nothing against *that*.'

'Oh yes . . . but this tiger is making a nuisance of itself, after all.'

Harry gazed at her calmly.

'So everybody keeps telling me,' he said.

The contest progressed through the morning. It was now approaching midday and the heat was rising steadily. Harry had to grudgingly admit that there was something awesome about the Australian's abilities on the firing range. He acted as if he had never heard of the word 'lose' and round after round he came up with a perfect score of six bulls. But, thought Harry, there was also something very disagreeable in the way he swaggered out to take his turn, a certain assured arrogance that suggested that he knew only too well that he was unbeatable in this particular game. There was a marked insincerity whenever he shook the hand of the man he had just vanquished. Melissa, however, seemed blind to these traits. Whenever he was on the firing line, he had every little bit of her attention, and as each successive round went by, she would applaud wildly and say, 'That's another one to Bob!'

Harry said nothing. He just sat quietly and observed. The final round came. Bob was matched against one of the Gurkha officers, the only man who had ever seemed to pose a threat. In the first round, they both scored a maximum of six points. Likewise with a second and third round. The heat now was becoming unbearable and a sudden death play-off was suggested. The men would fire alternately at two separate targets. The first to score anything less than a bull was out of the match. The round progressed in this

101

fashion for a considerable time, but it was noticed that while the officer took longer and longer over his shots, Bob cracked away quickly, almost carelessly, yet his aim never faltered.

'The day that young man misses an important shot,' thought Harry to himself, 'there will be hell to pay. Somebody that sure of themselves could never live with failure.'

At last, on his ninth successive shot, the Gurkha's luck failed. A shot went wide, well into the outer rings and Bob Beresford was the winner. He strode back, basking in the applause, to receive his crate of beer and, more importantly, the money.

'Well, it looks like you should have put your five dollars on our friend there,' observed Harry drily.

Melissa squeezed his hand. 'That's alright, Uncle Harry! You were marvellous anyway. Besides, five dollars isn't exactly a fortune, is it?'

Bob was now the centre of a large crowd of people, mostly officers, and more money was changing hands. A Malay youth had suddenly appeared amongst the crowd and people were talking excitedly to him. He was grimfaced but after a while he nodded. There was some laughter and Harry saw that several notes were passed to the boy. He turned away from the crowd and began to walk towards the targets, carrying a beer bottle in his hand.

'This must be the trick-shooting,' announced Melissa gleefully.

'Trick-shooting?' Harry stared at her quizzically.

'Bob said something about it before . . .'

The boy came to a halt by the targets. The crowd had backed away and now Bob went down on one knee. Abruptly, the boy reached up and put the bottle on his head. Then he waited, a look of silent dread on his face.

'Good God,' whispered Harry. 'He's going to . . .'

He stood up, horrified, and began to walk towards the firing line. But he had taken only two steps when he heard the report of the rifle and saw the bottle shatter above the boy's head. The crowd applauded enthusiastically, the boy ran forward, much relieved; but Harry felt a sudden surge

102

of anger erupt within him. He strode purposefully forward, an expression of pure rage on his face. He reached Bob just as the Australian was getting to his feet.

'You jumped-up bloody idiot!' exploded Harry. 'What the bloody hell do you think you're playing at?'

Bob gazed at him, open-mouthed in astonishment.

'What's the matter, Mr Sullivan?' he cried.

'What's the matter? Of all the irresponsible, downright bloody dangerous tricks I've ever seen— Supposing you'd missed? Supposing the cartridge had misfired? That boy could have been killed and you stand there asking me what's wrong!'

Bob reddened a little.

'Hey now, steady on. The boy was in no danger. I do that trick all the time!'

'Do you now?'

'Sure . . . and besides, he was well paid for that, twenty dollars. That's more than he'd earn in a month!'

'I'm quite prepared to believe that Mr Beresford, but it would be of little consolation to him if your bullet had gone through his forehead, would it?'

Some laughter went up from the onlookers nearest at hand and Bob realized just how public this little scene was.

'Now look,' he said quietly. 'You're making too much of this. If I've pulled that stunt once, I've done it a thousand times. It's perfectly safe . . . here!' Melissa had just hurried over to referee the bout and now Bob grabbed hold of her arm. 'Just to show you how simple it is, I'll shoot a bottle off Melissa's head too!'

'You damn well will not!' exclaimed Harry.

'Oh, why not?' retorted Melissa brightly. 'It sounds like fun!'

'Fun?' roared Harry. 'For heaven's sake, girl, you're as mad as he is.' He took hold of her other arm. 'Come along now, it's time you went home,' he said.

'Uncle Harry! Don't be ridiculous, let go of me!' For a moment Melissa was the object of a furious tug-of-war between the two men, but it was Bob who relinquished his hold first, embarrassed by the looks of pure delight on the faces of onlookers. Harry began to drag Melissa forcibly through the crowd. 'Let go of me! How *dare* you!' Her face was crimson. She had never felt so humiliated in her life. The laughter of the people she passed rang in her ears. 'Uncle Harry, I don't want to go yet! For God's sake, I'm *eighteen years old*!'

'Not old enough to have learned any sense though,' growled Harry. 'I'm sorry, Melissa, but I refuse to leave you here with that . . . that maniac. I'm merely doing what your father would do if he were here.'

'Don't be ridiculous. My father hasn't pulled a stunt like that since I was twelve!' They were moving away from the crowd now and Melissa's voice rose in volume. 'The plain fact is that you're *jealous*!'

He rounded on her in amazement.

'I'm not jealous, Melissa, I'm concerned. Concerned for your welfare, that's all. That *oaf*, Beresford . . .'

'Oh, he's an oaf is he?' Melissa had tears in her eyes now and she wanted to hurt the old man for humiliating her so thoughtlessly. 'An oaf who can shoot better than you. An oaf who's young and handsome, not a dried-up old stick who lives on memories!'

Harry shrank from her, as if she had physically struck him. He closed his eyes for a moment and Melissa saw, quite clearly, mirrored in the hard lines of his face the misery, the loneliness of long years of solitude. She regretted her words the instant they had left her lips. Harry stood still for a moment, his head slightly bowed. He looked weary, suddenly rather ill. Abruptly, he opened his eyes, turned away, began to walk in the direction of the gates. She followed, a few faltering steps.

'Oh, Uncle Harry . . . I didn't mean that . . . I didn't mean it . . .'

He stopped for a moment, not looking back at her.

'Of course, you did, my dear. And you're quite right. I am a silly old man. I don't understand, that's all. You go back to the others now. As you said, you're eighteen years old. You can do whatever you like.' And he walked on again.

Melissa stood where she was a moment, shocked by the cruelty of her own words. How *could* she have said such a thing? How could she? Through a blur of tears, she glanced back at the crowd she had just left. They were applauding some new stunt now and she could see Bob on the firing line, the object of their attention. Ahead of her, the lonely figure of an old man trudged slowly away, his head hanging in dejection. She hesitated for only a moment longer.

'Uncle Harry, wait for me!' She ran after him, until she was walking alongside.

'You were quite right, it *was* a dangerous thing to do. I wasn't thinking very carefully, that's all . . .' She bit her lip. 'We could . . . share a taxi home if you like . . . Uncle Harry? I'm so sorry, I was just angry. You aren't angry with me, are you?' She walked along for several moments, gazing at him intently.

He said nothing, but after they had walked a short distance, his lean gnarled hand reached out and took her own hand into its grasp. And they walked together towards the barracks gates in silence. Harry seemed to have retreated into a world of his own making. He kept hold of Melissa's hand, but he did not speak once all through the taxi journey home.

Chapter 11

Haji limped sorrowfully along a cattle trail. His body was stiff and ached in every joint, and loss of blood had weakened him considerably. The hunting that night had been more fruitless than ever, hampered as he was by his wounds. He had caught a couple of muddy frogs at the edge of a swamp earlier that evening and they had served to allay his hunger to a tiny degree. But he could not survive on such a diet and he knew that if another two nights passed without a major kill, he would simply lie down in some quiet thicket and die.

He prowled hopefully around the outskirts of another *kampong*, seeking to find evidence of cattle, but in this he was disappointed. There was nothing but the strong, all-pervading smell of Uprights. A fleeting image stirred through his mind's eye, a time when he had lain up close to a village and an Upright cub had come very near to him. . .

He moved on, clambered awkwardly up a slight rise and slumped down in a spot where he could gaze into the mass of buildings before him. A soft night wind brought the smell of the Uprights wafting straight up to him and he grimaced, dropped his head onto his paws, gave a long low rumbling growl of discontent.

The idea came abruptly to him that if he were to survive the hard nights and days to come, then he had only one choice. He must seek slower game.

Melissa's hair was dry already. Ten minutes earlier she had been splashing aimlessly about in the cool waters of the local swimming pool with her friends; now she was walking homeward beside them along the grass verge that bordered the road. The two girls with her were schoolmates, a year younger than her, agreeable enough company but, she thought, rather on the empty-headed side. For this reason she rarely bothered to seek them out during the holidays even though they lived quite nearby; but they had called at her house earlier that morning to ask if she would like to go swimming with them, and there was hardly any reason why she should say no. The girls' names were Victoria Lumly and Allison Weathers. Victoria was a rather plump girl with medium-length curly red hair and attractive green eyes. Though she possessed an innocent air, she was a holy terror where boys were concerned and some of the stories she came out with at school were rather lurid. Allison, on the other hand, was a tall thin girl with a rather homely face, the most striking feature of which was a set of buckteeth that had earned her the rather cruel nickname of Rabbit. Her one saving grace was her long blond hair, which fell down in a series of silken tresses that would not have disgraced the heroine of a pre-Raphaelite painting. She was one of those unfortunate creatures who was prone to fits of giggling whenever the subject of boys was brought up. As this was the chief interest of both Victoria and Melissa, she had consequently been giggling uncontrollably all afternoon and was now looking rather worn out. Still, for the moment at least, the subject had switched to a more general topic – going home.

'It's alright for you, Melissa,' observed Victoria enviously. 'We'll be going back to another year in school. You'll be free!'

'I suppose. But I imagine school in England will be more fun than it is in Singapore.'

The two girls looked extremely unconvinced by this.

'Actually,' confided Allison cautiously. 'I'm going to miss Malaya.'

'What?' The other two stared at her.

'Well . . . we won't have servants and things . . . and it's supposed to be very cold in the winter . . .'

'Bullshit!' cried Victoria. She was able to say this with some authority. Her parents had only been posted to Malaya for two and a half years, whereas the other girls couldn't remember what the old country was like. 'You'll soon get used to it. Besides, there's so much to do there, you'll be spoiled for choice! Pubs . . . discos . . . pop concerts . . . fish 'n' chip shops . . .' She raised her eyebrows. 'Boys . . .'

Allison began to giggle. The other two girls gazed at her wearily.

'Listen to it!' sighed Victoria. 'And this is the girl who claims she isn't a virgin!'

'I'm not!' retorted Allison crossly. 'I've told you before. I was interfered with by my *amah*'s brother.'

'You ought to see him,' chuckled Victoria with a wink at Melissa. 'Fourteen years old and five foot nothing with his socks on.'

'Well, he was certainly passionate enough, I can tell you! He . . . he came into the room where I was changing and . . . well, you know. . .'

'And where was your *amah* while all this was going on?' demanded Melissa.

'Out shopping.'

'It sounds very dubious to me,' persisted Victoria. 'Anyway, I bet he didn't go all the way.'

'He put his hand under my bra!' said Allison defensively.

Now it was the other girls' turn to laugh. Allison blushed a deep shade of red.

'Oh dear,' gasped Melissa. 'I'm not sure that qualifies as losing your virginity, somehow. Still, nice try. A for effort!' They walked on for some distance in silence, letting the mirth subside. 'Anyway,' said Melissa after some thought. 'I can't wait to kiss this place goodbye. Nothing ever happens here.'

'*Some* of us are alright,' said Victoria meaningfully. '*Some* of us get invited to shooting contests!'

Melissa smiled.

'Just a question of knowing the right people,' she replied. 'Anyway, how did you know I was there?'

'Oh, a little bird, dear, a little bird . . .'

Melissa frowned. She was well aware just how accurate the local grapevine was.

'I also understand,' continued Victoria, 'that you were in the company of Mr Bob Beresford.'

Allison began to giggle uncontrollably.

'Yes, well, I was talking to him quite a bit,' admitted Melissa. 'What's wrong with that?'

'Nothing! He's *gorgeous*. Give me half a chance and I'd be in there myself . . . What a shame he's tied up though.' She glanced sneakily at Melissa to gauge her reaction and it was one of surprise.

'What do you mean?' asked Melissa suspiciously. 'Oh for God's sake, Allison, stop giggling!'

Victoria sauntered along for a moment, relishing her own power.

'I thought everybody knew,' she said.

'Knew what?'

'Well . . . by all accounts, he's very fond of his little Chinese *amah* . . . I mean, *very* fond. I've seen her, she is an extraordinarily pretty girl.'

'They sleep together,' whispered Allison fearfully. She was about to lapse into another fit of giggles, but warning glances from her two companions kept her silent for the moment.

'I don't believe it!' snapped Melissa.

'Oh, it's true enough.' Victoria was quite adamant. 'They're quite open about it apparently. It's the talk of our estate, it's a wonder you haven't heard about it before.'

'Bob and I are very good friends,' persisted Melissa. '*Very* good. He's promised to give me shooting lessons.'

The two younger girls gazed at her with new respect.

'Lucky you,' Victoria murmured meaningfully.

'In fact, that's not all I'm planning to do with him!' Having got their attention, Melissa was determined to press home her advantage. 'He's been very . . . attentive . . . if you know what I mean.'

'Do you fancy him?' enquired Allison breathlessly.

'Of course, she fancies him, you gonk! Who wouldn't? Did you see him at the tennis club last week? Talk about poetry in motion . . .'

'And he does look quite *clean*,' reasoned Allison. The other two looked at her in quiet desperation.

'What's that got to do with it?' demanded Victoria irritably.

'Well . . . it's important. I wouldn't like to go with a man who wasn't nice and clean. For one thing, you can pick up all kinds of horrible diseases . . .'

'We are talking about sweaty animal passion!' cried Victoria. 'We are talking about a man who would grab you in his tanned muscular arms and throw you roughly onto a bed, raining passionate kisses down on your yielding lips . . .'

'He'd still have to be clean,' insisted Allison.

Victoria thought for a moment.

'What about your *amah*'s brother? Was *he* clean?'

Allison glanced at her feet for several moments.

'Not very,' she said at last.

Victoria smiled.

'Now, Bob Beresford,' she murmured. 'I wouldn't care if he'd just crawled through a cesspit. A *real* man like that – How old is he, Melissa?'

'Twenty-four.'

'Mmm. Do you really think you've got a chance of making home base with him?'

'Sure! Just a question of time, really.'

'I bet you won't go all the way with him.'

'I bet you I will!'

'How much?'

'As much as you like.'

'Twenty dollars.'

'Alright then.'

'This is silly!' said Allison. 'For one thing, how will we know?'

'That's true,' agreed Victoria. 'You could simply tell us that you'd been with him, and we wouldn't know any better. We'd have to give you a physical or something!'

'Well, I wouldn't lie to you.'

'You might. No we'll have to think about this more carefully . . .'

The three of them walked for some distance in silence, while Victoria thought out the possibilities.

'One way,' she mused at last, 'would be for you to perform the act somewhere where Allison and I could watch . . .'

'You must be joking!' retorted Melissa.

'Yes, well I didn't think you'd agree to that idea. Another way, I suppose, would be to bring something of his back to show us . . . sort of a trophy . . . but what? An item of underwear perhaps . . .?'

Now Allison began to screech with laughter. Melissa was quickly losing her temper with the girl.

'Shut up,' she snapped. 'This is serious.'

Victoria snapped her fingers.

'I've got it! Bob wears a special medallion, doesn't he?'

'I . . . don't know . . .'

'Oh yes. Angela Cartwright told me she got talking to him at the swimming pool a couple of weeks ago. He was wearing this thing around his neck, a silver charm shaped like a bullet or something. He told her it had belonged to his father and that he never took it off, because it really meant a lot to him. Now, if you brought *that* back to show us, I think that would be proof enough, don't you Allison?'

Allison nodded gravely.

'Better than underwear,' she reasoned.

'But supposing he won't give it to me?' asked Melissa. 'Bob was very fond of his father, you know. You can tell by the way he talks about him. He might not want to part with it.'

110

'My dear girl . . .' Victoria smiled mysteriously. 'I'm told that when a man wants a woman enough, he'll give her anything she asks in return for . . . sex.' Instinctively, she grabbed hold of Allison, before the giggles could start.

'Alright,' agreed Melissa, reluctantly. 'I'll try.'

'There's no need to set a time limit either, seeing as you'll be heading back to England in three months time. If you haven't caught him by then, you never will. I'll draw up a couple of papers for us both to sign, saying that if you haven't presented the medallion for me to see no later than three days before you leave, then you pay me twenty dollars. And of course, if you *do* show the medallion, I'll pay *you* the twenty dollars.'

'Do we really need papers?' enquired Melissa.

'Of course. Makes it more legal!'

'My daddy was telling me,' said Allison unexpectedly, 'that during the war they used to send the Gurkhas out after the Japanese and the Gurkhas got paid a bounty for each one they killed. To prove it, they used to cut off the Jap's ears and bring them back in pairs . . .'

'Now there's an idea!' cried Victoria in delight. 'You could sneak a knife into the bed with you Melissa and cut off something of Bob's, to bring back as proof!'

'Ooh horrible!' cried Allison, with a shiver of revulsion. 'Imagine poor Melissa bringing back Bob's ears in her handbag.'

Victoria winked. 'It wasn't his ears I was thinking of,' she announced, and she and Melissa lapsed into a bout of hysterical laughter. Allison stood staring at them in puzzlement, wondering just exactly what it was that they were laughing at. But they wouldn't tell her and she was left to conjecture about it all the way home.

Harry was snatched from a shallow dreamless snooze by the sound of a car engine roaring up to his garden gate. He sat up, blinking, unsure for the moment of where he was. He found himself in his favourite rattan chair on the verandah. A cup of tea stood on the table in front of him, but when he reached out to touch it, it was quite cold. He muttered something vicious beneath his breath and then turned his head at the sound of the garden gate. Bob Beresford came strolling up the driveway.

'Hello there!' He waved a greeting. Harry just sat staring at him in silent disbelief. 'Er . . . am I a little too early?'

'Early? Early for what?'

'Well, don't you remember? We made an arrangement yesterday. Here . . .' He reached into his back pocket, pulled out a wallet and extracted fifty dollars, which he set down on the table in front of Harry. 'There y'go. Cash in advance.'

'Yes, but . . . that was before you pulled that bloody silly shooting stunt! Naturally I didn't expect you to show up after that . . .'

Bob grinned, spread his arms in a gesture of goodwill.

'Well, forgive and forget, Mr Sullivan, that's my motto. As far as I'm concerned, I'm prepared to forget all about it.'

'*You're* prepared!' In spite of himself, Harry had to smile. The Australian's sheer gall was unbelievable. 'Well, Beresford, if you promise not to try shooting bottles off the heads of any tigers we meet . . .'

'You've got yourself a deal there!'

'Very well . . . but you'll have to hang on for a moment while I get changed.' Harry disappeared into the house and Bob sat down to await his return. He had expected a delay of five minutes or so, but it was nearer to twenty before Harry emerged again. He was now wearing strong canvas jungle-boots that laced up almost to the knee. Into these were tucked a pair of long khaki trousers, and he wore a matching shirt and a bush hat. His rifle was slung over his shoulder and he had a thick ammunition belt around his middle which was heavy with cartridges; also, hanging from this was a formidable looking *parang* in a leather sheath and a water flask.

'At least he's not wearing jodhpurs and a pith helmet,' thought Bob to himself. But he said, 'You look like you're ready for a nine-day march!'

'It's always been a rule of mine,' replied Harry firmly. 'Never go into the jungle even for a few hours unless you're prepared for every eventuality.' He leaned in at the doorway, said good-bye to Pawn, who was busy in the

112

kitchen, and then followed Bob along the driveway to the Land Rover. Soon they were racing along jungle roads en route to the scene of Bob's unsuccessful hunt.

Bob tried to make conversation with Harry, asking questions about his experiences as a hunter and as a commanding officer with the Gurkhas, but the old man's answers were mostly monosyllabic. He made it quite clear that he was there under duress and that, while he had agreed to help the Australian out, he had in no way consented to be his friend.

'Cantankerous old bugger,' thought Bob grimly. He wondered if other people had this much trouble making friends with the man. Harry, meanwhile, sat stolidly in the passenger seat, staring at the road ahead.

'That was some shootin' yesterday, Mr Sullivan. It's hard to believe that you haven't practised recently.'

'Well, it's the truth.' Harry glanced at Bob. 'You, on the other hand, clearly practise whenever the opportunity presents itself.'

'Yeah . . . I am a bit fanatical about shootin'. I get it from my father. He was the best shot in Australia . . . I dunno if you ever heard of him, Mr Sullivan? Roy Beresford, the Queensland Crackshot? He was the greatest.'

Harry shook his head. 'No, I er . . . can't say that I have.'

'Yeah, well . . . more of a *local* legend, really. Still, I owe it all to him. It was his huntin' stories that got me interested in the first place . . .'

They were nearing Kampong Wau now, and Bob brought the Land Rover to a halt beside the road, where a cattle trail led into the depths of the jungle.

'This is where we go in,' he announced. They clambered out of the vehicle and Bob led the way in. As they stepped into the shade, Harry remarked to himself that it was the first time he had entered the jungle in many long years. It was exactly as he remembered it, and as he walked along he found his gaze sweeping instinctively left and right of the trail, looking for pugmarks. After they had gone a little way, he spotted some wild pig tracks, but they looked to be weeks old. Harry knew that a good way of telling if a tiger was in the neighbourhood was to see how many pigs were

113

encountered on the trail. If they were abundant, it quickly became apparent that the cat had moved on to a new part of its range; when there were none, it indicated that he was around somewhere, looking for food. But in such instances, one usually found evidence of their recent presence, pugmarks, droppings . . . As they moved along, Harry was puzzled to find nothing but occasional old signs of their passing. This was strange because this part of Trengganu had once been abundant with wild pig. He asked the Australian if he had encountered any wild pig on his marches through the jungle.

'No, not one. Why?'

Harry shrugged.

'I'm just wondering if something's happened to diminish the pig population. They're the tiger's main source of food. A shortage of them could explain these cattle killings.'

'Hmm. Well, I'll keep my eyes open for them in future. Ah . . . now this is where we join the drag, I think.'

Sure enough, a trail of crushed vegetation and broken grass stalks moved directly across their path and they could see two trails where the calf's hooves had ploughed furrows on the damp earth. Bob let Harry take the lead from here; he was interested to see what the old man could do. Harry moved along the drag, stopping occasionally to examine half-formed pugs. At last, he found a place where the cat had crossed a patch of softer ground and here there were some quite clear imprints. He kneeled down beside them and studied them for a moment.

'Well, it's a male,' he announced at last. 'And old, I'd say very old.'

'How do you know all that?'

'Well, the forepaws of a male cat are larger and squarer than the average female; also, the feet splay out as he gets older, you see the large gaps between his toes? The pads seem very scarred too. Remember that long diagonal scar on his left forepaw, it'll be easy to spot again.'

'What about these smaller tracks here?' asked Bob, pointing. 'The *penghulu* at Kampong Panjang reckons there's two tigers, male and female.'

Harry chuckled.

114

'Standard Malay mistake,' he replied. 'A tiger's back feet are smaller than his front ones, that's all. No, there's only one cat there and a big devil too, judging by his pugs.' He stood up again and followed the prints across the soft ground. 'Hmm, that caps it,' he murmured. 'He's wounded in some way, in the right foreleg.'

'How the hell can you tell that?'

'He's dragging the foot to the side at each step, see there? That must be quite a pronounced limp. Either somebody took a pot-shot at him or he's had an accident of some kind. Porcupine quills, I shouldn't wonder. They tend to fall for that a great deal, though I've seen it more in India than here.'

Bob scratched his head.

'Strewth, you do know a thing or two, don't you? Here, I reckon with this kind of information behind me, we'll soon have him bagged.'

'Well, yes, perhaps it's not such a bad thing after all. He's badly wounded and most probably in pain. Be best to put the poor devil out of his misery.'

Bob stared at Harry, surprised by his about-face on the subject.

'Don't get me wrong, Mr Beresford,' warned Harry. 'It's not the sport I'm condoning. This would simply be a mercy killing. Besides, there is always the distinct possibility that a cat as badly handicapped as this one could turn man-eater.'

'You think so?'

Harry nodded. Then he continued along the trail, watching for more signs as he went. They travelled on in silence for nearly a mile, the trail leading across the most difficult terrain imaginable. The men had to clamber over fallen tree trunks, push their way through thickets of bamboo and wade through shallow, leech-infested streams. Bob noticed with grudging admiration that Harry scrambled about with an energetic wiriness that belied his years.

At last they reached the place where Bob's *machan* still hung in the branches of the Kapok tree. Bob was about to point it out to the old man, but Harry had already spotted it.

'No wonder the tiger didn't get taken in!' he exclaimed.

'You can see that damned contraption a mile away.' He turned back to Bob. 'You mustn't assume that because he's just an animal, he's stupid, you know! A tiger's eyesight is much more developed than yours or mine. If he sees the slightest thing out of the ordinary, he'll be alerted to the fact that something's wrong. Next time, you must disguise the *machan* with a covering of foliage . . . but also make sure you cut the extra branches from another place some distance away. A tiger will notice cut down shrubbery in the area of a kill. Believe me, the least thing can serve to warn him off; and when that happens, the normal reaction is to leave the kill alone and never go back to it.'

'Well, this fellow didn't react like that. As I told you, he came and stole the pegged meat when I was asleep.'

'Yes . . . curious that. He must be a wily old devil. I imagine he could hear you snoring or something; oh, that's the other rule about sitting up on a *machan*. Keep the noise down. Don't even fidget. Anyway, let's have a look around . . .'

Harry strolled around the area of the kill in a wide circle, casting left and right, until he came across some pugmarks, emerging from the jungle to the left of the *machan*.

'Here's where he came from,' announced Harry.

'That close! Strewth, it's a wonder I didn't spot him.'

'I've a feeling he's going to get a lot closer than this before he's finished. You see the way he circled around here? He probably saw you up in the tree and decided to check out all the possibilities.' They followed the tracks around and then they came to the place where Haji had moved to within a few yards of the carcass.

'Bloody hell!' snapped Bob. 'I was watching all the time. How could he have got this close without me seeing him?'

Harry said nothing. He saw that the tiger had doubled back again and he retraced his own steps, back in a wide detour until he came around behind the Kapok tree.

'Well, I'll be damned,' he murmured. He indicated a longish depression in the soft ground. 'He must have been lying here for some time.'

'Here?' Bob looked horrified. He glanced up at the *machan*, a few yards above his head. 'But . . .'

116

'Exactly, Mr Beresford. He's obviously not too shy of people. If he'd taken it into his head to reach up and grab hold of one of your legs, you wouldn't be talking to me now. In future, I should build your *machans* a little higher . . . also, I'd curb your need for cigarettes if you possibly can.' He indicated a couple of cigarette ends scattered at the base of the tree.

Bob frowned.

'Did I do *anything* right?' he mumbled sourly.

'Just one thing. You consulted me. Next time, I'm sure you'll be much better.' Harry glanced at his wristwatch. 'Well, that's about all I can tell you,' he concluded. 'There's nothing much you can do now except wait. Sooner or later, when he gets hungry enough, he'll kill again. Then you'll have another chance.'

'Alright, thanks, Mr Sullivan. Now, I've just got to get the *machan* unroped so I can put it back in the Land Rover . . .' He glanced at Harry hopefully, but the old man sat himself down on a tree stump and brought out a pack of cigars.

'You carry on,' he suggested. 'I'm in no great hurry.' And he sat smoking thoughtfully, watching with some interest as the Australian clambered into the tree alone.

Chapter 12

In the early hours of morning, before the dawn had crept into the eastern sky, a thick, low-lying mist wreathed the surface of the road to the north of Kampong Panjang. Haji went swiftly as he moved down into a monsoon ditch, along it for some distance and then up, to haunt the perimeter of an isolated stretch of *padi*. There was considerable urgency about his movements for he knew that to go without killing for a few hours more would prove fatal. He had summoned his last reserves of strength for this quest, a quest that had taken him out of his familiar jungle haunts into places where he believed he might find the slower game he had been seeking. But the *padi* was deserted and he slunk into a straggle of secondary jungle, moving across this for some time and then emerging into an area of land that was unfamiliar to him. This was a large rubber plantation and the countless numbers of evenly spaced, regimented trees, rearing up out of the mist, looked somehow threatening. Haji paused uncertainly on the edge of the land, made nervous by the strangeness of its appearance; but then his attention was caught by a moving, bobbing light out in the very midst of the trees and he began to creep cautiously forward, hugging what cover was available, even though it was unnecessary in such a mist.

The light proved to be a strange helmet with a lantern fixed into it; and the helmet was worn by a solitary Upright. Anxious to earn extra money for his family, he had come early to the plantation in order to collect the little cups of rubber that had been left out overnight. He had a large container slung over one shoulder and he was moving slowly along a line of trees, removing the small cups, tipping their contents into the larger vessel and then replacing the tin cup in a new position on the tree trunk. He spent several minutes at each tree, his back turned away as he fiddled over the task of transferring the fluid. Haji watched the Upright for some time, plagued by memories of old fears . . . but his instinct for survival asserted itself and he moved forward again until he was hidden behind the line of trees that moved parallel to the one at which the Upright busied himself. Now Haji trailed him from trunk to trunk. He could see that the Upright was moving gradually nearer to the perimeter of the field. Haji would wait until he reached the very last tree. From there, it would be a fairly simple task to drag the kill away into the cover of secondary jungle.

The Upright was four trees away from the end of the line. He was humming thoughtfully to himself as he worked. His hands went about their simple tasks quickly, almost mechanically. Haji watched with calm silent intent.

The Upright moved to the next tree. There was a terrible silence in the plantation, for at this early hour no birds sang, no insects stirred. The Upright seemed to become suddenly nervous. He stopped humming, glanced up from his work and stared this way and that into the mist; but he did not

118

see Haji, crouched some fifteen feet away from him. He frowned, shrugged, then smiled at his own foolishness. He thought of the extra money he was making and this served to cheer him up. He moved to the next tree.

Haji watched for a moment, then slunk forward, placing his wounded leg with great care. The Upright's humming sounds were serving to unnerve him for he had never heard the like before. The concept of a 'song' was alien to him. He knew only of sounds that articulated moods or desires. The Upright took down the little tin cup. Raw rubber sloshed into the large container. Mirrored in Haji's yellow orb eyes, two tiny Uprights stood, replaced the cup, moved on to the last tree. Haji tensed himself. He crept out to his own last tree. Now, it would require only one short rush. . .

A shout from out amongst the trees! Haji snapped his head around to stare. A second yellow light, bobbing like a spectre amidst the forest of upright trunks. The Upright stood up, called something to his approaching friend, then broke off as a brief snarl at his rear alerted him to the fact that he was not alone. He saw a long striped phantom emerging from a sea of mist and he opened his mouth to scream . . .

Haji struck the Upright with terrible force, flinging him back against the base of the tree by which he had been standing. The man's spine snapped with a dry crack and the large container of rubber clattered to the ground. The breath was driven out of his body in an instant and his scream died to a brief whimper of pain and surprise. His arms dropped marionettelike to his sides and then Haji's great jaws were clamped like a bloody vice around his throat. His eyes bulged grotesquely, but he put up no struggle whatsoever. Haji was momentarily surprised by the ease with which he had taken his prey. He gave the Upright's skinny neck a couple of mighty wrenches to left and right, as though afraid that he might be bluffing. More vertebrae splintered, the head lolled at an impossible angle. Haji began to pull the dead meat away from the scene, aware that the second Upright was now dangerously close.

A few moments later, the second man reached the trees. His smile of greeting faded as he realized that his friend was no longer there. The man frowned, glanced about. Then a smile came to his lips as he heard a brief rustle in the undergrowth ahead of him. He surmised that the other man was probably having a joke at his expense and that, at any moment, he would come crashing out of the fog, howling like a demon.

'Come on out!' he called in Malay. 'I've no time for fooling about this morning. Some of us need to earn . . .'

He broke off in surprise as he saw the overturned container, its precious contents spilled onto the ground. Moving closer, he noticed a small splash of crimson on the smooth bark of the tree. A feeling of dread overtook him. He ran a little distance to the edge of the secondary jungle and there he found his friend's bloody sarong, which had snagged on a root, and two narrow lines in the dust where the dead man's heels had dragged as his killer bore him away into the jungle.

The man let out a scream of pure terror, and turning on his heels he fled back toward the buildings at the far end of the plantation, the light of his lantern bobbing and leaping weirdly through the mist.

Bob woke abruptly from sleep. Somebody was shaking him.

'Bob! Bob, you must wake up! Somebody comes to see you . . .'

He blinked up at Lim's excited face. Then he shifted his attention to the bedside clock. It was past ten o'clock, he had slept late.

'What's the matter?' he demanded roughly. He dashed the moisture from his eyes with the back of his arm, not wanting her to see that he had been crying in his sleep. But it was too late, she had already noticed.

'Bob Tuan is upset?' she enquired with obvious concern. 'In sleep, you cried out for your moth –'

'Why did you wake me?' demanded Bob sourly.

'The *penghulu* from Kampong Panjang is here. He asks to speak with you.'

'Right. Tell him I'll be out in a moment.'

Lim frowned, shrugged, went out of the room. Bob sat where he was for a moment, cradling his face in his hands.

The dream had shaken him, though he couldn't exactly say why. He had thought himself beyond caring for his mother, but now he was not so sure. He swore dismally beneath his breath, then clambered out of bed, pulling on his dressing gown. The *penghulu* could be here for only one reason. Another damned cow. Christ, but he hadn't wasted any time getting here! Bob strode out of the bedroom, calling to Lim to make some coffee. He went out onto the porch, where he found the *penghulu* standing with another man that Bob did not recognize.

'Good morning, Tuan,' said the *penghulu*. He indicated his companion. 'This my brother from Kampong Machis. *Si-Pudong* strike again near there, early this morning. Brother come down on bicycle special to tell me; I pass word to all my family and friends. . . He take you to place – rubber plantation just outside the *kampong*.'

'A rubber plantation?' Bob scratched his head, thinking that in his sleepiness he had misheard the man. 'Since when do they keep cows on a rubber plantation?'

The *penghulu* shook his head emphatically.

'No, no, Tuan. This time he not kill cow. This time he kill man, a rubber tapper. Come up behind him and drag him .'way . . .'

Bob's face drained abruptly of colour. It occurred to him that only three nights ago that same bloody tiger had lain under a tree gazing up at him for some time, waiting for him to go to sleep. Supposing it had taken the notion into its head to turn man-eater then? He thought of the sheer horror of being dragged from the tree by a pair of great striped paws and he shuddered involuntarily.

'The Tuan is ill?' enquired the *penghulu*, stepping forward.

'No . . . no, I'm fine. Wait here, while I get dressed.'

Bob hurried back into the house, sorted out some clothes and fetched his rifle. He sipped hastily at the coffee that Lim brought him. Luckily, he had no lessons to give that day. Ten minutes later, he, the *penghulu*, and his brother were bouncing along the road to Kampong Panjang in the Land Rover and the *penghulu* was richer by twenty dollars. Once there, he alighted and he lifted the other man's bicycle into the back.

'My brother now guide you to Kampong Machis,' he announced cheerfully. 'He not speak any English, so you follow his hand signals!' The two men continued on their way, kicking up great clouds of dirt from the surface of the road. Bob drove even more recklessly than usual, for he was anxious to get to the scene of the kill as quickly as possible. The *penghulu* had been quite right about his brother. The man evidently couldn't speak a word of English and his directions consisted of a series of points, nudges, and gesticulations while he just sat in the passenger seat, grinning and nodding. Bob was quite relieved when they passed Kampong Machis and came to a halt by the entrance to the rubber plantation. The two of them alighted and the *penghulu*'s brother led Bob inside. A lot of worried natives were standing around chattering to each other and Bob was quickly seized upon by all and sundry and bundled in the direction of the foreman, a grim-faced Chinaman in a white short-sleeved shirt. He was standing on the edge of the crowd, his hands on his rather plump hips, and he looked very unhappy.

'You speak English?' asked Bob.

'Sure, Boss! You come shoot tiger?' It was refreshing to find somebody who didn't mind using the word.

'If I can.'

The foreman indicated his men.

'They no go back to work till tiger dead,' he said, in obvious exasperation. 'I tell them there is nothing to worry about. Foolish men!'

Bob could not bring himself to blame them. In similar circumstances, he would be far from eager to go out into those trees until he had seen for himself the tiger's lifeless body. He asked the foreman to take him to the scene of the kill, and the two of them strode away, leaving the men to chatter amongst themselves.

'This most annoying,' grumbled the Chinaman, as they went along. 'Very bad for business. Such a thing not happen for many years now . . .' He seemed very annoyed about the whole incident, but purely from a monetary angle. He did not express any regret for the poor devil who had been eaten.

They found the place where the killing had occurred. There was little indication of a struggle, just a couple of pathetic items of bloodstained clothing leading off into the undergrowth.

'I'll need a couple of men to help me,' announced Bob. 'There's a shooting seat in my Land Rover. Once we find the body, I'll rig that up over it . . .'

But the foreman stared at him.

'The body already found,' he replied and then grimaced. 'Very horrible. All chewed up. The workers bring it back hours ago.'

'Well, where is it now?'

'With family in *kampong*, of course. They arrange for burial . . .'

Bob cursed beneath his breath. Of course, he should have expected something like this. A human corpse was not like the carcass of a cow. No grieving family could really be expected to leave the body of a loved one lying unattended in the jungle for even a few hours. It was against all the rules of decency. He thought for a moment about alternative moves. Well, he could tie up some live bait in the area, a cow or a goat . . . but if this cat was as wily as old Sullivan seemed to think, its suspicions would surely be aroused by such a move. He would come back expecting to find a man and there would be a live goat in its place . . . and the chances of bribing one of the workmen to act as a human decoy seemed extremely slight, to say the very least. What else then? Bob's gaze fell on the blood spattered sarong and an idea formed itself in the back of his mind. It was a long shot, but it might just work.

'Well, I've got an idea,' he told the foreman. 'I'll still need a couple of men to come with me and help prepare.'

The foreman frowned.

'They may not want to come, Boss,' he said. 'They are very afraid.'

Bob slapped the butt of his rifle.

'This will protect 'em,' he retorted. 'Anyway, listen, if you want to get this plantation working again, you get the buggers organized! Another thing. The best chance of

123

getting the tiger is to have him come back for another feed on the kill, savvy? I've got a plan for tonight and I'll sit up and try and get a shot at him, but if I don't and this happens *again*, you spread the word. The body must be left where it is until at least the next day. Now you do all you can to let everyone know that.'

The foreman shrugged.

'I tell them,' he said. 'But they not like it.'

'They don't have to like it,' replied Bob. 'Now come on, let's get these two men organized. We've a lot to do before nightfall.' He went over to the articles of clothing belonging to the dead man and snatched them up. The foreman glanced at him in surprise.

'What you want those for, Boss?' he enquired; and an expression of revulsion came to his face as he saw a large smear of blood across the back of the torn white shirt.

'In the absence of a dead man,' explained Bob calmly, 'we'll have to make one of our own.' And he strode away, while the puzzled foreman trotted patiently along in his wake.

Harry was engrossed in the morning's edition of the *Straits Times* when the peace and quiet of mid-afternoon was rudely shattered by a human whirlwind in the shape of Ché. The boy came pounding down the driveway, his flip-flops slapping loudly on concrete. Pawn had been at the house all morning and this visit was entirely unexpected. So was the commotion that accompanied it.

'Tuan, Tuan! The great *tok belang* that killed Majid's cow has turned man-killer!'

Harry glanced up sternly from his reading as Ché thundered onto the verandah.

'Has he now?' he replied icily. 'And is that any reason to come here making so much noise when I'm trying to rest?'

The boy looked grieved.

'But I thought you would want to know, Tuan,' he said.

'Well, it's very kind of you to come all this way to tell me about it Ché. But you know, I could just as easily have read about it in tomorrow's papers.' He indicated the periodical in his own grasp. 'Wonderful things these . . . when a fellow

124

gets the chance to read them.' Harry felt decidedly crotchety today. The weather wasn't helping much; the atmosphere over the last few hours had grown muggy and oppressive, the air smelled strongly of sulphur. A storm was due before many more hours had elapsed.

'Are you not going to *do* anything, Tuan?' Ché moved closer now, staring at the old man enquiringly.

'Do?' Harry folded the paper carefully, slapped it down on top of the rattan table. 'What would you have me do, Ché?'

'Why . . . kill the creature of course! You are the greatest hunter for miles around. You have killed many tigers before, and now it is only right that you should be the one to put an end to this devil.'

Harry could only laugh at the boy's certainty.

'Ché, I haven't killed a tiger in . . . ten years! And most of the ones I've told you about were shot in India, during the war . . .' A note of exasperation crept into his voice. 'When are people going to realize that I'm an old man now! All I want is a little peace and quiet; but ever since this damned tiger stuck his nose out of the jungle people have been pestering me to have a go at it. Well, I'm not interested, it's as simple as that. And the sooner everybody gets that idea firmly into their heads, the better.' He frowned. 'Besides, I've no doubt that Tuan Beresford will be after the poor devil's hide soon enough.'

'But Tuan Beresford has never killed a tiger,' persisted Ché doggedly. 'It is not right that the glory should go to him . . .'

'What bloody glory?' cried Harry, losing his temper. 'You think there's any glory in seeing off a poor old beast who's too old and too lame to live as nature intended him to? Eh? Well, do you?'

Ché looked confused. He gazed self-consciously at his feet.

'He *is* a killer, Tuan,' he finally murmured.

'Do you think *we're* not? Just because we use guns and insecticides and poisons, while the tiger uses claw and fang . . .' Harry broke off as a sharp pain lanced across his chest. He massaged it with the palm of his hand and took a

125

deep breath. 'There, you see, now you've given me heartburn,' he complained bitterly.

Ché was still intent on the one theme he had pursued since his arrival.

'I do not think you are too old, Tuan. Besides, I have heard about the shooting contest at the barracks . . .'

'Yes, then you will also have heard that Tuan Beresford beat me; therefore, he should be the one to kill this bloody tiger, not me.'

'But I have heard that it was a very close thing.' He thought for a moment and then added, 'The people wanted you to win; they would always wish you to shoot the *tok* –'

'By God, you don't give up easily, do you?' cried Harry. 'I just think that . . .'

'Oh, go away Ché! Your chatter's beginning to tire me!'

Crestfallen the boy backed away a little, an expression of pain on his face as though he had been physically struck. Then, grimfaced, he turned abruptly on his heels and strode into the house in search of his grandmother.

Harry felt like a villain, but he was too annoyed to call after the boy. Mumbling to himself, he got up from his chair, thrust his hands into his pocket and stalked out into the garden. The late afternoon sun was being choked as the sky took on a flat, bruise-black tone and all birdsong had ceased as the creatures that inhabited the large garden anticipated the advent of rain and storm that would inevitably come with the brief tropical twilight. The very air seemed to crackle with electricity and the dank humid heat was almost suffocating.

Harry moved past rows of carefully tended orchids, past banana and papaya trees but he was hardly aware of them. His mind was black with resentment. Why was everybody so keen to associate that bloody tiger with him? How many times had he openly disclaimed any glory from his former failings; for that was what they clearly were to him now. Beresford was the one who was so keen to assume the mantle of 'great white hunter.' Let him wear it with pleasure!

A large olive-green lizard skittered along the base of the garden wall, searching for a safe nook to shield him from the rain. Harry sighed, then turned, and moved back to the house. He ignored the verandah and instead searched out the relative cool of his bedroom. As he went in, he could hear Ché jabbering earnestly in Malay to his grandmother. Harry closed the door quietly. Then he went to his wardrobe and took out the leather case that held his rifle. He removed the gun, cradled it in his hands, enjoying the reassuring touch of its smooth wooden stock. Then he snapped the rifle up to his eye and sighted upon an imaginary target.

Out in the garden, there was a peal of thunder and white lightning split the sky in two.

Chapter 13

Haji sniffed at the air. The storm was close now and he was lying under cover near the place where he had left the kill. He was a little stronger now, but still not up to wandering very far abroad. Still, for all that, he sensed that something was not right. The kill appeared to be where he had left it, for circling past the area earlier on he had caught sight of a huddled shape stretched out amongst the bushes. But somehow it seemed to have changed in a way he couldn't understand. Also, Haji detected a brief movement in a tree some twenty yards off to the left and this, more than anything else, had dissuaded him from approaching his meal directly. He was hungry now and needed sustenance but his all-powerful sense of caution warned him to wait for a while and approach in darkness.

The electrically charged atmosphere served to make him even more nervous. He kept glancing this way and that, growling softly to himself. He was only too well aware that this was no longer his territory, that he resided here only by the grudging allowance of its new lord and master. As soon as he was strong enough, there would come a time for moving on. Till then, recklessness could only plunge him deeper into trouble; so, for the moment, he chose to wait.

The first drops of rain began to fall, large fat globules that burst loudly amongst the broad-leaved ferns and bushes. For a few moments, it was halting, sporadic, as though uncertain of itself; but then, abruptly, it was as though a great hand had plunged a knife into the very fabric of heaven, ripping it asunder. The deluge came down from the sky, soaking everything that lay beneath it. In the midst of the torrent, his head resting on his paws, Haji waited patiently.

Bob Beresford was getting soaked to the skin. He had been in position on the *machan* for a little over three hours, but the last thirty minutes or so had been a nightmare. The canopy of foliage above him offered no respite from the downpour of water and now every article of clothing was sodden and he was cold and miserable; yet for all that, he would not give up his position, for while there was even the faintest chance of the tiger coming back to feed, he was going to hang on. From time to time, a flash of searingly bright lightning illuminated the crudely made mannikin that he had substituted for the corpse. Consisting of the victim's bloody clothing stuffed with straw, it certainly looked convincing enough from a distance, half-obscured as it was by its covering of foliage; but whether it would fool the tiger was another matter. Bob was far from hopeful that the tiger would even be abroad in such foul weather; and if that was the case, the hunted was displaying far more sense than the hunter. The cold rain gushed down Bob's collar and into his shorts. Even his sturdy boots were waterlogged and the horrible sensation of being wet through made the uncomfortable task of sitting on hard wooden planks even more disagreeable.

'I must be crazy to do this,' thought Bob glumly. For the first time that night, he considered the possibility of giving up, of simply clambering down the tree, and wandering back to the nearby *kampong* in search of some hot tea. But a characteristic stubbornness made him reject the notion almost as soon as he had thought of it. He found himself asking why he really wanted to kill the tiger. He had told Harry Sullivan that it was purely because he wanted a trophy . . . but there was more to it than that, wasn't there?

128

In his mind, he had dedicated this tiger to his father's memory, and in shooting it he would be perpetuating the ideals that the old man had stood for. It was still a terrible regret, a guilt, that he had lost touch with his father for several years, when Bob had gone away to study at the agricultural college. When he had left, his father had been a strong, active human being. On the infrequent visits home, Bob was appalled to see the rapid deterioration in him. By the time the three-year course was over, Roy Beresford was an emaciated, bedridden vestige of his former self. The diagnosis was terminal cancer. He had died only a few weeks after Bob's graduation. Among the effects left to him in his father's will was the old man's hunting equipment, and it was from that point that Bob fell to filling his father's shoes with an obsessive drive that amounted to fanaticism. The strange thing was, he was aware of his own motives, but felt powerless to do anything about them; in fact, he was not sure he *wanted* to do anything about them. He enjoyed the hunting, he really did, even when he found himself in an uncomfortable predicament like this one.

Bob reached into the pocket of his shirt and pulled out his cigarettes; or more accurately, he pulled out a sodden lump of cardboard and tobacco. He flung it away with a curse and a flash of lightning lit up the sky, followed by an awesome clap of thunder. Bob stiffened in surprise. For an instant, the eerie light had picked out everything in incredible detail. The tangled stretch of undergrowth below him, the blood-spattered shirt and sarong on the straw mannikin, the myriad of falling raindrops, momentarily frozen in mid-air . . . and something else. A long lithe shape slinking from a patch of long grass off to the left. Bob had glimpsed it but briefly; there was no mistaking the characteristic shape of a tiger. His heart leapt into his mouth and he literally had to stifle a cry of excitement. Instead, he brought his rifle up to bear on the bait, the faint whiteness of which he could barely see through his lightning-blitzed eyes. He waited for the next flash, hardly daring to draw breath, anxious to avoid switching on the torch mounted on his rifle barrel too early. It seemed an age before the next one came, though in reality it was no more than thirty seconds. The first glance was disappointing. He could see nothing moving in the clearing and he was beginning to think that he had hallucinated the creature. The accompanying thunder was now directly overhead and the power of it made the tree shake, but Bob kept his gaze pinned directly ahead. Now, in the darkness, he thought once again he detected movement . . . but he made himself wait for more light, while he counted the seconds in his head.

Again the lightning flash, and this time his senses thrilled as he saw, quite clearly, a large tiger prowling nervously from the undergrowth in the direction of the bait. Now there was not a moment to be lost. The tiger would soon realize that a switch had been made. Bob would have to be ready to fire at the next stroke of lightning, flicking on his torch at the same instant in order to prolong the light. He steeled himself, tried to settle into a comfortable shooting position. He was aided here by the fact that it could hardly matter if he made some noise amongst the din that was already going on. He sighted along the rifle, keeping it trained as near as dammit onto the faint glow of the shirt and sarong. Then he waited, for what seemed a long, nerve-wracking eternity. A succession of images shot through his mind's eye. His father, lying in a hospital bed, thin and horribly emaciated, his skin curiously yellowed by illness; a great stag's head trophy glowering from the wall of his father's study; his mother, dressed in black at the funeral, not even having the decency to cry, just looking down at the lowered coffin with a curious expression of finality on her face; and the memory of something she had said to Bob, the day he learned that she was to remarry.

'What do you think your father was, a damned plaster saint? He was the most selfish man who ever lived! Where was I when he was off on his hunting trips? At home, bored out of my mind! What did he ever do for me, you tell me that?'

She'd been hysterical, of course. His father was not like that. He was the greatest man that ever lived and it was typical that she should attempt to drag him down that way. Well, Bob had shown *her*, right enough. He'd fixed her wagon— For Christ's sake, where was that lightning?

Abruptly, unexpectedly, it flared in the sky. Bob hit the

torch button and there was the cat, standing over the mannequin, sniffing at it suspiciously. He looked enormous, how could anybody miss a target like that! Bob sighted up high behind the creature's shoulder and then events seemed to slip into a hazy slow motion. The cat sensed that something was wrong. The glare of the lightning was still on him even though the thunder roared from the sky. He turned his head to gaze up into the trees and the two orbs of his eyes glowed red in the torch beam.

Bob squeezed the trigger, the gun bucked against his shoulder. The tiger began to wheel away in alarm but then a concussion shook his whole body, a patch of hair flew up from his shoulder. He reeled drunkenly sideways, seemed to recover and then began to race forward towards the jungle on his left. Bob worked the bolt of the rifle, ejecting the spent cartridge, but another shot was unnecessary at this moment. The tiger's front legs seemed to fail him and he flipped upwards in the rain, turned a slow, agonizing somersault, his mouth open roaring pain and surprise, his long tail thrashing from side to side. Turning the complete circle, he crashed down onto the ground, rolled over sidways and lay for a moment, clawing the air with a single front paw. He attempted to get up, just once, but then the last vestiges of life deserted him and he slid back again, his tongue lolling from his mouth.

Bob stood gazing down at the dead beast for a few moments, his heart beating wildly. For the moment, he could hardly believe that he had achieved what he set out to do. He had been extraordinarily lucky. Then he gave vent to a cry of pure exaltation and he fired three shots into the sky, one after the other, the signal for the villagers that the man-eater was dead. He hoped that they would hear the shots in the middle of the storm. Then, clambering up, he threw his rifle down to the ground and half climbed, half fell after it. Retrieving it, he snatched it up and sloshed through the sodden undergrowth to claim his prize. The tiger lay quite close to the bait, looking strangely ethereal under a haze of deflected rain. His great yellow eyes were already clouding over in death. Bob felt a ridiculous sense of elation fill him and be began to dance childishly around his victim, laughing

131

out loud. Then he came to a halt, wheeled almost drunkenly back to the carcass and planted his foot on the tiger's flank, as though posing for an imaginary photo.

'Got you, you bastard,' he whispered.

Lightning flashed, but it was weaker now, moving away to the east. The rain was easing off and the thunder that sounded a few moments later was now just a rumble of discontent, not a roar of anger. Bob fired off another three shots at the sky, making sure there would be no mistake.

'Hope the buggers bring some cigarettes with 'em,' he murmured. He glanced down at the tiger's face, but something in the beauty and dignity of it gave him a twinge of remorse. He did not look at it again for a while. Instead, he squatted down in the grass and waited patiently for the villagers to arrive. The rain faded away almost as quickly as it had begun and a strange, funereal silence settled over the jungle.

Chapter 14

After the commotion of the previous night, the morning seemed a gentle absolution. Harry rose a little after dawn, made himself some tea, and took it out onto the verandah where he enjoyed it in a silent, thoughtful mood. He felt rather grieved at the way he had treated Ché the evening before, and since this was the boy's more usual day for visiting he was determined to make it up to him in some way. But he was disappointed and a little shocked when at eight o'clock, Pawn arrived for work without her grandson. She came slowly up the garden path, smiling rather sheepishly, for she was well aware of the old man's affection for Ché.

'Good morning, Tuan,' she murmured. 'Ché not here yet.' She waved her arms apologetically. 'He go to Kampong Machis to see dead man-eater, but he promise to come 'long later . . .'

'Dead?' Harry frowned. He had not expected Beresford to be successful so soon. The hunting down of a cat usually

132

required considerable persistence.

'Yes, Tuan!' Pawn grinned and nodded. 'Tuan Beresford shoot him. Now he bring into *kampong* for all to see. Much excitement. When Ché and his friends hear of it, they must go!' She shrugged expressively. 'Boys . . . what can one do with them? But I make him promise to come here after . . .'

'Yes, well, never mind, never mind,' snapped Harry gruffly. He did not want his concern to show. 'I expect he will come along when he wants to.'

'Tuan ready eat now?' enquired Pawn hopefully.

'Ah, no . . . not just yet. Later perhaps.'

Pawn bowed slightly and went on past him into the house. Harry remained where he was, a faint scowl on his face. 'It's only natural,' he thought to himself. 'Any boy in the world would rather go and see a dead tiger than pass the time of day with an old man.' Still, for all that, he felt rather put out by the affair, and though he sat gazing at the garden for the next few hours Ché did not come.

Harry fell into a shallow doze that was rudely interrupted by the creak of the garden gate. He opened his eyes and sat up, expecting to see Ché running up the drive, but in fact it was Melissa. She waved cheerfully to him as she approached. Beyond the gate, Harry could see her father's car with Dennis at the wheel.

'Hello, young lady, what brings you here?' asked Harry, with a smile.

'Daddy and I are going over to Kampong Machis to look at Bob's tiger. We, er . . . we wondered if you'd like to come along.'

Harry was somewhat taken aback.

'This tiger seems to be the biggest thing to happen around here in a long time,' he observed drily. 'They'll be organizing coach parties next.'

Melissa laughed.

'Don't think we haven't considered it,' she replied. 'Anyway, what do you say?'

Harry thought out his reply for a few moments. His initial reaction was to refuse, to say that he simply wasn't interested, though that really wasn't true. He was as curious as the next man to see what the man-eater looked like; also, he might have the opportunity to apologize to Ché if he was still there. Besides, Harry knew that any refusal on his part would almost certainly be interpreted as jealousy, and while he generally didn't give a tinker's damn what other people thought about him, he was anxious in this case not to lose the friendship of Melissa, who was quite obviously infatuated with Bob Beresford.

'I'll get my jacket,' announced Harry simply and he got up, went into the house, slipped on a khaki jacket and told Pawn that he was going out. She protested that he had had nothing to eat yet, but he told her that he would do that when he returned. Pacified, she went on with her other household duties. Harry went back out to Melissa and the two of them strolled arm in arm to the car. Dennis looked pleased, if a little surprised, that Harry had consented to the trip.

'Hello there, old chap! I'm glad you decided to come along.' He swung open the door on the passenger side and Harry climbed in beside him. Melissa clambered into the back beside her mother. Harry glanced at Kate in astonishment. It took a great deal to tempt her away from the home at the best of times.

'My goodness, it *must* be an event,' murmured Harry. 'Hello, Kate. I haven't seen you in ages . . . I wouldn't have thought this was your sort of thing . . .'

'It isn't!' Kate assured him. 'Going along to gawp at a poor dead animal is certainly not my idea of fun. But as everybody took such great pains to point out to me, this may be the only chance I'll ever get to see a real Malaysian tiger before I go home . . . besides, I'm more interested in getting a look at this man that Melissa's taken such a fancy to . . .' She winked slyly at Harry and Melissa blushed bright red.

'Mummy!' she protested. 'Really . . .' Harry smiled. Seeing mother and daughter together like this, it was astonishing how alike they looked. The same thick dark hair, the same piercing hazel eyes. Kate concealed her age remarkably well and it was sometimes hard to believe that she could be the mother of a girl Melissa's age.

'You've met this Mr Beresford, haven't you?' asked Kate

134

innocently. 'What's he like?'

Dennis hastily hit the ignition and accelerated away, sparing Harry the need to give a suitable reply. There was a slightly uncomfortable silence for a moment, and then Dennis started chattering to fill it in.

'Beresford had some remarkable luck, apparently. Managed to bag the tiger in the midst of that storm last night. I mean, it's amazing he even managed to stay up the tree in that lot, it was coming down in torrents . . .'

They sped on along the coast road, until they reached the place where a bumpy dirt track diverged to the left, leading up to Kampong Machis. They parked the car on the outskirts of the village and continued on foot from there. A large crowd of people was gathered in the very centre of the *kampong*, all of them pushing excitedly around some obscured object on the ground. In the midst of them, Harry could see Bob Beresford looking rather harassed by all the attention.

'People have come from everywhere!' observed Kate in surprise. Though most of the crowd consisted of villagers from the local *kampongs*, there was also quite a few white people in evidence and the atmosphere was rather like that of a public holiday. There were large numbers of young children racing excitedly about, and amongst one group Harry spotted Ché. He was carrying a crudely made wooden rifle with which he was energetically shooting all his comrades. Harry detached himself from Dennis's party and went over to talk to the boy.

'Hey there!'

Ché stopped, gave Harry a guilty glance, and then wandered slowly over to him.

'Good day, Tuan,' he murmured. 'I was going to come later . . .'

'Oh, that's all right! What have you got here?' Harry took the wooden rifle from the boy's hand and examined it critically.

'It is . . . only a toy, Tuan.' Ché changed the subject quickly. 'Have you seen the tiger yet, Tuan?'

Harry raised his eyebrows at this unexpected show of recklessness.

135

Ché laughed.

'I have no need to fear it now,' he explained. 'Tuan Beresford has killed him, so he can no more hunt me.' And he glanced in Bob's direction with an expression on his face that could only be described as hero-worship. 'Such a fine beast, Tuan! Such a *monster!*'

This last remark saddened Harry considerably.

'Not a monster, Ché, but a very beautiful animal. One of God's creatures. You mustn't be fooled into thinking otherwise.'

But Ché plainly wasn't listening. He snatched back his toy rifle and aimed it at some imaginary target.

'When I grow up, Tuan, I too will be a great hunter. I will go into the jungle and I will myself kill all the tigers that hide there. I will set the people of the *kampongs* free!'

Harry stared down at the boy in dismay, wondering just what in the world had got into him.

Meanwhile, Harry's companions had managed to push their way through the crowd to get a look at the slain beast. Bob was squatting beside it now, looking tired but proud. Melissa kneeled beside the tiger, ran her hand experimentally along the striped fur.

'Bob, he's fantastic!' she exclaimed. 'So huge . . .' A cough from her mother prompted her to make a hasty introduction. 'Oh, this is my mother, by the way.'

'Pleased to meet you, Mrs Tremayne.' The two of them shook hands across the dead tiger. 'Well . . . what do you think of him?' asked Bob.

'I'd rather see him alive,' replied Kate thoughtfully. 'But as Dennis keeps reminding me, he *was* a man-eater, I suppose.'

'He's a magnificent specimen,' observed Dennis. 'Look at that coat. No doubt you'll be having him skinned, Mr Beresford?'

'I intend to, just as soon as I can find somebody who knows how to do it! I expect we'll get it done tonight, when everybody's had a good look at him and it's a bit cooler.' Bob indicated the crush all around him. 'I wasn't expecting so much interest.'

'Of course everybody's interested!' exclaimed Melissa.

'You've made the area safe again. You're a hero, Bob!' And impulsively, she leaned forward and kissed him on the cheek. 'A kiss for the victor!' she announced dramatically. Bob stared at her for a moment, then grinned.

'I can see I'll have to go and shoot a few more tigers,' he chuckled. But he gazed directly at Melissa, an intense searching look that she returned brazenly.

Dennis gave an embarrassed cough.

'Ahem! Perhaps ah . . . Harry Sullivan might know some skinners. Now where did he go to?'

'I think he's over there talking to his *amah*'s grandson,' said Kate, smiling at her husband's discomfort.

'Mr Sullivan's here?' said Bob in surprise. 'Well, that's a surprise!'

'Why?' enquired Kate.

'Oh well . . . it's just that he doesn't like me very much, Mrs Tremayne.'

'Indeed? Why ever not?'

Bob shrugged. 'Your guess is as good as mine.'

'I must say, I hadn't expected him to agree to come along,' said Melissa. 'Perhaps he's decided to bury the hatchet . . .'

'Yeah. In the back of my neck, no doubt!'

'Oh, I'm sure it's not as bad as all that, Mr Beresford.'

Dennis swivelled around, shielding his eyes with the palm of his hand, while he scanned the crowd. After a few moments, he spotted Harry talking earnestly to Ché, but the boy hardly seemed to be listening to him. Suddenly, a group of children raced past and Ché took off after them, leaving Harry in mid-sentence. The old man gazed after him, a reproachful expression on his face. Then he shook his head sadly.

'Harry! Come over here! You haven't seen the tiger yet!' Dennis beckoned energetically and Harry glanced up in surprise, as if he had forgotten all about his main reason for coming here. Then he forced a smile, came trudging slowly over. It was quite plain that he was upset about something. As he reached the outer edge of the crowd, it seemed to part magically to let him through, a modern-day Moses passing between the waves of a human sea.

'That's Harry,' thought Dennis, with a smile. 'The rest of us have to push a way through, but for Harry everybody moves aside.'

'Hello there, Mr Sullivan. Come and take a look at this little beauty!' Bob stood up, as if making an involuntary sign of respect to the old hunter. He watched as Harry stooped to examine the kill. The old man crouched in silence for a few moments, gazing fixedly at the long striped carcass. His silence communicated itself to the rest of the crowd. Everybody, it seemed, was waiting for his blessing. After a little while, the tension became unbearable and Dennis prompted him.

'Well, what do you think Harry? A fine specimen, wouldn't you say?'

'Beautiful,' murmured Harry, his voice barely more than a whisper. 'Beautiful . . .' Abruptly, he snapped his head up and glared at Bob. 'You bloody fool,' he said coldly.

Bob's jaw dropped open, and he took a step back as though struck in the face. Clearly even he had not expected such a hostile reaction.

'Now just a minute, Mr Sullivan! I'm getting a bit damned tired of being victimized like this. Why, only the other day you told me this cat ought to be shot, to put it out of its misery . . . and that was before it turned man-eater . . .'

Harry sighed. He glanced briefly around the circle of shocked faces on either side of him. Then he returned his gaze to Bob.

'You're quite correct, Mr Beresford, I *did* say that. And I meant it. You may also recall that I checked out some pugmarks for you and . . . correct me if I'm wrong here . . . I gave you a fairly concise description of the . . . "man-eater" as you like to call him.'

'Well, yeah, of course I remember . . .'

Harry nodded slowly.

'Would you like to explain to me then, Mr Beresford, how it is that you've managed to go out and shoot the wrong tiger?'

'The what?'

'The wrong tiger, Mr Beresford. The cat that we tracked

138

that day was around fifteen to twenty years old and had a wound in its right forepaw. This cat is barely in its prime, it must be four years old at the most. I don't see any evidence of a wound in the leg, do you?'

Bob just stood there, his mouth open, staring down at the tiger. It had never for one moment occurred to him that another cat might be in the area.

'But –' he managed to blurt out. 'I . . .'

Harry held up one of the creature's front paws for inspection.

'You may also remember that the cat's pugs showed that his front feet were splayed out and badly scarred. Does that look like it might be capable of making such tracks? Well, does it? Good God, man, didn't you even think to look?'

Bob gestured helplessly with his hands.

'It must be the man-eater! I mean, it came down to take the bait . . . it just has to be . . . otherwise . . .'

'Otherwise you've shot a beautiful rare animal that has caused no harm to anybody. Well, Mr Beresford, that is exactly what you've done. I hope you feel very proud of your efforts.'

'Uncle Harry, leave him alone!' Everyone turned to stare at Melissa. 'Why, I've never seen such out-and-out *jealousy* in my life! You're just fed up because Bob's managed to do something that you're no longer capable of!'

'Melissa,' Kate cautioned. 'I don't think that's entirely fair . . .'

'To hell with what's fair! Everybody's so afraid of hurting Uncle Harry's feelings, but it clearly doesn't work the other way around, does it? He's been picking on Bob ever since he found out what a good hunter he is. Well I'm not afraid to say what I think, even if everybody else is.'

Harry gazed at her for several moments.

'You silly girl,' he said calmly. 'I'm not victimizing anyone. Don't you understand? He's shot the wrong animal. That isn't the man-eater, it's just some poor brute that happened to wander in the wrong direction.'

'Well, what does it matter *which* tiger it is? It's still a perfectly good trophy, isn't it?'

'Well, of course it matters.' Harry raised his eyes

139

heavenwards. 'Have you any idea how effective the grapevine is around here? By now, everybody will have heard that the man-eater is dead. So people aren't going to worry about strolling about on jungle roads in the middle of the night, are they? The next thing you know, there'll be another victim announced . . .'

'I still say you're just trying to find fault,' persisted Melissa.

'And besides,' added Bob. 'For all we know, the tracks we found under my *machan* might have belonged to another tiger that was just . . . passing by. I don't see any reason why this shouldn't be the killer. All we've got to go on is the word of an old man who hasn't been hunting for over ten years. What makes you so sure you know better than anybody else, Mr Sullivan?'

Harry's body suddenly went rigid, his face drained of colour. When he spoke again, his voice shuddered with emotion.

'Mr Beresford. I have had some considerable experience of so-called man-eating tigers. I have shot them on six different occasions, and in each case the cat was either very old or wounded in some way. Now you can believe me or disbelieve me, just as you wish, but I tell you, sir, that this poor devil is not the man-eater that you set out to shoot; not that I think it matters overmuch to you anyway, because people of your creed regard one dead brute to be just as good as the next. Furthermore, Mr Beresford, I think you have a moral obligation to inform the local villagers that you have made a mistake. Otherwise, the next death will be on your conscience. One more thing. You probably like to think of yourself as a *sportsman*, but it's quite obvious to me that you don't know the meaning of the word . . .'

'Now look here, you silly old bastard! . . .'

Bob broke off in alarm as Harry stepped impulsively forward and brought his hand across the Australian's face in an unexpected powerful slap. Bob reeled back with an oath and Dennis rushed forward to stop any escalation; but it was not needed, for Harry turned smartly on his heel and strode away through a shocked and silent crowd. The others stared after him in amazement.

'Well of all the . . .' Bob massaged his stinging cheek. 'I ought to go over there and knock his head in. I would if he wasn't old enough to be my father!'

'Are you all right?' cried Melissa anxiously.

Kate smothered a smile.

'I'm sure Mr Beresford is still in one piece, dear,' she murmured.

Dennis scratched his head.

'Well, whatever got into the poor fellow?'

'I don't know dear, but hadn't we better go after him?'

'Er . . . yes, I suppose we had. Melissa?'

'Oh, I don't think I want to face him at the moment, Daddy. I'll stay on here a while. I'm sure Bob will give me a lift home later on . . .'

'Uh . . . yeah, sure, if you like.' Bob shrugged, turned away, mumbling to himself. Kate gazed thoughtfully at her daughter for a moment. Her eyes said, 'We'll talk about this later, my girl!' but her mouth said, 'Good-bye, dear. We'd better get after Uncle Harry before he wrecks the entire village.'

'Whatever can be wrong with him?' sighed Melissa.

'I wonder . . .' Kate smiled. 'Well, good-bye Mr Beresford. I hope next time we meet it will be under pleasanter circumstances. Come along, Dennis.' The two of them edged their way through the crowd in the direction that Harry had taken. The villagers, having quickly recovered from their shock, were now all talking excitedly about the incident.

'It's not like old Harry to fly off the handle,' murmured Dennis.

'It was Melissa's fault; she shouldn't have turned on him that way. There was a time when she would never have dreamed of doing such a thing.'

'She's interested in Beresford, that's all.'

'Hmm. Well, I'm not sure I approve of her choice.'

'Oh, for God's sake, don't you start! What's wrong with the poor fellow?'

Kate frowned. 'It's hard to say . . . but I got a certain impression about him. I think Harry was right when he said that Mr Beresford regarded one dead tiger as being just as good as another. He didn't shoot that cat because it was a man-eater, but for the glory of it. He was obviously enjoying all that attention...'

'Well, perhaps, perhaps... but really, Kate, people have been shooting tigers around here for centuries...'

'Well, then perhaps it's time they stopped. Oh look, there he is!'

Harry was standing beside Dennis's car, leaning on the roof as if to support himself. His head was bowed and his shoulders seemed to be heaving. Fearing that the old man was suffering another attack similar to the one he had experienced at the tennis club, Dennis ran forward and grabbed Harry by the arm. Harry glanced up in surprise and Dennis could see quite clearly two trails of moisture running down Harry's cheeks.

'Here, here now... let me get the car open...' Dennis was flustered. He had never seen his friend so openly displaying emotion.

'No, I'm alright, really.' Harry straightened up, dashed at his eyes with his sleeve as Kate approached. He cleared his throat awkwardly.

'Silly of me. Shouldn't have lost my temper like that.' He ran one hand through his hair in exasperation. 'Damned idiot Beresford, you can't tell him anything. He'll discover soon enough, when that tiger gets hungry again...'

He quietened as Kate took his hand in hers and squeezed it gently.

'I feel I should apologize about Melissa,' she told him. 'She had absolutely no cause to go for you like she did.'

Harry forced a smile.

'Children are different these days,' he said. 'So strong-willed. It's perfectly alright. I'm sure when she's had a chance to think about it, she'll see that I was right...'

'She's not a child anymore, Harry. She may act like one, but she's not.'

Harry sighed.

'Well... after all that excitement, I could use a drink!' He was trying to sound hearty, but it was somehow unconvincing. 'What say we go back to my house for a cold beer?'

'Yes, why not?' replied Dennis. He glanced at Kate, and

142

she nodded wordlessly. Dennis fumbled for his keys and unlocked the car. The three of them got inside. The car had been standing in direct sunlight for some time and it was rather like climbing into a large metal oven. They wound all the windows down, and turning the car around Dennis headed back to the coast road. Harry lapsed into a sombre silence and neither Kate nor Dennis could think of anything that might distract him from his present mood. Consequently, it was a long and uncomfortable drive back to their destination.

The small cave was cool and comforting, a welcome respite from the fierce heat of the day. Haji felt much stronger now and he had come here with the intention of napping, but the incidents of the previous night still troubled him, as a succession of vague images. He remembered that he had lain in the bushes, while the storm exploded all around him, hungry but as yet too nervous to go out and reclaim his kill. Then, from the bushes on the other side of the clearing, his archenemy had emerged, moving towards Haji's kill with the bold, aggressive stride of the victor. He had seen Haji, lying up in the grass ahead and now he was going to brazenly snatch the old tiger's food away from under his nose. But then there had been the roar of a black stick, and the young tiger had whirled up beneath the rain to die in the tall grass. Terrified, Haji had slunk down into the deepest cover of the bushes and from there, he had watched as an Upright descended from the tree and had performed some kind of gleeful dance around his victim. Later, more Uprights had arrived and, cutting down some stout logs, they had bound the dead tiger between them and in the newfound silence after the storm they had carried the body away, whooping and shrieking their triumph to the treetops.

Still afraid, Haji had stayed put for another hour before at last cautiously emerging and making his way over to the kill for a belated supper. And behold, the strangest mystery of all! For the kill was no longer the kill, just a tasteless piece of Upright's skin filled with dead jungle, and the long wait had all been for nothing. And that would have been the end of the story for Haji, but for an unexpected slice of good fortune. Slinking dejectedly away along a cattle track, Haji had come face to face with a young tapir who had somehow got separated from his parents in the confusion of the storm. Not even possessing the sense to run away, he just stood there, bawling pitifully, until Haji's great jaws closed around his throat. The calf had provided just enough meat for a sumptuous late night repast; after which, Haji sought out a favourite resting place, where he was able to stretch out and reflect upon his good fortune. The Upright had unwittingly been of great help to Haji. No longer would he be forced to leave his home territory. With the outsider eliminated, the range was now returned to its original owner. The usurper's rule had been brief but eventful and, if nothing else, had taught Haji how easy it was to turn his attention to the new, slower game that would feed him through his declining years. Though in many ways he still feared the Uprights, he had tasted them now and knew that they were good to eat. He would not hesitate to take another should the opportunity present itself. Meanwhile, he would rest and allow his strength to return. For the moment, he was well-fed and there was no need to hunt . . .

In the reassuring coolness of the cave, Haji stretched out and let his head rest on his paws, while out in the jungle the afternoon sun burned down with relentless ferocity. He slept and dreamed of Uprights.

Chapter 15

It was late afternoon and the shadows were lengthening rapidly. Bob Beresford's Land Rover sped along the coast road, its engine growling a noisy protest at the rough treatment being administered to it. Sitting in the passenger seat, her long hair streaming back in the wind, Melissa clung grimly to the dashboard and tried to think of something interesting to say. She glanced slyly across at Bob, who was hunched over the wheel, his gaze intent on the way ahead. Melissa wondered if he always drove like a maniac or if he was simply trying to impress her. She hoped for the latter, but somehow suspected the former to be true. She glimpsed a glitter of metal beneath the open collar of his kahki shirt and for an instant she could see the bullet-shaped medallion that Victoria Lumly had mentioned. This provided her with a chance to strike up a conversation.

'What an interesting necklace!' She reached forward to examine it.

'Yeah. Present from my old man. He always wore it when he was out huntin'. Sort of good luck charm . . .'

He swerved the Land Rover recklessly around a tight bend and for the first time he noticed the look of alarm on Melissa's face. He grinned apologetically, dropped down to a more reasonable speed.

'Sorry . . . I suppose I'm just a bit anxious to get back to the tiger. That feller I left to guard it, I don't really know . . .' He shrugged. 'I guess I won't relax until the bugger's skinned and hung on my wall.'

'You've done very well,' she reassured him. 'I'm just sorry about all that fuss with Uncle Harry.' She sighed. 'Jealousy can be a terrible thing.'

'How come you call him uncle? He's not really related, is he?'

'No. Just a good friend really. I've known him since I was a little girl. The sad thing is, he's old now and he can't do the things he used to. It's not really surprising that he's so crotchety.'

Bob nodded. 'Saw the same thing happen to my father,' he told her. 'It's sad, but you know, there's nothing you can do. Mind you . . . I keep wondering about what he said. He certainly seemed to know what he was talking about when he tracked for me. Supposing the man-eater isn't dead? I can't help wondering if I ought to spread the word for everyone to take care . . . just in case . . .'

'You've got to remember,' retorted Melissa firmly, 'It must be over ten years since Uncle Harry was involved in anything like that. Memories fade with time. The whole thing was done just to discredit you, that's all.'

He gazed at her for a moment. 'You really think so, Melissa?'

She smiled, nodded. 'I'm sure of it.'

Bob reached out a hand impulsively to stroke her arm. She stared at it oddly for a moment, but made no attempt to pull away from his touch. She felt excited and oddly flattered by the gesture.

'How old are you, Melissa?' he asked.

'Eighteen.'

He smiled. 'You're quite legal then,' he observed, with a dry little chuckle; and she felt her face colour. 'It's the best age,' continued Bob easily. 'This is your estate on the left here, isn't it?'

'What? Oh . . . yes . . .' She had momentarily forgotten where she was. 'My house is over the back there . . .' But he was already easing the Land Rover to a halt on the outskirts of the estate. The light was fading rapidly and there was nobody about. Bob glanced at Melissa for a moment, then switched the ignition off. The two of them sat for a few moments, abruptly awkward in the silence. Now that the glib talk was over, there was a tenseness between them, and Melissa felt the old mingling of anticipation and fear come flooding back to her. She wanted something to happen, but she was not sure what. All the confident scenes of her fantasies evaporated like steam and she was left tongue-tied, fidgety, and hoping desperately that he would take the initiative and say something. When at last he did speak, it was an inanity.

'So, er . . . this is where you live,' he muttered, and he glanced mechanically about as though inspecting the place.

'Yes, this is it,' agreed Melissa. 'The most boring estate in Malaya! I keep waiting for something to happen, but it never does . . .'

'Well, what about these lessons then?' asked Bob, with a renewed sense of urgency.

She stared at him. 'Lessons?'

'Yeah . . . the shooting lessons, remember? I could get in touch with the lads at the barracks, find out when we could use the range . . .'

'Oh yes, of course. It would be great to be able to shoot. Of course, I don't expect I'd ever be as good as you.'

Bob considered the statement for a few moments.

'No,' he replied bluntly. 'I don't expect you would.' He

146

laughed and there was a trace of mockery in his voice that flustered her. She lowered her head, glanced at her wristwatch. 'Well I . . . I suppose I ought to be —'

She broke off in surprise as he edged suddenly and decisively against her. His arms came around her in a powerful embrace and his mouth was against hers. She resisted only for an instant, a token display of indignation; then she relaxed and returned his kisses, allowing him to push her back against the seat. The experience of kissing a mature male was new to her and oddly exciting. The rough stubble of his cheeks was like fine sandpaper against her skin and his body smelled of a mysterious mingling of tobacco and perspiration. But somehow, here in the cramped confines of the Land Rover, it was not as she had imagined the scene. His kisses became more hungry, his tongue exploring her mouth with increased confidence; and then his hands were caressing her breasts through the thin fabric of her blouse. She allowed this to continue for a few moments, but she was nervous at being so near to the estate and when his hands attempted to move upward beneath her skirt, she pushed him away and sat up.

'What's the matter?' he gasped. His voice was now coarse with desire.

'Not here,' she whispered breathlessly. 'I'll meet you somewhere else, another time . . . somewhere where we can be alone . . .' She reached out and stroked his face reassuringly. He took hold of her arms and tried to push her down but she shook her head.

'Somebody might see us,' she pleaded and he frowned, nodded.

'When then?' he said simply. There was a trace of irritation in his voice, and she feared that she might have offended him.

'Tomorrow . . . I'll go to the Chinese Swimming Club with some friends. Can you meet me there?'

'I've got classes in the morning, but I could get there at two o'clock.'

'That would be fine. You could offer me a lift home and we'll go somewhere off by ourselves . . .' She hesitated, embarrassed by her own boldness. 'That is, if you *want* to.'

'Of course I do!' He gave her a fierce glare, then reached out and stroked her leg with a slow, deliberate motion. His eyes promised excitement, but there was a familiarity in the gesture that worried her. 'We'll have a great time,' he promised her. 'You'll see.'

She nodded. 'I'd better go in now,' she concluded. She reached forward, kissed him briefly, and then pulled away, as once again he tried to embrace her.

'Tomorrow,' she assured him; and she clambered out of the Land Rover. 'You . . . will be there, won't you?' she murmured.

'Try and stop me!' he retorted. He gunned the engine, reversed the Land Rover back in a tight circle and accelerated away down the road, without glancing back.

Melissa stared after him until he disappeared round the bend. Then she gave a slow smile of satisfaction. Well, that hadn't been so difficult after all! The trap was set, the prey was in sight. Now she looked forward to the excitement of the kill.

Humming tunelessly to herself, she turned and strolled in the direction of her parents' house.

Harry sat alone in the darkness of his sitting room, staring fixedly in front of him, with eyes that saw nothing. He had been sitting in this way for several hours now, refusing both food and drink, and Pawn was concerned. She had lingered on hours later than usual, hoping that he might change his mind and have some dinner. But whenever she had broached the subject, he had simply grunted a monosyllabic refusal and had returned to his thoughts. Now it was dark outside and Pawn realized that her own family would be worried about her.

She went and stood in the doorway of the sitting room, but Harry did not even notice her presence.

'I go now, Tuan,' she said softly. 'You would like eat, before I go?'

Harry glanced up at her for a moment, then shook his head silently.

'Food is in oven, if you change mind . . .' She stepped forward. 'Tuan is ill?' she enquired. 'Like for me to get

148

Doctor man?'

Again Harry shook his head.

'You go now, Pawn. It must be way past your time.'

She smiled.

'No matter . . . if Tuan wish, I come back later, see you alright . . .'

'I'm fine, Pawn. Run along now, I'll see you tomorrow.'
He turned away as if dismissing her and with a sigh she went back to the kitchen to collect her bag. She had never seen the Tuan looking so miserable and she had an idea that Ché might have something to do with it. She resolved to have a good talk with the boy when she got home. With a sigh, she let herself out of the back door, locking it behind her. Then she strolled down the driveway and out through the gate. It was a cool, fine evening and a full moon lit up the surface of the road. She walked briskly out of the estate, her flip-flops slapping on the ground. Across the road, in one of the gardens, another *amah* was taking in some washing from the line and the two of them called briefly to each other as Pawn moved past.

'Soon the British will all be gone,' thought Pawn sadly, 'and then what will the *amahs* do for work?' She would be alright of course, for she was old and her family would care for her. Besides, Tuan Sullivan had already told her that he would be staying on. But many of the younger girls depended on the British Army and Air Force families for their livelihood. It was a sad state of affairs and no mistake.

Pawn went out of the estate and moved along the road to Kampong Panjang. To her left, a screen of jungle flanked its edge, thick and impenetrable. To her right, a flat stretch of *padi*, the shallow water glittering in the moonlight. The dark silhouettes of several fruit-bats flitted silently overhead and vanished amidst the trees. Pawn realized that she should not have stayed so late. Her family would doubtless be worried by her nonappearance at home and it was a good thing that the man-eating tiger had been shot, otherwise they would be combing the jungle in search of her body. Pawn grinned. She had a good family but they would insist on thinking of her as a helpless old woman when in fact she was more capable than the lot of them put together.

149

The night vibrated with the song of a million unseen insects and the road ahead was completely deserted. The mile walk to Kampong Panjang would take her a little more than half an hour, for she was still wiry and agile.

She was passing by a large clump of ferns that bordered the jungle undergrowth when an unfamiliar sound made her stop in her tracks. It was a dry rustling noise, the sound of vegetation being brushed aside to allow something to pass through it. Pawn turned her head to stare at the bushes and sure enough, she could see some agitation there. Now she heard the unmistakable crack of dry twigs breaking beneath a heavy tread. In the silence it sounded so loud that Pawn almost jumped out of her skin.

With an exclamation, she began to hurry on along the road, not wanting to examine the source of the commotion too carefully. She kept glancing back, half expecting to see some unfamiliar shape following her, but the road remained empty in the moonlight. After a few moments, she began to relax, but then another sound told her that she had not left the problem behind her, that it was simply following through the thick vegetation that bordered the road. A screen of bushes shook as a low moving shape disturbed them. Pawn began to walk more rapidly. Of course, it might be nothing more dangerous than a stray dog or a *berok*, but she certainly didn't intend staying behind to find out. She had heard too many *kampong* tales of weretigers and other hunters of the dark and like most Malays, she had a healthy respect for such stories. She came to a long curve in the road and the movements seemed to have stopped for the time being. She slowed her pace a little for she was getting out of breath and she moved cautiously forward, the slapping of her rubber flip-flops seeming to echo in the silence that had settled around her. Even the insects had stopped their chirruping. She slowed even more now, almost coming to a halt as she glanced this way and that in nervous anticipation, while she told herself not to be silly, there was nothing hidden in the trees that could possibly harm her.

Then, to her horror, she saw that a large patch of bushes directly ahead of her had begun to shake, as though the creature, whatever it was, had cut through the jungle in order to overtake her. Now it was waiting for her cautious advance, there, in that very bush! Pawn glanced helplessly around. There was no other route, short of going into the undergrowth herself, and she dared not leave the relative normality of the road. She moved forward slowly, never taking her gaze from the bush for an instant. It continued to shake with a constant, steady motion that abruptly aroused her suspicion. What creature of the jungle went around making such an unearthly racket, anyway? Pawn's eyes narrowed and she began to walk more steadily towards the bush, her hands on her hips.

'So,' she murmured. 'A wicked beast of the jungle is waiting to make a meal of me, eh? A wicked beast that feeds on weak old women like myself . . . well then, let's see how you like this!' And she ran the last few feet to the bush, swung her heavy rattan shopping bag into the air and brought it down with a thump into the midst of the bush. A howl of pain and surprise emerged and a creature burst out from cover, a black-haired, two-legged creature by the name of Ché.

'So, playing a nasty trick on your poor old grandmother are you?' shrieked Pawn. 'I'll teach you better manners!' And she struck him again and again, while he scrambled this way and that, trying to evade her.

'No, mercy, Grandmother, mercy! It was only a joke . . .'

'A joke is it? Well let me see you laugh this off, you little devil!'

Another powerful swing sprawled him down onto the road, where he lay with his hands cupped protectively over his head, while Pawn administered some more energetic thumps.

'Stop, Grandmother, you'll kill me!' cried Ché in desperation.

Pawned grinned.

'I doubt it,' she chuckled and aimed one last blow at his unprotected rear. Then she stepped back and viewed his crumpled form triumphantly.

'A fine thing to do to your poor ancient grandmother,' she observed. 'You could have given me a heart attack!'

'Not you, you're as strong as an ox,' observed Ché

151

ruefully, rubbing his backside as he clambered to his feet.
Pawn made a threatening move toward him, and he skipped
away a few steps.

'What are you doing here anyway?' she demanded.

'Mother was worried about you so she sent me to . . .'

'Scare me to death?' finished Pawn, with a glare of
accusation. But then she smiled, to show she wasn't really
angry. 'Come along then, little lizard, or the family will be
thinking something's happened to us.' She reached out and
took his hand and the pair of them continued on their way
to Kampong Panjang. 'I'm glad you're here,' said Pawn. 'I
wanted to have a little talk with you.'

'What about, Grandmother?'

'About the Tuan.'

'Oh . . .' Ché glanced guiltily at his feet.

'You may well look down like that,' cried Pawn. 'If you
could have seen him tonight. Ché! Never have I seen such a
poor sad old man.'

Ché feigned innocence over the matter.

'What is that to do with me, Grandmother?' he asked.

'I think you know! You must be aware of how the Tuan
likes you . . . how he looks forward to your visits. When I
arrived without you this morning, he could not hide his
sadness, it was written in the lines of his face. And you
promised to come along later but you did not.'

'But I saw him, Grandmother! He came to Kampong
Machis to see the great tiger that Tuan Beresford had shot.
He said then that he did not mind me not coming to visit
with him . . .'

'You believed that?' cried Pawn scornfully. 'And what
makes you so careless with your words now? Don't you
know that you will turn the wrath of the striped one upon
yourself?'

Ché laughed.

'But Tuan Beresford has killed the man-eater!' he
reasoned.

'So? Do you think he was the only one of his kind in the
jungle? The people of Kandong Balok never sleep. Old Dato
Uban, he keeps his ears open for foolish little boys like you;
and when one of his warriors falls, he sends another to take

his place ... so watch your step!' She glanced at him slyly. 'He also notices naughty boys who misbehave themselves and play terrible tricks on their grandmothers ... boys who don't do what they are told ...'

Ché swallowed nervously, but maintained an air of unconcern.

'Oh, I don't really believe those old stories any more!' he murmured, but he glanced quickly around at the moonlit road and the dark forbidding silhouette of the jungle trees against the sky.

'That's as it may be,' conceded Pawn. 'Anyhow, I think you'd better come to work with me tomorrow, so you can say sorry to the Tuan.'

'Sorry for what?'

'For not going to see him, of course!'

'But, Grandmother, I told you, I *did* see him. Besides, I'm not sure I should say sorry to him.'

'What's that?' Pawn turned and raised her shopping bag threateningly. 'Why, you ungrateful puppy, I ought to tell your father to give you a good thrashing!'

'But Grandmother! The Tuan himself was ungrateful ... he attacked Tuan Beresford – He struck him, and all because he was jealous.'

'I don't believe that for one moment.' Pawn lowered the bag and walked on again. 'The Tuan is a good man. I have known him for many years now. He would not let such a silly thing rule his heart. Besides, I heard differently. He came home with Tuan and Missy Tremayne afterwards and Missy Tremayne, she told me what happened. She said that the Tuan believed that the man-eater was still alive, and that your precious Tuan Beresford killed the wrong animal.'

'But how can that be when we all saw the man-eater lying there dead?'

Pawn raised her eyes heavenward.

'Foolish boy! Did anybody cut upon the creature's stomach and look inside? How can anyone know if it was the right beast?'

'Tuan Beresford would know,' said Ché with great conviction. 'He is a hunter.'

'And are hunters not men, like all others?'

'They are *special* men. One day, I shall be such a man.'

'Pah! If I have any say in it, you won't!'

They walked on for some distance without speaking. From the jungle to their left came the strange sonorous croaking of vast numbers of tiny green tree frogs, filling the night with an unearthly clamour. A bank of tumbling white clouds passed across the face of the moon, sending a great scudding shadow sliding across their path. They moved into the shadow and abruptly the visibility dropped to half of what it had been. It was a most unsettling effect. Ché glanced nervously at his grandmother.

'Does Dato Uban really send another t – another striped one to replace each fallen warrior?' he murmured fearfully.

'You can be sure of it! So you'd better start behaving yourself, my lad! You can start by accompanying me to work tomorrow and by telling the Tuan how sorry you are for letting him down yesterday.'

'But I can't!'

'And why not, may I ask?'

Ché pouted defiantly.

'Because tomorrow, Majid and I are going tracking together . . .'

Pawn gave another exclamation of disgust.

'There you go again, such ungratefulness. Tell me something, who was it gave you those fine English books that got you interested in the subject? And who explained to you all the little parts that you could not understand? And whose stories, in the very first place, made you interested in knowing all about the creatures of the jungle?'

Ché did not deign to answer these questions. Instead, he changed the subject.

'Majid and I, we have decided to practise the craft every day, so that we get better and better at it. Then, if we do well enough at it, perhaps Tuan Beresford will take us hunting with him!'

Pawn gave a derisive laugh.

'Oh, you children and your shifting affections,' she lamented. 'Two days ago, you thought nothing of that man. Indeed, I remember you complaining that he was a young usurper, come to take the Tuan's territory away from him.

Now, simply because he has killed the man-eater . . .'

'Not "simply," Grandmother! It was a fine and noble thing to do. The Tuan had a chance of it, but he let it pass him by. It makes me wonder if any of the Tuan's fine tales are true –'

He broke off as Pawn shot him a look of pure venom.

'When will you children realize,' she intoned coldly, 'that the greatest of men must one day grow old? It comes to us all in the end, just as in turn death must also come . . . Oh, but age is more terrible, more unspeakable than death, for while at the end of life you can sleep in darkness and forget your pains and worries, in age you must carry them around with you on aching, breaking legs. You must go through life doing all those things that are so familiar to you, but at half the speed, with twice the effort. And worst, Ché, the very worst of all, is that you must watch with tired and failing eyes as the youngsters go bounding past you and you realize that try as you might, you can never catch up with them. When I was your age, I could climb to the top of a tall Kapok tree in a few moments. I was as agile as a *berok!* Now, it's all I can do to climb a flight of stairs without getting out of breath. Think, boy. One day it will be you that is old and weary, long after my bones have turned to dust in the earth. And when you tell the stories of your youth to the *kampong* children, do you think for one moment, that they will really believe you were ever capable of such things?'

They strolled on again in silence for some distance. Ché stared thoughtfully at the ground, humbled by his grandmother's words. When at last he spoke, it was only to say, 'Let me carry your shopping bag, Grandmother.'

She let him take it from her hand and she couldn't help but smile at the glum expression on his face. 'You will come to the Tuan's tomorrow?' she asked again.

'I can't tomorrow, Grandmother,' he replied meekly. 'I promised Majid that I would meet him and I never break a promise. But I will come to the Tuan's another time, soon.'

'Good.' She reached out and stroked his head affectionately. 'You see that you keep your word now.'

And they strolled on in silence again. They could see the twinkling of kerosene lamps in the near distance, and it was

155

a comforting feeling to know that they were almost home.

Chapter 16

As soon as Bob arrived back at Kampong Machis, he knew that something was wrong. In the glare of the headlights, he could see that the open area of grass in the centre of the *kampong* was now deserted. The oil lamps that had been left beside the tiger for lighting-up time were still not in use and there was no sign of the man that Bob had paid to stand guard over his property. He brought the Land Rover to an abrupt halt and clambered out, gazing this way and that, but it seemed that everybody had retired to their homes for the night. Bob hurried over the the place where he had left the tiger, suspecting for a moment that it had been stolen. He breathed a sigh of relief when he perceived the dim shape of its long striped carcass stretched out on the grass. Cursing the uselessness of the guard who had wandered off, he took a box of matches from his shirt pocket and squatting down he lit one of the lanterns. He still had to organize somebody to do the skinning, and this would probably necessitate a trip into Kuala Trengganu, the only place where he knew for sure that he could get the job done properly. He still had to decide whether he wanted a head-trophy, a rug, or a fully stuffed and mounted animal.

He moved over to the carcass and held the lantern above it. The smile of triumph on his face turned abruptly to an expression of horrified amazement. He stood for several long moments looking down at the tiger, not wanting to believe what he saw. His eyes widened, then narrowed down to slits of anger.

The carcass had been decimated. Bob had not realized the attraction that tiger charms and talismans held for the villagers. During his absence and no doubt with the full cooperation of the 'guard,' there had been a massive free-for-all of souvenir-taking which must have escalated to ridiculous dimensions. First of all, they had wrenched out the teeth, leaving nothing but one or two deep-set molars;

156

likewise, they had pulled out the creature's claws. Either of these artifacts, worn as an amulet or talisman, would protect the bearer from attack whenever he ventured into the jungle. The less superstitious villagers would find a ready market for the items amongst the Chinese merchants in Kuala Trengganu. Mounted in silver and hung from chains or earrings, they would fetch a pretty price when transported over to England or America. The whiskers had been snipped away and these would find their way into the potions and balms of the Chinese herbalists, who were always interested in buying anything remotely tigerish. Even the ground-up bones of its skeleton were sought after for their supposed healing qualities, and a wine made from the substance could cure rheumatic ailments. The tail had been crudely lopped off, and because the ashes of burned tiger hair were also a highly prized ingredient in 'magic charms,' large patches of the tiger's beautiful hide had been hacked away with knives. The resulting mutilation ensured that the carcass would be of no use whatsoever to a taxidermist.

Bob gave a low moan and sank to his knees beside the carcass. He saw that one enterprising villager had even gouged out the beast's eyes and twin trails of redness had trickled from the empty sockets. He kneeled there for several minutes while he moved the lantern to and fro over the tiger's still form, as though hoping that some magical transformation might take place, that his ruined prize might somehow be made whole again. But each successive glance appalled his horrified gaze and a deep, cold rage settled in his heart. He turned away from the tiger and stared up at the dwellings around him in silent accusation. Now he could perceive faces peering fearfully from the windows. Emotion welled up like a great heat in his chest and his vision blurred. He threw back his head and screamed.

'Bastards!' He felt cheated, betrayed. The cat was his, it was he who had taken the trouble to seek it out, he who had tracked, connived, paid off natives by the dozen for their paltry help. Now they had robbed him at the moment of his triumph. How could they do such a thing? How could they even envisage such a vile, despicable trick? He stood up, the lantern swaying precariously in his grasp. He strode toward the nearest building, where he thought he saw the faces of children peering from the windows. 'Come out of there!' he shrieked. 'Come out, you bloody little thieves, and see what you've done. The tiger was *mine!* He belonged to me, I took him . . .' He aimed a kick at one of the thick supporting poles on which the building stood, and the rickety construction shuddered visibly for a moment. The children's heads vanished from the windows and shouts of alarm sounded from within, but still nobody came out. Raging impotently, Bob moved across to the next building and directed a few well-chosen curses in that direction, but the natives, perhaps wisely, chose to stay put inside the sanctuary of their homes.

'Gutless bastards!' screamed Bob. 'I should have let the fucking tiger go on killing you all!' A sudden wild impulse took him and he ran to the Land Rover, snatched out his rifle. Ramming a cartridge into the chamber, he sighted up on the first object that caught his attention, an innocent goatskin gourd full of water that was hanging from the side of a house. He squeezed the trigger and the gourd jerked convulsively, its contents streaming out through the rent in its side.

Abruptly, the windows were crammed with pale staring faces. Bob laughed almost hysterically, pumped the rifle bolt and took playful aim at the windows nearest to him. He could hear quite plainly the shouts of alarm from within, and he grinned with malicious intent. But at the last moment, he jerked the rifle upwards and fired at a clay chimney pot on the roof. It shattered and came down in a shower of broken bits, bouncing noisily off the corrugated iron roof. Lights were going on all through the village and shouting people were running out of doorways, then just as quickly ducking back in again, when they were greeted by the sight of an angry white man with a loaded rifle.

'Yeah, run and hide!' yelled Bob. He began to stride through the village, cracking off shots in every direction, channelling his aggression into an excess of sheer delinquency, making a target of any paltry possession that caught his eye. It was a pathetic little revenge for the trick that had been played on him, but for the moment he was totally

158

immersed in it.

'Stop this!' The command came from behind him with unexpected force. Bob whipped instinctively around and for a moment, he was on the very verge of shooting the man who stood before him. It was the *penghulu* from Kampong Panjang. The little man stood with his arms spread out and an expression of alarm on his face. He kept his eyes fixed unwaveringly on the threatening barrel of the rifle that pointed straight at his chest.

'The . . . Tuan is . . . angry?' he asked cautiously in a voice that was barely more than a croak.

Bob glared at him for a moment and then, he slowly lowered the rifle. The *penghulu* gave an audible sigh of relief.

'Yes, I'm angry,' snarled Bob. 'Bloody angry. Anyway, what are you doing here?'

'I come today to see *Si-Pudong*. . . I stay with my cousin, here.' The *penghulu* gestured vaguely at the buildings behind him. 'But Tuan, why do you do this? We all thought you were a good man . . .'

'A good man! A mug you mean! Have you seen what they've done to my tiger? Here, look for yourself.' He grasped the *penghulu* roughly by his skinny elbow and frog-marched him over to the mutilated carcass. 'There, look at that!' Bob took the lantern and held it over the corpse. 'You see what the thieving bastards have done to my tiger . . .'

'*Yours*, Tuan?' The *penghulu* glanced at Bob slyly. 'Forgive me, Tuan, but surely this was a creature of the jungle. Who can say that it belonged to anyone?'

'Don't give me that! A tiger belongs to the bloke who went out and got him. That's me, in case you don't remember. Now, I paid one of these monkeys to look after the carcass and when I returned, he'd buggered off and this had happened. When I catch up with him . . .'

'Oh, never fear, Tuan, the man shall be caught and punished just as soon as I tell this to the Kampong Machis *penghulu* . . . er – That is, soon as he plucks up the courage to come out here himself. But this man you leave on guard. What is his name?'

Bob shrugged.

'Well, I don't know.'

'And what does he look like?'

'Well, er . . . he was . . . small . . . and dark . . .' Bob slapped his own leg in exasperation. 'Anyway, what the hell does it matter? The point is, this should never have happened! I went out into that jungle and risked my neck for this village, and this is how they repay me. I mean, where's the fairness in that?'

The *penghulu* frowned, shook his head. He clearly did not know the answer to that one.

'The Tuan must remember,' he said. 'These people who live in the *kampongs*. To them, *Si-Pudong* is a great and magical beast. To own a part of him is everyone's wish.'

'Well, then why don't they go out and shoot one themselves?' snapped Bob bitterly.

The *penghulu* gave a little laugh.

'To say such a thing, you do not know Malays very well,' he observed. 'A Malay has a special outlook on life, Tuan. Things are done only when they must be done. A man's roof leaks, water falls on him . . . then he fixes roof, not before. You understand?'

'Yeah, basically it means he's bloody lazy!'

The *penghulu* shook his head.

'No, you say this because you think like a white man, and the white man must be always doing something. For a Malay to hunt *Si-Pudong*, there must be a strong reason, like revenge – Si-Pudong eat his wife or children, or he badly need money for some reason.' The *penghulu* pointed at the scarred corpse. 'Many of the people who do this, they do it because they believe a piece of the body will save them from harm, will make them brave and strong like *Si-Pudong*, will give them children, make wife love them more . . . And others, Tuan, others will use their tokens to sell when times are hard. It will put food into their bellies when they are hungry, will buy special presents for the ones they love.' The *penghulu* spread his arms in a gesture of inquiry. 'What would you have done with the beast, Tuan? Stuffed him and stood him in your fine house? Made a rug of him for your good friends to place their feet on? Cut off his head and fix it to a wooden board to hang from a wall? You have no beliefs about him yourself, for you are not of the same land

160

as he was. You do not share the same trails as he, you do not drink of the same water. Surely if *Si-Pudong* belongs to anyone, then he belongs to us . . .'

The *penghulu*'s carefully considered words had shamed Bob, but he did not want to admit it.

'It's easy for you to talk,' he blustered. 'You didn't sit up that bloody tree in the rainstorm! Anyway, I'm damned if I'm going to leave the rest of the carcass here for those ungrateful parasites.' He strode to the Land Rover, threw his rifle into the back, and then returned to the tiger. Going down on one knee, he attempted to drag the beast along, but he could not even budge it a few inches. 'Give me a hand with this,' he grunted to the *penghulu*. 'At least I should be able to get a few quid for it in Kuala Trengganu. They say the bones bring a good price.' The two men heaved ineffectually at the tiger for a few minutes, but it had taken four strong men to carry him out of the jungle and it was apparent that they would never lift the carcass high enough to get it into the Land Rover.

'Call some of your friends down from their houses,' gasped Bob. 'We need a hand here.'

The *penghulu* shook his head regretfully.

'Alas, Tuan, I fear they will be too frightened by your shooting before!'

'Don't be bloody silly! The gun's in the jeep now and it will only take a moment. Call them down.'

'They will not come, Tuan. Perhaps if you were to offer a few dollars . . .'

Bob's face reddened with anger.

'I bloody well will not,' he retorted. 'I've handed out enough cash these last few days to pay for an army.' He took a long silent look around him at the grim faces watching from the doorways of houses and then he gave a formless shout of exasperation. He stood up and went back to the Land Rover, clambered into the seat, and kicked the engine alive. The *penghulu* ran after him.

'The Tuan is leaving?' he enquired politely.

'Damned right I am. You can keep the bloody tiger and good riddance to it! It's no use to me in that state, anyway.'

'But Tuan, perhaps if both of us try again . . .'

161

'No, no, forget it! I'm going home to get some sleep.' A glint of moonlight caught something lying on the passenger seat. Bob picked it up and examined it carefully. It was a silver lipstick case. In the midst of his rage, Bob found an unreasonable target on which to focus his disappointment. If it hadn't been for her, he would never have left the tiger.

'Bitch,' he muttered. He flung the case carelessly away, wrenched the vehicle into gear and accelerated out of the *kampong*, leaving the *penghulu* staring after him with a bemused smile on his wizened monkey-face. The *penghulu* reached thoughtfully beneath the open neck of his white shirt, where the tiger's claw hung in a tiny leather pouch around his neck. He had felt quite confident about coming down to confront the white man and, sure enough, the power in the claw had saved him from being shot. He glanced at the carcass and grinned. It was his own cleverness that had secured the remains of the beast and the *penghulu* of Kampong Machis could hardly deny him a share in the profit they would make from the herbalists. On impulse, he walked over to the tiger and placed one foot on it, mimicking the traditional pose of the victorious white hunter. For this, he received a burst of sporadic applause from the watching villagers, who appreciated that he'd scored a sizeable victory over the aggressive Australian. Now, satisfied with the outcome of the adventure, they began to drift back into their houses to resume their interrupted repose.

But the *penghulu* sat up a little while longer at the scene of his victory, gazing thoughtfully at the dead tiger and smoking a last, incredibly satisfying cigarette.

Haji awoke to a familiar sound: the distant mournful cry of Timah, who, oddly enough, was still avidly seeking a mate. The force of her roars suggested that the young male, for all his apparent strength, had been unable to mate with her because of his lack of experience. Haji felt much stronger now and he did not hesitate to leave the cool sanctuary of the cave and go in search of Timah, responding occasionally to her call with his own deeper roar.

After half an hour's search, he managed to find her. She

162

had taken up residence beside a wide jungle stream and she was pacing restlessly up and down beside it, for she was now at the height of her oestrus and would find no rest until she was fulfilled. She displayed no surprise when Haji emerged from the undergrowth, but moved forward to greet him and as she had on the previous occasion, she patrolled up and down in front of him, rubbing her flank against his, and pausing to give a slow sensuous stretch that was primarily designed to excite him. He responded quickly, for Timah was certainly no stranger to him. He nuzzled at her neck with his mouth and she flopped down in the grass for a moment, purring luxuriously as his warm tongue lapped at her ear. Abruptly, she rose to her feet, prowled a short distance, then went down again, presenting herself to him with her tail slightly raised. Haji followed silently, clambered astride and entered her with well-practised ease.

The union was brief, twenty seconds at most, with Timah emitting a series of low guttural moans indicating her pleasure. As the union came to climax, Haji lowered his head and gripped the fold of skin around Timah's neck tightly in his jaws, then gave a peculiar, high-pitched squeal as he ejaculated. Now, the first consummation completed, Timah felt abruptly insecure and began to protest that she must be released. She dislodged Haji with an unceremonious jerk, whipped around, and launched a boisterous attack on him, boxing at his head with her heavy forepaws. He fell back before her, blocking the most severe of her swings, but not attempting to counter the attack. After a few moments, Timah seemed to lose strength and she simply flopped down in exhaustion, rolling onto her back and letting her legs hang awkwardly above her. Haji sat down quietly a few feet away, watching her intently. The only movement was the occasional spasmodic twitch of her tail. Five minutes passed and it was deadly silent in the jungle, the birds shocked to silence by the tigers' earlier commotion. Now, Timah's head lifted a little and Haji crept forward to nuzzle at her face again. She rolled onto her side, growling softly as the yearning to copulate reasserted itself. She got to her feet, walked a short distance and flopped down to present herself for a second bout of lovemaking. The entire process was

163

repeated, right down to the brief quarrel afterwards, and indeed it was repeated again and again all through the day and the following night at intervals of between five and twenty minutes. During this time, Haji and Timah had no thought of food and only during the late hours, after they had mated some forty or fifty times, did they allow themselves the luxury of a brief nap between sessions. While the oestrus lasted, Haji and Timah would stay constantly together, and only when it was at an end would they separate and return to their more usual life patterns. If the union was successful and Timah found herself pregnant, then she would have the unenviable task of raising and feeding the resulting litter for up to two years, when they would be capable of looking after themselves. In that time, save for chance encounters, she would not normally expect to have Haji's companionship again. Such was the simple and solitary life that nature had evolved for the tiger.

Fending off another of Timah's bouts of boisterous insecurity, Haji had a brief vision, a memory of other times when he had performed this strange old ritual, and there came to him the conviction that, if he was successful in siring offspring this time, then it would surely be the last time, for he was very old now and was already past the age when most male tigers lost their ability to reproduce. He had no way of knowing how many cubs he had fathered and there was still, in his mind, the vague, fretful memory of his other mate Seti, who had died trying to deliver her last litter.

He dropped patiently down into the grass and watched as Timah slumped yet again into exhaustion. For a moment, an image of Seti's blind eyes assailed him, but then it was gone, lost in the jungle of half-formed visions and images that surfaced occasionally in his brain. He concentrated on the slow, serpentlike coiling of Timah's tail, and he waited for desire to come to her again.

Chapter 17

Melissa was fuming. She stalked silently along the road, her hands in the pockets of her shorts, painfully aware that she had made a complete fool of herself. Bob Beresford had not turned up at the swimming pool that afternoon. That much would have been bad enough, but so confident had she been about her conquest that she had herself invited Victoria Lumly and Allison Weathers along to witness the triumph. At first she had been quietly confident about the assignation, but as the afternoon wore slowly onward and there was still no sign of Bob she had begun to feel quite wretched, a creature of ridicule. Of course, the acid-tongued Victoria had lost no opportunity to press home the point, feigning wide-eyed innocence as she said 'helpful' things like, 'Perhaps his jeep broke down,' or 'Are you sure it was today you told him to meet you?' Meanwhile that dreadful Allison had just snickered and giggled the entire day away. At last, Melissa could stand it no more and she had simply sneaked away, leaving the two insufferable creeps to their own devices.

Now, walking back along the coast road in the direction of her estate, Melissa began to examine the possibilities. Had she come on too strong with him, perhaps? She'd always been led to believe that men liked girls who showed a little initiative; and besides, he'd been keen enough the night before, there was no doubt about that. Perhaps he really had got himself into an unavoidable situation at work ... maybe he would get in touch with her soon ...

She snapped her head up as a strange, distant sound reached her ears. It seemed to come from the direction of the jungle, an eerie, prolonged caterwauling that culminated in a short highpitched shriek. Melissa put her head to one side and listened, but all was silent now. She frowned, shrugged, trudged onwards again. Monkeys, no doubt ...

'I bet *they* don't have this trouble,' she muttered to herself.

The sound of a familiar car engine interrupted her thoughts and she turned, half expecting to see a battered Land Rover pursuing her. In seconds, a succession of brief images flickered through her mind's eye: Bob had been unavoidably delayed, but now he would leap from the Land Rover and take her roughly in his arms ... and Melissa of course, would insist that the two of them go back to the

165

swimming pool, if only for a brief time, just so that Melissa could see the looks of shock on the faces of those two arrogant Medusas, Victoria and Allison . . . and then, she and Bob would ride off to some quiet little spot where they could . . .

The images died abruptly. It was not the Land Rover at all but her father's car, returning from the barracks. He was smiling at her from the driver's seat and opening the passenger door for her to get in. He must have been vaguely surprised by the look of disgust she favoured him with.

'Is there something wrong, dear?' he asked mildly.

'Yes, there is!' she complained bitterly. But she walked to the car and clambered into the passenger seat, slamming the door shut behind her.

'What have you been up to today?' enquired Dennis.

'Swimming pool.'

He raised his eyebrows slightly.

'Did you forget your towel then?'

'I didn't go there to *swim*.'

'Ah . . . that would explain it.' He accelerated the car away from the verge. 'Go by yourself?' he asked.

'With Victoria and Allison.'

'I thought you didn't like them.'

'I don't. They're disgusting.'

'Ah . . . yes . . .' Dennis noted to himself that his daughter was in a singularly strange mood today, but he had learned from long experience that it was pointless to try and pursue any of her more puzzling remarks in search of some explanation.

'Did you er . . . see Bob Beresford at all, today?' asked Melissa.

'No, I didn't. But I did hear something interesting about him . . .'

Melissa sat up and took notice.

'Oh? What was that?'

'Well, it seems he had a bit of a nasty trick played on him last night. He left somebody to guard the tiger while he went away for a while and when he got back, the villagers had taken a few trophies of their own . . .'

Melissa stared at him.

166

'What do you mean?' she demanded.

'They chopped the tiger up, dear. Took the teeth and claws from it, hacked it about with knives. Apparently it was good for nothing by the time Beresford got back to it, so he ended up just leaving it there. Damned shame, really . . .'

Melissa turned to gaze blankly at the straight strip of road ahead. On either side, the jungle was a thick impenetrable screen of fronds and behind the treetops over to the west, the sky was rapidly reddening as the sun began to journey west down to the horizon.

'Oh my God . . .' she whispered.

'What's the matter?'

'It must have happened while he was driving me home.'

'Uh . . . yes, I suppose it must.'

'Well, don't you see? He'll blame me for it! He obviously thinks it's my fault!'

'Surely not . . .'

'Yes, of course he will!' She sank her face into the palm of her hand with a groan of misery. 'He won't even want to know me now,' she concluded glumly.

'Oh, now Melissa, I do think you're being dramatic about this,' reasoned Dennis. 'It's hardly your fault, after all.'

'The point is, if he hadn't had to drive me home, he'd have been with the tiger all the time . . . the villagers wouldn't even have had the chance to get at it. It stands to reason that he's going to blame me. For God's sake, that's obviously why he didn't turn up at the swimming pool today!'

'Oh, I see . . .' Dennis frowned. He did not have much experience of discussing this kind of thing with his daughter and he felt distinctly uncomfortable. He gave what he thought was a reassuring smile. 'I'm sure he'll soon get over it,' he murmured lamely.

Melissa looked far from convinced.

'How long will that take?' she retorted sulkily. 'There's not much time . . .' She turned to gaze silently out of the open window.

'What peculiar little plot is she hatching now?' thought Dennis uneasily. It occurred to him, not for the first time, that he really knew very little about his daughter. Oh, she'd inherited Kate's wilfulness right enough, a determination to achieve any goal she set her sights on, that much he knew. But unlike her mother, Melissa seemed to possess an ability to divorce herself from her emotions. She was always working on some calculated little scheme or other, but the secrets of them were never divulged until it was too late and the prize, whatever it was, safely netted. For once, the object of her attention seemed well and truly transparent. Bob Beresford. But something told Dennis that it couldn't be as straightforward as that. For one thing, Melissa wasn't acting like somebody who had been smitten by an infatuation; anyway, she was too sensible for that kind of thing. Beresford was simply a means to an end, but what that might be was anybody's guess. One thing was for certain. For Beresford, it was only a matter of time. Regardless of her reasons for pursuing him, Melissa always got what she wanted in the end. That much had been proved time and time again in the past.

She sat now, leaning slightly forward, her chin resting on her clenched fist, her elbow resting on one knee and her face bore an expression that suggested earnest concentration.

'Penny for them,' said Dennis drily, and was not unduly surprised when he received no reply. Melissa had retreated to her own world, where she was the only real inhabitant and the rest of mankind merely pawns to be manipulated. This was the familiar pattern. Whatever it was she was plotting now, it ultimately meant trouble for somebody . . .

It was late and it was Mess night, but for the first time since he had begun the regular visits Harry could not raise the necessary enthusiasm to go. He sat alone in his sitting room, with just one small reading lamp lit behind him. He had told Pawn to go home, that he would not be going out tonight and eventually, with great reluctance, she had agreed. She had realized only too well that something must be very wrong, for the Tuan was a creature of habit and the visits to the Mess were as much a part of his weekly routine as the cups of tea he liked to enjoy out on the verandah.

'I'm just tired,' he had said, by way of explanation. 'I

need to rest.'

He knew himself that this was nothing but a poor excuse. What he really felt was an acute sense of betrayal. Quite unexpectedly, the two people he loved most in the world had turned against him. Not only that, but both of them had gravitated towards a man that he disliked intensely, a man who according to Harry's code of living had no moral ethics whatsoever.

Harry sighed. He gazed thoughtfully about the room in which he sat and he seemed to be seeing it for the first time. What a grim, cheerless place it looked, doubly so in the harsh limited glow of a single light bulb. The bare, red-tiled floor was covered here and there by worn rush matting and though Pawn kept it beautifully polished, it had none of the appeal of a good soft carpet. The heavy teak furniture, brought over from Burma, was at least an improvement on the ghastly tubular steel and Formica stuff that the armed forces tended to furnish their officers' quarters with, but against the nondescript pale-blue walls, it tended to look oppressive and only served to emphasize the emptiness of the rest of the room. There had been paintings and some wood carvings once upon a time, but these artifacts were more Meg's influence than his and he had got rid of them shortly after her death, for they only served as constant reminders of her existence. There were no plants in the house either, the only other living occupants being a pair of chit-chats, busily searching the corners of the ceiling for tasty insects.

'Dead,' thought Harry sadly. 'Even the room is dead.' For the first time in his life, he felt near to resigning himself to a similar fate. There seemed little to go on for now. The community here was falling apart at the seams. In a short while Melissa would be gone, and it grieved him to think that she might leave before their quarrel could be repaired. As for Ché . . . well, he was at an impressionable age. It was quite possible that he would simply forget about the old man who had once meant so much to him. Then what would be left for Harry? Would he go on haunting the Mess and the tennis club, until all the last stragglers had moved away to their British homes? Was he to be the last doddering old vestige of Empire, constantly hounded by well-meaning bores like Doctor Kalim? He shuddered at the very thought of it. He was in every way, in every little habit, a product of the strange colonial life he had led for so very long. With that life-style gone, he would be nothing more than a pitiful relic. A feeling of coldness settled over him. He stood up slowly and went over to the ornately carved writing desk that stood against the far wall. He pulled out the single drawer and extracted a heavy .38 revolver that had not been fired in many years. Reaching further back into the drawer, his fingers located a box of ammunition. He put the two items down on the desk and stood gazing at them for several moments, the palms of his hands resting on either side of them. He did not feel in the least afraid. He now opened the cardboard pack and let the bullets drop out onto the desk. Breaking open the chamber of the gun, he began to load it, carefully and methodically. Once all the chambers were full, he snapped the gun shut and stood, gazing at the weapon thoughtfully.

The doorbell rang. Harry glanced up in surprise. He had certainly not been expecting a caller. The only person who might be expected to call on Mess nights was the old Chinese *trishaw* driver, but Harry had not seen hide nor hair of the fellow since his illness. It was very silent in the house. Harry stood where he was for several moments, trying to decide what to do. Then he came to a decision. He raised the pistol, opened his mouth slightly and placed the tip of the barrel inside. A friend had once told him that this was the best way to do it; a shot through the side of the head could often deflect against the hard bone and a lingering, miserable death resulted. Harry closed his eyes and his finger tightened on the trigger . . .

The doorbell rang again, shrill, insistent. Harry snatched the gun away with a curse and slammed it down on the surface of the desk. How the hell was he supposed to make an end of himself with all these bloody interruptions? Mumbling to himself, he strode towards the door, unlatched it, and peeped out into the night. It was not well lit out there, and at first all he could see was the silhouette of a small, half-naked boy. Harry's first impulse was one of joy,

170

for he thought that this was Ché; but as he swung the door open and the boy stepped into the light, he could see that it was a Chinese youth, someone he had never seen before.

'Yes?' he enquired, puzzled.

The boy moved forward into the light. He was clad in just a pair of khaki shorts and some worn looking flip-flops. He was somewhat older than Ché, perhaps fourteen or fifteen, and he had that wide-eyed, undernourished look that many of the poorer *kampong* children possessed. When he spoke, it was haltingly, for his English was not good.

'I come take Tuan sol'ymess.'

Harry gazed at the boy for a moment, then scratched his head in puzzlement.

'What?' he asked simply.

The boy smiled self-consciously, aware of his own limitations. He repeated the phrase again, more slowly this time.

'I . . . come . . . take Tuan . . . sol'ymess.' Then he turned and pointed up the path, into the darkness. '*Trishaw*,' he added and patted his own thin chest to indicate that the vehicle was his property.

'Ah . . . I see . . . where's the other fellow?' He noted the boy's look of bafflement and amended his own question accordingly. 'Where is other man who always come for me?'

Recognition flared in the boy's large brown eyes; then he glanced regretfully at his feet.

'My grandfather, Tuan,' he said glumly. 'He dead . . . two days now.'

To Harry, the news was like a sharp blow beneath the ribs. It momentarily took the breath out of him and he had to lean against the door frame for support.

'Oh,' he murmured tonelessly. 'Oh God, I'm sorry . . .' So they were all leaving him, one by one. Even the ones who really belonged here. He glanced back over his shoulder and the pistol was waiting for him, a shiny mechanical ticket to oblivion.

'Grandfather leave *trishaw* to me,' explained the boy with difficulty. 'He also leave . . .' He struggled for a word he did not know, then brightened and pulled a piece of paper from his back pocket and handed it to Harry. The old man gazed

171

at it blankly. It had been scrawled on in pencil, but the characters were Mandarin Chinese and Harry could only shrug helplessly.

'Is *times*, Tuan. Times you allus go sol'yness. Grandfather make me promise to come for you ev'ry night. Also, not take money till pay back what you give him. You unnerstan'?'

Harry nodded, sighed.

'Yes, I understand. But there is no need to pay back anything . . .'

'I promise Grandfather. In return, get own business. *Trishaw* driver. So . . . we go now, yes?'

'I . . . I won't be going tonight son. Too tired . . . here, let me . . .'

He began to fish about in his pocket for change but the boy shook his head adamantly.

'I not take money, Tuan! Is promise I make.' He gazed at Harry imploringly. 'Why you not go, Tuan? Grandfather, he say you allus go. You think I not look after you?' He grinned fearlessly. 'Don't worry, Tuan! I small but strong too!' He indicated his skinny little legs. 'Go many mile aw'ready . . .'

'Yes . . . yes, of course, it's not that I don't trust you . . .'

'If you not go, how I pay back what Grandfather owe? It long way from *kampong* to here, but I allus come for you. You see!'

Harry gazed thoughtfully at the boy, suddenly struck by the determination in the boy, the will to fill his grandfather's shoes, to do a man's job. It couldn't be easy for him, for he was thin and puny and no doubt he crawled into bed every night in a state of exhaustion, every muscle aching. Harry felt ashamed, realizing just how easily he himself had given up. He thought of the old man who had not even let death prevent him from repaying what, to him, was a debt of honour. He could learn much from people like this.

'I'll get my coat,' he said simply, and turning he strolled back inside, pausing only to unload the pistol and replace it in the drawer.

'What is that, Tuan?' asked the boy, intrigued.

'Nothing. Just a toy I was playing with,' replied Harry

172

and he went to find his jacket.

A few minutes later, the *trishaw* was whizzing smoothly along the coast road. The night was humid and rich with the scent of wild orchids. As they turned a long slow bend in the road, Harry could see the ocean far below, half masked by a screen of thick foliage. The sea air wafting in over the treetops was a temporary cooling respite before they plunged back between flanks of screening jungle, but the vision of glittering moonlight on restless waves stayed with Harry as they journeyed on into the darkness.

The boy applied himself to the task of turning the pedals with silent dedication. His dark face shone with sweat.

'You're a good driver,' observed Harry, and the boy grinned with pleasure.

Harry leaned back with a sigh and took the cigar case from his breast pocket. He extracted two, lit them both and then handed one back to the boy. He had done this from force of habit, momentarily forgetting that it was no longer the old man who was driving him, but the boy accepted the cigar gratefully, put it between his lips and smoked as though he had been doing it for years.

'Thank you, Tuan,' he said brightly. 'Good cigar.'

And the *trishaw* whirred on into the night, its easy gliding motion calming the desperation that Harry had so recently felt in his heart. Once again, he was at peace with the world.

TWO

Chapter 18

Haji moved slowly through the screen of bushes that flanked the jungle road, placing his paws with delicate precision: he never took his eyes off the old Upright woman for a single moment. She was moving with surprising speed for her age, as she had done now for several miles. She was totally unaware that she was being followed and that she had already had several lucky escapes. Every time Haji tensed himself for the short dash that would end the woman's life, something happened to disrupt the plan: a bullock cart passed along from the other direction, or a group of Uprights would call noisy greetings to her from the roadside. Haji would then be obliged to hug cover and wait for some time, before another opportunity presented itself and now the woman was dangerously close to Kampong Panjang, the place where she was headed.

It was getting increasingly difficult to secure an Upright. Over the two and a half months since Haji had resumed his rightful territory, he had killed five of them. He had also picked up several dogs from around the *kampongs* and some stray cattle, but his presence was now so feared that people did not wander about after dark and Haji had been forced to operate in broad daylight. He still hunted his more usual prey whenever the chance arose, but there seemed to be a terrible shortage of game in the jungle and, anyway, he had quickly learned that an Upright was much easier to catch and kill. His right foreleg was now almost completely useless and though he had learned to live with it, it slowed him down terribly.

Haji was certainly having to keep his wits about him now. It seemed impossible to return to a kill without finding it disturbed in some way and with an Upright lying up in wait for him, with the inevitable black stick. He had been shot at on two occasions, the roaring fire coming dangerously close, and as a consequence he hardly ever returned to a kill anymore without first patrolling the whole area and assuring himself that the coast was clear. It very rarely was and if the victim was an Upright, it *never* was. The most suspicious creatures of all were the live cattle that Haji sometimes encountered tethered in the very midst of the jungle. They made no attempt to run when they saw Haji, they simply tugged ineffectually at the ropes that held them and bawled pitifully. There was something so *wrong* about this behaviour that Haji steered well clear of the creatures, even when he was very hungry. He had once encountered Timah on one of the cattle trails and saw that she was stalking one of these strange cattle. Haji had intimated his fear to her and she too had abandoned the scheme, bowing to his greater experience. Haji had noticed that she was heavy with cubs and realized that his litter might be born in a few weeks' time. This had given him a brief sensation of well-being, though he had quickly forgotten the incident when he and Timah went their separate ways. He hoped that he had instilled in her the good sense to avoid anything that seemed 'unnatural' for there was, in nearly every case, a strong indication that Uprights had been in the vicinity and these were dangerous times.

The road seemed deserted again. Haji glanced to left and right, and for the moment nothing else moved. He fixed his gaze on the old Upright, moving his head backwards and forwards, like a cameraman taking focus, and he crept to the very edge of the undergrowth, bunching his leg muscles to propel himself across the road . . .

An unexpected yell startled him and a large band of Upright cubs spilled from out of some bushes to his left. He dropped back with a growl of frustration as they rushed past him along the road, waving their arms and shouting greetings to the old woman, who they quickly surrounded. Haji was furious. He dared not attack so large a group and he could only slink along, keeping pace with them, in the vague hope that he would get one more opportunity to strike before the woman reached the sanctuary of the *kampong*. But even now she was turning in at an open entrance that led along a short lane to the houses of the village, no more than twenty yards away. The cubs, who had

178

no doubt appointed themselves as some kind of escort, deemed her to be safe this near the *kampong* and they turned away, waving and yelling their goodbyes. Smiling, the old woman turned and trudged slowly along the lane, while the others continued along the main road.

Glancing wildly around, Haji cut through the intervening cover at a steady trot, hoping to surprise the Upright in the narrow confines of the lane, but he had reckoned the distances badly, for when he reached the lane she was already emerging into the area beyond and was passing into the shadow of the first house. The *kampong* seemed quiet in the heat of the day and Haji was loath to follow her in there; but then he noticed that she had come to a halt beside the second house and that this house was still near the very perimeter of the village. Making a quick decision, Haji burst from the cover of the bushes and loped across the intervening distance, a lithe, striped form that made no sound. He came around the far side of the house she had already passed, instinctively keeping to the shadow it threw on the hard earth. The old Upright had begun to climb the ladder to the open door of the house. She was on the third rung and she was calling out to someone within . . .

Inside the house, the woman's daughter was sitting cross-legged on the floor in the corner of the room, attending to some sewing. She lifted her head at the sound of her mother's voice and was slightly puzzled by an abrupt bump that followed it. She stood up and placed her sewing carefully where it would not be disturbed; then she turned, strolled to the open doorway with a smile of greeting on her face. The smile faded when she saw that there was nobody there. Outside was deserted and silent save for the maddening song of a brain fever bird. The woman thought she saw a brief flutter of dress fabric, disappearing around the corner of the house and she leaned forward a little, called her mother's name. But there was nothing there. She began to think that she must have imagined the call and was about to turn back into the interior of the house; but then she noticed something strange on the ladder below her, something soft and brown that was caught in one of the Vs, between the upright and a horizontal slat of wood.

179

Something that was wedged there. The woman frowned, began to clamber down the ladder curiously. Now a dark viscous liquid began to pump from the thing, spattering the rungs further below. The woman recognized one of a pair of elaborate embroidered slippers that she had given to her mother some years before as a present. It dawned on her slowly, horribly that her mother's foot was still inside, torn raggedly away at the ankle.

She screamed until she fainted.

Bob Beresford sat in the bare cheerlessness of his sitting room, cleaning his rifle with an oily rag and taking occasional swigs from a can of Tiger beer. For him, the last two and a half months had been a frustrating time. Although he had practically redoubled his efforts to catch the man-eating tiger, he was still no nearer to his goal. The beast was very lucky, very cunning, or possessed a combination of both. At any rate, none of Bob's ruses had worked, the closest he had got were a couple of fleeting glimpses of the tiger as it took off into cover and the shots he had tried on both occasions nothing more than useless gestures that stood not a hope in hell of hitting their target. He had also managed to shoot a leopard which had attacked a tethered calf he had put out in the vicinity of one of the tiger's kills and that particular beast had since been converted into a rather tatty-looking rug, that looked singularly out of place in Bob's otherwise spartan abode.

The greatest blow of all to Bob's pride had, of course, been the realization that Harry Sullivan was quite right about Bob's mistaken shooting of the first tiger. When the news had come through about a second kill, Bob had felt vaguely ashamed of himself, but not enough to apologize to the old man. He had encountered Harry once or twice at the Mess since then, and though nothing was actually said the venom in Harry's eyes suggested that it would have been useless to try to be friendly; so, perhaps wisely, Bob kept his distance and simply got on with rectifying his own mistake to the best of his ability. Of course, as time went on and more lives were claimed, the Malayan Game Department had dispatched one of their own men to take care of the tiger. His name was Mike Kirby and he was an affable enough fellow. Bob had gone drinking with him on a couple of occasions and there was certainly little competition between the two of them. The fact that Bob lived locally and had already organized a good 'jungle telegraph' for himself meant that the Australian tended to be onto the scene of the kill first and as Bob seemed to know what he was doing, Kirby was content to work from a series of staked-out baits.

'Between the two of us, we'll get the bugger sooner or later,' he reckoned. He had also come up with an interesting explanation for the sudden spell of man-killing. The Game Department had, he told Bob, discovered that the local wild-pig population had been decimated by a virulent disease in the last few months, a malady rather like domestic swine-fever. The result was that the tigers' main food source had been drastically reduced and this might account for the spate of attacks by the area's resident tiger. Kirby had a good knowledge of the animals, but he surprised Bob by asking if 'old Harry Sullivan' was still in the area. He went on to explain that in his estimation there was nobody in the area who knew more about them than Harry did.

'I've only been on this job a few years,' he continued. 'It takes a lifetime to learn about an animal as secretive as a tiger. You need any help, Bob, mark my words, Harry Sullivan's the feller to see. Get the experience of an old hand behind you.' Bob had simply gritted his teeth and said nothing. And so the last couple of months had passed and still the tiger was at large. Now it was not simply a question of getting him eventually. The hunt had developed into a race against time. In a few weeks, Bob's assignment here would come to an end, as his last batch of pupils headed home. He had sworn to himself that he would not quit Malaya without taking the beast's head away with him.

Lim bustled into the room from the direction of the kitchen.

'Food ready soon,' she announced brightly. She had a duster in her hand and she began to busy herself with unnecessary cleaning, lifting the few ornaments that Bob had acquired and dusting underneath them. After a few moments, she came across to the table where Bob was working and began to tidy up his jumble of cleaning apparatus.

'Leave that be!' he snapped irritably and she moved quickly away, as though he had slapped her. Her pretty face collapsed into an expression of misery and she attempted to hide the fact that she was crying by turning her back on him.

'For Christ's sake, what's the matter now?' he shouted. For the last few days, Lim had been acting rather strangely, crying at the least little thing and Bob was rapidly beginning to lose patience with her. She did not answer him but simply ran back into the kitchen, slamming the door after her.

Bob swore beneath his breath. After a few moments, he could quite clearly hear the sounds of her frenzied sobbing from the bare, echoing kitchen. He sighed. He was well aware that his inability to bag the tiger was making him more irritable than usual, but he did think that she was overdoing it a bit. But then, he reflected, Lim was all too aware that soon the 'Tuan' would be heading back home and that she had absolutely no chance of going with him. What would happen to the *amahs* in general was anybody's guess. It was obvious that they would have to find themselves an alternative line of work, or simply remain at home with their families, tending to a series of depressingly menial chores. The job she had now might be menial in itself, but at least it gave Lim independence.

He suddenly felt ashamed of his snappiness, and getting up he went to the kitchen door, opened it, and peered in. Lim was standing by the sink, directing her sorrows into a large white handkerchief. She glanced up as he came in.

'Hey, listen, Lim I'm sorry. I didn't mean to bawl you out like that . . .' He slipped an arm protectively around her, a rare gesture on his part. He never extended any affection towards her, unless it was in the form of foreplay before sex. She hugged him gratefully, putting her head on his chest and he stroked her dark hair gently.

'Now what's it all about, eh?' he asked her gruffly.

She sniffed softly.

'I . . . I just wish you could kill that tiger, Tuan. Then perhaps you not be so angry with me.' She gazed up at him earnestly through eyes that were brimming with tears.

'I'm not angry with you,' he assured her. 'I'm angry with myself, that's all. You wait and see, I'll get him before much longer. Anyway, how come you aren't afraid to say "tiger"? Most of the people up at the *kampong* wouldn't say it for a hundred dollars.'

She shrugged.

'I not like them, Bob Tuan. They believe old tales ... I think like Western woman. I know better.' She dabbed at her eyes with the handkerchief, then glanced at him slyly. 'Soon, Bob Tuan go home, yes?'

'Er ... yeah ...' Bob turned quickly away from her. 'I haven't heard anything definite about that yet, Lim. When I do, you'll be the first to know.' He changed the subject quickly. 'Hey, how about a nice cup of coffee? I could use that!'

She brightened a little, forced a smile.

'Of course, Bob. If that's what you want ...'

'Sure thing. And look, no more tears now, okay?' He tousled her hair briefly and then went back into the sitting room, closing the door after him. He resumed his former seat, swigged down the last of his beer, and then picking up the rifle he sighted on an imaginary target, beyond the open doorway. Leaving would be difficult, he realized that now. Perhaps he should have thought twice before getting involved with the girl, but it was already far too late.

'Tuan!' The shouting of a distant but familiar voice roused him from his thoughts. He stood up and hurried to the door, still carrying the rifle in his right hand. He stood on the verandah, shielding his eyes with the flat of his left. A battered bicycle was clattering towards him and seated on the perilous vehicle was the *penghulu* from Kampong Panjang. His little monkey face was shining with sweat and as he slowed the bike to a spectacular, shuddering halt, he shouted, 'Another one, Tuan! Kampong Panjang again!'

Bob did not waste any more time on useless conversation, for by now this had become a well-drilled operation. While the *penghulu* loaded his bicycle into the back of the Land Rover, Bob rushed back into the house to grab the one or two bits of equipment that were not stored permanently in his vehicle. Reemerging a few moments later, he dashed straight to the Land Rover and scrambled into the driver's seat.

'How long ago?' he demanded tersely as the *penghulu* climbed in beside him.

'Maybe half hour at most. I come soon as I hear.'

'Good. Let's get after the bugger!' Bob hit the ignition, threw the Land Rover into gear and accelerated away. The dust of its passing hung on the air in a great brownish cloud for several moments, before sinking slowly back to earth.

The house was silent again, except for the rhythmic clinking of crockery in the kitchen. Lim was feeling better now and she hummed some half-remembered pop song as she poured out two large cups of coffee. Then placing them carefully on a small silver tray, she went to the sitting room door and opened it.

'Coffee ready, Bob!' she called out. She stood in the doorway a few moments, gazing around. She frowned, noticing that his rifle was no longer lying on the table. She set down the tray and walked slowly to the open front door. She stood on the verandah for a moment, her hands hanging limply by her side, her face impassive. The Land Rover was gone and the streets beyond the gate were quite empty. Across the road, another young *amah* in a brightly patterned trouser suit waved briefly as she toted a heavy bucket of water onto the yard to wash it down. Lim returned the wave, but it was a slight, half hearted affair.

She went back into the empty sitting room, sat down at Bob's worktable and began to drink her own cup of coffee, sipping at it mechanically, because it did not seem to taste of anything. She glanced down at the leopard skin rug. The head had been badly stuffed, the expression manipulated into something intended to represent the creature in mid-roar. Instead, it simply looked comical, as though the head had been inflated with a bicycle pump. It was a desecration of the animal's own natural beauty and in no way suggested that the creature could ever have been *alive*. The blind glass eyes stared dully at Lim and she returned the gaze for a few moments. She had never had cause to think much about the beasts of the jungle but now she hated them, for they were

184

constantly taking the Tuan away from her. He was never around when she needed to talk to him and now, more than ever, she needed to do just that. She both loved and feared the Tuan at the same time; feared his quick hard words, his fierce temper, his heartless mocking laughter. Sometimes, lying in bed at night while he lay asleep beside her, Lim would begin to wonder if she herself were not some kind of trophy to him, an animal that he had trapped and mastered. Soon he would be going back to his own country and no doubt he would be taking his animal trophies along with him to show off to all his Australian friends . . . but not little Suzy Lim, oh no, she would be nothing more than a fond memory, something to boast to those same friends about. She could almost hear Bob's strident voice, as she lay in the darkness, weary but far from sleep.

'Had me a nice little servant girl out there . . . Chinese, eighteen years old, attended to all my needs, if you know what I mean! Well hell, you don't have to *marry* a girl like that, fer Chrissakes! Where's the sense in buying a sweet shop just so you can have a lick of the lollipop!' And then Lim could imagine the raucous laughter of Bob's drinking friends as they clustered around him, slapping him on the back. The hollow mocking echoes of it rang in her ears until she had to bury her head in the pillows in a vain attempt to block it out. But it refused to go away, and even her dreams were filled with terrible images of fear and rejection.

The time was quickly running out and there was something that she had to tell the Tuan before he left her forever; but Lim doubted that she had the necessary strength to raise her tiny voice so that he might hear her. And meanwhile, the tigers and the leopards, whether they lived and prowled the jungle or lay still and silent on the living room floor, were taking him away from her, were ruining the last few weeks that she might share with him.

She could never forgive them for doing such a terrible thing. If all the tigers in Malaya were to vanish overnight, it would be enough to make her dance with joy. For perhaps, then, the Tuan would stay in one place long enough for Lim to tell him all the things she felt in her heart. As it was, she was alone and her coffee tasted of nothing. With a sigh, she set her cup back down on the tray, picked this up and getting to her feet, she went back into the kitchen, closing the door behind her.

Melissa rolled slowly onto her back, in order to allow the sun to scorch the stretched out front of her swimsuited body. With just a few weeks left before her return to England, she was doing what everybody else was occupied with – deepening her tan to the necessary 'going-home' shade of dark brown, one that would make the 'moonies' back home suitably envious. At any rate, there was certainly nothing else to do. For her, too, the last couple of months had been frustrating to say the least. Over that time she had encountered Bob Beresford on only three occasions, all of them chance encounters, during which he had been polite, civil, and quite indifferent to her charms. The subject of their previous assignation had not even been mentioned and it was painfully clear to Melissa that Bob equated the loss of his tigerskin trophy with her. She had thought that the discovery of the continued existence of the man-eater would have in many ways lessened the blow to his pride but this did not seem to be the case, and now Melissa was faced with the uninviting prospect of eating humble pie and presenting the hideous Victoria with her twenty dollars. The mere thought of it made her blood boil, but there really seemed to be no alternative.

Melissa sighed. She stared up at a vast expanse of lapis-blue sky above her, darkened slightly by the twin frames of polarized glass before her eyes. A couple of fishing eagles were performing slow, lazy gliding patterns at an incredible height and she watched them intently for some time, until their repeated circular flight took them away to her left and out of her vision. Suntan oil tickled her shoulders and the sun was so fierce it was an effort simply to lie motionless beneath it. From the small kitchen behind her came the sounds of her mother preparing a meal. The day was absolutely still with not the slightest breath of wind to provide relief. The ball of flame suspended in the sky above Melissa seemed to be sapping every ounce of energy from her body and it was all she could do to simply turn her head

186

to one side.

'If only he'd shoot that bloody tiger,' she found herself thinking. 'Then maybe he'd be *approachable*. His ego would be boosted. Men are easier to get when they're feeling good . . .'

Her thoughts were interrupted by the creaking of the metal gate. She glanced up hopefully, as she always did at such times, but was dismayed to see Victoria Lumly advancing up the path with a smug grin on her face.

'Oh shit,' murmured Melissa beneath her breath. She made no effort to get up; indeed, she gave no indication that she had noticed the other girl's arrival.

'Hello, Melissa,' ventured Victoria hopefully. 'Mind if I sit down?' She got no reply to this question, but sat down anyway on the sun-dried grass beside Melissa's lounger.

'That's a *fantastic* suntan you're getting,' she murmured patronizingly. 'I wish I could get one, but it just turns into freckles. Waste of time really . . .'

Melissa cringed involuntarily, knowing that Victoria only handed out compliments as a preamble to delivering less friendly overtures.

'Where's the bride of Dracula?' murmured Melissa at last, referring to Victoria's more usual companion.

'Allison? Oh, she went into Kuala Trengganu with her parents. Panic souvenir buying for the folks back home.' She grimaced. 'I don't expect I shall bother to take much back. How about you?'

Melissa shrugged, kept her gaze fixed firmly on the sky.

'Haven't thought about it,' she said.

'My mother's going berserk. She's buying a collection of the most frightful odds and ends to take back to aunts and uncles from Land's End to John O'Groats. I had no idea we had so many of them.'

Again Melissa said nothing. She was waiting, waiting for Victoria to turn the one-sided conversation around to her favourite subject. There was a long pregnant pause, interrupted only by the distant barking of a dog.

'Any luck with Bob Beresford?' asked Victoria at last.

'You know the answer to that well enough,' snapped Melissa icily.

Victoria simply smiled. She was so thick-skinned it was unbelievable.

'Only it *is* getting late,' she continued. 'I know we didn't actually set a date for you paying up . . .'

'We bloody well did!' retorted Melissa. 'Three days before I leave, that was the deal as I remember it!'

'Oh, was it?' Victoria gestured vaguely. 'Yes, well, whenever it was . . . surely now that there's no chance of you bringing it off you wouldn't mind paying up a bit earlier; I could really do with the money at the moment . . .'

Melissa's temper flared, bringing out the obstinate creature that always lurked below her more rational exterior.

'Who said there's no chance?' she retaliated crossly.

Victoria glanced nervously towards the house as though afraid of being overheard.

'Well, it certainly looks as if . . .'

'If you must know, I'm not doing badly at all, thank you very much! The fact is I've just been playing him along up till now.'

'Playing him along?' Victoria raised her eyebrows mockingly. 'From where I'm sitting, it seems like he's doing all the playing. Besides, I've just heard something about your precious Mr Beresford that puts an entirely different complexion on things. If you must know, he –'

'Oh, stuff your silly gossip!' cried Melissa. She was impassioned enough to sit up on the sun-bed and lean towards her tormentor. 'Why don't you mind your own business and leave this to me?'

'You're just trying to get out of the bet,' whined Victoria bitterly.

'No I'm not. In fact . . . I was thinking of raising it!' said Melissa, in a sudden rush of bravado.

'You wouldn't dare!' sneered Victoria.

'How does fifty dollars sound?'

'Fifty!' Victoria gazed at Melissa for a moment, her eyes narrowing to suspicious slits. 'You'd be throwing your money away,' she announced flatly. 'If what I just heard is anything more than a rumour . . .'

'Oh, stuff the rumours! I told you, I don't want to listen

to them. The fact is Bob Beresford is crazy about me and I could have him any time I wanted. It's just a question of snapping my fingers, that's all.'

Victoria put her hands on her stout hips and shook her head knowingly.

'If he's crazy about you, he certainly knows how to hide it,' she chuckled. 'And if that is the case, why didn't you exercise your uncanny powers some time ago?'

Melissa thrust her jaw forward.

'Two reasons,' she snapped. 'One, so I could make more money out of it. Two, just to make you *sweat!*'

The two girls squared up to each other in silent defiance for several moments.

'You're lying,' murmured Victoria, at last.

Melissa extended her hand.

'Fifty dollars,' she said coolly.

Victoria gazed at the hand thoughtfully for a few moments.

'You're going to lose,' she whispered.

'Fifty dollars,' repeated Melissa.

Victoria glanced nervously at the house again.

'Three days before you leave,' she warned. 'You've got to honour it!'

'Fifty dollars!' Melissa's gaze did not flinch and she made no attempt to disguise the look of out-and-out contempt on her face.

'Alright!' And the girls shook hands briefly.

Chapter 19

The mood in the *kampong* had changed considerably. Bob was aware of it as he strolled past the first few houses, the heavy, all-pervading atmosphere of silent terror. The groups of people standing around in the village were for the most part sullen and silent. This was the third killing in Kampong Panjang in as many months; and the neighbouring villages had suffered too. People were frightened and they saw the gun-wielding Australian as their only hope of salvation.

'It is very bad, Tuan,' murmured the *penghulu*, as he led Bob toward the scene of the killing. 'Everyone is afraid to leave the *kampong*. I will be glad when you bring *Si-Pudong* down.'

Bob grunted noncommittally.

'That might not be so easy,' he replied. 'This one's a cunning devil. I've tried everything . . .'

The *penghulu* nodded.

'This is because he is no ordinary beast, Tuan. He is a werecat. The old *bomoh* who lives by Kampong Machis . . .'

'What, you too?' Bob had heard the same accusation several times over the last few weeks. 'I thought you had better sense than that,' he said accusingly.

'But Tuan, it is the truth,' protested the *penghulu*. 'Why, only last week two villagers came across him in the jungle; he was on all fours and he was growling and foaming at the mouth, having just changed back from his animal state. They ran away screaming.'

Bob grinned.

'I'll bet they did!' he chuckled. The two of them moved around the side of a building and came across a large crowd of people clustered around the entrance ladder of a house. The *penghulu* called for them to disperse, and reluctantly they began to drift away to their own homes, muttering darkly amongst themselves. The *penghulu* gazed after them anxiously.

'They begin to lose trust in me,' he complained bitterly. 'If we don't get *Si-Pudong* soon, I'll be out of favour.'

'We?' echoed Bob, raising his eyebrows. 'Excuse me, but I seem to be the one who's doing all the work around here. If you like, I'll bring a spare gun and you can –' He broke off in surprise as he caught sight of the grisly object wedged in the angle of the wooden ladder. It was now surrounded by a halo of flies, but the *penghulu* had forbidden anyone to touch it until the Tuan had examined it. 'Jesus Christ,' breathed Bob, with extreme revulsion. The sight of it made him feel nauseous and yet, perversely, he was unable to take his eyes from the thing. 'It must have caught at an angle,' he murmured. 'The tiger pulled . . .' He shuddered, forced himself to turn away. 'Anybody see anything?' he asked the *penghulu*.

'The woman's daughter just saw a flutter of cloth around the side of this building. She is too ill to talk further now; but she said that she heard her mother call and a moment later, when she went to the door, her mother was gone. So quick, Tuan! Surely only a werecat could . . .'

'It's not a monster we're looking for!' snapped Bob angrily. 'Just a plain, four-legged, common or garden tiger.'

The *penghulu* looked puzzled.

'Please, Tuan . . . what is . . . common . . . or garden?'

'Never mind. Have you found which way it went?'

The *penghulu* spread his hands in a gesture of defeat.

'Alas, Tuan, the ground here is very hard . . . hardly a mark shows! There is another thing! What ordinary cat would come into a *kampong* this way?'

'I didn't say he was *ordinary*. Oh, he's smart alright, never doubt it. But you can forget all this nonsense about weretigers and *bomohs*. When I finally get the chance to have a crack at him, he'll fall just like all the rest.' He turned away abruptly. 'Wasted enough time already,' he announced. 'I'd better try and find some pugs. Maybe if you look over there . . .'

'Oh, I am sorry, Tuan, I must go now. My wife, she is afraid to be alone. She gets very cross if I leave her . . .' He gave an apologetic little shrug and moved away. 'Farewell, Tuan, and good luck,' Bob gazed after him contemptuously. Considering the man's authority in the village was at stake, he was surprisingly reluctant to involve himself in the hunt. The strain of going it alone was beginning to tell on Bob. Though ridding the locals of an increasingly nasty problem was only a secondary aim in his schemes, Bob felt that he deserved a little appreciation on that score; but as the kill rose steadily, so did the Malays' desire not to get involved in something that might conceivably take them nearer to the tiger's jaws. Just getting people to help him put up the *machan* was hard enough, and the going rate for the job had risen dramatically.

Fear of the tiger had more widespread repercussions. Some of the victims had been rubber-tappers, and plantation owners were finding it difficult to persuade their workers to go out in anything but large groups, and even then only when the sun was fully up, allowing perfect visibility. Some villagers had been sufficiently worried to set up illegal gun traps along remote jungle paths. These were dangerous affairs, consisting of ancient rifles loaded up and fixed in the fork of a tree, with a long length of trip wire connected to the trigger. More often than not, it was some hapless human who set the device off and a couple of people had already been committed to hospital with bullet wounds. *Trishaw* drivers were extremely reluctant to make journeys along jungle roads, *amahs* were refusing to travel to work unless collected in a motor car, and even the postal service was being disrupted in more remote areas where letters were delivered by bicycle.

It was years since the district had been subjected to the depredations of a man-eating tiger and there were very many people who looked forward to the creature's demise. But, reflected Bob soberly, there was still only himself and Mike Kirby engaged on the actual job of hunting the cat down, and meanwhile the tiger seemed to be staying one step ahead of them at every turn.

Bob paused to gaze around at the area into which the cat had ventured. In front of the luckless victim's house, there was a large open area of flat, dry ground; off to the left, more buildings led off into the heart of the *kampong*. Directly ahead of him, across the intervening space, was the side of another long dwelling, around which, Bob surmised, the tiger must have crept up on the victim. Beyond that, there was a thick stretch of secondary jungle, flanking the main road and this screen of vegetation was bisected only by a narrow lane down which the old woman must have walked. For the tiger to have crossed an open area of land where there was not the slightest bit of cover suggested that he was becoming either reckless or hungry to the point of near-madness. It seemed logical to suppose that the cat must have taken the corpse across the main road at some point and into deeper jungle; but how to find that point of entry without the evidence of pugs would prove a difficult task. Bob stooped to examine the ground but could find no clues there. Any disturbance of its surface had long been disguised by the baking hot sun, and after checking over the whole patch of earth he found nothing but a tiny patch of dried blood, which gave no indication of direction.

Shouldering his rifle, he moved forward to stand at the corner of the building that flanked the jungle. Gazing around it, he was surprised to see a young Malay boy crouching on the ground in front of him, examining something that he had found there.

'Hello, what have you got there?' asked Bob.

The boy glanced up in surprise. He was a lively looking boy, perhaps twelve or thirteen years of age, with large dark eyes, and a thick mop of straight black hair. He was wearing nothing but a pair of khaki shorts and some worn flip-flops. When he saw who was standing before him, he got to his feet, pointed solemnly at the ground and said, 'Tiger pass this way.'

Bob smiled at the certainty with which the boy said this and he moved nearer, stooped to follow with his eyes the direction indicated by the boy's finger. All he could see was a stretch of seemingly unmarked ground.

'I don't see anything,' he murmured.

'The stone, Tuan! See . . .' The boy picked up a tiny pebble and held it out for inspection. 'You see, it has been moved. This side clean and smooth where rain and wind polish it. But it was lying the other way up.' He displayed the other surface, which was ever so slightly rough with a coating of dry earth.

Bob frowned, rubbed his chin.

'You think so, do you?' he muttered. 'Well, maybe . . .' He moved away, dismissing the boy from his mind and he began to cast left and right in the direction that the boy had suggested, but again the ground seemed devoid of any clues. Bob was unaware that the boy was following close on his heels, until the child gave a small cry of triumph and, rushing forward, snatched up a tiny fragment of a brown substance caught on a sharp rock. Similar in colour to its background, it would have evaded Bob's eyes completely.

The boy handed his prize to Bob proudly.

'From woman's slipper,' he announced, then turned away and continued ahead, bent low, his gaze fixed steadfastly to the ground.

193

Bob scratched his head and examined the substance. Sure enough, it did look like a sliver of soft leather. He gazed after the boy with a little more respect this time.

'Blood here, Tuan, and see, a scratch mark in the dirt. This is where tiger stopped to change his hold.'

'Really?' Bob hurried over and examined the place. Sure enough, there *was* blood and a faint, almost imperceptible mark. He glanced up at the boy. 'What's your name?' he asked drily. 'And where have you been all my life?'

The boy grinned with obvious pleasure, displaying a set of even, dazzlingly white teeth.

'My name is Ché. I live here in Kampong Panjang!'

'You do, huh? And how come you know so much about this stuff?'

Ché kept tracking.

'I practise very much. One day, hope to be best tracker in Malaya!'

'You're not doing too badly so far,' observed Bob. 'How come I didn't come across you when I first started asking for trackers?'

'Because then I had not decided to become one.'

'Ah . . . that would explain it.' Bob was mystified and delighted, all at the same time. Such a stroke of luck seemed almost too good to be true. He mopped at his clammy forehead with the sleeve of his shirt. 'Well look, uh . . . Ché, is it? How about showing me what else you can do?'

The boy's grin widened joyfully.

'You want me to find body, yes?' he cried.

'You bet, kid!'

'Okay, boss.' The boy bounded ahead and began to run forward in a semi-crouch, stopping every now and then to inspect some new evidence. Bob followed behind, bemused and highly grateful for such timely assistance. It quickly became apparent that the boy knew exactly what he was doing. He kept pausing for Bob to approach, and then he would explain some little detail before bounding away again. Here, Tuan, was where a little sarong fabric had snagged on a bush! Here was where the tiger's injured paw had dragged crossways in the dirt! Here was where the woman's heel had carved a shallow furrow in the earth! Bob

194

was vividly reminded of the time Harry Sullivan had tracked the pugs that the tiger had left beneath a *machan*, that time; there was the same wealth of information, the same quick, confident assessment of what had happened. But if anything the boy, aided by his youth and agility, seemed even more accomplished than the old man.

The trail continued for several hundred yards parallel to the secondary jungle, then plunged abruptly into it. The boy bounded in without hesitation, with Bob struggling along behind him. Here, the drag marks were easy to follow, but it got more difficult again when the trail veered to the left and followed the narrow, dry dirt lane for some distance before moving left again and back into the undergrowth. At last, Bob and Ché emerged into the main road and Ché pointed out where a few bits of twig and grass had scattered onto the surface of it.

'Tiger cross here,' announced Ché. He made as if to bound across the road like an excited terrier, but Bob grabbed his arm for a moment.

'Let me get my breath back,' he gasped. 'Anyway, where did you learn to track like that?'

Ché shrugged.

'From books mostly. My friend Majid and I, we decided we would become great trackers! He soon got fed up with it, but I . . .' The boy tapped his chest proudly. 'I practised every day. I went out into the jungle and followed every track I found. And I read every page of the Tuan's books, until I remembered it all . . .'

'The Tuan?' echoed Bob, suspiciously.

'Yes, I mean, of course, Tuan Sullivan. He gave me the books a long time ago, but before, I only looked at the pictures. This time I read every word *and* I had nobody to help me.'

Bob snapped his fingers. So the old bastard *was* involved!

'Well, well . . . so you know Harry Sullivan do you?'

'Oh yes, Tuan, everybody knows him; just as everybody knows you and how you shot one great tiger and how you are hunting the weretiger, the demon that hunts the people of the *kampongs*.'

'Hmm. Another one who goes for the spook theory, eh?

Aren't you afraid of the tiger, Ché? You say you go into the jungle to track all the time, and most people round here won't even say the word.'

Ché sighed.

'Alas, it is too late for me now, Tuan. When I thought that you had shot the man-eater, I began to take his name in vain, many times. For that reason, his curse is already on me; but I do not fear, for I know that soon you will kill him and then I shall be safe from his jaws. Besides . . .' He pulled something from his pocket, a small thing wrapped in leather. He untied the bundle and held the object out on his palm. It was a tiger's claw. 'My grandmother was so frightened for me that she bought me this for a talisman. It came from a man in Kampong Machis and was very expensive; but it keeps me safe when I go into the jungle.'

Bob nodded slowly and watched as the boy rewrapped his precious item and replaced it in his pocket.

'And I bet I know where that bloody thing came from,' thought Bob drily. A vivid image of the tiger's lacerated body, stark in the lantern-light, came briefly back to him. But he could not bring himself to blame the boy, who probably knew nothing about the theft. He experienced a sudden flash of guilt when he realized that he had been quite unreasonable transferring his resentment to Melissa Tremayne. She too was innocent of any blame, yet he had let his anger linger on for several months, an irrational and immature way to behave. He remembered their petting in the Land Rover, the soft feel of her warm flesh beneath his fingers, the heady aroma of her perfume . . . an abrupt rush of desire stirred within him and he had to force his mind to move back to more immediate problems.

'Well, let's move on, shall we?' he suggested.

Ché was off across the road, like a greyhound let off the leash. Bob followed at a more cautious pace, unslinging his rifle in anticipation.

'Don't get too far ahead,' he warned the boy. 'Just in case . . .'

They moved on into thicker jungle and once again, after a little casting around, the drag marks became evident: a wide trail of flattened leaves and disturbed grass, leading over

196

rough and fairly inaccessible terrain.

'The boy's worth his weight in gold,' thought Bob, as they trailed onwards. 'If it had been left to me, I'd still be back at the *kampong*.' Luckily, the boy seemed eager enough to be involved and Bob decided to offer him some kind of partnership, whereby he would pick up the boy whenever there was a kill and make use of his considerable skills. Ché would probably be prepared to do it for nothing, but the offer of a few dollars would doubtless be an extra incentive to him. The children were currently on holiday from their various schools and would be for the next month, so there should be no problem about his availability.

The trail led onwards for about half a mile and then, at last, they came to a broad stream where they found the corpse of the woman lying. It was not covered with foliage in any way.

'He must have heard us coming,' whispered Bob, gazing around. 'I'll bet he's not far away.'

He reached out an arm protectively to draw the boy back from the dismembered body, not wanting him to see it, but Ché pulled away and walked boldly over to the grisly remains. He stood gazing down at them thoughtfully. The old woman had been mostly consumed. All that was recognizable was her head and shoulders and her left arm. Everything else from her torso downward was mangled meat and bone. There was still an expression of shock on her grizzled face.

'He was very hungry,' observed Ché, with surprising calmness, but then he turned quickly away, doubled over and was violently sick on the grass. After a few moments, he straightened up, his eyes streaming with tears.

'You alright?' asked Bob helplessly.

'Yes. Tuan. I am sorry.'

'Don't apologize. I often feel like puking myself . . .' Bob frowned, turned to take a long slow look at his surroundings. It was terribly quiet in the jungle, not the sound of a single bird broke the silence.

'He's watching us alright,' murmured Bob. But there was any number of places where the cat might be lying in wait. That long stretch of grass there. Behind the vine-covered

197

trunk of that fallen tree. The thick patch of bamboo over to the right. Bob sighed. His desperation had not yet reached the point where he was prepared to go after the tiger on foot.

'Alright, Ché, let's go back for the *machan*,' he suggested. 'Think you can get another man to help us fix it up?'

Ché nodded.

'My friend, Majid, will help.'

'Alright then. We –'

Bob broke off in alarm as there was an abrupt rustle amongst the dry grass to his left. He swung the gun around to bear on the movement, which was progressing quickly towards him, travelling to the very edge of the long grass. Whatever was making the commotion should burst forth from cover at any moment . . .

A large magpie flapped out into the open, then took off at a steep angle with a few quick strokes of his powerful wings. Bob swore viciously beneath his breath and lowered the rifle. He felt uncharacteristically jittery today and he decided that the length of this hunt was beginning to get to him. The thought of another night spent out on a hard *machan* made his spirit sag, but he would not allow himself to give in now. The chances were that if he let one opportunity go, along would come Mike Kirby and put the bugger down with one lucky shot.

'The cat belongs to me,' he thought grimly. 'I've earned him.' He mopped at his sticky brow with his shirt-sleeve. He still could not rid himself of the distinct conviction that the cat was watching him, somewhere close by. He turned back to Ché and saw that the boy was gazing at him curiously.

'We go back now, Tuan?' he enquired.

'Yeah, sure. Look kid, you did a good job here. How would you like to track for me again?'

Ché smiled, nodded eagerly.

'I would like that very much, Tuan!'

'Good boy.' Bob reached into his pocket, took out his wallet and produced a couple of crumpled dollar bills. 'There now. You get that each time you track for me. And a special bonus when we finally put an end to old stripey.' He pressed the money into Ché's hands and then patted him gently on the back. 'You just hold yourself ready to go whenever I call for you. There's not much time and I ain't going back without him.'

'Maybe you'll get him tonight,' suggested Ché encouragingly.

'Tonight. Yeah, maybe.' But Bob was dismayed to realize that he already doubted this. Too many failures were leading him to believe that the tiger had some kind of charmed life, that he would never be shot from a *machan*. But what alternatives did that leave? Again, Bob stared off into the long grass from which the magpie had recently emerged. Then he glanced at the mutilated corpse of the old woman and he shuddered involuntarily. He remembered something that Harry Sullivan had once said to him.

'The only possible reason for following a cat into the jungle is to put it out of its misery after your first shot has failed to finish it off.'

The trouble with Sullivan was, he seemed to know exactly what he was talking about. So far, he'd been right all down the line. Maybe it was potential suicide to go after a man-eater on his home ground. But the way things were, there couldn't be many more opportunities to finish the cat off and maybe the time would come, when he'd have to follow up through the long grass with just his wits and his gun to aid him.

He shrugged and moved away. For the time being, he'd give the *machan* another try. He retraced his steps back into the jungle, and Ché followed close on his heels. Soon their figures were lost in the dark shadows of the trees. Several minutes passed in silence. Then there was a slow swishing motion in the grass. A bird perched high in the treetops gave a single warning shriek and flew away. The movement progressed to the edge of the grass and then a lean striped shape emerged and went to continue the meal that had been so rudely interrupted.

Harry strolled in through the open doorway of the Mess. It was Wednesday afternoon, and although Dennis had warned him earlier that he would not be able to keep their usual appointment Harry had decided to come in anyway, rather than break with his usual habits. He was shocked and rather saddened to see that he and Trimani were the sole occupants of the place. Over the last few weeks, attendance had been steadily dwindling, so this should really have come as no great surprise; and yet it was the first time that Harry could remember such an occurrence in this hallowed place. He approached the bar, his hands in his pockets, and Trimani must have shared his feelings because the little Tamil shook his head sadly and gestured with his hands, as if to say, 'Ah yes, Tuan, how sad it has come to this.'

Harry leaned on the bar, hardly knowing what to say. He accepted the glass of Tiger that Trimani gave him and drained it in one swallow and indicated that he would like another. He took out his cigar case, handed a smoke to Trimani, and took one himself. He lit the two cigars and there was a long moment of silence as the two men inhaled and exhaled, both of them lost for the moment in their own memories. At last, Harry broke the silence by asking, 'How much longer do you stay open, Trimani?'

'Until the very end, Tuan. There are still some officers left to take care of things.' He shrugged. 'Two, maybe three weeks. Then, close down.'

'And what will happen to you then?'

'Me, Tuan? Oh, it is not too bad! I am old now, ready to step down. I have a good family, who will take care of me . . . did I tell you, Tuan, that my eldest son is now a lawyer in Kuala Lumpur? He sends money home to us every week . . .'

'Yes, Trimani, I believe you did, but I'm very pleased for you anyway. Will you not be getting a pension from the British government?'

Trimani shook his head.

'There has been no mention of it, Tuan.'

'And how long have you been working here?'

'Fourteen years.'

Harry nodded slowly. He felt ashamed of his own race, amazed that such brazen ingratitude could be dealt to a man as loyal and trustworthy as Trimani. He glanced up at the large, framed equestrian photograph of Queen Elizabeth II hanging above the bar. He knew that Trimani loved this photograph and that the little barman polished the glass that covered it every day of his life. But now the queen's stern expression and patriotic salute seemed nothing more than a hollow mockery, a travesty of what it had once stood for.

'Have a drink with me, Trimani,' suggested Harry suddenly.

The barman shook his head.

'Thank you, Tuan, but you know it is not allowed. The rules . . .'

'Oh hang the bloody rules! D'you really think that they have the right to impose any? Fourteen years you've stood behind this bar and not once have you been able to have a drink with me; what difference can it make now, for God's sake?' He gestured around at the empty building. 'Besides, who's here to see you break the rules? Pour yourself a beer, and I'll have another one too.'

Trimani frowned. He still did not much like the idea, but after another glance around to assure himself that the chances of being caught were very remote he stooped down, removed two cans of beer from the refrigerator and poured them out into glasses. He handed one to Harry.

'That's the spirit, Trimani! Now, what shall we drink to?'

Trimani turned and indicated the photograph above his head.

'Let us drink to this fine lady,' he suggested.

'I'm surprised that you should want to, considering what's happened,' said Harry.

'It is not her fault, what's happened here, Tuan. It is British government who give the orders. The queen is no more than their puppet. My eldest son told me that.'

Harry smiled drily.

'Sounds like a bright boy,' he observed. And he raised his glass to the photograph. 'Queen Elizabeth II!' he announced.

'One fine lady!' added Trimani. The two men drank deeply. Trimani banged down his empty glass on the counter. 'Ah, very nice!' he exclaimed. 'Tiger is very good beer.'

'Pour yourself another one,' suggested Harry.

'Oh, but I should not, Tuan. I am not a great drinker and I may get drunk . . .'

Harry gazed around at the empty bar.

'Do you see anybody here who's likely to complain?' he asked.

Trimani grinned.

'No, Tuan, I don't!' And he took another two beers out of the refrigerator.

'What shall we drink to now?' asked Harry. His mood was improving by the moment and he was beginning to feel ever so slightly tipsy. He usually made it a rule not to drink more than two Tiger beers during the heat of the day, when its effect seemed even more powerful than it was at night, but now he had cast his usual caution to the winds.

'Let us drink to our friend Captain Tremayne,' suggested Trimani brightly. 'He has always been most kind to me.'

'Dennis, it is!' agreed Harry. 'In fact, I can't think of anybody more deserving of being drunken to . . . of being drunk to . . .' He scratched his head. 'Of having a drink drunk to them . . .' His words weren't coming out quite as he meant them.

'To Dennis!' he cried.

'Captain Tremayne!' The two men drank their beers.

'Ah, that's better,' observed Harry, wiping his mouth on his sleeve. 'You know, Trimani . . .' He leaned across the counter as though confiding a secret. 'Poor Dennis has so much work, he couldn't even be here to drink with us in person . . .'

Trimani took a deep breath.

'I feel very strange, Tuan,' he murmured.

Harry slapped his shoulder encouragingly.

'That means you're ready for another one!' he explained. 'Come on, line 'em up!' He took a handkerchief from his pocket and mopped at his brow. 'Whew, it's damned hot in here.' He gazed up at the large electric fan suspended from the ceiling above his head. Turning rhythmically, it seemed to be largely ineffectual and simply serve to move currents of already warm and stale air around the room. Harry took of his jacket, laid it across the bar and rolled up his shirt-sleeves, a rare break from decorum on his part.

202

'Now, let's get down to some serious drinking!' he suggested. 'Come along Trimani, thash another two beers . . .'

'Oh, Tuan, I'm not sure I should . . .'

'Nonsense, m'boy. You don't want me to have to drink alone, do you?'

Trimani sighed, shook his head. He took two more beers out of the refrigerator.

'What shall we drink to this time?' wondered Harry.

An hour passed. Nobody else came in, and Harry and Trimani steadily drank their way past the point of no return. During the course of their drinking, they proposed toasts to an increasingly obscure series of subjects. They drank to the health of Trimani's family, Doctor Kalim, various former officers of Kuala Hitam barracks, alive or dead, the manufacturers of Tiger beer, the late Chinese *trishaw* driver and his grandson, and other subjects that suggested themselves as blurry phantoms looming through the grey mists of their drunkenness.

'Whash next?' enquired Harry blankly. He was leaning rather unsteadily on the bar for support and Trimani was, with great difficulty, pouring out the next round of drinks.

'Oh Tuan,' he groaned. 'The room is going around my head . . .'

'Nonsense!' Harry waved an admonishing finger. 'Once you begin to believe that my friend, you are halfway to being . . . halfway to being . . .' Harry considered this statement carefully and decided that in spite of Trimani's blank expression, it did make perfect sense. He grabbed the next glass of beer and stood there, swaying dangerously from side to side. 'Whash next?' he demanded again.

'My family?' suggested Trimani.

'We've drunk to your family already.'

'Oh yes, so it is. Well, your family then.'

'Yesh, my family.' Harry raised his glass, hesitated, then brought it down again. 'No good,' he muttered. 'Haven't got a bloody family.'

'Oh yes, Tuan. I am sorry.'

Harry patted the barman reassuringly on the shoulder.

'Don't worry about it. Whash next?'

'Ah Tuan, I know!' Trimani pointed excitedly to the tiger's head over the doorway of the Mess. 'Your old enemy. You always drink to him, but today when we are toasting, you have not!'

'That's it! Trimani, you're a genius.' Harry gazed up at the snarling face. 'Trimani, did I ever tell you how I came to shoot that fellow . . . ?'

'No, Tuan. I asked you before, many times, but you would never speak of it.'

'I wouldn't?' Harry looked puzzled. He set down his drink, fumbled in his jacket pocket for his cigar case and then realized that he was no longer wearing the jacket. He abandoned the scheme.

'I'll tell you now,' he announced grandly. 'It was . . . 1958. I wasn't quite as old as I am now . . . reports started coming in that a big tiger was taking cattle from the *kampong* stockades. He wasn't a man-eater or anything like that, he'd just wandered out of the jungle, looking for food . . . but of course, everybody was *convinced* that he would become one in time . . . so they all got on to me to go out and have a crack at him. 'Course, in those days, I was always ready to have a go . . . I still thought of it as some kind of sport, God help me! So I tied out a cow and built myself a *machan*. That night, the tiger came down to eat and I put a bullet through him; but it was a bad shot. I heard him howl and then he ran off into the jungle. Naturally, the *sporting* thing to do was to follow him up and put him out of hish misery.' Harry laughed bitterly. 'Even more sporting would have been to leave the poor bugger alone, but still . . . he went into a patch of long grass and I waded in after him, like the bloody arrogant fool I was. In those days, I believed totally that carrying a gun put you above all retribution . . . then . . . thish is hard to explain. . .' Harry reached forward and grabbed Trimani's arm. 'I tell you what, I'll *show* you. You be the tiger, climb up on the bar here. That'sh right, up here.' He half pulled, half assisted Trimani up onto the wooden bar-top, where the little man crouched unsteadily on his knees. 'Now then . . . the tiger . . . that'sh you . . . was up on a small outcrop of rock, lying flat so's I couldn't see him. Now, we need some thorn bushes between us –' Harry reeled away from the bar and began to overturn chairs, heaping them into a pile in front of the bar.

'Tuan, what are you doing?' cried Trimani.

'These are the thorn bushes in front of the rocks,' explained Harry. 'Thish is hard to explain...' He kept on adding to the pile until he had a large spiky pile of wooden chairs heaped up in front of him. Now he stumbled over to the corner of the room and snatched up Trimani's broom, which he wielded as though it were a rifle. 'Now then,' he explained. 'You'll have to use your himagination here... these tables at the front, these are the long grass and that pile of chairs there are thorn bushes... meanwhile, up on the rocks there, is the tiger; thatsh you. Now get down low!'

Trimani sank obligingly onto his hands and knees.

'It'sh dark, remember, and I've only got the moonlight, because coming down the tree, I knocked the flashlight on the rifle barrel and smashed the lens...' Harry began to move stealthily forward, the broom held ready to fire. 'I crept through the long grass, looking from side to side,' he narrated. 'I couldn't see much, but from time to time, I heard the tiger'sh roar...' Trimani responded with a low rumbling growl. 'That'sh very realistic!' observed Harry. 'Now, sneaking forward, I didn't see the thorn bushes until it was too late!' Harry thrust one foot into the tangle of chairs and began to thrash noisily around in them. 'I was caught!' he yelled. 'Immobile! And the more I struggled, the more my clothing seemed to snag. Now, the tiger, hearing the movement below him, began to creep forward acrosh the top of the rock until he was directly above me –'

Trimani leaned forward over the edge of the bar and gave a blood-curdling roar.

'I say that'sh really very good, you know... but I was held with my back to the rock and couldn't turn to face the attack. My left arm was held back like this, and the right side of my shirt hooked too. I could sense that the tiger was about to come down on me, so I stopped thrashing about and gazed upwards.' The recollection of the incident seemed to sober Harry up abruptly. His voice became more lucid. 'I could just make out the glint of its eyes as it began to move down toward me. I've never been more terrified than I was in that moment, Trimani. I thought I was going to die, I really did. But at the last instant, the instinct for survival asserted itself. I still had the rifle in my hands and I twisted it around, so that it was resting on my left shoulder, pointing upwards . . . There was no time to aim. Small rocks began to fall on me, and I could hear the noise of the tiger's body sliding off the rock and into space. It was coming down right on top of me . . . right on top, mind you! The weight of it alone would be enough to crush me and the claws and jaws would be ready to tear me to pieces. The tiger was cornered and in pain, it would kill me if it could . . . I squeezed the trigger! *Bang!* The shot echoed in my ears! I heard a squeal and the tiger seemed to fly over my head suddenly, as though the impact of the shot had given it wings. It came down in front of me, landing hard, its striped body shuddering. It lay there for a moment and I thought it was finished, but then it lifted its head and it looked at me. It looked at me! And then . . . then . . .' Harry broke off in alarm as a sudden savage pain erupted in his chest. He gasped, clutched at his heart and the broom clattered to the barroom floor. Trimani, still crouching on the top of the bar, looked down at him in alarm.

'Tuan? What is wrong?'

'Trimani, I think I –' Again the sentence collapsed into a brief exclamation of pain. The colour drained from Harry's face. Trimani began to scramble down from the bar. Harry tried to take a step, but his leg was still amongst the chairs and he fell forward in a sprawl, bringing several of them clattering around him. He slumped down onto his face but then Trimani was beside him, turning him over.

'Tuan, what is the matter with you?'

Harry's face was ashen.

'Too much to drink,' he hissed through teeth that were gritted in pain.

'I get help!' cried Trimani desperately. He leapt up and raced out of the bar, his footsteps pounding on the wooden floor.

Harry groaned softly. He tried to sit up, but another spasm shook his body and he thought it better to lie still and wait. From where he lay, he could see the stuffed head of the tiger snarling down at him from above the doorway. He gazed back calmly, unafraid. The tiger's head seemed to grow slowly in size and it lost definition, dissolved into a huge orange blob that sizzled in front of Harry's eyes like a great ball of flame. Heat enveloped him now but then it was abruptly cool and there was a firmness beneath his back. His vision focused briefly and he saw a grey anonymous ceiling above his head. Set into the ceiling at regular intervals were a series of glowing orange tigers' heads, which whizzed past over him and away as he sped down a corridor on oiled silent wheels. Then hoods slipped down over his vision and he thought it better to rest, so he let the clouds of sleep that were tugging insistently at his brain take over and float him downwards into a deep and dreamless world. He no longer felt any pain and a last vague thought wheedled its way up from his subconscious mind.

'Death. That's one thing we forgot to drink to.'

Chapter 20

The night was calm and humid. Haji lay some twenty yards away from the body of the female Upright that he had killed earlier that day. He was concealed by the stout limb of a fallen tree and he lay on his side, occasionally dozing or lapping at the festering wound on his right foreleg. From time to time, a slight breeze carried the stench of decaying meat in his direction and his stomach churned at such torture; but the young Upright was on the scene as usual, perched in a tall Kapok tree off to the right of the kill and Haji had already resigned himself to losing what was left of the meat. Still, he lingered at the scene, hoping perhaps that the Upright would fall asleep or, better still, give up and return to his own lair.

The great silvery orb of a full moon hung suspended in the sky, casting an eerie illumination that infiltrated the dense jungle in a series of slender rays that minted the bushes and swaying grasses with patches of restless dappled light. Haji was incapable of napping for more than a few moments at a time, for there was a terrible sense of insecurity in him this night, a nagging, fretful mood that he was unable to shake off. There had come to him, quite suddenly, the powerful conviction that his days were numbered, that he was doomed. Old age had destroyed him. It had made him incapable of following the old ways, and instead had transformed him into a *kampong*-thief, a devourer of Uprights.

He got to his feet and began to pace up and down behind the log, growling low in his throat. The Upright would probably hear him, but for the moment, he did not care about that. His useless paw hampered him even in such aimless movement, and the insecurity in him turned quickly to a powerful rage, an all encompassing anger that for the moment he was unable to direct at anything. A first long rumbling roar escaped from his throat and it seemed to echo in the night.

There was a brief silence and then Haji's sharp ears detected a brief rustle of movement in the Upright's tree, as the young Australian shifted position. Haji stopped pacing and fixed the tree with an intense glare. He could see it quite clearly in the moonlight, could even discern the low fork where the Upright had fixed his wooden seat no more than twelve or fifteen feet from the ground. Haji's rage continued to grow in intensity, a brooding powerful mood that quickly began to blot out the tiger's limited powers of reasoning. Soon even his healthy fear of the black stick was forgotten, for now the Upright was a focus for Haji's rage, the object against which all his bitterness must be directed. Pressing his body low against the ground and keeping his gaze fixed on the tree, Haji began to circle around to his right, slipping silently through the tangle of undergrowth that separated him from his goal. The distance shortened rapidly and Haji could now see quite plainly that the Upright was looking in the opposite direction, that he was totally unaware of the vengeful creature creeping up behind him.

Now Haji could see the hated black stick and this, more than anything else, served to antagonize him, racking his hatred up into a brief, senseless bout of madness. Without further hesitation, he began to race directly at the tree, covering the remaining yards in a matter of seconds. With a bellow of rage, he launched himself directly at the *machan*.

Then all was chaos. At the last instant, Bob turned and found himself gazing full into the face of death. Haji's forepaws struck the broad fork of the tree, and for an instant the cat hung suspended by his claws while he tried to lever himself forward to tear at the creature that had for so long tormented him. Bob screamed aloud in pure terror and made a clumsy attempt to bring his rifle around to bear on the cat that was mere inches away from him; but the barrel hit a stout branch and the gun went off prematurely, firing harmlessly into the treetops. The shattering roar of it assailed the night and the tiger's eyes were momentarily lit with fire. Bob, caught fast in the worst nightmare of his life, felt the hot gusting raw-meat breath of the cat on his face. Hanging precariously by its claws, it was inching toward him, its face a mask of demonic fury. A roar spilled from the open jaws, seeming to shake the entire tree down to its roots. Desperately, Bob struck out with the butt of the rifle, slamming it full into the tiger's face and the cat snatched it in his foaming jaws, gave it a quick sideways wrench and sent it spinning away like a useless toy. Without waiting to see anymore, Bob scrambled away further up the tree, but Haji, pulling himself higher into the lap of the fork, came after him. Somebody had once told Bob that tigers had very limited climbing ability and he could only pray to God that this was the case as he clambered out along a network of thinner branches with the tiger's jaws slavering at his heels. He edged along as quickly as he dared, terrified that a branch might break and send him down to the jungle floor, where the tiger would make very short work of him. He felt the branch beneath his feet bow dramatically, and glancing back he saw to his horror that the tiger was inching his way out along the limb on which he was standing. With an oath, he scrambled higher, lost his footing, dangled precariously for several moments by his hands, while his flailing feet searched for a new hold. Haji reared up and swung at his feet with his forepaws but this extra action caused the branch on which he was crouching to give out a long agonized splitting sound and he was obliged to move quickly back to the fork with a snarl of baffled rage. Once there, he turned back to watch the struggles of the Upright. Bob was beginning to panic. His feet could find no suitable hold and his hands, wet and slippery with his own sweat, were failing to grasp the smooth bark of the limb above him. He glanced desperately down at the jungle floor. He could see his rifle lying there, but doubted that he could drop to the ground, retrieve it, reload and fire, all before the tiger dropped onto him from above. The only substantial limb below him was the one which had already been splintered by the tiger's weight. It was drooping down at an alarming angle and looked incapable of supporting more than a few pounds. Bob realized that his only hope was to somehow pull himself more securely onto the limb from which he was already hanging. He clenched his teeth, and digging his fingers as much as he could into their precarious hold he flexed the muscles of his arm and began to raise himself tenaciously toward the branch.

Haji's rage had suddenly dispersed itself and now it was replaced with a sense of curiosity. He turned away, dropped down to the forest floor and padded out beneath the Upright, gazing up curiously at the man's frantic struggles.

Bob was, for the moment, unaware that the cat was no longer in the tree with him. He was horribly aware that his shaking fingers were losing their grip and he began to reconsider the possibility of dropping to earth and snatching his rifle; but glancing briefly downwards, he saw the tiger's amber eyes gazing patiently up at him; the shock of it galvanized him into making one last heave and he swung his legs upwards in a desperate ploy and wrapped them like a vice around the branch. The limb bent downwards with heart-stopping abruptness but then it held and Bob was able to take a better hold with his hands. Hugging himself tightly against his perch, he craned his head around to stare triumphantly down at the tiger.

'Beat you, you bastard,' he screamed. 'Let's see you get up here!'

But Haji was already strolling away, the heat of the rage that had consumed him forgotten now. He paused to sniff at the kill for a few moments but it had been disturbed and he did not trust it. He glanced back at the Upright in the tree. The man was screaming and gesticulating like some agitated tree ape.

'You thought you had me, didn't you, you bastard! Well, you won't get another chance! D'you hear me? I'm going to put a bullet through you if it's the last thing I do!'

Haji gave a low growl of irritation and continued on his way, strolling slowly away into the undergrowth with as much dignity as he could salvage after such an untypical outburst. After a few moments, he was lost amidst the undergrowth.

Bob clung to the branch, trembling violently. He was drenched in cold sweat and now the shock of the experience was fading, he was beginning to realize just how close he'd been to death. In the darkness, the tiger's great jaws had been mere inches from his face, and in his mind there was a vivid image of the cat's eyes lit up by the flare of the rifle. They had been full of hatred, those eyes, and they would haunt Bob's dreams for many long nights to come. Glancing wildly about to assure himself that the cat was really gone, Bob inched clumsily back along the branch and half clambered, half fell back down the tree, swearing rhythmically to himself as he did so. He could remember no experience in his life that had terrorized him as much as this event. The instant his feet struck the ground, he ran to his rifle and snatched it up, rammed a fresh cartridge into the chamber. The stock of the gun bore several deep gouges where the tiger's teeth had sunk into it. Bob imagined those same teeth tearing into his flesh and he felt nauseated. He loosed off three shots into the air in quick succession and then he moved back against the trunk of the tree, pressing his back against its reassuring hardness. He squatted there, cradling the gun in his arms and glancing nervously this way and that while he waited for the villagers to come. For the first time in ages, he wanted there to be lots of people around him, the more the better. Even in the humid tropical night, he was very cold, and the trembling had become so bad that his shoulders were heaving up and down and he could scarcely control his breathing.

211

It was some considerable time before it occurred to him that he was crying.

Bob brought the Land Rover to a halt in front of his house. He took his hands off the steering wheel and sat in the seat for a moment with his head slumped forward, his hands hanging limply by his sides. It was afternoon, but only in the last hour or so had he felt capable of driving home from Kampong Panjang. As the shock of his brush with the tiger wore off, his nervous reaction to it had increased and he had spent the morning wandering numbly around the *kampong*, trying to pull his frayed nerve endings together. Now he felt exhausted, grateful to be alive, and more resolved than ever that he would get the tiger before much more time elapsed. He shook his head and clambered out of the Land Rover.

Lim came running out of the house to greet him.

'Bob Tuan!' she cried. 'I was so frightened . . . I thought the tiger had eaten you.'

'He nearly bloody well did!' Bob threw his arms around her, for once not caring what the neighbours might think. 'Strewth, I need a drink,' he croaked.

'Tea, coffee?'

'Whisky. But first I need a shower –' Bob broke off in surprise. A tall gaunt Malay was standing on the verandah, a strange-looking fellow with piercing black eyes and a thin, pock-marked face. He was naked, save for a sarong and the inevitable rubber flip-flops. 'Who the hell's this?' demanded Bob irritably. He had had enough surprises for one day. 'If he's selling anything, we don't want any!'

Lim shook her head.

'This man has come from the *bomoh* at Kampong Machis,' she explained. 'He came this morning, asking to see you. When I told him you were away, he told me he would wait. He would not go . . .'

'Wouldn't he now?' murmured Bob.

The man stepped forward.

'I am student of the *bomoh*,' he explained. 'He ask me come fetch you. He needs to talk wid you.'

'Oh yeah? I suppose he's going to tell me that *he's* the

212

tiger that's been doing all the killing, is he?'

The man looked horrified.

'Oh no, Tuan, not at all! The *bomoh* is concerned that many people *say* he is the man-eater. He want to set record straight; also, give you advice how to catch striped one.'

'Very nice of him,' sneered Bob. 'Well look, you just go back to him and tell him that I don't for one moment believe what I've been hearing about him, alright?'

'Just the same, he want to talk wid you. Bid me fetch you . . .'

Bob ran a hand through his hair and took a deep breath.

'There's only one place I'm going right now and that's to bed,' he snapped irritably. 'So you go back to the *bomoh* and tell him that maybe I'll look him up later on, when I've had some rest . . .'

But the man shook his head adamantly.

'He tell me not return without you. I wait here for you. You sleep.' The man crossed his arms and took up a resolute stance on the verandah, his legs slightly apart, his dark eyes staring out toward the garden.

'But – I may be asleep for hours,' warned Bob.

'No matter. I wait.'

Bob stared at the man for several moments in silent antagonism. He felt too tired to attempt throwing the fellow off the verandah, and it was quite plain that it would take more than a few well-chosen words to move him on.

'Well, suit yourself!' snapped Bob at last. 'You'll soon get fed up with it!'

And with that, he turned and strode into the house, slamming the door behind him. Lim met him with a large tumbler of iced whisky, which he drank down in one gulp.

'What happened?' she asked him, but he silenced her with a wave of his hand.

'Tell you about it later. First I need to sleep. Forget the shower. I'll have one after.' He thrust the empty glass back into her hand and left her standing where she was, dumbfounded by his abruptness. He strode into his bedroom, stripped off his clothes, and clambered into bed. Lim came to the door. She stood gazing at him thoughtfully. 'Is there anything you need?' she asked him.

213

'No. Just sleep, that's all. Leave me be, will you?'

She nodded sadly, moved away.

The moment Bob's head touched the pillow, he was asleep, but it was not a peaceful slumber.

When he woke, he was sobbing violently. He was sitting up in bed in the darkness of his room, his own arms wrapped protectively around his body. Above him, the metal blades of the electric fan clicked rhythmically around, disturbing the humid air. With a gasp, Bob groped for the switch of his bedside light and flicked it on for reassurance. He sat blinking in the glare for a moment, but his dream had made even the mundane seem irrational. The room looked alien, unfamiliar, as though he were seeing it for the first time. He fumbled for the pack of cigarettes that always lay beside the bed, extracted one and lit it with shaking fingers. Then he took a long drag, blew out smoke and slumped back onto his pillow. The bedroom door opened, and Lim peered in at him.

'Bob Tuan alright?' she whispered. 'I see light under door . . .'

'Fine. I'm fine. What time is it?'

''Bout six o'clock.'

'Strewth, have I slept for that long?' He frowned, took another big drag on his cigarette. 'I'd better get up,' he announced. 'Run the shower for me, will you?'

'Alright.' Lim smiled happily at the prospect of having a little company and she hurried off to the bathroom, closing the door after her. Bob lay staring up at the ceiling, watching the thin trail of smoke from his cigarette, which rose vertically for a short distance and then went crazy as it was caught by the wind from the fan.

He felt edgy, unable to relax. After a few moments, he stubbed out the cigarette in an ashtray and went to the bathroom. The cold water of the shower brought him fully awake and set all his nerve endings jangling ferociously. He washed his hair, noting a line of itchy red bumps around his scalp where mosquitos had feasted on him the night before.

'Little bastards,' he murmured ruefully.

He dried himself, sprinkled his body with a liberal helping of talc, and went back to his bedroom, where he dressed in

214

clean clothes. He began to feel happier and he strolled into the sitting room. Lim was watching television, a Chinese film with English subtitles. She was clearly not too interested in it, though, because she reached out and switched it off as soon as she noticed Bob's presence.

'Bob Tuan like drink?' she asked.

'Yeah, please. A straight whisky with a little ice.' She virtually ran to the kitchen to fetch it. 'Have something yourself,' yelled Bob after her, though he knew quite well that she never drank alcohol.

'Thank you, Bob Tuan, I have Coke,' she called back.

Bob grinned. He put his hands in his pockets and began to pace silently around the room, unable to settle. When Lim returned with the drinks, he took his and drank half of it in one gulp. Lim stared at him thoughtfully for a moment and then she sat down.

'What happen to you last night?' she asked cautiously. 'You promise to tell me about it later . . .'

'Did I?' Bob frowned. He had a strong suspicion that he'd said nothing of the kind, but he didn't see any reason why he shouldn't tell her. 'Well, the tiger came after me, that's all. The bastard jumped into the tree where I was sitting . . . he . . . snatched the gun right out of my hand . . .' Recalling the events now, they seemed unreal, ridiculously farfetched. 'Then he came up the tree after me. I had to climb for my life – He just seemed to go berserk all of a sudden and then, after a few moments, he lost interest and went away . . .'

Lim was staring at him open-mouthed.

'Oh, Bob Tuan!' she exclaimed. 'What would I do if anything had happened to you? You must leave this tiger alone now. That was a warning!'

'Nah . . . I don't believe all that stuff. He went after me, it's as simple as that. Anyway, I was too quick for 'im and I don't intend to give the bugger another chance to get so close, I can tell you.' Bob strolled slowly towards the open front door. Out in the calm evening, the crickets had begun to sing and the occasional dark silhouettes of bats flitted across the dark blue backdrop of the sky. 'No, the next time I get my rifle between me and that tiger, I'll make sure that –'

Bob broke off in surprise and his half-finished glass of whisky slipped from his hand and smashed loudly on the tiled floor. From the darkness of the verandah, a pair of glowing eyes had fixed Bob with a stare that almost caused him to jump out of his skin.

'What the – ?' For a moment, Bob was literally rooted to the spot with fear; then his instincts reasserted themselves and, with an oath, he reached out and snapped on the switch that controlled the verandah lights. He was both relieved and surprised to see the *bomoh*'s assistant standing in exactly the same place where Bob had left him several hours earlier. The man's arms were crossed, his legs were set well apart and he seemed not to have moved so much as a muscle in the time he had been waiting there.

'Tuan ready to come along now?' enquired the man hopefully.

Bob stared at the man in disbelief.

'You don't give up easily, do you?' he snapped. He turned and glanced accusingly at Lim.

'I told him to go three times,' she protested defensively. 'He take no notice!'

'You could have told me he was still out there. Damned near scared me to death.' Bob turned back to the man and gazed at him thoughtfully for a few moments. 'Why's it so important that the *bomoh* see me?' he demanded.

'I tol' you, Tuan, he very worried what *kampong* people are saying. He want help you catch real man-eater, so people know the truth.'

'And how does he intend to help me?'

'You must talk wid him. I cannot say . . .'

Bob stared down at the fragments of ice and broken glass on the floor. He probed them with the toe of his shoe as if trying to divine some meaning from them. Then he broke the spell by saying. 'Lim, get a brush and clean this mess up, will you? I'm going along with Doctor Caligari here . . .' He strode back into the hallway to get a jacket. Lim hurried after him.

'Bob Tuan,' she gasped. 'I think you should not go along with that man!'

'Oh . . . why?'

'The *bomoh* is supposed to be a very wicked man, very powerful. Many people in the *kampongs* are afraid to go anywhere near his hut . . .'

Bob chuckled.

'I thought you were the one who didn't go in for all this superstitious claptrap,' he taunted her. 'I thought you prided yourself on being a *modern* girl.'

Lim frowned.

'Just the same,' she murmured. 'You do not know what these people want of you. Perhaps they plan to kill you and steal your money . . .'

'Don't talk nonsense, Lim! They just want to spout a bit of mumbo jumbo at me, that's all. It's all harmless nonsense.'

'If you believe that, then why are you going?'

Bob shrugged.

'Well . . . just out of interest really – Besides, let's face it, the way things are going with this bloody tiger, I need all the help I can get!' He went into his bedroom, took a clean khaki jacket out of the wardrobe, and slipped into it.

'You are always leaving me alone in the house,' complained Lim bitterly.

'I won't be long,' he assured her and then gave her a reproachful glare. 'Seems t'me that somebody around here is forgetting their place. I could always get another *amah* you know . . .'

'I clean up the mess now,' Lim assured him, and she hurried off to search for a broom.

Laughing to himself, Bob went back through the sitting room to the front door, where the *bomoh*'s assistant was still waiting.

'Come on then, Gunga Din, let's see what your boss has got to say for himself. How did you get here, by the way?'

'I walk.'

'Strewth, all the way from Kampong Machis? Bugger that for a lark, we'll take the Land Rover.' He motioned the man to follow him down the driveway, and the two of them clambered into the front seats. As Bob started up the engine, he glanced back at the doorway. Lim was standing in the

217

oblong of light, gazing out at him with a worried expression on her face. She was holding a broom in her hands, but was clearly too distracted to do anything with it. Bob felt a wave of fondness pass through him. Lim was a good kid, she gave him everything she had and got precious little in return. He would have to make an effort to be nicer to her, one of these days. He waved briefly and accelerated away down the road, but turning the bend at the far end of the street, he noticed that she was still standing there, gazing out into the darkness that lay all around her.

Chapter 21

The television screen faded gradually up from greyness and then flickered into life. Melissa stared at it for several moments. It was a Chinese melodrama with English subtitles, the kind of programme she detested. With a groan, she reached out and hit the off button. The screen went blank.

'I'm bored,' announced Melissa, dramatically.

Kate glanced up from the novel she was reading and gave her daughter a sympathetic smile. 'I sometimes wonder why we have a television set,' she murmured. 'There's never anything worth watching. Why don't you read? I could lend you a good book . . .'

'I hate reading,' retorted Melissa wearily. This was not altogether true, but when she was in this kind of mood there was very little that would serve to distract her.

'Oh dear, oh dear. You're not happy at all, are you?' Kate closed the novel and put it aside, realizing that when her daughter was unhappy she tended to prevent everybody else from having a good time. 'Perhaps we could go out later, when your father gets home. The Mess or something . . .'

'No thank you! Anyway, I don't know what you're talking about. You loathe the place more than I do . . .'

'True,' admitted Kate wearily. 'But if it would help to lift you into better spirits – Who knows, you might bump into Mr Beresford there.' This was intended as a casual tease, but it quickly became apparent from the expression of Melissa's face that something was wrong. 'Well don't tell me you're even fed up with *him!*' cried Kate imploringly.

'It's not so much that *I'm* fed up with him,' pouted Melissa. 'More the other way round really. Since that incident with the dead tiger, he's just had no time for me . . .'

'Oh, I'm sorry about that, darling.'

'You're not!' Melissa fixed her mother with a glare of accusation. 'You don't like him anyway.'

'Why, Melissa, I've never said a word against him . . .'

'Not to me perhaps, but I'm willing to bet that you've bent Daddy's ear on the subject from time to time – There, you see, there's no need to answer! You look as guilty as anything!'

Kate flushed a little. She glanced at the floor.

'Well, darling, I won't pretend that I don't find him a little . . . brash . . . but you see, my opinion of him has nothing to do with it. So long as a man interests you, you know neither I nor Daddy would try to stand in the way of a romance . . . well, unless he was married, or something of that kind. I'm sure Mr Beresford is . . .'

'Yes, well it's purely academic at the moment, isn't it! Like I said, he's been avoiding me for months, so there's an end to it.'

Kate sighed.

'Well, dear, perhaps it's just as well. After all, you'll be going back to England soon and the last thing you'd want is some kind of romantic entanglement that would make it difficult for you to leave with a clear mind . . .'

'Ah, good old Mummy! Always so practical . . .' Melissa felt an uncharacteristic surge of fondness run through her, and getting out of her seat she went to give her mother a fierce hug.

'Goodness!' exclaimed Kate in mock surprise, but she responded by stroking her daughter's hair, something she hadn't done since Melissa started school. She abruptly felt rather sad as she visualized her only child leaving home, something that would surely happen before many more months had elapsed. There had only ever been the one child.

There were serious complications with the first birth and doctors had warned Kate that it might be dangerous to try for another baby.

'Tell me something,' murmured Melissa. 'I've often wondered. How did you manage to ensnare Daddy?'

Kate smiled.

'Well, I think "ensnare" is perhaps an unfortunate word . . .'

'Nonsense! Don't all women go out to trap their men? Don't we use perfume and makeup as our bait and don't we attempt to entice them all down that one-way tunnel that ends in matrimony?'

'Well dear, it's a rather cynical way of looking at it, don't you think? I prefer to think that we just make the men aware of a simple fact that they've for some time overlooked: the fact that they can't do without us!'

Melissa giggled.

'I see and how did you make Daddy aware of that?'

'Well . . . as I remember, I'd been on the scene for a very long time. Of course, we were in civvy street then, it was before the war . . . your father had just finished university and had come home to his parents' house. I lived with my parents quite close by. Of course, the two of us had known each other for years, but I think he'd always regarded me as nothing more than a "pal" really. I'm sure he wasn't even aware that I was female, for all the interest he showed. We went out together a great deal at that time, but just as friends you know, there was no . . . well, you know. Then, Sandra Buckingham came on the scene!'

'Who was she?'

'You may well ask! She was this simply ghastly girl who I'd been at school with, and for some inexplicable reason your father met her at a dance and became totally besotted with her. My dear, if only you could have seen her! She was a frightful creature with a pronounced lisp and a mop of blonde curls that would not have looked out of place on Shirley Temple. Added to this was the most appalling dress sense I have ever witnessed; and there was your father going all goo-goo-eyed over her. It was a nauseating spectacle, I can tell you.'

'She sounds horrific. Whatever did you do?'

'Well, my first intention was to wash my hands of him completely and look into other possibilities. There was no shortage of interest from other young men . . . and yet, deep down inside, I knew that I was the right one for him and that this awful . . . gorgon that he was mooning over would prove to be the end of him. Anyway, that was when I discovered the secret weapon.'

Melissa was intrigued.

'What was that?' she enquired.

'A simple enough ploy, my dear, but one that has aided womankind since time immemorial. I refer, of course, to the ancient art of *playing hard to get!*'

'Ahah!'

'You see, while I was just . . . available, your father took me for granted. So, quite suddenly, without any warning. I deserted him and went about my other interests. When he called, I wasn't in. When he wrote, I didn't reply. When I saw him on the street, I crossed to the other side. Of course, with Sandra Buckingham still on the scene, it was a calculated gamble, but the change in your father, when presented with such indifference, was astonishing to behold. Inside a couple of months, the hideous Sandra was forgotten and your father and I were engaged to be married.'

'Marvellous!' Melissa applauded the story heartily. 'And here am I, living proof that the technique works – Golly, I must look up this Sandra Buckingham when we get to England. I want to see if she's as repulsive as you say!'

'You will do no such thing,' said Kate, holding up her hands in mock-horror. 'There are some spectres from the past that are best left buried. Besides, there's an interesting little postscript to the story, which I will tell you if you promise not to breathe a word to anybody else.'

'Yes, I promise! What is it?'

Kate sighed.

'After her romantic letdown, Sandra sought to console herself by taking on a career in acting. She went to a drama school and, shortly after leaving it, she changed her name to Sandra Bennet . . .'

Melissa stared at her mother.

'What? Not . . . *the* Sandra Bennet? Not the film star, Sandra Bennet?'

Kate nodded silently.

'But, Mother, she's absolutely *gorgeous!*'

'Yes . . . well, I suppose it goes to show what a little voice training and beauty consultation can do; she was an absolute baboon when I knew her. The irony is that Dennis still doesn't know about the transformation. In fact, he's seen her in films on two different occasions and never made the connection. Somehow, I've never been able to bring myself to tell him about it. I'd hate to think that he felt cheated in some way.'

Melissa threw back her head and laughed, her boredom, for the time being at least, quite forgotten.

'Oh, Mummy, how could he ever feel cheated? Sandra Bennet is just a boring old film star but you, you're absolutely unique!'

'Well, thank you for that dear.' Headlights played across the slatted panes of the sitting room window, as a car pulled in through the open gates of the garden. 'There's your father now . . . remember, Melissa, not a word about this to him, or anyone else for that matter.'

'Don't worry, my lips are sealed; gosh though, it's funny to think of Daddy married to her! With all her money, he'd be a kept man . . .'

'Yes, well, I can't see him enjoying that much, can you? Ssh now, here he comes! Melissa, do stop giggling, you'll give the game away . . .'

The front door opened, Dennis hurried into the room and the bleak expression on his face quickly dampened Melissa's amusement. It was quite apparent to the two women that something was wrong.

'Harry Sullivan's had another heart attack,' announced Dennis gravely. 'Worse this time though. He was admitted to the hospital at Kuala Hitam but discharged himself this morning.'

'Discharged himself?' echoed Kate. 'Was that wise?'

'Not at all, dear, but you know Harry. I just got the story from Trimani before I came home. Apparently, Harry had been drinking heavily and he was horsing around in the

Mess, pretending to be shooting tigers or some such nonsense. Honestly, sometimes you'd be forgiven for thinking he was a six-year-old instead of sixty-five . . .'

'Sixty-seven,' corrected Melissa, knowing that this was exactly what Harry would have done if he were present.

'We'd better go up and visit him after dinner,' suggested Kate. She and Dennis both directed their gazes in Melissa's direction.

'You've not been up to see Harry since the two of you had that last run-in,' observed Dennis admonishingly. 'You haven't even apologized to him about it. He was right about Beresford's tiger, after all . . .'

Melissa's mother took a more persuasive tack.

'It would mean so much to him if you were to come along with us,' she reasoned. 'Why not bury the hatchet once and for all?'

Melissa nodded.

'Of course I'll come,' she said simply.

It was a fine clear evening. The sky was cloudless and the stars were particularly striking, twinkling like great handfuls of polished diamonds scattered across the blue velvet heavens. Far off to the right, the richly forested hills plunged down to meet the placid tranquil waters of the ocean. Abruptly, Melissa found herself reflecting that there *were* some things she would miss about this country. She knew that England had its own cold, rather austere beauty but where in that far-off land would she ever find a scene so wild, so relatively untouched by civilization at the vista that she could glimpse now through the car window? And also, in that moment, she realized that Harry would never be persuaded to leave this place; the hot sun and the palm trees and the great shimmering sweep of ocean were in his veins and were as much a part of him as he was a part of them.

They turned in at the small estate where Harry lived and Dennis brought the car to a halt outside the familiar white bungalow. They all got out and stood for a moment, gazing apprehensively at the closed doors and darkened windows. They could see no light inside.

'I hope he's alright,' murmured Kate.

Dennis led the way in through the gate and they advanced

slowly up the drive, paused at the front door. Dennis reached out and rapped politely with his knuckles. The house seemd ominously silent. After a few minutes' wait, he knocked again. At last they were rewarded with a soft tread beyond the door and the sound of the latch being withdrawn. The door opened and there was Harry looking just as he always did, in the peak of health. He peered out into the night and then his tanned face broke into a grin.

'Hello there, Dennis . . . Kate! Well you two are a sight for sore eyes, I must say! Well, come in, come in . . .' He ushered them inside and then, for the first time, he noticed that they had not come alone. Melissa stood on the doorstep, an expression of uncertainty on her face.

'Hello, Uncle Harry,' she murmured.

He stared at her in silence for a moment, surprised and a little taken aback by her unexpected visit.

'Hello stranger,' he said at last and his voice was rather tremulous. 'Well now . . . come along in. It's good to see you again . . .'

'It's good to see you too, Uncle Harry. But, before I come in . . .' Melissa glanced self-consciously at her parents, and they obligingly moved further into the house in order to let her make her peace with Harry. 'Before I come in, I rather think I owe you an apology.'

'Indeed?' Harry raised his eyebrows. 'And why is that, may I ask?'

'I think you know. The argument we had . . . about Bob's tiger. I was a little fool, Uncle Harry, shouting my mouth off about something I didn't know anything about. Then, afterwards, when you were proved right . . . well, I suppose I was just too proud to admit that I was wrong. Pride's a terrible thing.'

'Well, that's true enough,' admitted Harry. 'And I've got more than my fair share of it myself, I can assure you.' He smiled, extended his hand. 'Here, come along inside . . . or are you going to stand around on the doorstep all night?'

Melissa smiled, accepted his hand, and squeezed it gently. It was good to be back. She let Harry pull her slowly through the open doorway, into the house.

*   *   *   *   *

'Stop here, Tuan,' said the *bomoh*'s assistant.

Bob pulled the Land Rover to a halt and sat for a moment gazing cautiously around. They were on a deserted stretch of dirt road, a short distance beyond Kampong Machis. On either side of them lay thick, shadowy stretches of jungle, dank and forbidding in the darkness. Bob did not much fancy the prospect of wandering in there at this late hour. He turned to ask his companion a question, but the man was already clambering out of the Land Rover.

'Hey, hang on a minute!' Bob groped around in the back of the vehicle, found his rifle and a powerful flashlight that he always used for hunting at night. He slung the rifle over his shoulder and, flicking on the torch, he climbed down and hurried after the *bomoh*'s assistant. The man was already striding fearlessly through the long grass that flanked the road. 'Hold on a bit . . . I've got a light here,' called Bob.

'I know my way,' replied the Malay, matter-of-factly. He ducked beneath a tangle of low-hanging branches and disappeared momentarily into the gloom of the jungle. Cursing to himself, Bob hurried after the man, tripping and stumbling over the unfamiliar ground. At last, with an effort, he managed to catch up with him, and despite the fellow's assurance that no light was needed he directed a powerful beam of yellow light across the ground in front of them. He was momentarily startled by the alien appearance that the jungle took on at night. Features that would have seemed quite ordinary in the daylight took on a decidedly weird quality in the stark glare of the flashlight. Tree trunks and hanging creepers possessed a twisted, serpentlike look that was disconcerting. Ferns and leaves cast dappled moving shadows that suggested that they had somehow come alive and were gradually closing in on the two men. Birds, resting in the lower branches of some of the trees, flapped away in alarm as the light sought out their leafy sanctuaries, and the beat of their wings in the silence was enough to set nerve endings jangling like a peal of bells.

'Nice place to visit, but I wouldn't want to live here,' muttered Bob grimly. His companion did not even acknowledge the statement. He was seemingly intent on wherever he was going and nothing was going to keep him from his goal. Exercising a good deal more caution, Bob was on the alert for possible dangers. It was he who saw the snake first, a small dusty-brown creature, wriggling violently in the glare of the flashlight. It was a krait and, despite its lack of any great size, Bob knew it was one of the most venomous of the local snakes, possessing a poison in its tiny fangs that worked neurotoxically, acting on the nerves and causing paralysis of the limbs, jaws, and eyelids. More often than not, bites proved fatal. But the *bomoh*'s assistant gave no indication of having spotted the danger. He was striding straight towards it and the creature was suspended in the grass at a height where it must surely brush against the Malay's bare legs.

'Hey, watch out!' yelled Bob. 'Snake!' He pointed into the beam of the light, but the Malay simply smiled, did nothing to check his speed or alter his direction. He brushed roughly against the snake, knocking it down to the ground by his feet; then, instead of moving quickly on, he stopped stock-still. Gazing down in horror, Bob could see the krait coiling and writhing against the bare flesh of the man's ankles.

'For Christ's sake, move!' urged Bob. 'That thing is deadly poisonous!'

'But of course, Tuan.' The man turned his head to smile mockingly at Bob but he still made no attempt to move away out of harm's reach. Instead, he stooped abruptly down and to Bob's astonishment, snatched the krait up in one hand and held it out for inspection. 'See! Beautiful, is it not?'

'Jesus Christ —' Bob stepped back instinctively and gazed in sheer disbelief. The creature thrashed and writhed in an attempt to escape the man's grasp, but it did not attempt to bite him. The man's smile deepened into a grin. His teeth were very white in the darkness.

'Why . . . why doesn't it bite you?' asked Bob weakly.

'A snake only attacks that which fears him,' replied the Malay matter-of-factly. 'Since I am not afraid, he does not bite.' He stared at Bob thoughtfully for a moment. 'He would bite you though,' he added and seemed to be on the point of handing the snake over to his companion.

'I'll take your word for it,' said Bob hastily. The man gave a short derisive laugh and then flung the krait contemptuously aside. Then, the incident seemingly forgotten, he strode away again, his gaze fixed straight ahead. Bob took a long deep breath in order to calm himself and he stumbled after the Malay again. He was beginning to feel very uncomfortable.

'Look, how much further is it?' he demanded irritably. 'I wasn't expecting a bloody marathon.'

'Not far now, Tuan.'

'Well, I hope not. Listen, if the *bomoh* was so anxious to talk, why didn't he come and see me himself?'

'The *bomoh* never leaves his hut . . . at least, not on *two* legs.'

Bob gave a sneer of contempt.

'What's that supposed to mean? Look, mate, don't try pulling the old mumbojumbo on me, it won't wash!'

The man shrugged indifferently.

'I only say what I know,' he replied calmly.

The *bomoh*'s assistant had come to an abrupt halt.

'We are there,' he announced tonelessly. Bob was taken by surprise. He stopped too and stared in the direction in which the Malay was pointing. At first he could see nothing but an unrelieved backdrop of undergrowth, but then the beam of his torch picked out a low, flimsy wooden shack that was virtually surrounded on three sides by trees and bushes. It was a crudely constructed ramshackle affair, not even raised off the ground in the familiar local tradition of building. The tiny window apertures were glassless and covered with lengths of mouldy sacking, and the only element that suggested any life within was a thin plume of grey smoke issuing from a roughly made hole in the corrugated iron roof.

'That's it?' enquired Bob dismally. Now that he had arrived at his destination, he felt strongly reluctant to go into the place.

'The *bomoh* is waiting for you,' murmured his companion.

'Aren't you coming in?'

227

'No. I wait here.'

Bob frowned, shrugged, and hoped that he didn't look as apprehensive as he felt. He approached the hut slowly, keeping one hand on the stock of his rifle, so that he might snatch it from his shoulder if necessary. The low doorway at the front was also covered with filthy sacking. Bob reached out to grip it in his fingers and a large black spider skittered abruptly down the material and away across the ground. Bob shuddered involuntarily, and his skin began to crawl. He dreaded to think what other nightmarish creatures might be creeping about on the floor of the dingy little hut. He glanced back and saw that the tall Malay was still watching him, so he pulled the sacking roughly aside and entered the hut, stooping low to avoid banging his head.

Inside, there was a low wood fire burning dully in the very centre of the floor, the air was thick with fragrance of woodsmoke, and a powerful smell of incense mingled with hashish. A small, half-naked man was sitting in front of the fire, his legs crossed comfortably beneath him. He was wiry, apish-looking, with a completely bald head. Several diagonal scars ran across both his cheeks, some kind of ceremonial markings, Bob supposed. The man's eyes were tightly shut and he seemed to be in a trance. Bob felt unsure of what to do, but then, unexpectedly, the man spoke, without opening his eyes.

'So you are here at last, Mr Beresford. I was beginning to think that you would not come.' The voice was surprisingly cultured, the command of English excellent. 'Come, sit opposite me. There is a place by the fire.'

Bob lowered himself awkwardly onto the floor, half afraid that he would sit on a scorpion or, worse still, a tropical centipede. It was oppressively hot in the cramped interior of the hut, and a thick sweat began to ooze from his armpits and chest.

'Why are you afraid?' asked the *bomoh*. 'There is nothing to fear here.'

Bob was about to reply but at that instant the *bomoh* chose to open his eyes, and the Australian was transfixed by the sight of them. They were two pale orbs that caught the flickering glow of the firelight. In the very centre of each eye

228

a tiny, tar-black pupil rested like a pinprick of black emptiness. They were not the eyes of a man at all, but the cold malignant eyes of a cat. Despite the heat, a cold shiver tingled its way down Bob's spine. The *bomoh* smiled, displaying tiny white canine teeth that had been carefully filed to sharp points.

'I . . . I'm not afraid,' replied Bob at last.

'Oh, but you *are*. You have been unsettled from the moment you dropped your glass of whisky on the floor of your house.'

Bob stared at the *bomoh* for a moment in shocked silence. 'How did you know that?' he demanded.

'How does a man know anything? I watch. I listen. And then all is revealed to me.'

Bob took a deep breath, but the thick cloying atmosphere only served to make him feel lightheaded.

'It's some kind of trick,' he said with conviction. 'I don't know how you did it, but it's some kind of trick.'

The *bomoh* chuckled, a low, guttural unpleasant sound.

'Is that not typical of the Western mentality?' he observed. 'Always suspicious of that which they cannot readily explain – But, since you like to call it that, I shall not argue with you. The Malay people would perhaps have another, more accurate name for it.'

'Yeah, well cut out the clever talk, mate. It might impress the people in the *kampongs*, but it doesn't cut any mustard with me. Let's get down to brass tacks, shall we? Why did you ask me to come out here?'

The *bomoh* gave a short, mocking bow of agreement.

'We have similar aims, Mr Beresford. We both wish to see the old man-eater disposed of. I, because I fear that the wrath of the local people may turn against me; and you, because you are driven by a desire to prove yourself.'

'What are you talking about?' Bob fixed the *bomoh* with an outraged glare. 'I hunt that tiger because he's a menace, that's all. *Somebody's* got to put a stop to the killing.'

'Well, whatever your reasons, I feel I can be of help to you.'

'You think so, huh?' Bob frowned, stroked his chin for a moment. 'Listen, if you're so worried about the talk in the *kampongs*, why don't you just go and explain the situation to them?'

'Perhaps my assistant did not make it clear to you before. The form I take when I leave this hut would not make me very welcome in the habitations of humans.'

Again, Bob found himself wondering how the *bomoh* could know about this; but, he reasoned, it would be a simple enough thing to set up beforehand.

'Oh yeah, I forgot,' he murmured sarcastically. 'You're the tiger-man, right? Must make things very awkward for you, no doubt.'

'Indeed, it does. For instance, Mr Beresford, the lateness of your arrival does not give us very long to talk. In a short while, I must go out to hunt for my evening meal.'

Bob gave a short derisive laugh.

'Well, I'll have to stick around,' he said. 'I'd like to see that.'

The *bomoh* shook his head.

'Oh no, Mr Beresford, I don't think you would. However, since you are a free man, you must do as you think fit. Meanwhile, let us consider the ways I might be of use to you. For one thing, I know the tiger that you are seeking. I have seen him on several occasions. As I said before, he is an old devil, very cunning. He has some porcupine quills embedded in his right foreleg and the wound has made him lame. They cause him considerable pain and that is why, for instance, he has begun to suffer terrible rages, such as the one that made him leap into your tree last night.'

Again, Bob was amazed, but he replied stolidly, 'You could have heard about that from anyone at Kampong Panjang.'

'Of course, Mr Beresford. And they too, could have told me how the tiger tore the rifle from your hands, leaving deep teeth marks in the wooden stock; and how only your agility and presence of mind saved you from becoming his next victim. But really, Mr Beresford, I do not particularly care what you think or believe about me. Only the outcome of this meeting is important. The tiger must die if I am to enjoy the continued assistance of the *kampong* people.'

'Assistance?'

230

'For many years, the local people have turned a blind eye to my preying upon their livestock; but as the wildlife here in the jungles declines, it becomes necessary to hunt nearer to places of habitation. The people allow this because they have a healthy respect for me, a respect born of fear; allow that fear to turn into anger and eventually they will fight back . . . Do you understand?'

Bob took a deep breath. The thick perfumed atmosphere in the hut was making him feel distinctly dizzy. Coupled with the *bomoh*'s fantastic conversation, the event seemed to possess a vivid, hallucinatory quality.

'Tell me something,' muttered Bob. 'Where the hell did you learn to speak such good English, huh?'

The *bomoh* shrugged.

'How does a man learn anything?' he enquired. 'I watch. I listen. And then . . .

'Yeah, yeah . . .' Bob waved him to silence. 'Christ, it's hot in here.'

'I can tell you one thing for certain, Mr Beresford. You will never catch the old tiger by putting out baits, or by lying up in the treetops. He has lived too long and learned too many tricks to allow himself to be trapped.'

Bob nodded. 'I've about come to that conclusion myself,' he muttered.

'To kill him, it will be necessary to follow on foot across his own terrain. It will require great courage and even greater skill, but only this way will he be laid finally to rest.' The *bomoh* turned away and picked up a small leather pouch that lay at his side. He untied a thong that bound its neck. 'Now, hold out your hand,' he instructed.

'What for?'

'Don't worry, there's no trick involved. Trust me.'

Hesitantly, Bob held out one arm and the *bomoh* upended the bag, dropping several small brownish bones into Bob's open palm.

'I want you to cast these onto the floor in one throw,' explained the *bomoh*. 'With them I can foretell your future.'

'More mumbo jumbo,' chuckled Bob. But he threw down the bones and watched in amusement as the *bomoh* puzzled over them for several moments in silence. Then, abruptly, he began to talk quickly in a low toneless voice, hardly pausing to take breath.

'There are more deaths to come. One who dies has skin of white. The tiger will be found on a day when the sun is unobscured. There are *two* tigers. The first shall not die till the second has looked him in the eyes. The gun . . . the gun . . .' The *bomoh* paused for a moment, his fingers twitching on empty air. Then he leaned quickly across the low fire, snatched Bob's rifle from his shoulder and held it against his chest, his fingers moving slowly up and down the length of the barrel. '*This* gun,' he crooned rapturously. 'Ahh yes, *this* gun will bring the tiger low . . . but there will be a terrible price to pay . . . a terrible price –' He glanced suddenly up at Bob. 'You will fire this gun once more!' he cried. 'Then never again. Never!'

Bob stared at the *bomoh* for a moment, shocked, despite his lack of belief in the man's magical powers. He leaned across the fire and snatched the rifle back.

'Yeah, well thanks, Doc! Is that all for now, or do I get a long-range weather forecast, too?'

The *bomoh* gazed at Bob blankly for a moment as though still lost momentarily in some kind of trance. In the flickering firelight, his face looked gaunt and alien.

Then he said softly, 'Did my words not please you?'

'Well, you got one bit right. This *is* the gun that will bring the tiger low. But I'm not so keen on the rest of it. What did you mean when you said I'll fire this gun once more and never again? And who's the man with white skin that's going to die?'

The *bomoh* shrugged.

'I speak the words of prediction many times. But it does not mean that I understand them.'

Bob nodded.

'That's very convenient for you,' he observed drily.

'Perhaps. Sometimes, it is better not to have the burden of knowing the truth.' The *bomoh* seemed to suddenly tire of his audience with Bob. 'It is getting late. You had better go now. I wish to prepare myself for tonight's hunt.'

Bob smiled maliciously.

'But I wouldn't dream of going now,' he replied. 'Don't

you remember, I said I wanted to stick around and catch the act?'

The *bomoh* nodded.

'Yes, I remember, Mr Beresford. And do you not remember that I told you that you would most assuredly *not* enjoy what you saw?'

'Sounds like a poor excuse to me, Doc.'

'Perhaps I am worried that you will forget yourself, and in the excitement you will use your rifle and attempt to make a trophy out of me.'

'Well now, Doc, I'd hardly do that after what you've told me, would I? Use up my one and only shot on you, when it's reserved for the man-eater? I should say not!'

The *bomoh* stared at Bob for several long moments in silence. Then he said quietly, 'You are indeed a most obstinate man, Mr Beresford. But you may do as you think best.' And he closed his eyes.

A silence settled inside the hut, broken only by the crackling of twigs in the fire. The *bomoh* sat stock-still, but his chin sank gradually downwards to his chest. Only the slow rise and fall of his breathing indicated that he was alive. Bob sat sweating uncomfortably in the thick, incensed atmosphere of the hut. He was fascinated that the *bomoh* was actually going to go ahead with the 'transformation.' No doubt he'd just sit like that for hours until Bob got bored and went home. It was funny how these magical devices never worked under close scrutiny. Still, Bob didn't feel inclined to let the *bomoh* off the hook that easily. The Australian reached into his shirt pocket, took out a cigarette, and lit it in the embers of the fire.

'I've got all night,' he told himself.

Time passed.

Abruptly Bob became aware of a sudden change in the atmosphere of the hut. It was an inexplicable thing, a tingling against the flesh, as though the very air had become imbued with a subtle charge of electricity. And then a powerful smell filled the room, a musky, animallike odour, the sort that might be associated with caged creatures at zoos. Bob was intrigued. Now that *was* impressive! He felt like applauding, but as he turned his gaze back to the *bomoh*, he saw that the man's eyes were opening again; and that now there was a new quality in those already disturbing eyes. They were staring fixedly at Bob, but the light of reason had vanished from them and seemed to have been replaced by a bestial cunning that was badly out of place on a human being. The *bomoh* was breathing very heavily now, his sweat-beaded chest rising and falling, his mouth gaping open to reveal the sharply chiselled teeth. Bob felt the hairs on the back of his neck begin to rise and a terrible shiver convulsed his body. He tried to tell himself that this was just another device designed to play upon his imagination, but though his reason assured him that this was the case, his other senses did not seem able to agree with him.

For now, the *bomoh*'s face was changing, dissolving upon itself, the features rearranging, horribly, inexplicably. The shape of the head became squat, rounded, *inhuman*.

'No . . .' The word was barely a whisper. Bob shook his head from side to side, trying to dispel the image that hovered before his terrified eyes, but it remained, growing ever more hideous. The cigarette dropped forgotten from his shaking fingers and he stumbled back, away from the fire, until his shoulders connected with the wall of the hut.

'No!' he screamed more forcibly. 'It's a trick!'

A deep guttural boom of laughter exploded from the mouth of the changeling.

'No!' Bob's nerve broke completely. In an instant, he had grabbed his rifle and was scrambling for the door, scattering ashes and sparks from the fire in his headlong panic, while behind him another burst of laughter exploded in the confines of the hut. His head reeling, Bob struggled through the screen of sacking into the world beyond. He began to run, blind in the heat of his own panic. He tripped over something lying in the grass and sprawled down on top of it. It was the *bomoh*'s assistant. The man was lying down on his back, mumbling incoherently. A thick white foam was oozing from his lips and his hands came up to grab at Bob's wrists, as if to hold him fast.

'Let me go!' Desperately, Bob struck out with his knees, wrenched his arms free and tumbled away. He was on his feet in an instant and racing back through the jungle, ducking beneath outspread limbs and branches. There came to him the intense conviction that something silent and unseen was racing along on his heels and he blundered through the dark undergrowth in a direction that he prayed would lead him back to the Land Rover. Vines and thick ferns clung to his legs, and he became exhausted very quickly. He was forced to rest for a few moments with his back up against the trunk of a tall tree. Out in the clear air, away from the incense and hashish of the *bomoh*'s hut, he was able to gain control of himself more readily. He unslung the rifle and waited to see if indeed anything was following him along the trail. Nothing emerged from the bushes and he had to concede that *that* part of it, at least, had been his imagination. But what of the rest of it? Here, in the cool light of reason, the misadventures seemed already unlikely, a fable, a product of his overwrought imagination; but there, in that claustrophobic hut, for an instant he had believed – really believed that . . .

He shook his head. The sheer impregnable logic of his strict Western upbringing asserted itself, prevented him from believing in what he had seen, or thought he had seen. It had been a trick, brilliantly orchestrated perhaps, but a trick all the same. If he were to go back to the hut now, he would find the *bomoh* and his assistant laughing with each other over the way they had put the fear of the devil into the nonbelieving white man. Or was he really supposed to accept that the *bomoh* was out in the jungle somewhere, prowling on four legs instead of two?

All the same, he didn't feel much inclined to actually go back. Instead, he slung the rifle back over his shoulder and moved away at a more leisurely pace in search of his vehicle. He took the flashlight out of his shirt pocket and directed a beam of light onto the narrow track ahead of him. He had taken no more than a dozen steps, when he stood stock-still with an exclamation of shock. For an instant, caught in the beam and framed amidst a tangle of bushes, was the surprised and scowling face of a large tiger. But by the time Bob had unslung his gun again, the creature had slipped away into the undergrowth.

Haji gave a long low rumbling growl of discontent.

He had only followed the Upright for a short distance, attracted by the noisy headlong flight of him as he raced through the jungle. Haji had overtaken him and dropped down to lie in ambush at the far end of a narrow cattle trail. But instead of blundering right into Haji's hungry jaws, the silly creature had come to an abrupt halt and rested for a while with his back to a tree. He had taken out the dreaded black stick, as though expecting some kind of attack; and then, most alarming of all, there had been the blinding, unnatural river of light, rushing straight into Haji's eyes, and then and there the tiger had promptly given up all thought of eating this troublesome Upright and had gone off in search of more predictable prey.

Now, here he was some considerable distance away from the scene of the incident, heading for the nearest *kampong* and quite unaware of the fantastic notions he had stirred in the mind of his would-be victim.

Off to the east, an argus pheasant called several times, a lonely haunting 'Cuau-Cuau!' that faded gradually into distance as Haji slipped like a scarred shadow through the silent trees.

Chapter 22

The sound of a car horn intruded upon Harry's midday nap, with all the delicacy of a brick thrown through a plate-glass window. He blinked owlishly, sat up in his rattan chair and gave a brief exclamation of irritation, tilting his sun hat back on his head so that he might search out the source of the noise.

Paarp! Paarp! PAAAAARP!

'What the bloody . . . ?' Harry got up out of his chair and leaned over the rail of the verandah. There was a bright blue Volkswagen parked by the garden gate, a vehicle he had never seen before, but the sun's reflection on the windscreen prevented him from seeing the driver. Harry strode quickly down the pathway, with every intention of punching the inconsiderate fellow on the nose.

'Making a damned bloody row in the middle of the afternoon,' Harry muttered to himself. 'Don't know what this place is coming to –' He broke off in surprise as the car door opened and the driver got out.

It was a middle-aged woman, rather stout but with fine striking features. She was dressed in a shapeless green khaki shirt and a skirt of the same material, while on her head she wore a crumpled faded hat of the kind favoured by the Gurkhas for jungle warfare. Some wisps of iron-grey hair emerged from the back of the hat, and, most incongruous of all to Harry's mind, she appeared to be smoking a cigar. His intentions quite forgotten in his rush of surprise, Harry just stood by the gate, staring open-mouthed at the woman.

She fixed him with a glance from a pair of steely blue-grey eyes.

'Lieutenant Colonel Sullivan?' she enquired hopefully.

'Retired,' he added. 'Yes, that's me.'

'Ah excellent!' There was the faintest trace of a Scottish accent in her voice. 'I hope I'm not disturbing you.'

'Er . . . no, not at all.'

She stepped up to the gate and stretched out a hand to him.

'The name's Burns. Marion Burns. I've had quite a time looking for you – er . . . now look here, I can't go on calling you Lieutenant Colonel Retired, now can I? It's far too time-consuming! What's your first name?'

'It's uh . . . Harry.'

'Well then, Harry it will be! I trust you'll forgive the familiarity?' She opened the gate and stepped through onto the drive. 'What a lovely little house you have here! Perhaps we could sit on the verandah for a while. It's damned hot today.'

'Uh . . . yes . . . of course.' Harry was confused and beginning to wonder if this, in fact, was some mystifying dream that he was having. 'I'm sorry, I don't believe I've had the pleasure of . . .'

'No, of course not. Forgive me dropping out of the blue like this, Harry.' She was already heading towards the verandah and Harry trailed along beside her. 'Let me explain. I'm a feature writer for the *Straits Times* and I've been sent down here to put together an article on the man-eating tiger that's giving you so much trouble at the moment. Of course, so far we've given it the usual news coverage, but the fellow's arousing so much interest, it's been decided to give him the full-page spread treatment. Goodness, what lovely chairs!' She settled herself into the seat where Harry had just been sleeping. 'You see,' she continued, 'this is the first major man-eater the country's had since the mid-fifties. Oh, we've had them carry off the odd one or two rubber tappers, but they generally get caught before they can take matters any further. This fellow has reached seven, and we seem to be no nearer to catching him than before.'

'I see . . . but –'

'There's a certain fascination in the subject, this is the thing. Of course, we all know the popular view of the man-eater as some kind of rampaging, blood-lusting demon on four legs, but I'd like to try another angle. I want to get at the truth behind the myths, more or less present the tiger's side of it, you know? I'd also like to tie it in from a conservationist angle. I find it rather ironic that the tiger is our national emblem and yet, the way we're going, he's liable to be extinct before very many years have gone by.'

A coin dropped in Harry's memory.

'Well then, you must be M. Burns!' he exclaimed. 'Why I've read many of your articles . . . but I always assumed you were a man!'

Marion smiled good-naturedly. 'Sorry to disappoint,' she chuckled.

'Good heavens, not at all. I – Would you like some tea . . . er . . . Marion?'

'Indeed I would!'

'Right. Pawn! Pawn, are you in there?'

Pawn bustled to the door, wiping her hands on a tea-towel.

'Yes Tuan?'

'Some tea for the Missy and myself, please.'

Pawn gazed at Marion for a moment and grinned excitedly.

238

'Oh, yes indeed, Tuan! Right away! And she hurried away in the direction of the kitchen. Harry turned back to his guest.

'So . . . where were we?' he enquired.

'I think you were bewailing the fact that I'm not a man,' she chuckled.

'No, no, not a bit of it, really! One makes assumptions, that's all. So you intend to write an article on the man-eating tiger, eh? Well I think it will make splendid reading, particularly if you do er . . . get the right angle, as you call it. But the question is, what's all this got to do with me?'

'What indeed!' Marion reached in to her shirt pocket and pulled out a folded, crumpled sheet of paper. She handed it to Harry. 'Remember this?' she enquired.

He took it from her and opened it out carefully. He was amazed to see that it was an old article he had written for the barracks magazine, *Parade Ground*. The title of the piece was, 'Hunting in Tiger Country.'

'Good heavens!' exclaimed Harry. 'This is years old. Where on earth did you get a copy of this?'

'You may well ask! Well, naturally enough, when I got to Trengganu, the first place I headed for was the Game Department, telling myself that if I was going to find a tiger expert anywhere, that would be the place.'

'Seems like a fair assumption.'

'Right. But there I talked to a nice chap called Mike Kirby.'

'Ah, Mike! Yes, I know him well. I would have thought that if anybody could have helped you out . . .'

Marion shook her head.

'He told me that I would not find a more informed source of information anywhere in Trengganu than his old friend Harry Sullivan. And then he produced this article, which he himself has used as a textbook on the subject for several years. So, naturally enough, here I am.'

Harry smiled fondly.

'Mike said that, did he? Well, that's most kind of him, I must say.'

'Then you'll help?'

'Well, of course, if you think I can be of any use, I'll be

glad to.'

'Excellent! I will, of course, give you a mention in the article.'

'Really? You know, I've always wanted to see my name in the *Straits Times*. I was beginning to think I'd have to wait to see it in the obituary column.'

Marion tilted back her head and laughed happily. She had a bright, infectious kind of laugh and Harry found himself chuckling, too. He watched her for a moment as she inhaled thoughtfully on her cigar, staring out across the lush garden.

'I must say you have a delightful little home here,' she observed. 'How long have you been a widower now?'

The frankness of the question shocked him momentarily.

'Seventeen years,' he replied tonelessly. 'But how did you –'

'I always make a point of finding out about people,' she replied. 'Part of my reporter's training. Actually, it's interesting. I was widowed myself, six years ago; so you see, we've got a bit in common.'

There was a brief, rather uncomfortable silence, but luckily it was effectively broken by the entry of Pawn carrying a tray of tea and biscuits. She placed it reverently on the table, all the while grinning happily at Marion. She was clearly waiting for an introduction.

'Er . . . Pawn, this is Mrs Burns. She's a writer for the newspapers.' Harry mimed the action of opening and reading a newspaper to make the point more clear, and Pawn grinned even more and bowed low. 'This is my *amah*, Pawn,' he told Marion.

'Hello, Pawn. I'm pleased to meet you.'

'Hello, Missy. I hope you like tea.'

'I'm sure I will.'

Pawn moved backwards into the house, bowing and grinning at regular intervals.

'She's a funny old coot,' explained Harry, as she disappeared into the house. 'But a great worker and a marvellous cook.'

'She's obviously a treasure. Shall I pour?'

'Oh, yes, please do.' Harry watched as she stubbed out the butt of her cigar in the ashtray and picked up the silver

240

tea pot. She had small, dainty hands that belied her somewhat unfeminine appearance. Harry was usually rather formal and uncomfortable with strangers, but with Marion this was certainly not the case. She struck him as being very interesting, and he found himself wanting to know more about her. He picked up the stub of her cigar and examined it carefully. It was of the small, mild Dutch variety, the kind of thing that one usually smoked with coffee.

'I like Havanas myself,' he murmured. 'Perhaps you'd like to try one of mine?'

She shook her head.

'No thank you. I'm sure it would be too strong for my taste. But you go ahead if you've a mind to, it won't bother me in the least.' She smiled. 'A lot of men don't like the fact that I smoke cigars,' she observed. 'They feel *threatened*, I think.'

'Rather strange attitude,' said Harry, reaching for his cigar case. 'Good lord, if a woman can smoke a cigarette, she can have one of these. You can smoke a pipe for all I care!'

'Now that would cause some *controversy!*' She sipped experimentally at her tea which she took without milk or sugar. 'This is delicious.'

'It's Darjeeling. I acquired a taste for it when I was out in India.'

'I must say, you're not like most military men I've met. Some of them are so set in their ways! Are you planning to head back to England when it all folds up here?'

'Oh no, I rather think I'll be staying on.'

'Good. That's refreshing. I hardly seem to meet anyone these days who isn't looking forward to "dear old Blighty."' She grimaced. 'Personally, I don't think I could stand the climate anymore. I've lived here most of my life and the thought of returning to cold, blustery Scotland would be most unappealing.' She switched the subject back to more immediate problems. 'I expect it will take me two or three days to put the article together. Can you recommend a hotel in the area?'

Harry frowned. He struck a match, lit his cigar and inhaled thoughtfully.

'Well now, that might be a problem. I really don't know anywhere nearer than Kuala Trengganu, and to be honest with you I've no idea how good the amenities are.'

'Hmm. Well, perhaps you've a spare room here that I might commandeer for a few days?'

'Well, er . . . there *is* a spare room, but –'

'Oh, but of course, I could hardly impose on you that way. No doubt, you'd be worried about what your neighbours might have to say. . .'

'Not at all! I don't give a damn what my neighbours think . . . it's just –'

'Well, that's settled then! I've only one small suitcase and a typewriter. I must say, it's very hospitable of you.'

'I . . . er . . . yes . . . right.' Harry was slightly dazed by the skill with which she had handled the situation, but he couldn't honestly say that he wasn't looking forward to having a little company. 'Well . . . I'd better tell Pawn to tidy the room out a bit. It hasn't been used for a very long time.'

'Now, don't go to any great trouble on my behalf,' she told him. 'Any old corner will suit me, so long as there's a place to stretch out and a roof over my head. You know, I've slept in some strange places since I started this job, I can tell you!' She gave that infectious laugh of hers again, bright, bubbly, appealing. Harry felt the corners of his lips rising almost involuntarily.

'Well, I'm sure Pawn will make it comfortable for you. Perhaps you'd like to have some dinner with me later on? . . .' He asked the question cautiously, afraid of being rejected, but she looked genuinely pleased at the prospect.

'Yes indeed, that would be lovely.'

'Oh . . . good. I'll get Pawn to cook up something special for us. I hope you like Malay food?'

'Nothing better.'

'Right then. If you'll excuse me for a moment. I'll just pop and get things organized. Do help yourself to more tea.'

He got up from his chair and hurried into the house. In the sitting room, the large electric fan was whirring purposefully around, fighting a losing battle with the humid air. Harry found himself thinking wryly about this strange, forceful newcomer, Marion Burns. What an extraordinary creature she was, only here a few minutes and already she had wangled free accommodation for herself, but the strange thing was that Harry had let her get away with it. Furthermore, he felt not the slightest bit put out by the incident and was actually looking forward to finding out more about his unexpected guest. He had to admit to himself that he found her very interesting, and it was a plain fact that he had not been interested in any woman since Meg had died.

He found Pawn on her hands and knees, scrubbing the already sparkling tiles on the kitchen floor. She glanced up in surprise as he came in, for the kitchen was a place that he very rarely entered.

'Ah Pawn, leave that for now please. Something more important. The Missy will be staying for a few days –'

'Missy stay *here?*' cried Pawn delightedly. 'With you?' she added hopefully.

Harry cleared his throat.

'The Missy will be sleeping in the spare room, Pawn, so would you please make sure that it's clean and tidy?'

Pawn grinned and nodded.

'Yes, Tuan, I clean very well. I start now!'

'Just a moment, there's something else. Will you stay a little later tonight and prepare dinner for the Missy and me?'

'Dinner? Oh Tuan!' Pawn clapped the palms of her hands to her face. 'There is not much food for me make good dinner!'

'Oh, that's alright.' He put a hand on her shoulder to reassure her. 'I'll give you some money and you can take a taxi to the nearest market and get whatever you need to make a special meal. Now don't worry about the expense, you get the best there is, alright?'

'Oh yes, Tuan! I get very best!' Harry took his wallet from his back pocket and handed her two fifty-dollar bills. She stood staring at them for several moments almost in disbelief. 'There is plenty here, Tuan,' she said at last. 'This will buy wonderful dinner for you.'

'Good. And if there's any change, perhaps you might like

243

to buy that nephew of yours a little something.'

Pawn's grin faded and she shook her head.

'He not deserve anything from you, Tuan. That boy promise me he come see you before, but he not come again. I am 'shamed of him. Now all he want do is talk 'bout hunting, be like Tuan Beresford.'

Harry frowned. 'I expect it's just a phase,' he murmured sadly. 'Anyway Pawn, there's lots to do and not much time to do it. You'd better run along to the taxi rank now.'

'Yes, Tuan, I go now. Clean room when I get back. Can I stop at *kampong* on way home, tell family I shall be late?'

'Yes, surely. Don't forget now, get the best you can buy!'

Pawn bustled away to collect her shopping bag and parasol. Harry smiled at her eagerness to please. He wandered back to the verandah, humming softly to himself. Emerging into the glare of daylight, he saw to his surprise that both the rattan chairs were empty. For a moment, a dull sense of shock hit him and various irrational ideas flashed through his mind. Marion had panicked. Rather than go through the ordeal of having dinner with a dry old stick like Harry, she had made an escape and was now driving back to her newspaper offices, hell bent for leather. Worse still, she had never existed, she was a figment of Harry's lonely imagination, the inevitable result of years of living alone. Or she was . . .

The gate clanged open and to his relief Harry saw Marion coming back along the drive, holding a small case and a portable typewriter. Harry strode down the steps of the verandah, hurried up to her, and relieved her of the luggage.

'Thank you! I thought I'd just get my things out of the car . . .'

'Certainly. We'll put them on the verandah for now, until your room's ready. Pawn has promised to make us something really special tonight.'

'Lovely . . . ah, don't look now, but I think your neighbours are having a good look at us.'

Harry glanced up just in time to see a curtain swish back into place in the front window of the house next door.

'Damned impudence!' muttered Harry blackly.

'Inevitable though.' Marion smiled. 'What are they like,

244

your neighbours?'

Harry stepped up onto the verandah and put down the luggage.

'I've no idea,' he replied truthfully.

'Then you've not lived here long?'

'About eighteen years.'

Marion raised her eyebrows. 'Well ... then your neighbours must be fairly new. Are they?'

Harry shrugged. 'I think they've been here ... oh ... five or six years.' He had never stopped to consider the matter before but it did seem a ludicrous state of affairs. 'I tend to keep myself to myself,' he added, by way of explanation.

'That's no understatement by the sound of it,' observed Marion. She followed him up onto the verandah and settled down again in the same chair she had occupied earlier. 'At our time of life, we have to be careful,' she observed. 'After all, no man, and no woman, for that matter, is an island. A person could get terribly lonely out here, you know.'

Harry nodded. 'I have a few good friends,' he said. 'But sadly, most of them will be heading back to England in a very short while.'

'You should move out to Kuala Lumpur, Harry. Things are a little faster there. There's more to do.'

'Well ... I'm not so sure about that. I've never been much of a one for socializing. Too fond of my own company, that's the trouble.'

Marion nodded.

'I used to be that way, until after my husband died. When you're married, you're rather spoiled for company ... but of course, since then, the newspaper work has helped to introduce me to any number of people. And now there's nothing I hate more than my own company. Friends are very sacred and important and the older you get, the more important they become.'

Harry frowned. 'Well, that's your opinion.'

'I think it's most people's opinion. But strangely enough, a lot of elderly people become frightened to admit how lonely they are. Perhaps it makes them feel too vulnerable, somehow.'

Harry coughed nervously, taken somewhat aback by the

accuracy of the observation. Marion noticed the discomfort she had caused him and quickly switched the subject. She took a small notebook from her jacket pocket.

'I suppose we could start right away,' she suggested. 'For starters, let's be specific. Can you tell me anything about our man-eater, for instance?'

Harry frowned again.

'Precious little in the way of facts . . . of course, I could speculate until the cows come home. But if we're going to begin with what I know for sure, then there isn't much to tell. To begin with, he's old, which in tiger terms will mean that he's anything over ten years; but from what I've seen myself, I'd put his age at around fifteen years, which is quite exceptional for an animal living in the wilds.'

'You keep saying "he." What makes you so sure it might not be a female?'

'Oh, there's no doubt about it. I've seen the tracks. He's an old gentleman and, furthermore, he's badly wounded in his right foreleg, makes him walk with a pronounced dragging motion. I imagine it must slow him down considerably and that's no doubt one of the chief reasons why he's become what he is.'

'Does there have to be a reason?'

'Oh yes, absolutely. Contrary to what many people may have told you, a healthy tiger would never dream of attacking a human being. It's not their style. They have their natural range of prey and they prefer to stick to it. Let's say that they're traditionalists. Tigers, like all other animals, have a natural and perfectly understandable fear of mankind. The only difference between your average tiger and our man-eater is that the latter has managed to conquer that natural fear, and you can bet that the major factor involved was the prospect of slow starvation if he didn't adapt.'

Marion nodded. 'So why hasn't he been caught yet?'

'Well, you see, already we're into the realms of speculation. I imagine his great age hasn't dulled his wits in any way; on the contrary, it will have made him cunning in every sense of the word. The mistakes of youth have all been made long ago and luckily enough, he's survived them. He's not about to start making any more at this stage of the game.'

Marion smiled. 'It sounds very much to me as if you admire the tiger,' she announced.

Harry nodded slowly.

'Admire him? Yes, I suppose you could say that,' he replied thoughtfully. 'He's survived a long time, in a world where survival for creatures like him is becoming increasingly difficult.' He sighed. 'Tigers and dinosaurs. There's not much room for either of them in this new Malaya they're building . . .'

'Dinosaurs?' Marion looked puzzled. 'I'm sorry, I don't follow.'

'Oh, forgive me. Just something a friend and I were talking about. Nothing really . . . but you know, I can remember this place when it was nothing but a few huts and brick buildings perched on the edge of the jungle. How quickly it grew. Estates hacked out of the forest. The British needed homes for their troops, who was going to tell them that the jungle should be preserved? So in went the bulldozers and the trees came down like ninepins. Wrong, all wrong. I couldn't see it then, of course. You don't, when you're a part of it all.' He frowned, shielded his eyes from the sun. 'Now here we are, years later, and there's precious little jungle left to cut down. The British are leaving, but the process will go on. The Malays have learned from our glorious example. Every time I go out, it seems there's a new building under way, a new road being constructed. And every day they cut a little deeper into the green, whittling away at it, destroying the habitat at a terrific rate. Progress, they call it. If the animals of the jungle could speak, no doubt they'd come up with something far more appropriate.'

'Basically, you're an ecologist,' observed Marion.

'No.' Harry chuckled, shook his head. 'I'm a dinosaur.'

'What is all this dinosaur nonsense?' pleaded Marion.

'Oh, nothing. Just a little foolishness. But tell me, Mrs Burns, do you think this article you're writing will make any difference to what's happening here?'

Marion shook her head. 'I lost that kind of naivety years

247

ago,' she replied. 'But somebody might stop to think about it for a few moments. That's got to be worth something surely?'

Harry did not offer a reply. He relit his cigar, which had gone out some time before, and sat quietly gazing out across his garden like a king surveying his domain. Marion stared at him for a few moments, but he had temporarily retreated to a world of his own making.

The sun was warm, and it was very quiet in the garden.

Chapter 23

Melissa strolled aimlessly along the road, her head down, her gaze fixed thoughtfully on its sunbaked surface. Her recent dip in the swimming pool had only served to cool her for a brief while. She had gone but a short distance in the direction of home and already she felt sticky and uncomfortable. There had been nobody at the pool she recognized, but she had geen grateful for that. She had simply floated on her back in the cool, blue-green depths and let her mind empty itself of all the nagging worries that had so recently assailed her.

She was glad that she was no longer feuding with Uncle Harry. Looking back she could scarcely believe that she had treated him so abominably; but he had been very kind to her the other night – cheerful, open, and so forgiving it had made her feel ashamed of herself. And to think it had all happened because of that stupid obsession with Bob Beresford, that ridiculous bet she had taken on with Victoria Lumly. How could she have allowed herself to be –

'Hey there? Want a lift?'

Melissa nearly jumped out of her skin. The vehicle had come up behind her but she'd been so lost in her thoughts that she hadn't even noticed it. She spun around and found herself staring into the tanned and smiling face of Bob Beresford.

'Uh . . . I . . .'

'Sorry, I didn't mean to startle you. Climb aboard!'

This was such an unexpected turn of events that Melissa was stunned by it. She stood at the roadside for several moments, debating what to do. Then she remembered a recent conversation with her mother and this provided her with an answer.

'No thanks, I think I'd rather walk.'

Now it was Bob's turn to register surprise.

'No?' he echoed incredulously. 'But why ever not? You surely don't want to walk all that way in this heat, do you?'

'Oh . . . I enjoy walking,' retorted Melissa. 'Thanks anyway!' And she turned and continued on her way. Bob stared after her for a minute. Then he started the engine and brought the Land Rover gently up alongside her.

'All right, I get the picture,' he said. 'You're still mad at me, right?'

'Mad at you, Mr Beresford? Why on earth should I be mad at you?'

'For not turning up at the pool that time when we arranged to meet.'

Melissa smiled. 'Oh, you mean that you didn't turn up either? And to think all this time I've been worried about standing you up, when in fact, neither of us bothered to go.'

'Well I . . . I was detained . . . I *wanted* to go – Here look, why don't you get in? It'll make it easier to talk.'

Melissa paused again, feigning indecision. Then just as Bob began to reach over to help her in, she recommenced walking.

'I really do enjoy walking, you know,' she announced airily.

The Land Rover cruised alongside of her again. Bob was beginning to look faintly harassed.

'Look, I said I was sorry,' he growled. 'Can't you see I'm trying to make it up with you?'

'Make *what* up?' Melissa directed a smile of sweet innocence in Bob's direction.

'It's all very well giving me the freeze-out treatment,' muttered Bob. 'I seem to remember you were far from cold the time we made the little appointment. In fact, the way I remember it, you were very friendly indeed.'

'You were rather friendly yourself,' retorted Melissa

sharply. 'But of course, that was before the people at Kampong Machis stole your tiger.'

Bob looked indignant.

'What? You surely don't think that's why I . . . ?'

Melissa shrugged. 'I did sort of get that impression,' she said, and she began to walk on again. This time she managed to travel some considerable distance before the Land Rover pulled alongside of her again. Bob looked rather shamefaced, like a child caught with his hand in the biscuit tin.

'I guess I owe you an apology,' he murmured uncomfortably. 'The fact is that you're right about the tiger. I think in many ways I've got a lot of growing up to do. It was just so important to me, that's all. And remember, at the time, I thought it was *the* tiger, the man-eater. But of course, old Sullivan was right all the time . . . and to think I nearly bit the poor old bastard's head off.'

'He doesn't bear a grudge. I was 'round there last night, the matter wasn't even mentioned. Really, I think he's forgotten about it.'

'I can hardly see how. Perhaps he's already done his growing up.' Bob sighed. 'But I keep thinking about something he said at the time. You remember, he told me it was my duty to go out and warn the villagers . . . he said that if I didn't, the next death would be on my conscience. Well, he was right about that too. I keep thinking that maybe, if I'd done as he said . . .'

'Oh, you mustn't think like that! You're the only one who's trying to do something about the tiger, after all. It's not your fault if he keeps eluding you.'

'Maybe not.' He glanced at Melissa hopefully. 'You sure you won't accept a lift? I'm going your way, you know.'

Melissa sighed. She could feel her resolve weakening by the moment. But really, wasn't it absolutely typical? Just when she had made up her mind to forget that the wretched man even existed . . .

'Alright,' she conceded at last. 'Just a lift. No strings attached, okay?'

'Sure, whatever you say!' Bob reached out and helped her into the passenger seat. 'It's good to be friends again,' he observed. Melissa stared at him, amazed by his simple code of ethics. 'He thinks everything's fine and dandy now!' she thought to herself bitterly. 'One simple apology and everything's as right as rain again. Honestly, the sheer impudence of the man . . .' For a moment she experienced a powerful desire to instruct him to hold on, while she clambered out, and calmly informed him that she wouldn't be his friend if he were the last man on earth; but then his handsome tanned face was smiling winningly at her and the Land Rover was accelerating away down the road. A second, more appealing notion formed itself in Melissa's mind. She would get Bob to take her home by a slightly more circuitous route than usual, a route that would take the vehicle past the front gate of Victoria Lumly's house, where, with any luck, the hideous Victoria, and perhaps even her drippy friend, Allison, would be sunbathing in the garden. The looks of sheer terror on the faces of her two archenemies would be the high spot of an otherwise tedious day, and if Bob behaved himself on the journey homewards. Melissa might . . . she just might . . . invite him to dinner on Saturday night.

Doctor Kalim tapped the end of his pencil repeatedly against the scarred wooden surface of his desk while he waited patiently for the young girl to stop crying. She was hunched up in her chair, a portrait of perfect misery, and she was sobbing her despair away into the large white pocket handkerchief that Kalim had lent her. Kalim found himself unable to go over and comfort her, he felt oddly remote from her despair. That was not to say that he did not pity her, it was just that over the years he had grown more and more accustomed to this scene. The first time the girl had visited him, he had known only too well that it would end this way. A shame. Such a pretty little thing. Eighteen years old and, at this moment in time, very confused.

Her sobbing had subsided a little and now she gazed imploringly up at him, her eyes thick with tears.

'I'm afraid there can be no mistake,' murmured the Doctor. 'You're two months pregnant. I am sorry that my diagnosis brings you no joy.'

Lim sniffed, nodded, dabbed at her eyes with the handkerchief. She had known in her heart that she was with child, but she had put off coming to a doctor for as long as possible, hoping that, like any other troublesome ill, the condition would simply go away. Now, the truth could be avoided no longer.

'I am . . . sorry, Doctor,' she murmured.

'Don't be. It's not your fault. And remember, it's not too late for the condition to be terminated – You understand my meaning?'

She nodded, but looked away, was unable to meet his gaze.

'You can . . . cut the baby out?' she said tonelessly.

'Abortion is a simple enough operation. You need be in hospital for no more than a day . . . but of course, it requires money.' He glanced at her enquiringly. 'Have you spoken to your parents of your suspicion?'

Lim shook her head.

'Well then, you must tell them now.'

'Oh, but I could not tell them! They would kill me!'

Doctor Kalim frowned.

'I doubt that very much,' he retorted. 'Oh, they will hardly be pleased of course, but I'm sure –' He broke off in mid-sentence, seeing from the look of determination on her pretty face that she would never take that course. 'Very well. Do you know who the father is?'

'Yes.'

Doctor Kalim looked at the forms in front of him. There it was in the girl's own laboured scrawl. Occupation: AMAH. How many times had he been obliged to go through this next series of questions?

'Is it your employer?'

The girl glanced away, reluctant to speak.

'I can assure you that anything you are telling me will be treated in the strictest of confidences. Now, come along. Is it your employer?'

Lim nodded.

'Is he British?'

'No. From Australia . . .'

'A white man, nonetheless. And have you told him

252

anything of your suspicions?'

'No, Doctor. I could not.'

'Well, then you must! You need have no fears on that account. Why you silly girl, what consideration has he displayed for your feelings? The story is always being the same! He is clearly to blame for your condition and now he must be made to be bearing the consequences. I have not the slightest doubt that once informed, he will be only too eager to pay for the abortion.'

Lim shook her head.

'But supposing I do not want the baby cut out of me?' she cried. 'I want to have the child. I want to be its mother!'

Kalim stared at her for several moments in utter despair.

'What are you saying?' he snapped. 'Foolish girl, do you think for one moment that your employer will be willing to marry you? Such men are not prepared to do what they call "the honourable thing."' The doctor got up from his desk and paced over to the window, his hands in his pockets. 'If you had been studying as I have, you would know that the history of the white man has always been one of domination and misuse of the people whose lands he appropriated. Why, not so very long ago, you would be lucky to escape being driven into the jungle to fend for yourself. The women of the colonies were there to be dishonoured and deflowered as the white man saw fit.' He turned away from the window and paced back to the desk. 'No doubt this man will soon be returning to his homeland. Are you honestly believing that he will want to take a Chinese wife home with him?'

Lim gazed helplessly at the surface of the desk.

'I . . . cannot say,' she stammered.

'Of course you cannot. Now, you go home and tell this man what he has done to you. Then tell him to come and see me, and we can be arranging this abortion. But do not be wasting much more time, or it will be too late! You understand? And no more foolish talk of keeping the child. One day you will be meeting a handsome young Chinese boy who you may talk into marrying you. But not if you are already having a baby tucked under your arm, do you see? Go along now, and send in the next patient.'

Lim nodded silently. She got up, gave her eyes a last wipe

with the handkerchief and placed it carefully on the desk. The doctor was sorting through his papers, he had already dismissed her from his mind. She gave a small shrug of resignation and moved slowly towards the door, her gaze fixed vacantly on the ground beneath her. She could picture Bob Tuan's face contorted with anger and disbelief, and she flinched involuntarily from the cutting edge of his outraged voice. She knew that despite Doctor Kalim's advice, she could never bring herself to tell Bob the truth. She would just have to hope and pray that he would offer to marry her. There seemed no other hope for her.

She let herself out of the office and drifted through the waiting room in a daze. She emerged into blazing hot sunshine and a cacophony of noisy traffic, and for the first time the realization hit her that as she travelled homewards, she was carrying a new life deep in the pit of her belly, a small soft formless thing that would grow day by day until it acquired the form of the baby she so badly wanted. Even at this early stage, she was determined that nobody would ever take this new life away from her. Come what may, she intended to be its mother.

Chapter 24

Harry tapped politely on the door of the spare room.

'Hello in there! Mrs Burns ... Marion? The dinner's served ...'

The door opened and Marion emerged. Harry stared at her for several moments in undisguised surprise. He had known that she intended taking a shower and changing her clothes before dinner, but he had not been prepared for such a transformation. She was wearing a blue silk evening dress, cut quite low at the neck, but still, Harry thought, tasteful. She had carefully brushed her short grey hair and had applied the merest touch of makeup to her eyes, emphasizing their lovely blue-grey tone. At her throat, she wore a single strand of natural pearls and she also sported a pair of matching earrings. The effect was uncanny but she looked five years younger and several pounds lighter than the woman who had arrived at the house earlier that morning. Harry hadn't realized how openly he was staring at her until Marion said defensively. 'Well, I don't wear khakis *all* the time, you know!'

Harry coughed self-consciously.

'Er . . . no, of course not. You look very . . .' He waved his hand ineffectively, realizing that he had forgotten how to go about giving compliments to a woman. He reddened slightly. 'Shall we er . . . go in?' he suggested lamely.

'Yes, let's! I'm absolutely ravenous.'

'Well, that's good. From what I saw going on in the kitchen earlier,' Pawn's prepared enough food to feed a regiment.' They strolled along the hallway and into the dining room. Pawn had laid out the feast on the teak dining table and it was the first time in many years that it had been laden with a meal worthy of its grandeur.

'Good lord,' said Marion softly. 'You weren't exaggerating, were you?'

If the meal had tasted only half as good as it looked it would still have been delicious. It was set out in typical Malay fashion, a plethora of small hot dishes from which the diner might choose at will. There were, of course, various curries, thick and fragrant with coriander and wild lime varying in their degrees of fierceness from a mild chicken mixture, pale and creamy with coconut milk, to a fiery green curry that was laced with chilies and peppercorns, only bearable to the most well-seasoned palate. There was the much milder *Nasi Goreng*, a delicious concoction of rice and prawns, lightly spiced and flecked with scraps of beaten egg. There was *Kari Kapitan*, shreds of tender chicken cooked with onions, chilies, yellow ginger and lemon juice. *Satay*, barbecued kebabs of beef soaked in a rich peanut sauce. *Laksa Assam*, fish and noodles flavoured with tamarind juice and *Nasi Kandar*, white rice ladled over with a piquant shellfish and vegetable sauce. For sweets, there was an equally magical array. Freshly sliced papaya and winter melon were a mouth-watering alternative to the hot curry dishes. There was a large platter of mangosteen, a succulent white fruit, sliced into thin segments and sprinkled with wild lime juice. Rambutans and chilled lychees in custard. And of course, the greatest delicacy of all, the magnificently malodorous durian in all its thick glory.

'Where do you start?' enquired Marion wonderingly.

'Start by sitting down,' Harry told her with a chuckle. He pulled out a chair for her and waited politely while she settled into it. Then he sat himself opposite her. He indicated a large champagne bucket filled with iced water. Inside it floated half a dozen cans of Tiger beer.

'I suppose it really ought to be wine,' he murmured. 'But you can't get hold of any decent stuff out here . . .'

Marion shook her head.

'I was raised on this stuff,' she assured him. 'I wouldn't dream of drinking anything else with dinner.' She surveyed the multitude of offerings in silent anticipation. 'Now then,' she mused thoughtfully. 'What shall we try first?' She reached out experimentally and lifted up a forkful of one of the milder curries, savouring its delicate aroma for a moment before putting it into her mouth. 'It's absolutely delicious,' she announced. 'You were right about Pawn. She's a treasure.'

The *amah* chose just this moment to bustle into the room, beaming all over her wizened face.

'I go now, Tuan. Hope you and Missy like dinner.'

'Pawn, this is the finest meal you've ever made,' said Harry.

'Thank you, Tuan!' The beam broadened into a wide grin and she bowed slightly from the waist. 'Now I go cook for own family,' she announced happily. 'You enjoy. I come 'morrow morning, wash dishes.' And she backed slowly out of the room, delighted by the praise she had received. She closed the door after her and a few minutes later the back door slammed and they glimpsed her tiny bent figure as she hurried down the driveway into the brief tropical twilight.

Harry poured Marion a glass of ice-cold beer.

'Cheers,' he said, and they both drank.

'Now, come along,' Marion urged him as he set down his glass. 'You'll be left at the starting gate, if you're not careful.'

'Hmm?'

256

'The food! You've not eaten a thing yet.'

'Well, that's easily fixed,' he replied. He took up his fork and spoon and set to the happy task with gusto. For the first time in ages, he felt that he had a keen enough appetite to do the meal justice. For several minutes, the two of them ate in silence, applying their full concentration to the enjoyment of the food. But then as the keen edge of their hunger diminished, they became more leisurely and soon enough, they fell into conversation.

'And what does your average tiger eat for dinner?' enquired Marion, as she reached out for a second helping of *Kari Kapitan*. 'When he's not chewing the leg off some unlucky native, that is.'

Harry smiled at the ghoulishness of her phrasing.

'Well, hereabouts, it's mostly wild pig . . . or at least, it should be, under normal conditions. But the fact is, there don't seem to be many around lately. Once upon a time, you couldn't take a stroll in the jungle without seeing several of them, but the last time I went out I didn't even see any evidence of them. Strange . . .'

'I believe Mr Kirby, up at the game department, mentioned something about that. Some disease apparently is killing off the wild pigs in Trengganu . . . though he's not sure about the cause. I got the impression he thought that it might be a man-made epidemic . . . pollution of some kind; but he was very vague . . .'

'Well, it wouldn't surprise me if he was right about that,' growled Harry bitterly. 'As far as the businessmen and developers are concerned, the jungle is just a temporary obstacle to be torn down at the earliest opportunity and replaced with highways and tower-blocks. It's sickening.'

'You sound bitter about it; and if it's any consolation, I agree with you entirely. But going back to the food thing. If there are no pigs left, what's next on the agenda?'

'Perhaps a *rusa* . . . oh, that's just a local name for the sambar deer. Of course, if this was India, they'd be number one on the menu, but they're nothing like as plentiful here. Then, perhaps a *gaur* calf, provided he can get it away from the parents without being trampled for his pains. After that . . . well, tigers are adaptable you know. Monkeys, crabs, fish, frogs, rats . . . if he's hungry enough, he'll eat them. But of course, it's around about that stage that the local cattle start to look very tempting. And where there are cattle, there are usually people. And the more they see of people, the more they are liable to realize that we're really a rather vulnerable and puny species. Rubber tappers are often the most likely victims. They work alone and they're often out at strange hours . . .'

'Oh yes, I remember one of our coolies being scared by a prowling tiger many years ago. It was difficult getting the men to go back to work after . . .'

'Coolies?' Harry gazed at her in puzzlement. 'I'm sorry, I don't . . .'

'My fault, I should explain. That's what I used to do before I took up journalism, you see. My husband owned a big plantation near Ipoh. Michael Burns, his name was. A Scotsman, naturally. He came out here just after the first war with the object of making his fortune and my goodness, he certainly succeeded. Brought a young and very green wife with him too.' She shook her head and smiled sadly. 'Honestly, I didn't have the first idea what to expect. I'd never been further than the next village up till then. Looking back, I sometimes wonder how I survived. But Michael was an adventurer of the old school, there was nothing too daunting for him. He thrived on difficulties, and we prospered because of it. We came through the second war battered but still intact and that's when the plantation really began to take off. We had a long and very happy marriage.'

Harry nodded. 'Uh . . . how long ago . . . did you say . . . ?'

'Oh, there's no need to be uncomfortable. Michael was always a plain speaker, he'd not be pleased if I were to beat around the bush on his behalf. He died a little over six years ago. He had a private plane and he was making a routine business trip to K.L. His plane exploded shortly after take-off and crashed into the jungle. At least it must have been a quick death . . . a search party was sent out to the wreckage, but I knew from the start there could be no hope of survival.'

'I see . . . I'm very . . .'

258

'Of course you are, but don't be!' She reached out and squeezed his hand reassuringly. 'It was all a long time ago, Harry. It's true what they say about time healing all wounds. *Then*, of course, I was desolate. I walked around inside my grief for several months, never going out, never seeing friends. It was the most miserable period in what had otherwise been a fairly full and very happy life. Grief is a strange companion, you know. There's a side of you that loves . . . really relishes . . . the awful Shakespearean tragedy of it all. That's not to say that the grief isn't real either . . . it's just that there's such an all pervading need to be *seen* to be suffering. You understand what I'm saying?'

'Yes. Yes, I think so.'

'Well, I let it ruin my life for quite some time; and then, one morning, it just occurred to me that Michael would have hated to see me that way. You know, he always used to say that the greatest gift I ever gave him was happiness. I could make him laugh any time of the day or night . . . even in the middle of a terrible row; and lord knows we had enough of those!' She smiled fondly, then shrugged. 'So that morning. I took a good long look around the big empty colonial-style house and the big empty gardens beyond and further on, the big empty plantations full of rubber trees that were slowly dripping money drip, drip, drip . . . into little tin cups and all for my benefit . . . and I realized that if I was ever going to pick up some of the pieces of my life, then I'd have to go right away from that place and start afresh. I was safe and secure, I had enough money to keep me in creature comforts for the rest of my life . . . but where was the challenge? Where was the motivation to carry on? I had no children to hand the estate on to . . . we'd tried for them, you understand, but I turned out to be absolutely barren I'm afraid. We bought a puppy instead and that seemed to suit us both very well, so we didn't worry about it unduly . . . the easy option, I supose, would have been to carry on. as the Memsahib, find myself a houseboy who doubled as a lover, consume a bottle of gin a day, and end up thoroughly hating myself. The other option was to find something else to occupy my time. But what to choose? I thought about it very carefully for at least an hour and then

I remembered what the green little Scottish girl had been doing when she married her wayfaring husband. Namely, working as a reporter on a tenth-rate local newspaper. I sat myself down there and then and I composed a letter to the *Straits Times*, explaining that I was the greatest feature writer in Malaya and that they would be totally insane if they didn't employ me. To my amazement, a few days later, I received a reply, asking me to send some samples of my work. Now, this took me very slightly unawares. I suppose at the back of my mind had existed the firm conviction that I was just whistling at the moon. Now I had to back up my idle boast with something of substance! I put together an article about the rubber industry . . . after all I had as much information as I needed for the research side. Of course, I neglected to mention that I was myself a plantation owner of some considerable experience, I wanted them to believe that all that gritty realism came from my sheer journalistic *expertise*. At any rate, the *Times* people liked it and used it, and it wasn't long before I had a politely worded letter offering me more permanent employment. I sold the estate, lock, stock and barrel, moved myself to a little bungalow in K.L., and never regretted it for one instant. And that, in a nutshell, is how I came to be sitting here with you, eating this delicious meal. Would you pass the *Satay*, please?'

'Uh . . . yes, of course.' Harry had become quietly mesmerized by her conversation. He was getting to like and admire this lady more and more by the moment. 'Er . . . another drink?' he asked her.

'Yes, I think that would be very nice,' she replied.

'You'd . . . never go back to the old way now, if the chance came up? I mean, now that you've proved to yourself that you can do it?'

She glanced at him slyly.

'Why, Mr Sullivan! Is this some kind of proposal?' she murmured.

Harry reddened.

'Good heavens, no! That is . . . I mean . . . I didn't –'

'Relax,' she chuckled. 'I was pulling your leg. No, I wouldn't dream of leaving journalism. It's my life now and a very full and rewarding one, I might add; also, taking it on

260

taught me a very important lesson in life, one that I wish a few more people would get into their heads.'

'Indeed? And what's that?'

'Simply that a person isn't automatically finished once they pass their fiftieth birthday. It's a widely held belief that such is the case, I'm afraid . . . and if others let you know it often enough, it's possible to get yourself into the state where you begin to believe it also. Hence, you end up doing nothing. You vegetate. But there's no reason . . . no reason in the world, why this should be the case. I, for instance, have produced the best, most fulfilling work of my life in the last few years. I may have grey hair, a weight problem and a slight case of deafness in one ear, but it doesn't mean I'm ready for the scrapheap yet.'

'Bravo! I'll drink to that,' said Harry, raising his glass.

The conversation continued late into the night. The bottles of Tiger beer were drained and as much of the food that could possibly be eaten was consumed. For Harry, the time passed all too quickly. He couldn't remember when he had last enjoyed female company so much; when Meg was still alive, he supposed. Ah, such a long, lonely eternity ago. Thinking of her made him lapse momentarily into a melancholic silence, and Marion took the opportunity to observe that it was really high time she went to bed. Harry nodded and, getting up from the table, he escorted her politely down the hallway and showed her where the bathroom was. Then, bidding her goodnight, he strolled back to carry out his nightly routine of securing the doors and windows, switching off the fans. Before locking the front door, he strolled out onto the verandah for a few moments. The insects had long since fallen silent and the night air was warm and fragrant with the smell of frangipani blossoms. Harry took a deep breath, let the air out in a long slow sigh. He felt rather sad now that the conversation was over. It had taken the presence of someone like Marion to make him realize how desperately lonely his life had been, for such a very long time. He shook his head, went back into the house, locking and bolting the door behind him. As he walked slowly out of the room, he switched off the fan and the lights. The big-bladed fan creaked gradually to a halt in the darkness. Harry moved on, along the hallway. The bathroom was empty now and he went in. While he was washing, he noticed several unfamiliar objects by the basin; a green toothbrush, a bottle of skin-lotion, and a smaller one of perfume. He picked them up, examined them thoughtfully and then placed them down again, with great care. He dried himself, glanced critically at his reflection in the mirror. His hair needed cutting before too long, he decided. He went out of the bathroom, switching off the light. He was surprised to see that his bedroom door was ajar and that the light was on within. He hurried to it, peered inside.

Marion was standing beside the dressing table, wearing a white cotton nightdress. She was gazing thoughtfully at the framed photograph of Meg. She glanced up as Harry entered.

'Your wife?' she enquired softly.

Harry nodded.

'She was a beauty,' observed Marion. Then she put the portrait face-down upon the top of the dressing table and turned to look searchingly at Harry. 'The way I see it,' she murmured, 'there are two things we can do. We can be terribly British and go to our own beds and pretend that the interest we have in each other doesn't exist . . . but that would be a lie. I am attracted to you, Harry Sullivan, and, from observing you this evening, I know that you are also attracted to me . . . On the other hand, we could, the two of us, have this night together with no ties and no expectations of any further developments. After all, we are two unattached, responsible, and fairly mature people . . .' She smiled wickedly. ' . . . and it could be great fun,' she concluded.

Harry scratched his head.

'But –' he began and then broke off, smiling sheepishly.

'Finish what you were going to say,' she told him.

'Well . . . I was just about to tell you . . . I'm sixty-seven years old.'

'And I'm fifty-nine, but does it really matter? I'm still a woman, you're still a man. You see, you've let yourself get brainwashed Harry. You're well past fifty, but you look just fine to me.'

Harry frowned, glanced at the floor.

'It's been such a long time,' he murmured. 'I wouldn't want to fail you . . .'

'Can you ride a bicycle?' she asked him unexpectedly.

'Why . . . yes? But what . . . ?'

'There are two things in life that you never forget how to do. That's the other one!'

Harry felt the corners of his mouth lifting into a grin. He shook his head in undisguised admiration.

'You make everything seem so easy . . . so right,' he said.

'I try to,' she replied. 'Anyway, what do you think?'

Harry thought for a moment. He gazed at Marion and he glanced at the overturned photograph on the dressing table and then he stared up at the restless circling fan suspended from the ceiling.

'Let's try,' he said simply. He closed the door behind him and, reaching out, killed the lights with a stroke of his hand.

Chapter 25

Harry woke abruptly from a deep, dreamless sleep. He lay for several moments, gazing up at the ceiling above his head. Then recollections of the previous night filtered back into his mind and he turned his head slightly to one side, but the bed next to him was empty. Marion had already risen.

Harry smiled. She had been right, of course, a man never really forgot how to make love and it had been so good, so fine, the soft reassuring warmth of another body pressed against his. But afterwards he had cried, sobbed like a child, feelings of guilt mingling with the powerful if temporary release from his years of loneliness. He had not cried like that since his father died, no, not even for Meg, though he had wanted to. It was plain that Marion Burns was to be a special influence on his life. He could scarcely believe that he had met her only a day ago and now here he was, jumping into bed like some promiscuous teenager. He chuckled to himself, wondering just exactly what the neighbours would have to say about the goings-on of the previous night were they to find out about them; no doubt tongues were already wagging over the mere presence of a woman in the house. Well, let them talk. Harry didn't give a damn for their opinions anyway.

He climbed out of bed, slipped into his bathrobe, and went out of the room into the hallway. Pawn's dusky little face popped out from the kitchen doorway.

'Good morning, Tuan!' she called with a knowing grin. Harry coughed uncomfortably. He hadn't realized how late it was.

'Good morning, Pawn,' he replied stiffly. 'Good meal last night. Excellent.' He coughed again and slipped into the bathroom, where he showered and shaved, humming tunelessly to himself. As always, he examined his reflection critically in the mirror, and this morning decided that he had the kind of face that a woman could possibly bring herself to love. He went back to his room, changed into his clothes and went out to face the heat of the day.

He found Marion on the verandah. She had placed a battered portable typewriter on the rattan table in front of her and was pounding away on it, her eyes screwed up tightly against the blaze of sunlight streaming in over the porch, a half-smoked cigar clenched determinedly in her mouth. She had reverted back to more practical dress, a loose khaki bush jacket and a large pair of knee-length shorts. She looked so unprepossessing that Harry was momentarily struck by the thought that this was the creature with whom he had just spent the night. It seemed somehow rather unlikely. He gave a loud 'ahem' to announce his presence but she was seemingly too intent on her work to give him any attention. He strolled nearer and glanced over her shoulder. The title of the article was, 'The Hunter and the Hunted.'

'Which is which?' enquired Harry politely.

Marion glanced up.

'Oh, good morning!' she exclaimed. 'It was such a lovely day, I thought I'd get up early and make a start . . . and as for the title, that's just the idea! From one point of view it's the tiger who's the hunter and the people from the *kampong* the hunted . . . but then one could just as easily say that it's the big property developers and highway builders who are the real hunters and our old tiger just another victim. It's that kind of double-edged view that I want to develop through the article.'

Harry nodded gravely.

'Well, I shall certainly be interested to read it when it's finished. Have you had any breakfast yet?'

'No, I thought I'd wait for you. Besides, after last night's feast, a cup of tea is about all I can manage.'

'Hmm. I'll second that. I'm sorry I slept so late . . .'

'Late nothing! It's barely nine o'clock. A man should be allowed the luxury of a good long snooze now and then, it does no harm whatsoever.'

Harry slipped into the chair next to her.

'It is a beautiful day, though,' he observed. 'Anything in particular you'd like to do?'

'Just get down several thousand words onto paper. I'm afraid I'm terrible company when the writing bug gets me.'

'Not a bit of it. You carry on and I'll order up some tea for us. Then I might just have that snooze you mentioned, right here on the porch . . .' He frowned. 'Marion, about last night. I want to . . . I . . . hardly know what to say . . .'

'Then don't say anything,' she announced brightly. 'Last night was last night. This morning is this morning. Where's the sense in harping on about the past?' She smiled, reached out and squeezed his hand gently. She was about to release her hold but Harry retained it, lifted the two hands up into the air, above the level of the rattan table.

'What *are* you doing?' asked Marion, puzzled.

'I just wanted to give the neighbours something to talk about,' replied Harry, with a chuckle.

The morning passed pleasantly enough, while Marion continued with her typing and Harry alternated between chatting, sipping tea, smoking cigars, and having forty winks. It was nice to wake up to the realization that, for the moment at least, he was not alone. The day was imbued with the brilliant clarity that was so much a feature of the later months of the Malay year. High up above jungle-clad hills, solitary fishing eagles drifted effortlessly on the air currents that would carry them out over the glittering sea to where their dinner waited. Harry sighed. To exchange these noble birds for a handful of dowdy sparrows shivering in the rain of Britain seemed to him to be the poorest trade he could imagine. He began to drift in the direction of sleep again but was interrupted prematurely by the puttering of a car exhaust. Opening his eyes, he recognized Dennis's car, easing to a halt by the garden gate, but it was actually Melissa who got out of the car and came strolling purposefully along the driveway. She hesitated a few moments when she saw an unfamiliar figure on the porch; but then she continued, no doubt intrigued by having stumbled onto something new.

'Good morning, Uncle Harry,' she called, well before she reached the porch.

'Good morning, Melissa. Isn't your father coming in?'

'No, we can't stop, we're on our way to the *amah*'s market to get some provisions. I was hoping I'd catch you in. I didn't know you had company though . . .' She glanced at Marion in silence, obviously waiting for an introduction.

'Ah . . . yes, well, Melissa, let me introduce Mrs Marion Burns. She's a journalist, she writes features for the *Straits Times*. She's going to be staying here for a few days. I'm er . . . helping her with the research . . .'

'Really? How exciting! And just what exactly are you writing about, Mrs Burns?'

'Tigers, my dear. Or more specifically, *the* tiger.'

Melissa nodded.

'Well, of course. I should have realized. There's nobody knows more about tigers than Uncle Harry.'

'So I've been told.' Marion turned to Harry. 'You didn't tell me that you had such a lovely niece,' she complained.

'Oh, but I haven't! I mean, she's not . . . she's not really my niece . . .'

'We're just good friends,' chuckled Melissa, with a sly wink.

'Oh, I see,' replied Marion, falling in with the joke. 'Well, Harry, I must say, you've got excellent taste!'

Harry coughed, reddened somewhat.

'Good heavens, Marion, you surely don't think . . . ?' He

266

realized that they were pulling his leg now and he lapsed into a silence, but not before Melissa had noticed his use of Marion's Christian name. 'Hello, hello,' she thought to herself. 'What's going on here then?'

'Well er . . . if you can't stay, then why –'

'To ask you to dinner, of course!' interrupted Melissa. 'We're having a little dinner party at our house tomorrow evening and, naturally, it wouldn't be any kind of a party without you, Uncle Harry . . . and since Mrs Burns will be staying with you for a few days, then she must come along too!'

Marion smiled.

'Well, I must say that's very kind of you,' she exclaimed.

'Not at all! It'll be a pleasure to have somebody new on the scene . . . and besides, it will save us having to fix up a date for Uncle Harry, won't it?' Melissa grinned mischievously. 'Also, Mrs Burns, it could be very useful for you in a professional sense . . .'

'Oh?'

'Yes, You'll be able to chat with our *other* resident tiger expert.'

'Oh no!' Harry's face fell. 'Don't tell me Beresford is going to be there?'

Marion glanced at Harry, intrigued by his reaction. Receiving no elaboration from that quarter, she returned her gaze to Melissa.

'Bob Beresford, Mrs Burns. The man who's doing his level best to shoot the man-eater. He happens to be a friend of mine.'

Marion nodded.

'Well, yes I'm sure that *will* be very useful.'

'As you may have noticed by Uncle Harry's reaction, the two of them don't get on particularly well, so if the evening ends in squabbling, I apologize in advance.'

'It sounds very interesting, I must say. I can hardly wait.' She glanced again at Harry, who had lapsed into a moody silence. 'That is, of course, if my host decides to go.'

'He'd better,' retorted Melissa, 'or he'll never hear the last of it!' A car horn blared in the silence of the day. 'Uh oh! I'd better run along or they'll be leaving without me. Tomorrow evening then, eight o'clock. It's informal, so don't dress up or anything. Lovely to meet you Mrs Burns, perhaps we'll have a chance to get to know each other better tomorrow.' And Melissa was off, racing up the driveway, anxious to tell her father about Uncle Harry's mysterious guest.

The *gaur* bull was nervous. He cropped away at the jungle vegetation, his jaws munching the ferns into green mush, but he kept raising his great horned head at regular intervals to glance this way and that into the surrounding trees. His flaring nostrils had caught no particular scent and there had been no calls from bird or monkey to alert him to any danger, but for all that he was edgy and could not totally abandon himself to the pleasures of eating. His mate did not share his caution. The graze here in the jungle clearing was just a little too lush and inviting for her to concentrate her attention on anything else, so she kept her head low, swinging it from side to side in slow rhythmic curves while her jaws and rough tongue tore up great big clumps of moist fragrant sustenance.

But it was not the cow that Haji was watching, nor the big, heavily muscled bull that grazed beside her, rather, it was the leggy six-month-old calf accompanying the pair that demanded the tiger's full attention. The trio had been something of a gift. Curled up asleep in the bushes, Haji's first notion of their presence had been the abrupt rasping of grass as it was torn from the ground. As luck would have it, he was positioned downwind of the beasts, and because of his lack of movement he had not been spotted by any jungle sentries.

Still, for all that, he had not exactly been handed his dinner on a plate. The bull was alerted by some strange chemistry to the fact that all was not well. The great curved horns on his head were capable of ripping Haji open from end to end, so it was necessary to ensure that there was some considerable distance between him and his more vulnerable offspring, if there was to be a chance of Haji bringing off the attack successfully. Luckily, there seemed to be some chance of this happening. The calf was impatient to

268

wander off on his own and seek his own graze. In the six months of his existence, he had yet to undergo a really frightening experience and this fact had made him a little cocksure, a little belligerent. He kept moving off across the clearing, his pink nose snuffling curiously amongst roots and grass, but each time he took more than half a dozen steps the bull would issue a low, guttural warning that would stop the calf in his tracks. However, after a few moments had elapsed, the calf would resume his course, one that was taking him nearer and nearer to the place where Haji was lying in wait.

Haji licked his lips in anticipation. If the hunting had been better, he might not even have considered so daring a raid, but the Uprights seemed to be very wary of him now. He hardly ever got the opportunity to catch one alone in the right place, at the right time, though he had been searching extensively. It was several days since anything more sustaining than marsh rats and frogs had entered his belly, and if his hunger grew any more intense he would be obliged to take on anything that came along, even the big bull if necessary. Here, there was at least a strong possibility of success. If he could get one good hold on the calf's throat, he could slip into the bushes through openings that would be far to small to admit the vengeful parents. Secure in there, he could feast to his heart's content, while the bull bellowed his rage to the wind. So Haji waited, keeping absolutely still, his long body pressed tight against the ground.

The calf's life had recently undergone a major change. He had spent the first months of it as a member of a sizable herd, and because of this he had received the best possible protection whenever danger was near. The adults would form themselves into a tightly packed circle with the youngsters locked securely in the middle, and then, lowering their heads, they would face the tiger (the only creature in these parts large enough to present a threat) with a near impenetrable wall of bristling horns. It was a very foolhardy animal indeed that ever chanced himself against such a terrible defence. But then, a month or so earlier, the sickness had come to the herd. Sudden, terrible, and debilitating, it had left grown bulls vomiting and bellowing, their bodies racked with pain, their hide covered in ugly, suppurating sores. Within hours, they would drop to the ground and no amount of nudging or lowing from their companions could entice them back up onto their shuddering legs. The herd moved on, leaving the sick behind them, and before death had settled on the *gaurs'* eyes, the carrion creatures of the jungle descended to take their share of the diseased flesh. In a matter of weeks, the herd had been completely decimated, cut back to just a few creatures. The calf was lucky in that his family was one of the very few to escape the sickness completely. Lacking a decisive leader, since the dominant bull had fallen some weeks back, the survivors had split up into small family groups and would remain that way until numbers increased sufficiently to facilitate the formation of another herd. Life for the calf was now a considerably more dangerous affair, but he had yet to realize it. He interpreted the gruff commands of his parents as overzealousness on their part and was determined to assert his own will. Glancing slyly at his father from time to time, he contrived to move gradually away from his parents' side. Every time the bull raised his huge head to stare in the direction of his offspring, the calf stood stock-still and cropped grass, giving the impression to his rather dull-witted father that he had not actually moved from the spot where he had last been standing. In this manner, the calf began to gradually put distance between his parents and himself and was well on the way to exploring the tangle of luxurious undergrowth that flanked the clearing.

Haji tensed himself, tiny muscles quivering on his shoulders and legs. He raised his body slightly so that it was just clear of the ground and focused his gaze on the calf completely now. He was anxious not to let his hunger make him too hasty. There would be a moment when everything was right, and then he would make his bid, not before. The calf was drawing nearer all the time, his brown eyes gazing directly at the bush where Haji was lying, but the shadows that dappled the tiger's hide made him melt completely into his surroundings.

The bull raised his head and gave a loud snort of warning.

The calf stopped, sank his head to crop the ground and the bull regarded him for several moments in glowering silence, aware at last of the considerable distance that separated them. Now the cow's head came up too and she added her own more plaintive voice to that of her mate. The calf stood his ground defiantly, refusing to come back to them. There was a brief silence. Haji waited, the calf's image trapped in the yellow orbs of his eyes, like a prehistoric insect in amber. Silently, he willed the calf to take another step closer . . .

Now the cow lowered her head and resumed her noisy ruminations, but her mate continued to stare challengingly at his disobedient offspring for several moments, an expression that threatened a powerful butt if it was not obeyed. The calf weakened a little. He knew only too well the force of his father's wrath, and now he lowered his head slightly, afraid to meet that terrible gaze. Reluctantly, the calf swung around, began to retrace his steps. Seeing this, the bull was satisfied. He put his own head down and resumed his meal.

Now! The moment had to be now, or it was lost forever! Haji froze the image in his mind, the calf in the midst of taking its first step away from him, the bull, nose to the ground, intent on tearing up a thick clump of ferns. The muscles in Haji's legs jolted like well-oiled machinery and shot him out from cover like a bullet from the barrel of a gun. His great front paws struck the ground, his back legs came in to power the leap that would carry him through the air onto the calf, who had heard the slight noise of the tiger's approach and was half turning around in a clumsy panic, not having the first idea of what to do to defend himself. In the fraction of a second that expired between leaps, Haji took careful aim and launched himself through the air.

It was the calf's own indecision that saved him. Urinating pathetically where he stood, his back legs gave way and he tipped sideways at the very instant that Haji's outstretched paws touched him. It was too late to adjust the angle of flight. Haji's claws gouged deep furrows in the calf's tender hide but impetus took the tiger over and across the body of

271

his intended victim to tumble in an ungainly heap amidst the undergrowth. With a roar of frustration, Haji thrashed back to his feet. The calf was flopping about helplessly on the ground, his vulnerable underbelly exposed, but a deafening bellow from the old bull's direction warned Haji that it was probably too late. There was a brief vision of a huge black shape bearing down on him, a pair of evil, curving horns. Instinctively, Haji flipped his body sideways and managed to avoid the full impact of the charge, but the thick part of one horn still caught him with a crippling sidelong blow to the ribs that drove all the breath out of his body. The force of it threw him sideways and he rolled over and over, several times, blasting out his pain and humiliation. The bull was not finished with him either. Wheeling around, it came back for another attempt. But this time, Haji wasn't prepared to give the creature an opportunity. Spotting a small opening in the bushes off to his left, the cat flung himself at it and vanished like a shadow into the half-light beyond.

The bull, maddened by the presence of a creature he hated most in the world, flung himself at the spot where the tiger's rump had been a moment before, pounding the bushes in a brutal senseless assault, until the undergrowth shook in every direction for some considerable distance. By the time the bull realized that his adversary had escaped, Haji was over a mile away, lying up in a bamboo thicket and licking the spot against his ribs where the bull's horn had carved a deep red stripe, a raw, stinging stripe that ran in the opposite direction to the ones that nature had given him.

Chapter 26

It being a Saturday, one of the nights that Harry habitually went to the Mess, the young *trishaw* boy turned up at the accustomed time and was surprised to find, that as well as a different destination, he had two passengers instead of the more usual one. Accepting this with his usual stolid shrug, he took a crumpled piece of paper from his back pocket, the worn stub of a pencil from behind his ear and placed another tick on his list.

'It ought to be two ticks tonight,' Harry reminded him. 'In fact, it really should be *five*, because this is a longer trip.'

The *trishaw* boy shook his head.

'Grandfather would not like,' he murmured. But after some careful thought, he did agree to put down an extra tick for Marion.

'Poor little devil,' whispered Marion as she eased her frame into the rather precarious seating. 'For carrying someone of my build, he should have a hundred ticks.'

Harry chuckled.

'Well, he's determined to work it off the honourable way, I'm afraid. At a dollar a trip, it's going to take a very long time.'

The *trishaw* glided them along remote jungle roads, the kerosene lamp shining brilliantly in the darkness. It was mercifully cool this evening and a lively breeze, fragrant with the scent of jacaranda and frangipani, rippled through the topmost fronds of the coconut palms. Off in the darkness, they could hear the restless sounds of waves crashing onto the beaches, far below. Nearer at hand, there was the weird rhythmic croaking of hundreds of tree frogs, the drone of a myriad unseen insects. Marion turned to gaze into the unfathomable green depths on the left-hand side of the road.

'I suppose he's out there somewhere,' she mused thoughtfully.

'Who?'

'Our tiger, of course. What do you imagine he's doing now Harry?'

'Oh, he's on the prowl, no doubt. They do most of their hunting at night.'

The *trishaw* boy took a deep breath and increased his rate of pedalling dramatically whizzing the rickety vehicle around a bend at such a terrifying rate that it threatened to tip over. Marion had an abrupt mental image of a lean striped shape loping silently along behind the *trishaw* and the idea was so horrible, she put it out of her mind instantly and did her very best not to think of it again. Both she and the *trishaw* boy were relieved to see the bright streetlights of their destination come into view, but Harry was lost for the moment in his own thoughts. The sight of a battered Land Rover parked outside Dennis's gates soon jerked him back to reality. He alighted and helped Marion to clamber out. The *trishaw* boy watched the two of them thoughtfully. The Tuan's female visitor was already the talk of the *kampong*, and he was as interested as anybody else to know what was going on.

'How Tuan get back?' he asked.

'Oh, that's alright. The Tuan at this house has promised to take me back in his motor car. Besides, it will be very late when we are ready to go. You'd best get back to your family.'

'Okay, Tuan. Have nice party. I go now!'

'Just a minute!' Marion stepped forward. She took a ten-dollar bill out of her purse and held it out to the boy. He stared at her bewildered for a moment.

'I not charge,' he protested.

'Just because you have a special arrangement with Tuan Sullivan, that doesn't mean that I have,' Marion told him. 'Besides, this isn't fare money. I noticed that your flip-flops are nearly worn through and everybody knows that a good *trishaw* man needs decent shoes to power him along.'

'But . . . I can buy many pairs flip-flops with this much . . .'

'I'm sure you'll think of other things you need . . . perhaps your mother would like a present?' suggested Marion.

The boy thought for a moment.

'She needs a new cooking pot,' he said hesitantly.

'Good! Well, you take this along and buy her one. Some new flip-flops too.' She pressed the bill into his hand, and after a few moments' hesitation he lowered his head slightly and crumpled the money into his pocket.

'Thank you, Missy,' he murmured. 'You good lady. I go now.' And with a brief wave he turned the *trishaw* around and headed back the way he had come. Harry and Marion stared after him for a few moments, until the swaying glow of his light was lost to them.

'Lovely boy,' murmured Marion. 'I hope he's safe out there in the dark . . .'

But Harry was already leading the way up the Tremaynes' drive.

'Let's get it over with,' he said flatly. He marched up to the front door and rang the bell. After a few moments' wait, the door opened and there stood Kate, wearing a simple white cotton dress.

'Hello, Harry,' she said. 'For once, you're the last person to arrive.' She smiled at Marion. 'And you must be M. Burns! I read your articles in the *Times* every week. I could hardly believe our luck when Melissa told us you were coming to dinner.' She took Marion's hand in hers and shook it warmly.

'Well, thank you, Mrs Tremayne, it was lovely of her to invite me.'

'Not at all, not at all . . .'

'Are you going to ask us in?' enquired Harry gruffly. 'Or would you like us to chat with you on the doorstep all night?'

Kate smiled.

'I see. It's going to be that sort of evening is it? Right, come along in and meet everybody.' She inclined her head closer to Harry, so she could talk in a quiet voice. 'We are going to do our very best to get on with Mr Beresford, aren't we?' she murmured.

'Well, of course!' retorted Harry acidly.

'Good. Just checking.'

They went in, along the hallway, to the sitting room, where they found Melissa and Bob Beresford deep in conversation and Dennis nursing a drink and staring vacantly into space. He leapt up as the newcomers entered and hurried over to them.

'Harry, old man! Nice to see you!' He was obliged to shout because of the presence of some loud rock music blaring out of the stereo. 'And er . . . Miss . . . er . . . *Burns*, isn't it?' He extended a hand awkwardly and Marion shook it.

'It's Mrs Burns, actually, but Marion will do fine,' she said. 'I'm very pleased to meet you.'

'Likewise. Can I get you a drink of something? We have sherry, martini . . .'

'Tiger beer, please, if you have any.'

'Oh yes, indeed we have!' Dennis glanced sideways at Melissa, who thus far had not so much as acknowledged the presence of the people she herself had invited. She was evidently far too enraptured by the conversation of Bob Beresford to even notice that they had arrived. 'Melissa,' he snapped. 'Can't you turn that row down a bit? I'm sure Mrs Burns doesn't want to be pounded by that terrible din . . .'

'This is at the top of the LP charts in Britain,' protested Melissa. 'Hello, Uncle Harry . . . Mrs Burns . . . besides. Daddy, if you knew the trouble I've had getting hold of a copy . . .'

'That's not the point, dear. Not everybody shares your questionable taste in music, you know.'

Marion stepped gracefully in to pour oil on troubled waters.

'Oh, don't turn it down on my account, Melissa. I rather like Jimi Hendrix.'

Melissa's jaw dropped wide open, as did Bob's, beside her.

'Golly, Mrs Burns . . . how . . . how the heck did . . .'

'An old fogey like me know about Jimi Hendrix?' chuckled Marion, completing the unfinished question. 'We don't all go around listening to Mantovani, you know!'

'Oh, gosh, no, I didn't mean . . . it's just unusual, that's all . . .'

Marion reached out and patted her shoulder reassuringly.

'I could go on to astonish you, Melissa. For instance, I could tell you that the *New Musical Express* recently described Jimi as a major force in the field of contemporary rock, also that his use of improvisation and his dynamic stage shows have set the old school on their heads . . .'

Now Melissa did reach out a hand to turn down the volume control. There was a look of awe on her face that suggested she was in the presence of some kind of divine being. Harry just stood where he was in amazement. It seemed that he was learning new things about Marion every time she opened her mouth. She was clearly delighted with the effect her words had produced.

'It's really quite straightforward,' she chuckled. 'You see,

276

Melissa, as well as writing weekly features for the *Times*, I also handle the music column. You may have read my article on Pink Floyd last week.'

'You? But . . . the music column is written by somebody called . . . Suzy Q.'

Marion took a little bow.

'That's me,' she announced. 'Or rather, it's one of several *noms de plume* I use. Incidentally Melissa, I get lots of review copies sent to me, more than I can possibly play. Perhaps I could send you some of them, when I get back to K.L.'

'Really? Wow, that would be fantastic!'

Dennis took hold of Harry's arm and steered him towards the kitchen.

'Come and give me a hand with the drinks,' he suggested.

'What? Oh . . . yes, of course.'

They went out of the room, leaving Melissa to introduce Bob to Marion. On the kitchen table were ranged a generous selection of drinks and the refrigerator was well stocked with cans of Tiger.

'I say,' murmured Dennis, 'she's marvellous, isn't she?'

'Who is?'

'Oh, don't play dumb with me! Marion, of course. How on earth did you come to be mixed up with her?'

Harry poured beer into a glass.

'Simple, really. She's writing about the tiger and she needed an expert. That's me. Cheers!'

'Yes, but Melissa told me that much,' complained Dennis.

'Nothing much else to tell, really.'

'Well, of *course* there is! Like . . . for instance, how did she come to be staying with you? You know, there's going to be all kinds of gossip flying around if you don't watch out.'

'Hmm, yes.' Harry smiled drily. 'Much of it from your direction I shouldn't wonder.'

'Not a bit of it, old chap!'

'Not much! Anyway, it's all quite above-board. There were no hotels in the area, so naturally Marion suggested that she stay at my place . . .'

'*She* suggested?' Dennis smiled, rubbed his chin thoughtfully. 'You know, she's got quite a way with her, that one.

277

You notice that she managed to get Melissa to turn that damned record down and that was without even asking her! I tell you what, old son, that's more than I can manage if I plead with her on my hands and knees.'

Harry nodded. 'Well, Marion is a . . . very interesting woman,' he said.

'What's that supposed to mean?'

Kate bustled into the kitchen.

'Come along, you two, there're people dying of thirst out there!' She paused, hands on hips, eyeing the two men suspiciously. 'Hello, hello, what's going on here?' she murmured. 'When you two get into a huddle, I know there's something fishy going on. Dennis, Marion's waiting for that drink.'

'Yes dear.' With a sigh of resignation, Dennis picked up the glass and went back into the sitting room, whereupon Kate closed in upon Harry.

'She's an absolute *beauty*, Harry! How did you come to be mixed up with her?'

Harry sighed. 'I think I've just had this conversation with your husband,' he said tiredly. 'The fact is that Marion and I are simply . . . collaborating on a newspaper article. There's nothing clandestine about it, I can assure you!'

'Well, of *course* not! I wasn't for one moment suggesting that . . .'

'Good. What are we having for dinner?'

'Well, it's a traditional British meal . . . to celebrate going home, really. I gave the *amah* a night off and made everything myself. We're going to have a prawn cocktail, then roast beef and Yorkshire pudding with all the trimmings, and finally, an apple pie and a lemon meringue. Oh dear, you *do* eat English food, don't you?'

'Yes, of course. Bit of a novelty these days, mind you . . .'

'Oh, I do hope everything's alright. Somehow, it all tastes different over here. Take a simple thing like a potato, for instance. It looks the same as normal, smells, peels, slices just the same. But the end result always *tastes* . . . foreign . . . if you know what I mean. Of course, I don't suppose you'd remember . . .' A furious hissing sound from the cooker told her that a panful of carrots was in the

278

process of boiling over. 'Uh oh! Excuse me!'

'Yes, well, you carry on, Kate. I'm sure everything will taste delightful. I'll go back and join the others.' He made his escape bid, before Kate could trap him and begin a full interrogation. Dennis he could easily handle, but his wife was rather more of an expert on these matters. He slipped out of the doorway and left his hostess to cope with the carrots.

The remainder of the time leading up to dinner passed without great incident. Harry and Dennis talked mostly about the Tremaynes' imminent departure to Britain. Now that the time was so close at hand, Dennis was experiencing very mixed feelings over the matter. While he was, for the most part, looking forward to his homecoming, there was a strong part of him that would miss Kuala Hitam and the regiment of which he had for so long been a part. Marion, meanwhile, was quietly weighing up Bob Beresford. She thought him an affable enough young fellow, rather attractive in a loose-limbed, macho sort of way. She could quite understand why Melissa was interested in him, a fact Marion had deduced from her first glance of the couple in conversation. But, she noted, there was a less agreeable side to the man, a swirling undercurrent of arrogance that he himself seemed unaware of. 'A man who's always had his own way,' she concluded. 'He may have a little growing up to do.' She had also noticed that the only two people who had not acknowledged each other's presence the whole evening were Harry and Bob. The feud between them was almost painful to behold and a person could spend hours looking into the reasons for it; but it seemed to her that, if anything, the resentment stemmed more from the older man than the younger. When Bob mentioned Harry, it was with a certain guarded reverence in his voice; he used exactly the same inflection a short while later, while mentioning his *father*.

'So that's it!' thought Marion. 'Bob sees Harry as a patriarch, the nearest thing to his dead father. He only wants to impress Harry, the same way any son seeks to impress his old man; and Harry, whether it's conscious or unconscious, is reacting *against* being placed into that mould. He doesn't want to be admired or consulted, he just wants to be left in peace ... so he snaps back, his resentment turns to dislike. Bob, in turn, having been rejected, goes along with the feud, but deep down that's not the way he feels at all. And the only way ... the only way he can prove himself, to Harry, to his father, to the world at large, is by *killing that damned tiger!*' Marion took a long rewarding drink of beer.

'I should have been a psychoanalyst,' she said aloud.

'Pardon?' enquired Bob, halting in mid-conversation.

Marion smiled sheepishly.

'People seem to like talking to me,' she said, by way of explanation. 'But do go on with what you were saying ...'

In the kitchen, Melissa was trying to explain to her mother that Uncle Harry was intending to wed Mrs Burns the very next day.

'I think he must have been pulling your leg, dear,' she replied calmly, as she poured batter into a tin tray.

'Well, don't say I didn't warn you, that's all!'

Half an hour later, everybody was seated at the long table in the dining room, and the meal was under way. Kate and Dennis sat at the far ends of the table, with Harry and Marion seated on one side of it and Bob and Melissa on the other. Thus far, the conversation had been sporadic and centred mainly on the food, which, despite tasting vaguely *foreign* as Kate had feared, was nonetheless rather successful.

'Of course, there are some people in Malaya who eat this kind of stuff all the time,' observed Kate. 'Really, they wouldn't dream of eating "local."'

'Damned disrespectful if you ask me,' muttered Harry. 'To go to a country and not eat the local delicacies ... well, it's ignorant. Of course, it's perfectly alright to remind oneself of your own traditions now and then ... but to completely ignore the ways of the people whose country you're sharing, that's just not on.'

'I couldn't agree more,' said Dennis, 'but honestly, you'd be surprised at the number of servicemen I come into contact with who will only eat English food – Did you know that they've opened another fish and chips shop on the coast road, just beyond the barracks?'

'Another one? Good lord . . .'

'Mind you, they're not short of customers, either. Every time I drive past, I see people queueing in there.'

Harry smiled grimly.

'Well, there won't be very many customers for them in a few weeks' time,' he pointed out. 'No doubt, they'll have to find something else to sell.'

'I've had fish and chips from there,' announced Melissa unexpectedly. 'I really enjoyed them.'

There was a brief, uncomfortable silence during which Melissa gazed rebelliously around the table, ignoring the admonishing glares of her parents.

'Well, I suppose once in a while isn't so bad,' murmured Dennis defensively.

'I've had them lots of times,' persisted Melissa. 'I can't see anything wrong with them myself.'

Marion hastily changed the subject. 'Mr Beresford, are you having much luck in your attempts to shoot the tiger?'

'Evidently not,' muttered Harry acidly, in a voice that was just loud enough to be heard by everyone present.

Bob frowned, shook his head. 'He's a clever old devil and no mistake; the nearest I've come to him is a couple of wild pot-shots in the dark. The fact is, *he's* come closer to getting me. Chased me up a tree the other night . . . or rather, he jumped into the tree in which my *machan* was fixed. He came sneaking up behind me. The first clue I had about his being there was turning around to see him staring me in the face.'

'My God!' Melissa was suitably impressed. 'How did you get away?'

'I shoved my rifle butt into his mouth. I know it sounds crazy, but it was the only thing I could do. He just snatched it out of my hands, flung it away; but luckily, it gave me a few seconds to climb and I went up that tree like a bloody monkey with his arse on fire.' Bob reddened a little, sensing a rebuff from Harry, but Marion threw back her head and laughed merrily.

'That's fantastic,' she gasped. 'But honestly, is it common for things like that to happen?'

'That I couldn't tell you Mrs Burns, I'm a self-confessed beginner in the tiger stakes ... but I'm sure Mr Sullivan there could tell you.'

Marion smiled. Again, the unmistakable traces of respect. She turned to Harry. 'Well?' she inquired.

Harry chewed methodically on a mouthful of food for a few minutes before replying. 'No, not common. But then, man-eating itself is comparatively rare. I've said before, this is a wily old brute. It's going to take a fair deal of wit ... and a large slice of luck ... to bring him down.'

'One way or another, I intend to do it,' replied Bob without hesitation; and Marion was slightly disturbed by the tone of rigid fanaticism in his voice.

'Of course,' offered Dennis, 'if you were to believe what the locals are saying, you could bag the man-eater very easily on two legs instead of four; though you'd have to be prepared to face a murder charge afterwards.' The three men chuckled and Marion stared from one to the other. Like any newspaper reporter, she resented not being in full possession of the facts.

'Somebody elucidate,' she demanded. 'Otherwise, heads will roll!'

'It's simply a bit of local legend,' explained Dennis. 'The local villagers are convinced that our man-eater is really a *weretiger*. No doubt, you're familiar with the myth?'

'Oh, surely. There's always some kind of changeling haunting every *kampong* ...'

'Ah, but in this case it's slightly different. There's a hot suspect – an old *bomoh* who lives out beyond Kampong Machis who has always claimed that he has the power to turn himself into a tiger. Of course, it's complete nonsense but ...'

'I'm not so sure,' interrupted Bob. Everybody turned to look at him in surprise, but he kept his head down over his plate and did not offer to elaborate on the subject. There was a brief, uncomfortable pause before Marion retrieved the thread of the conversation.

'What I can't understand, Mr Beresford, is why you and Mr Sullivan have never got together over this tiger business. I mean, surely with his experience and your prowess as a marksman . . .' It went abruptly very quiet at the table. The clatter of cutlery and the sound of munching jaws seemed painfully loud by comparison, but it was a reaction that Marion had expected, and she pursued the point with calm determination. 'I mean, when you consider that people are still being killed, surely any personal differences you might have should go by the board . . .'

'It's not a matter of personal differences, Marion,' said Harry softly. 'But as I've told Mr Beresford before, I'm far too old to go gallivanting about in the jungle after this tiger, it's as simple as that.'

'Too old?' murmured Marion tonelessly. 'That's not the impression I got last night.'

Harry reddened, fumbled with his knife and fork. Melissa clasped a napkin to her mouth to conceal a smirk, then winced as her mother kicked her on the shin beneath the table. 'Anybody like another drink?' asked Dennis uncomfortably but he got no reply. 'Yes . . . well I think I'll have one, anyway,' he muttered. Only Bob seemed to have missed the inference in Marion's remark.

'Mrs Burns, there's nothing I'd like better than to have Mr Sullivan along. I've tried often enough in the past, but he seems reluctant to get involved . . .'

'Not at all!' snapped Harry irritably. 'But it's been *years* since – '

'Surely tigers haven't changed all that much,' reasoned Marion.

Now Melissa joined the fray. 'I honestly think, Uncle Harry, that you should give it a try. We'll all be pulling out soon, what will happen if the man-eater is still at large?'

'Well, good heavens, girl, there are people up at the game department . . .'

'They haven't been much use so far, have they?'

'Well I . . .' Harry paused and gazed slowly around the table. Three of his fellow diners were obviously convinced. He gazed at Dennis for a moment.

'It *does* sound like a sensible suggestion, old chap,' reasoned Dennis.

Harry sighed. He glanced at Kate.

'Don't let people pressure you, Harry,' she said simply.

'Do what you feel is best.'

He smiled, nodded.

'Thank you for that, Kate,' he murmured. 'I'm glad to see somebody sympathizes.' He considered for a few moments, toying absentmindedly with the food on his plate. 'I suppose . . . if it was just in an *advisory* capacity . . . as a tracker, perhaps . . .' He switched the subject abruptly. 'You've been using a local boy as a tracker, I hear?'

'Ché? Yeah, smart kid. He helps me out when I'm working around his *kampong*. I know he learned the ropes from you though, Mr Sullivan . . .'

Harry nodded. 'I don't much like the idea of having the boy around that tiger. It's too dangerous. The cat's unpredictable, he's proved that much already.'

'Well now . . .' Bob grinned. 'If I had the master workin' with me, there'd be no need to employ the pupil, if you get my meaning.'

'Yes. Hmm. Well, I suppose it can't do any harm to give it *one* try.'

'Now you're talkin' Mr Sullivan! The next time that tiger makes a kill, I'll be calling for you. You just keep your gun oiled and polished, that's all.'

'I always have,' retorted Harry acidly.

But the atmosphere lifted dramatically with Harry's decision. It was as though the other diners had breathed an audible sigh of relief and the dinner party was able to progress much more smoothly after this point. For Marion, it was a minor victory, another step taken along the path to reforming Harry Sullivan. As far as she was concerned the more times a person told himself that he couldn't do a thing, the closer he came to complete vegetation. In Harry's case, the deterioration was well under way, though it should have been plain to any observer that he was frankly capable of a great deal more than he gave himself credit for. There was nothing for it but to bully him into action. After that, she could only hope that things would turn out for the best.

'Let's have a toast,' she said brightly, raising her glass. 'To the new partnership, and though I almost hate myself for saying it, to the death of the man-eater!' Everybody raised their glasses immediately, except Harry, who sat frowning

284

at his own drink for several moments. But then he shrugged, picked up his glass and tilted the cold beer to his lips, draining the contents in one long swallow. Melissa applauded happily.

'Let's all get drunk!' she suggested.

Marion smiled. It wasn't going to be such a bad party after all.

Chapter 27

Haji hardly dared to move. The Upright was not aware of him, he was sure of that. But the hunger was now so terrible, so all-consuming, the fear of missing yet another kill made the cat anxious to the point where his stalking was uncharacteristically timid. The fact that the Upright carried a black stick was also a worry; and then again there was the knowledge that this was not a stranger, but a tall pale Upright who often appeared at the scene of Haji's kill, the walker by night who concealed himself in the treetops and waited quietly for the tiger's approach. Haji knew his scent and it was this more than the other two factors that had kept him lying concealed for over an hour, watching and waiting for the right time.

Perhaps the Upright had learned that this was the place where Haji had made his unsuccessful attack on the *gaur* calf the previous day. Now, a sleek white goat was tethered in the centre of the small clearing. It was grazing calmly, unaware that it was being observed. The Upright, meanwhile, was gazing up into a large Kapok tree and barking instructions at two smaller, duskier companions, who were roping some kind of wooden contraption into place. The Upright's black stick hung carelessly across his shoulder, and he had one of the small white twigs in his mouth that gave out a strong smell of burning. He was no more than ten feet away from the place where Haji was lying.

The ball of emptiness in Haji's guts contracted spasmodically, and he ran his tongue nervously around the inside of his mouth. Already his strength was depleted. If another day were to pass without sustenance, he would surely sicken and die.

An abrupt feeling of decisiveness came to him. He raised himself slightly until his body was just clear of the ground. He fixed his gaze intently on a dark sweat stain that ran down the back of the Upright's loose-fitting tawny skin; he let the image burn into his vision until he had excluded everything else that surrounded him, until he saw nothing before him but the tall straight back of his next victim. He let a swift terrible rage burn up inside him, pushing aside the doubts and fears that had so far held him back. He came out of cover in a swift terrible run, an engine of destruction, a harbinger of death.

One of the dark Uprights screamed a desperate alarm from the shelter of the tree. The pale Upright whipped around, and for an instant Haji registered the white round face of his prey, frozen in a grimace of shock and terror. Then the face swooped nearer as Haji's legs propelled him upwards, the face was a great screaming moon that tumbled earthwards as Haji's jaws closed around the vulnerable throat beneath it. The black stick went clattering uselessly away, and the Upright could do little more than aim a few puny blows at the head of his assailant before his life hissed briefly from the gash in his ruptured neck. He shuddered violently for a few moments, his arms still hitting out ineffectually. Then he went abruptly limp, flopped back onto the ground and was still.

The Upright's two companions gibbered and shrieked like a pair of apes in the tree-fork, and Haji let go of the carcass for a moment to direct a great shattering roar in their general direction. With gasps of terror, they launched themselves higher into the treetops, their momentary bravado forgotten as they realized they were still within reach of a leap. In the confusion, one of the Uprights lost his footing, slipped, and came plummeting earthwards, to land with a heavy thud six feet from Haji's side. The tiger took an involuntary step back, then roared again, sending a blast of power and the stink of raw meat full into the face of the Upright, who promptly fainted.

Haji gazed at the fallen creature for a moment, then

286

padded over to him and gave him an exploratory sniff. There was no blood on the man, and luckily for him Haji simply did not associate him with the idea of food. Instead, he moved back to the meat he had already slain, gripped it firmly by the neck and began to drag it away from the scene of the kill. Hanging from a precariously slender branch, the remaining Upright gazed down, wide-eyed in amazement, scarcely believing the scene he had just witnessed. The tiger vanished into the bushes, taking the body of the Tuan with him; nevertheless, the man wisely allowed several minutes to elapse before he clambered down from the tree to revive his uninjured and incredibly lucky comrade. This accomplished, the two men headed for their *kampong*, screaming at the top of their lungs.

Harry put down the manuscript with an air of finality. He nodded. 'It's good,' he said simply. 'Very good.'

'It's only the rough draft,' Marion reminded him.

'Nevertheless, I think it's just right. You've stated all the angles very effectively, and the strongest point is that you've managed to evoke sympathy for the tiger while admitting that he must be killed.'

Marion smiled. 'Ah good, I'm glad you saw that in it. It was one of the points I was worried about . . .' She reached out, took the manuscript back from him, patted it softly. 'I shall have to have this in to my editor by tomorrow afternoon,' she told him. 'Means I'll have to be moving on tomorrow morning . . .'

'Oh.' Harry gazed thoughtfully at the rattan table. He had of course expected this, but had forced himself not to think about it. 'Must you . . . go quite so soon? I thought tomorrow, we might . . .'

She stilled him with a wave of her hand.

'Harry, it's my job. I *have* to go.'

He nodded, glumly. 'Yes, well of course . . .' He shrugged ineffectually. 'If that's the way the land lies, who am I to say different? But look here, surely one more day couldn't make that much – '

He broke off in alarm as a familiar vehicle came lurching dangerously up the street and slowed to a dusty, noisy halt at Harry's garden gate. An equally familiar figure leapt from the driver's seat and, in his haste to enter the garden, actually vaulted the gate and came running breathlessly up the path.

'Beresford! What the hell is the meaning. . . ?'

Bob waved him to silence.

'No time, Mr Sullivan, no time! Run and get your gear quickly, there's been another killing over by Kampong Wau. Only happened a couple of hours ago, I just got the news.'

Harry sat there, staring indignantly at the Australian. He was not in the mood to go racing off into the jungle and he silently cursed the agreement he'd made the night before. Perhaps though, if he could stall for time, the impatient Aussie might give up and be on his way.

'Now look here, Beresford; I know last night I agreed to come along, but how was I to know it would happen so soon? I . . . I haven't even got my kit sorted out yet and besides . . .'

Once again, Bob waved him to silence.

'I think you'll *want* to come along with me, Mr Sullivan,' he said. 'See, it wasn't some stranger who got killed this time. It was Mike Kirby.'

'Mike . . .' Harry's eyes widened in momentary disbelief. Then they narrowed suspiciously. 'There must be some mistake,' he murmured. 'Mike wouldn't be that careless. He's been hunting those jungles for years – He . . .'

Bob shook his head adamantly.

'Believe me, it's no mistake, Mr Sullivan. I've talked to the boys who were with him. He was setting up a *machan* and the cat came right up behind him. Poor bugger didn't have a chance. Now . . . are you coming, or do I go without you?'

Harry frowned, glanced at his feet.

'I'll get my things together,' he said, and getting up from his seat he strode into the house. Bob sat himself down impatiently on the steps of the verandah to wait.

'Mike Kirby,' mused Marion sadly. 'I've only met him once, but he struck me as such a *capable* man . . .'

Bob shrugged. 'It only takes one mistake, Mrs Burns. Besides, he had no reason to suppose the cat would sneak up on him at a time like that. It might just as easily have

288

been me.'

Marion frowned. She reminded herself that it was her own interference that had got Harry involved in this venture.

'Take care out there,' she murmured. '*Both* of you.'

'Ah, don't worry on that score, Mrs Burns. I'm not about to do anything stupid at this stage of the game. And I reckon Mr Sullivan knows how to take care of himself.'

Marion nodded.

'I hope so,' she said softly, and she gazed out across the hot silent expanse of the garden, wishing she could explain the sudden terrible fear that had settled in her heart.

It was cramped and uncomfortably hot up on the *machan*. Harry and Bob sat side by side, sweating profusely in the dank heat of the night. They were both in foul tempers, though up till now the older man had managed to suffer in silence, sitting up as rigid and unmoving as a dummy behind the thick screens of foliage he had so painstakingly erected, his rifle resting across one knee. Bob sneaked a glance at him and wondered how in the hell he could keep himself so still. Ever since calling at Harry's house, the Australian had regretted the idea. Firstly, the old man had taken so long to get himself ready; after nearly an hour's delay, he had emerged from the bungalow looking like the Great White Sahib himself, resplendent in two layers of clothing, a waterproof jacket worn over a thick khaki shirt, puttees, long drill trousers, and a battered jungle hat. Then he had spent what seemed an eternity packing odds and ends into a light haversack and an even longer one saying good-bye to Mrs Burns. By the time they were ready to drive away, Bob was positively screaming with impatience.

Finding the kill was a relatively smooth affair. The old man had followed up the pugmarks with commendable efficiency, but by the time they reached the hideous remains fo Mike Kirby's body, the tiger had eaten his fill and moved on. At this point, Harry insisted on saying a few prayers over the body, a gesture that Bob found quite pointless and merely a waste of valuable time. Next, Harry organized the two accompanying Malays into setting up the *machan*, and if he had been difficult before, now he was absolutely unbearable in his attention to detail. For one thing, he would not allow the Malays to gather wood and camouflaging from anywhere nearer than half a mile away; also, the exact positioning of the platform seemed of great importance to him, and he was continually ordering the builders to shift it an inch or so to the left or right. Meanwhile Bob paced restlessly up and down, cursing bitterly beneath his breath. When at long last the *machan* was erected to Harry's complete satisfaction, it was nearly dusk and the Malays scrambled off in the direction of their *kampong*, casting nervous glances over their shoulders as they went.

It was with a sigh of relief that Bob clambered up into position, but once Harry was beside him the older man issued a terse order.

'Don't forget now, not a sound, nor a movement if you can possibly help it. If you have anything to communicate, use handsignals.' Since then, the old man had not spoken so much as a word. Three hours had crept leadenly by with not the slightest interruption by any creature larger than the inevitable mosquitos of which there seemed to be thousands tonight. Bob felt as if he were being eaten alive and had begun to realize that shorts and bare arms were not the best outfit for night hunting, but he had been in such a hurry earlier on it had simply not occurred to him to call home and pick up something more substantial. Now the maddening itch of tiny jaws on every bit of exposed flesh was making him wriggle on the hard wooden seat like an agitated monkey. He kept slipping out a hand to slyly scratch a particularly irritating area, but each time he did so he received an indignant glare from his companion. At last, Harry was motivated to fumble in his haversack and pass a small bottle over to Bob. The Australian lifted the cap and sniffed at it exploratively.

'Strewth!' he gasped. 'What's this?'

'Sssh!' hissed Harry. 'Insect repellent. Put it on and shut up.'

So that was the smell that had been puzzling Bob all night; the old man must have plastered himself with the stuff. This explained why he had taken so long getting ready and also why he was able to keep so still. Bob was hardly surprised that the stuff was so effective, it smelt so bad it was liable to repel anything that came within range. Still, anything was better than the misery he was currently being subjected to. He began to daub the vile stuff discreetly over his arms and legs.

Harry watched the operation in silent disdain. For his part, he could scarcely credit a grown man coming out into the jungle in dress that was better suited to a day at the beach, and the fellow was such an infernal fidget it was a wonder that he had ever taken up hunting in the first place. There was much more to the business than simply being a good shot, but perhaps nobody had ever pointed this out to him.

Harry looked away, across the moonlit clearing below him. Through the tiny slit he had allowed himself in the covering foliage, he could see quite clearly the half-eaten corpse of his former friend. It was somehow hard to accept that this mangled hunk of naked flesh was Mike Kirby, the man with whom Harry had passed many a happy hour over the years. It made Harry feel cheap and degraded to sit up like this, using Mike as the bait in a trap; indeed, the first impulse upon finding the body had been to give it a decent burial. But the necessity of killing the tiger before it struck again had outweighed the demands of decency and a simple prayer service had had to suffice. Mike had no real family, at least that was a blessing. A bachelor, his parents long since dead, there would be nobody to mourn him. Harry wondered glumly if it would be like that for him too. With the Tremaynes gone to England, there would only be old Pawn . . . perhaps Ché . . . and Marion, he supposed. He might never see her again after tomorrow, but he knew that she would feel something when she heard of his death. He felt abruptly annoyed that he should be forced to spend the last night of her stay sitting up a tree in the middle of the jungle with a boorish Australian at his side. Life could be very unjust sometimes.

He started violently as a brilliant light flared up from just beside him.

'What the –' He stared at Bob in disbelief. The

confounded man had just lit a cigarette.

'Sorry, Mr Sullivan, but I was gasping.'

'You!' Harry gave a formless exclamation of disgust. 'Gaahhh! Don't you realize, you must have alerted every bloody animal for miles around!'

'Hey, calm down a bit, Mr Sullivan. It was only for a moment!'

'Good God, man, it's quite plain to me why you've never managed to kill this bloody tiger, if that's any sample of your bushcraft. Well, I've had enough of this fiasco; I'm going home!'

'Hold on, you can't give up that easily.'

'Oh, can't I? Well, we'll just see about that . . .'

'Look, I'll put the cigarette out, how about that?'

'You oaf! After the noise we've been making, do you honestly think the t – '

Harry broke off in mid-sentence as an abrupt flash of light and a loud detonation ripped through the bushes, several hundred yards to their left. Mingled with the noise was another sound, a deep shattering roar of animal power that faded abruptly as the echoes of the crash subsided.

'What the fuck was that?' yelled Bob, the cigarette dropping from his twitching fingers. 'Some kind of shot, wasn't it?'

'Yes, but I thought I heard – '

'Come on, let's find out!' Flicking on the torch on his gun barrel, Bob was thrashing down the tree, kicking the flimsy camouflage to bits.

'Just a minute!' snapped Harry angrily. 'Don't go blundering off into the dark, you fool!' He snapped on his own torch and followed the Australian at a slightly more dignified pace, his gun held ready to fire at anything that might come lunging out of the darkness. He could hear the man's voice yelling recklessly back through the trees and just occasionally he caught a glimpse of Bob's lanky body flailing through the bushes, his bare legs shockingly white in the torchlight.

'Over this way, Mr Sullivan. I think it came from . . . owww!'

'Beresford!' Harry leapt forward. 'What's wrong? Beresford?'

'Aww shit, I'm alright . . . just tripped over a branch!' And he was off again, moving off to the left. 'It's close now, I can smell cordite . . .'

'Beresford, will you please calm down and be cautious?' shouted Harry desperately. 'I'm sure I heard the tiger just now.'

'Yeah, me too, me too . . . that's why . . . Jesus!'

'What is it? What've you found?'

At last Harry caught up with his reckless companion. The Australian was examining a gun, that was jammed into the low fork of a tree. In the glow of the torch, Harry could see that it was an ancient rusted 12-bore shotgun. The barrel was still smoking, and it was pointed along a well-worn cattle trail. A length of cord was attached to the trigger, and this led off into the darkness further along the trail.

'An old-fashioned tiger trap,' muttered Harry. 'One of the locals must have got fed up waiting for you to finish off the man-eater.'

'Looks like it. These things are illegal, aren't they?'

'Very.'

'The thing is . . . did it work?' There was a strong hint of dread in Bob's voice. It was clear to Harry in that instant, that the Australian hoped the cat had escaped. He obviously believed that *he* was destined to shoot the tiger, he and nobody else. His expression was fearful as he shone his torch in the direction of the length of cord.

'My God!' His face drained of colour. 'What the hell is that?'

Now Harry added his own torch beam to the glow of light. Lying face up on the ground was a man, a naked man. Hardly believing their eyes, the two hunters approached the body. There *was* no face. The blast of the shotgun had dashed that away, leaving a mask of red pulp and a rapidly spreading pool of crimson oozing out on either side. But Bob could tell very easily who it was. The totally bald head and a pair of elaborate carved bone earrings were instantly recognizable.

'Good Christ, it's the *bomoh!* The *bomoh* from Kampong Machis . . .'

Harry nodded dumbly.

'But hell, Mr Sullivan, what was he doing out here . . . in the dark?'

Harry stepped forward and pushed the toe of his boot against something that lay beside the body. It was the freshly killed body of a mouse deer. There were deep red wounds sunk into its twisted neck.

'He must have been carrying this,' muttered Harry. He turned and glanced back at the gun barrel. 'On his hands and knees,' he added.

'What?' Bob stared at him. 'What do you mean?'

Harry pointed. 'That gun is no more than three feet off the ground, wouldn't you say? If he'd been standing upright, the blast would have hit him in the legs . . . so, he must have been moving along on his hands and knees.'

'Jesus – Are . . . are you saying . . . ?'

'I'm not saying anything, Mr Beresford. But it does look rather strange, doesn't it? And we both heard a tiger roar when the gun went off.'

Bob shook his head slowly from side to side, comprehending but not wanting to accept so outrageous an idea. 'No!' he said firmly. 'That's impossible. That's the craziest thing I *ever* heard.'

Harry shrugged.

'I wouldn't know about that. All I know is that a man's been killed and we'd better head back to Kampong Wau and report an accident. But I'll tell you something. The locals are going to have enough gossip to keep them going for months, once the news of this gets out. Come on, we'd better get going. I'm afraid that our hunting's over for tonight.' Harry had insisted that the Land Rover should be left parked at the *kampong*.

Bob stood his ground for a few moments, gazing from the corpse to the shotgun and back again, over and over, and at the same time, repeating the word 'impossible' to himself in a voice that was slow and toneless. He was glad he was not the policeman who would have the task of finding a suitable explanation for the mystery. Besides, Mr Sullivan had been right about one thing: They had both heard a tiger roar. There was no disputing that.

294

Bob turned and hurried after the bobbing glow of Harry's torch.

'What are you going to say?' he demanded.

'Nothing much. I'll let them work it out for themselves. I'm damned if I can think of anything.'

Bob frowned.

'Well, there's one thing for sure. After tonight, I'm giving up on the *machan*, it's a waste of time. The next kill happens, I'm going after that striped bastard on foot.'

'Don't be a damned fool,' replied Harry scornfully. 'You do that and you're liable to wind up as dead as Mike Kirby. He was a more experienced man than you, my friend, and look how it ended up for him.'

Bob shrugged. 'I don't care. Somebody's got to stop that cat before it causes any more damage, and with Mike gone, it's going to have to be me.'

Harry smiled wryly.

'Tell me something,' he murmured. 'What would you do if that damned tiger dropped down dead from old age before you got a chance to put a bullet in him?'

'He won't do that,' retorted Bob sullenly. But he fell silent and did not speak again through the long gloomy trek back to Kampong Machis.

Chapter 28

Marion's few belongings were packed into the blue Volkswagen, the sun was well up on the eastern horizon, and it was clearly time for her to go. She walked slowly along the driveway with Harry strolling awkwardly beside her. They had both been dreading this moment.

'It's another beautiful morning,' observed Marion lamely.

Harry nodded.

'I wish you didn't have to go quite so soon,' he murmured. 'Things will seem quiet here without you.'

'That could be a blessing,' she said.

'No, I don't think so.'

She squeezed his arm affectionately.

'Oh, come along you old sourpuss! You've got an expression on your face like a mourner at an English funeral. We'll see each other again . . .'

'Will we?' He sounded unconvinced.

'Here . . .' She took a plain brown envelope from her pocket and handed it to him. He gazed at it blankly.

'What's this?' he enquired.

'My address and phone number in K.L. Anytime you care to look me up, that's where I'll be. There'll always be a place for you to stay, Harry . . .' She gazed at him suspiciously. 'Not that I believe for one moment that you'll actually make the effort to get out there and see me.'

'I haven't been up to K.L. in years,' muttered Harry.

'All the more reason why you should get off your backside and come along! And of course, when work permits me to get up here and see you, I'll be more than glad to return the favour. Remember, you've got a lot more free time than me.'

'You'll be due for retirement soon, won't you?'

She chuckled, shook her head. 'When my newspaper decides they want to be rid of me, they'll have a fight on their hands,' she told him. 'As far as I'm concerned, the only person who is qualified to judge when my usefulness is past is myself. Incidentally, thanks for the story about the *bomoh* and the gun-trap. It's just about the most fantastic thing I've ever heard . . .'

'Will you use it?'

'Maybe as a piece of fiction. I can't see it working any other way, can you?' She glanced at her wristwatch. 'I really must go now, if I'm going to submit this copy on time.'

He nodded, reached out his hand to bid her a formal farewell, but she brushed his hand aside and moved forward, to touch her lips against the roughness of his suntanned cheek.

'Till next we meet,' she whispered. 'Remember now. Come and visit.' And she stepped back to the Volkswagen, opened the door, and climbed in. She slammed the door shut, wound the window down, and gave him a brief wave. 'Good-bye Harry. Thanks for everything!' Then the car was accelerating away along the street, kicking up a thin haze of

296

dust from the sunbaked surface of the road. Harry stood, staring glumly after it, shielding the glare from his eyes with the palm of one hand. The car rounded the curve of the road and Marion waved briefly, before vanishing from sight. After a few moments, the distinctive rumble of the Volkswagen's engine faded into distance.

Harry sighed, gazed at the brown envelope in his hand. He crumpled it into one of his pockets and, turning, he went in through the gateway and along the drive, his face expressionless. Somewhere, off in the treetops at the end of the garden, a brainfever bird was singing its maddening phrase over and over, the shrillness of its call an insolent intrusion into the otherwise silent morning. Harry climbed the steps to the verandah and went on through, into the shade of the house.

It had never seemed so big and empty before.

'That's the most fantastic story I've ever heard,' announced Melissa. 'I think somebody was putting you on.'

Bob shook his head. 'A pretty drastic practical joke though,' he observed. 'The *bomoh* is dead sure enough, and the local police are on the lookout for whoever set that gun-trap. I guess the charge will be manslaughter. Still, it's like Mr Sullivan said. If he'd been walking upright, the shot wouldn't have – '

'Let's not talk about it anymore, Bob. Makes me feel queasy.' She raised her glass of gin fizz. 'Let's get drunk,' she suggested recklessly.

'I already am!' he confessed. He glanced around the deserted confines of the Mess. Besides Melissa and himself, there were two other people drinking at the far end of the bar, who even now seemed on the point of leaving. 'Jesus, why did we come here?' he murmured. 'It's dead. Why don't we go into Kuala Trengganu? There's a few nightclubs there, we could do it in style.'

Melissa shook her head.

'I've got a better idea. We could get a few cans of drink and then we could just ride out somewhere. The beach would be a nice idea. Might be a bit cooler.'

Bob's face lit up at the notion.

'Yeah . . . sounds great to me.' He glanced at his watch. 'You have to be home any particular time?'

She shook her head.

'Not me. I'm a big girl now.' Melissa looked directly into Bob's eyes for a minute and then glanced quickly away.

'Right,' he murmured. 'That's what we'll do then. Cheers!' He raised his own glass and they both drank. 'I'll go and get Trimani to organize us some booze. Don't go away now!' And he was gone, hurrying off in the direction of the bar.

Melissa smiled triumphantly. She'd hooked him this time, sure enough. She could almost visualize the frustrated look of defeat on Victoria Lumly's face as the silver medallion was submitted for inspection. The whole thing would be doubly satisfying since the wretched monster so obviously believed she was in the clear now. Melissa would demand payment right there and then, on the spot. It would all be so very, very rewarding! With a grin, Melissa drained the last of her gin.

A peculiar warmth was spreading through her, and she felt pleasantly woozy. Even the grim, deserted surroundings of the Mess looked agreeable to her right now. She stared up at the snarling tiger's head above the door and she roared at it herself, curving her fingers into mock claws. The tiger seemed to momentarily register surprise and she stifled a giggle with her hand.

'Bloody silly tiger,' she murmured. 'If you'd changed back into a man in time, Uncle Harry would be a convicted murderer by now.' The idea seemed incredibly funny all of a sudden, and a vivid impression of Uncle Harry, dressed in a convict's suit, glumly sewing mailbags, made her giggle even more helplessly than before. A hand squeezed her shoulder. It was Bob, with a paper bag full of drink tucked under his arm.

'Hey, what's up with you?' he inquired.

'Nothing! Nothing at all. Let's go, shall we?' She clambered rather unsteadily to her feet, and Bob was obliged to support her with his free hand.

'Here, you *are* drunk!'

'I'm nothing of the kind,' she informed him, with mock

298

indignation. 'I'm just very slightly tipsy, that's all.'

He laughed.

'Well, whatever, you'd better take it easy. We don't want to spoil the rest of the evening, do we?' He gazed at her meaningfully and she laughed again.

'Why, Mr Beresford,' she murmured. 'I haven't the slightest idea what you're talking about. Come on, let's make a move! This place is the pits!'

The pair of them made a noisy and rather undignified exit but there was nobody to witness it, only the silent and melancholic Trimani, who was glumly polishing the already sparkling bar-top with a spotless white duster.

'Cheer up, Trim!' chuckled Bob, as he moved past. 'It might never happen.'

Trimani forced an unconvincing smile.

'It already has,' he replied tonelessly. 'Good night, Tuan. Good night, Missy.'

'Poor Trimani,' observed Melissa as she weaved out onto the steps. 'For him, it's nearly over . . .'

'Come on, I'll race you to the car!' interrupted Bob. He loped down the steps and she raced after him, catching him up just as he reached the Land Rover. He turned to face her as she approached and then his arms were tight around her, his mouth was on hers, and they were kissing with a fierce, eager desperation, in the half light of the car park.

It was Melissa who broke away first.

'Not here, Bob, somebody might see us . . .' Her voice was husky with suppressed passion. 'Later . . . by the beach . . .' He reached for her again, but she nimbly evaded his grasp and clambered up into the passenger seat. 'Bob, behave yourself!' she told him firmly. 'Otherwise you can just take me right home, this minute.'

'Alright, alright, take it easy. Let's go.' He climbed up beside her. 'I know a quiet little cove where nobody will disturb us.' He gunned the engine and accelerated abruptly forward, throwing out one arm to support Melissa as she swayed backwards. They roared out of the car park. Glancing back at the lonely white building, Melissa thought that she had never seen it so forlorn. The Land Rover swung out onto the coast road and Bob pushed the accelerator pedal down to the floorboards. A great rush of fragrant humid air blasted into Melissa's face, blowing her hair back behind her in a tangled flurry. She rummaged around on the floor for a moment, found the cans of beer, and opened two of them, sending twin plumes of chilled froth spattering out in their wake. She passed a drink to Bob and took a long swallow herself.

'Where are we going exactly?' she yelled, for the wind was snatching her breath away.

'Wait and see,' he retorted, with a mischievous grin. He leaned the Land Rover into a tight bend and powered into the straight, the engine protesting every inch of the way. Melissa winced, but kept a brave face for Bob's benefit. 'Not going too fast, am I?' he yelled.

Melissa shook her head.

'I like going fast,' she replied, and instantly regretted it as he took this for an excuse to drive even more recklessly. Up ahead the road took an abrupt rise, where it crossed a paddy field. The Land Rover zoomed upwards into the air, seemingly leaving Melissa's stomach somewhere back along the road. Then it came crashing down with a force that shook every bone in her body. She took another pull at her beer and clung grimly on, hoping desperately that Bob would tire of the game before very much longer.

Happily, the journey was not a long one. A few miles further along the road, Bob turned off along a deserted track and took the vehicle bumping and lurching along for some distance, through ranks of scrub jungle. Unexpectedly, the ground dropped away to a long silvery stretch of beach and an endless vista of dark blue ocean lapping tirelessly in to meet the shore. The sea air smelled fresh and cool after the humid dankness of the drive.

'This is beautiful,' sighed Melissa. 'How come I've never found this beach?'

'It's not that well-known,' murmured Bob. 'Apparently, the leathery turtles come to lay their eggs here, at a certain time of the year. The locals know about it and those are the only times you're liable to see people on this beach.'

'With our luck, it'll be tonight,' giggled Melissa. She turned to gaze at him enquiringly. 'Who told you about this place, Bob? Who brought you here first? Was it your *amah*, perhaps?'

'My . . .' He glanced at her in surprise, then looked away again, reddening slightly beneath his tan. 'What makes you say that?'

'Oh . . . it's just that I heard you had . . . a thing for your little Chinese maid, that's all. It's nothing to be ashamed about, you know. Lots of men . . .'

'The only girl I've got a *thing* about is you,' he told her. 'You don't want to believe everything you hear, my girl.' He edged closer to her, slipped an arm across her shoulder. 'You start spreading gossip like that,' he whispered, 'and I'm going to have to be very . . . strict . . . with you.'

She laughed.

'Strict in what way?' she demanded.

'Well, now, I just might have to – ' But she leaped from the vehicle and fled giggling along the beach, galvanized by the touch of his hand on the soft flesh of her thigh. 'Goddammit, come back here,' he shouted impatiently.

'No!' she shrieked defiantly. 'You'll have to catch me first! I'm the tiger and you, you're the great white hunter. When you catch me . . . I'm all yours!'

Bob swore colourfully. His frustration was rapidly getting the better of him, but he clambered out of the Land Rover and went racing after her, his long legs rapidly eating up the distance between them. They sped along the beach in silence for a moment, both of them sweating in the heat of the night. Sensing that she was losing the race, Melissa veered right towards the surf but Bob hardly faltered for a moment. Then they were crashing through the shallows, their feet exploding the restless surface of the water into shattered mirrors of flying foam. Steadying himself, Bob lunged forward in a well-timed flying tackle and the two of them went down into the shallows a bundle of flailing arms and legs. He grasped Melissa around the waist and dragged her out of the water, onto the damp, firm sand higher up. She was laughing uncontrollably and Bob could see the firm outline of her young body beneath the flimsy wet dress. He pulled her roughly against him and gazed at her face for a moment. In the moonlight, it looked oddly white, almost doll-like. The salt water had dissolved her mascara, and it was running in two trails from her eyes. Her mouth was open, he could see her firm white teeth. Desire shivered through him.

'I've caught you now,' he said hoarsely. 'You're mine. I can do anything I want with you.'

Melissa stopped laughing. She returned his gaze and then she relaxed in his arms, became passive. She did not resist as Bob's mouth closed on hers like a vice or as his fumbling hands began to pluck at the buttons on the front of her dress. She was both fearful and exhilarated now that the moment she had worked so hard for was at hand. She lay gazing up at the deep vastness of the night sky, only dimly aware of Bob's impatient hands as he fumbled with her clothing. She could scarcely control her own breathing. After what seemed an eternity of waiting, his handsome tanned face moved into the range of her vision. She was momentarily perturbed by a strange expression in his eyes, a cold ruthless aggression that she had never seen before . . . but she dismissed the idea. Nothing would spoil the perfection of this moment. Nothing.

She held her breath, savouring the moment: the warm perfumed air, the restless pounding of surf on sand a few yards behind her. In the darkness, she could see the glint of moonlight on the bullet-shaped pendant that hung around his tanned neck. She reached up a hand to finger it inquisitively. Afterwards, perhaps she would ask him for it. It would be a keepsake, a love token . . .

And then suddenly, inexplicably, pain tore through her, making her gasp, such was its intensity. A sharp, wrenching pain deep inside her, it felt like she was being violated with a knife.

'Bob!' she cried. 'Oh Bob, no, stop, stop! It hurts!'

'Don't be bloody silly! Just relax, it'll pass in a moment.'

But it did not pass. It simply got worse by the second. Melissa began to struggle. Inadvertently, without her even knowing it, her hand clenched tightly around the silver neck chain and snapped it, pulling it free.

'Bob, oh God, please, *no!*' The horror of the situation overcame her now, driving away the last numbing traces of

302

the alcohol in her system. All she could see was his face above her. The expression on it was that of a beast: feral, leering, gazing fixedly ahead, it seemed to possess not one iota of humanity. It occurred to Melissa in one horrible flash of conviction, that the man who was supposed to be making love to her was barely even aware of her presence, of her *participation* in the act. He was making love to himself; and she ... she could only lie there in miserable, helpless subjugation, praying for it to be finished.

The sound of the waves crashing onto the beach intruded into Melissa's confusion as the last of her tears subsided. She was dimly aware of Bob, sitting on the beach some distance away from her. His back was turned to her as if in disgust.

'What was all that fuss about?' he asked at last.

She sat up, glared at him, and with a great deal of effort she managed to calm herself enough to spit out a reply.

'You beast!' she sobbed. 'You filthy ... horrible – ' Words failed her. She was not schooled enough in the language of curses to articulate her real feelings.

'Hey, hey, steady on! What's the matter?'

'Don't you know? You were hurting me. I asked you to stop ... I begged you to, but you just carried on with it. Why?'

'It always hurts the first time,' he replied noncommitally.

'Oh I see. Something of an expert on the subject are we?'

'There's no need to be sarcastic,' he retorted. Seeming to dismiss the subject, he reached down and carefully removed something limp and glistening from his body, tossing it carelessly aside. Melissa felt abruptly nauseous.

'I want to go home,' she announced flatly. She stood up, collected her panties from the sand where they had fallen, and began to walk away from Bob, back towards the waiting Land Rover. She felt soiled, cheapened by the sordid abruptness of the encounter. What had happened to the romance, for God's sake? It had been nothing more than a squalid fumbling rut on the beach. She thought how Bob would boast of the exploit to his drinking friends and the shame of it brought fresh tears to her eyes. She lifted a hand

303

to wipe them away, and for the first time she became aware that she was holding something in her clenched fist. She opened her hand and gazed at the object blankly for a moment. It was the bullet-shaped pendant.

'Look, what's the hurry?' demanded Bob. He stumbled after her, pulling his trousers back up around his skinny legs. 'It's early yet. Let's have a few drinks. I tell you, it won't hurt half as much *the next time* . . .'

Melissa's eyes narrowed and she closed her fist back around the pendant. She whirled back to face him.

'What makes you think there'll be a next time?' she cried bitterly. 'You arrogant swine, you're disgusting.'

He could not have looked more shocked if she had struck him full in the face.

'Well . . . that's charming, isn't it?' he complained. The two of them were nearing the Land Rover now and he hurried forward, as if to bar her path. 'I take you out, give you a good time . . .'

'Give yourself a good time, more like!' She shook her head. The wooziness that a short while earlier had seemed so enjoyable had given way to a harsher, more disagreeable shifting sensation in the pit of her stomach. She took a deep breath and tried to push unsteadily past Bob, but he grabbed her shoulder and pushed her back again. 'Look,' she told him firmly. 'I want to go home.'

'All in good time, my girl,' he told her, as he fumbled for his cigarettes. 'Don't you think you're laying it on a bit strong, Melissa? After all, you're not the only reluctant virgin in the world, let's face it!'

'I'm not even *that* now,' she observed.

He lit his cigarette, blew a thick cloud of smoke into her face.

'The way I see it, you should be grateful to me. After all, I've saved you a lot of trouble for your wedding night. It means you'll be able to enjoy sex from the word go. No husband wants the bother of having to break his missus in, believe me. It's better when they come along already saddle-trained.'

Melissa gazed at him in silence for a moment. She wondered vaguely how she could have been so blind to his

304

failings. It was as though she was seeing him for the first time, and it was not a particularly agreeable sight.

'My God,' she murmured. 'I knew you were arrogant, but I just didn't realize how deep it went. You really are a nasty piece of work, aren't you?'

'Oh, I see . . . well, that's typical isn't it. Absolutely bloody typical! A girl gives you the old come-on . . . and let's get it straight, darlin', it was *you* that was asking for the business all the way along . . . then, once you've had a little bit, you find you don't like it so much and you start acting all high and mighty. Well, it won't wash, Melissa, because I know just what sort of girl you are. Believe me, in a week or so, you'll be sniffing around again, offering it to me on a plate, and by then I won't even be bothered to reach out and grab some.'

Melissa nodded sadly.

'You're right about one thing, Bob. It was me that wanted . . . the business, as you so delicately describe it . . . and I certainly got what I was asking for, didn't I? Believe me, I won't make the same mistake in a hurry. Because I'll tell you the sort of girl I am, Mr Lady-Killer Beresford. I'm the sort of girl who learns by her mistakes . . . so the next time I bump into a stupid insufferable pig disguised as a human being, I'll know better than to even give him the time of day . . .' She reeled aside and stumbled over to the Land Rover, rested her weight against it. The turbulence in her stomach was rapidly worsening and she realized with a sensation of abject resignation that she was going to be sick. It seemed a fitting end for the events of the evening. 'Please take me home,' she wailed miserably.

'I'll take you when I'm good and ready,' he retorted tonelessly. He stood there, his hands jammed into his pockets and the cigarette trailing from his lips, while he stared thoughtfully out to sea. There was a long uncomfortable silence, during which the pounding of waves in the middle distance seemed to rise to a crashing crescendo.

When Bob spoke again, his voice was quieter, more considerate.

'Look, alright . . . maybe I was a bit hard on you. I suppose it must be difficult the first time. But it's crazy to fight like this, isn't it? The two of us, we've only got a week or so left. Surely we can work it out. If we could just . . .'

The rest of his words seemed to fade into distance as a terrible queasiness filled Melissa's stomach. She gasped for air a couple of times and then she began to heave violently. She dropped to her knees beside the Land Rover and craned forward, her eyes blurring with tears. And the sickness came streaming up from her belly and out of her mouth and nostrils, spattering onto the sand in thick spurts. It was as though she was ridding herself of the poison she had accumulated over the evening – not just the drink, but the disappointment and shame instilled by her brief and pathetic union with Bob Beresford. She was dimly aware of his voice talking soothingly somewhere behind her, and there was the brief touch of his hand on her shoulder, but she felt quite indifferent to his presence now.

'Leave me alone,' she groaned at one point, and the hand and the voice were gone. She went on, grimly ridding herself of the last vestiges of the sickness that had so abruptly taken her; meanwhile, she had the presence of mind to keep her hand grasped tightly around the bullet-shaped pendant, telling herself that it was better to come through the ordeal with something to show for it than nothing at all.

Finished at last, she slumped down beside the Land Rover, taking long deep breaths of the cool sea air down into her scoured lungs. After a while, Bob came back from wherever it was he had wandered. Without exchanging a word, the two of them clambered into the Land Rover and drove homewards in silence.

Chapter 29

Melissa moved slowly along the street. Behind the twin screens of the sunglasses she wore, her eyes flitted restlessly left and right, as though afraid that somebody might be observing her; worse still, that somebody might know the dark secret of the silver pendant that she carried in the pocket of her shorts. She felt sure that Bob must have missed it by now, and she had spent a sleepless night anticipating a knock at the door of her parents' house and Bob's angry voice demanding the return of his good luck charm. But, happily, the event had not occurred. Now it was early morning, the sun had already driven the people from the streets and Melissa was heading for a long-arranged assignation, followed only by the thin black wraith that was her shadow.

Her parting with Bob the previous night had been swift and terrible. He had leaned over and attempted to plant a kiss on her cheek. She had brought her hand across his face with all the strength she could muster and had then stalked grimly into the house, where she had needed all her powers of imagination to spin her parents a convincing enough yarn to account for her dishevelled appearance. She was not sure how convinced they were at the end of it all, but anything was better than the truth. Her parents were fairly broad-minded as far as the species went, but they certainly drew the line at screwing on the beach, that much was for sure. So she had mumbled some hopeless story about falling into the sea after attempting to balance on a slippery rock. Her parents had exchanged looks and gone ominously quiet, and Melissa had taken the opportunity to shower and go straight to bed. This morning she had been up and about uncharacteristically early. The old saying about things look better in the morning could not be applied in this instance. She still felt desolate about her own stupidity, and the conviction that she had been somehow cheapened and soiled by the incident would not go away. She had spent a long time under the shower, scrubbing and soaping every inch of her body, and it was while she was preoccupied in this way that the realization first came to her that she had been raped. The word itself was shocking, but what else could one call it? It was true that initially she had been receptive to his advances, but she had made it plain that she wished him to go no further. By then it was far too late. He was stronger than her and intent on achieving his own aims. There was nothing she could do but submit to him. She had been raped on the sands of that idyllic little Malaysian beach and nothing could ever alter the fact. She used to laugh at the few girls in school who prized their virginity as some wonderful commodity, but now she thought she understood.

Melissa moved on, past the rows of identical gardens that flanked her route. Many of them were deserted now. The last occupants of the small white bungalows had already fled to their cool homelands, but here and there small groups of sunbathers lay spread out on garish sun-beds, taking the opportunity to soak up the last bit of real sunshine they were likely to see for quite some time. Melissa came to a halt outside a certain garden. Within, on the parched stretch of lawn, Victoria Lumly lay sunning herself in a ridiculously skimpy red bikini. Alongside of her, Allison Weathers did likewise, clad in a rather more sensible black number. Beside them, a transistor radio was spilling out the latest chart songs from Great Britain, and on a small portable table two tall glasses of Coke shimmered with helpings of crushed ice. Melissa stood watching them for a moment. Her initial impression was of a basking hippopotamus, sharing its favourite grazing spot with a huge stick insect.

The girls glanced up in surprise as the gate creaked open. They too were wearing shades and the three sets of secretive eyes gazed impassively at each other.

'Oh,' said Victoria at last. 'It's you, Melissa.' Her voice was flat and resentful, almost as if she had guessed the purpose of the visit. 'Haven't seen you for ages . . .'

'No, I've been busy.' Melissa strolled slowly into the garden. She glanced off towards the house, where the shadowy figure of Mrs Lumly waved briefly from the kitchen. 'Getting your panic tan in, I see,' she observed coolly. By this, she was, of course, referring to the mass of blotchy red freckles that covered every square inch of Victoria's body. 'Who knows, if you lie there long enough, you just might manage to mass them all in together?'

Victoria didn't bat an eyelid.

'That's always the problem for those of us with more *sensitive* skin,' she mused sweetly. 'Of course, there are those people with skin so *tough*, they could tan themselves with a blowtorch.' Beside her, Allison gave a brief giggle of amusement.

'Oh, I can recommend that treatment,' retorted Melissa sharply. 'You should try it some time.' She slid her hand into her pocket and let the tips of her fingers caress the hard cool shape of the pendant. She would not produce it just yet. She was savouring her triumph. 'When are you two shipping out?' she enquired.

'I'm leaving the day after tomorrow,' announced Allison glumly. 'Victoria's got another three weeks, lucky devil!'

'My goodness. What will you two do without each other?' wondered Melissa. 'The old team breaking up, eh? Why, it'll be like . . . Bogart without Bacall . . . Peaches without Cream . . . Mutt without Jeff.'

Victoria glanced up irritably.

'I hope you realize there's not much time left for that money you owe me,' she snapped.

'Money?' Melissa gazed down blankly at her reclining enemy. 'What money would that be, Vicky dear?'

'You know bloody well what money!'

'Yes,' agreed Allison. 'It's not fair, Melissa Tremayne! I'm a witness to the bet you made and you agreed to pay up. Victoria's got a piece of paper that *you* signed, and I think trying to back out of it is really mean of you.'

'Oh . . . that bet! Yes, but if you remember, Victoria, I was allowed until three days before I left. By my reckoning, that still leaves me – '

'What difference does that make?' interrupted Victoria sourly. 'The fact is, if you were going to come through with something, you would by now. You're all talk, Melissa, that's your trouble. Let's face it, you just can't accept that you've lost and you're playing for time.' She sat up on her sun-bed. 'And you needn't think I've forgotten that you upped that bet the last time I saw you.'

'That's right, I did, didn't I? Let me see now . . . how much was it again?'

'Fifty dollars! And any time you're ready to bring it over, I'm ready to go out and spend it. Let's face it, Melissa, anybody who doesn't keep up their part of a bet, isn't worth knowing.'

'I do agree with you,' said Melissa calmly. 'That's why I

know that you'll be ready to do the decent thing . . .' And she pulled the pendant from her pocket with a flourish and let it dangle in front of Victoria's shaded eyes.

There was a brief, terrible silence; then Allison wailed, 'She's got it, Vicky! She's won the bet!'

'I can see that, you ass!' growled Victoria. She snatched the pendant from Melissa and peered at it suspiciously. 'But how are we to know this is the real one? As far as I know, she could have bought this herself in Kuala Trengganu . . .'

Melissa gave a derisive laugh. 'I must say, Victoria, your faith in me is absolutely touching! Anyway, there's some sort of inscription on it that you can barely make out – For goodness sake, you can see how old it is. So . . . when you're ready, I'll have that fifty dollars please.'

'I . . . don't have it right this minute,' murmured Victoria ungraciously. 'You'll have to give me a day or so. I'll get it for you, don't worry . . .' She handed the pendant back to Melissa and then gazed at her thoughtfully for a few minutes. 'So . . .' she muttered at last. 'You finally rolled Bob Beresford, did you?' She paused for a moment to allow Allison's inevitable bout of giggling to subside. 'What was he like?' she enquired.

'What do you mean?'

'I mean . . . how was he?' She removed her sunglasses for a moment and gave Melissa a slow, sly wink. 'Was he a good lover?'

'Oh yes, tell us all about it!' enthused Allison, sitting up and taking notice. 'Where did you do it? At his house?'

'What, with his pretty little *amah* there?' chuckled Victoria. 'I should say not, eh Melissa! She'd be a bit upset about it, especially with things the way they are now.' She laughed and Allison joined her. The remark was so obviously intended as some kind of taunt that Melissa ignored the bait and simply kept talking.

'We went down to the beach if you must know. It was all very romantic, the stars and the waves beating on the sand. We'd had a few drinks of course . . .'

'Oh, so that's how you talked him into it!'

'Believe it or not, Victoria, he didn't need any persuading. Quite the opposite actually. He's been after me for quite

310

some time now.'

'Hmm. Well that's not the impression I got, dear. Especially that time at the swimming pool when he didn't show up.'

'Yes, well it might take a little while to get them hooked, but they always go down in the end.'

'Tell that to Bob's *amah!*' said Victoria; and she and Allison laughed again. Melissa was beginning to get very irritated by the constant innuendos.

'What the hell are you on about?' she demanded.

'Us?' Victoria feigned wide-eyed innocence. 'Oh nothing, dear, nothing at all. We're not ones to spread gossip are we, Allison?'

'I should say not!' But the girls continued to smile in a smug, knowing way that was beginning to make Melissa very angry indeed.

'And you know,' continued Victoria. 'Melissa never wants to hear these things either. Why, the last time I saw her, I offered to tell her all about it, but she just didn't want to know. Oh, Melissa, I do hope you were careful when you were *earning* your fifty dollars – I mean, I hope you made sure that Bob took er . . . precautions . . . since he so obviously didn't bother taking any with Lim . . .'

'What? What was that?'

'Oh, now look, I've gone and let the cat out of the bag!' Victoria replaced her sunglasses and settled herself back down on the sun-bed. 'Well, anyway, it's nothing that need concern you, Melissa. After all, you must have known he was the reckless type . . .'

'Are you saying that Bob's *amah* is pregnant?' demanded Melissa, her temper building to a slow steady simmer.

'So the grapevine says . . . of course, the really funny thing is that everybody knows about it. Everybody but Bob, that is.' She laughed briefly. 'To be honest with you, Melissa, that last time I was going to tell you about it, I wasn't really sure. *Then*, it was only a rumour. But now it's an ugly fact, I'm afraid. Lim made the mistake of confiding in Mrs Hoskin's *amah* and she told Mrs Blair's *amah*, then Mrs Blair's . . .

'Yes, alright, Victoria, I get the general idea.'

311

'Still, you've done alright for yourself, Melissa. A night of passion with Bob Beresford *and* you got paid for it. Actually, fifty dollars for one night is pretty good by standards, I should think. Plus, with any luck you won't end up like poor Lim, holding the baby. I bet Bob won't tell her about what went on between you either . . .'

An abrupt and all encompassing redness erupted in Melissa's head, a rage so sudden and so powerful that she was barely aware of her own actions. One moment she was standing gazing impassively down at Victoria's plump, reclining body; the next, she was leaning forward over the sun-bed, clawing viciously at the girl's unprotected face. Victoria gave a loud, indignant squeal of protest. Her sunglasses flew off and she twisted sideways away from Melissa's unexpected attack, upsetting the sun-bed and sending her heavy body sprawling onto the dry grass.

'Allison, stop her! She's gone berserk!'

Melissa ignored the protests. She dropped down onto Victoria's plump back like a vengeful cat and began to tear at the wretched girl's face and hair. Allison came stumbling warily into the fray. She began to tug ineffectually at Melissa's arm in a pathetic attempt to pull her away, and she received a slap in the face for her trouble. With a howl of pain, she sat down on the lawn and stopped taking interest in the proceedings. Meanwhile, Victoria was loosing off a series of shrieks and curses that would have done justice to an Irish navvy. The commotion was enough to bring Mrs Lumly out of the house to investigate.

'I say, what's going on out there? Stop it now, stop it at once!'

As suddenly as it had begun, Melissa's anger subsided. She got up and allowed a bruised and rather shaken Victoria to pull herself together.

'You little wildcat,' howled Victoria pitifully. 'What was that for?' She dabbed gingerly at her nose and found a tiny smear of blood on her fingers. 'It's probably broken,' she snarled ruefully. 'I'll get you for this, Melissa Tremayne, you just see if I don't.'

'Do what you like,' retorted Melissa casually. She glanced off across the lawn to where the portly imposing figure of

312

Mrs Lumly advanced like a harbinger of doom.

'You there! Melissa Tremayne isn't it? What on earth is the meaning of this shocking behaviour?'

Melissa offered no reply. Instead, she stooped, picked up the fallen pendant, and crammed it back in the pocket of her shorts. She glanced at Allison, who was holding both hands against her reddened cheek and was howling pathetically.

'For God's sake, shut up,' hissed Melissa. 'I didn't hit you *that* hard.' Allison gulped, paused for a moment, then resumed her noisy protest.

'You'd better clear off,' warned Victoria in a low, threatening voice. 'I always knew you were a roughneck under that hoity-toity image . . . and if you think I'm giving you that money now, you've got another think coming.'

'Keep your money,' growled Melissa, as she turned to walk away. 'Perhaps you could use it to buy yourself a night of passion with Bob Beresford. He's just about what you deserve!' Melissa went out through the garden gate, slamming it behind her and ignoring Mrs Lumly's strident demands that she stay where she was and be tongue-lashed. She set off down the street again, her hands thrust deep into her pockets, one clenched fist still holding the bullet-shaped pendant. The one aspect of her affair that she thought might still bring her pleasure had been yet another dismal failure. Only the sheer animal thrill of hitting Victoria Lumly's unbearably smug face had been worth anything at the end of the day.

'Your parents shall hear of this,' shrieked Mrs Lumly as a parting shot, leaning over the gate and shaking a huge pink fist.

Melissa sighed. Head down, eyeshades firmly in position, she simply kept walking in the direction of home.

Lim glanced up from the cheerless expanse of the dining room table, as the familiar sound of Bob's Land Rover ruptured the silence. She got up from the chair in which she had been sitting for nearly an hour and she resolved to herself that, this time, she would tell him. She turned to face the door. Through the opening, she saw the Land Rover screech to a halt, throwing up a thick cloud of dust that hung in a fine haze over the garden. A moment later, there was the creak of the garden gate, and Bob came hurrying along the path, an expression of intense preoccupation on his face.

Lim's hands came up to stroke her dark hair into position. She cleared her throat. He would be angry with her of course, he would shout and glare at her, and though she hated to be subjected to his displeasure she must bear it and speak her words, slowly and simply so that he would understand.

He burst into the room wearing a face that was a mask of irritability. He did not even acknowledge Lim's presence.

'Bob Tuan . . . ' she began; but he pushed straight by her and strode in the direction of his bedroom. She followed, meekly, awaiting her first opportunity to speak. But when she followed him into the bedroom, she saw that he was stripping the sheet off the bed that she had so carefully made up that morning. He yanked the cotton right back, searched through it for a moment, then dumped the whole thing unceremoniously on the floor. Now he searched under the pillows, stooped to examine the floor around and under the bed.

'Bob Tuan has lost something?' enquired Lim politely.

He nodded, scowled.

'My luck,' he replied tonelessly.

He shifted his attention to the chest of drawers beside the bed, pulling out each drawer one at a time and scattering its contents onto the already disrupted bed. Lim stepped forward.

'Let me look,' she offered hopefully. 'What have you lost?'

'My good luck charm. You know, the bullet-shaped thing on a chain?' He paused for a moment, stared at her. 'You haven't seen it, have you?'

She shook her head.

'No, Bob Tuan, I no see . . . but please, may I speak about something that I . . .'

'Well, it's got to be *somewhere*,' he reasoned. 'Things can't just vanish.' He emptied out the last of the drawers, turned his attention to the wardrobe. 'Could be in a jacket

314

pocket, I suppose . . .' He turned around and began to desecrate that shrine of order. Meanwhile, with placid acceptance, Lim began to remake the bed.

'Please, Bob Tuan, if I could just . . .'

'Nah . . . nah, this is crazy. Why would I have put into a pocket anyway? It can only be somewhere where it might have fallen . . .'

'. . . tell you of a thing, that causes much unhappiness now . . .'

'Somewhere like . . . ummm . . .'

'. . . and though I am almost afraid to speak of it, I know I must . . .'

'The bathroom!' Bob snapped his fingers. 'It could be in the shower basin, I suppose. It would be too large to go down the grill . . .' He hurried out of the bedroom. Lim gazed after him sadly for a moment, aware that he had not, as yet, heard a single word of what she had said. She followed him with dogged determination and found him crouched in the shower enclosure, examining every square inch of the tiled floor.

'Please, Tuan, can I speak of something . . . ?'

'Aww look, Lim, don't bother me now, alright? This is important.'

'But this of which I speak is also . . .'

'See, that pendant is my good luck, Lim. I can't go hunting without it, it's like a superstitious thing I have going. Now, I've got to think where I could have dropped it over the last day or so . . .' He moved past her again, rubbing his chin as he recounted all the possibilities to himself. 'I'm sure it's nowhere at work, I've already checked that out. The Mess, I suppose is a possibility . . . I'll have to wait till tonight to look around there . . .'

'Please, Bob Tuan, you must hear me now. This too is important, like you speak.'

Bob sighed, glanced at her.

'Yeah, yeah, go ahead, I'm listening.'

She paused for a moment, unsure of herself now that she had his attention. She began again at the beginning, halting and self-conscious.

'Bob Tuan, I must speak of something that is very hard

for me to say. You know I care very much for Tuan, but I would not have you think I say this because I want go to Australia . . .'

'Well, now I think we've had this conversation already, Lim. You know I've told you before that there's absolutely no chance of . . .'

'But please, Tuan, when you hear what I have to say, maybe you not think that way. Maybe you think of Suzy Lim different when you hear what I must speak . . .'

Bob sighed, shook his head.

'I don't think there's anything you can say that can make me change my mind on that one, Lim, and frankly, I'm a little surprised at you talking this way. I thought more of you than that. It's been a fine relationship in every sense of the word, but when the time comes to go, that's the way it has to be.'

'Yes, but Tuan, now I am . . . now I am . . .'

'The beach!' exclaimed Bob, and he swore curtly beneath his breath. He turned and headed towards the door. 'Listen Lim, we'll talk about this another time right; only right now, I have to go find my luck, savvy?' He waved her to silence. 'Now, while I'm gone, I want you to think very carefully about what you've been saying. I think you'll come to the conclusion that you've not been very fair. Frankly, I don't want to hear any more about the subject.'

'But Tuan . . . you have not listened to me! I try to tell you that . . .'

'Now, that's enough, Lim! I'll be back later on. Why don't you get working on a nice curry for dinner, eh? See you later . . .'

And he was gone again, striding across the porch in his heavy work boots. Lim stared after him helplessly, her face expressionless. After a few moments, she heard the roar of the Land Rover as he gunned the engine, and then the vehicle was accelerating away down the street, leaving her sad and alone in the silence of the house.

She shook her head slowly from side to side. She had tried. She had tried so hard to speak, but he had not let her finish, and in her heart she knew that even if she had been allowed to say everything that was troubling her, still he

316

would not have heard her words. She returned to her seat by the table. Staring down at her dull reflection in the cheerless brown Formica, she wondered desperately what she should do next.

Chapter 30

When the paper boy brought the copy of the *Straits Times* that morning, Harry was waiting eagerly. He slipped the boy a silver coin and opened the paper to the appropriate place, ignoring the lead items of world news that usually received his full attention. On page six, he found the article under the resplendent title of 'The Hunter and the Hunted.' It seemed to be the same basic article that he had read on the verandah only a couple of days earlier, but fleshed out here and there in the second or third draft. Harry thought it was probably the best piece he had ever read on the Malaysian tiger and he felt a warm glow of pride at his involvement in the project. What pleased him even more though, was a lengthy dedication that preceded the article itself.

The author would like to thank the people of Trengganu whose hospitality during my stay was so generous and heartwarming; also, a special thank-you to Lieutenant Colonel Harry Sullivan (retired), whose insights into the life-patterns of the tiger proved invaluable and without whose help this article would not have been possible.

Harry sighed. He folded the newspaper shut and laid it down on the rattan table. He settled back in his chair and stared thoughtfully off across the garden. The papaya trees seemed to shimmer in the heat haze.

'I'm missing her already,' he thought to himself, and he wondered if he might not act on her advice soon and travel up to K.L. for a brief visit. No doubt she had been correct in her assessment of him. A stubborn old creature of habit, forever patrolling those areas which he had designated as his home territory: the house, the garden, the Mess. Soon, now, the latter would no longer be open to him. The modern world was encroaching on his familiar ground, whittling it inexorably away. He had the choice of slinking back into his house for the remainder of his life, or simply changing his habits, finding new ranges to patrol. Perhaps he might even ask Marion to be his wife. At the very worst, she could only say no . . . He was tired of living alone. It had been for too long . . .

He closed his eyes and the heat of the morning settled around him in a heavy, all enveloping shroud. He slept and dreamed that he was young again.

Melissa approached Bob's house cautiously and was relieved to see that the familiar Land Rover was not parked by the gates. Nestled in her pocket, her hand was clammy around the small metallic medallion. She advanced cautiously along the garden path. The front door of the house was wide open and a radio was playing within, a Chinese pop song, the voice of the girl vocalist harsh and discordant to Western ears. Melissa stood on the porch for several moments, before stepping forward to knock politely at the door. After an interval of a few moments, a pretty young Chinese *amah* stepped into view. The two girls appraised each other in silence for several moments.

Despite herself, Melissa felt a curious twinge of envy run through her, because the girl *was* extraordinarily attractive, but then, as she looked closer, she experienced a sense of despair, because it was quite apparent that Victoria Lumly's ugly 'gossip' was nothing short of the truth. Lim *was* pregnant, as anyone could tell at a glance. Her hair and skin were in poor condition and the baggy shirt she was wearing did little to hide the fact that her tiny waist was beginning to lose its shape. Her eyes possessed the weak washed-out quality that suggested she had shed many tears over the last few weeks. Melissa wondered how Bob could be so blind as to be unaware of the girl's condition.

'Too preoccupied with himself, as usual,' she thought to herself.

Lim glanced down at her feet, as though she was aware of

318

Melissa's thoughts.

'Yes, Missy?' she enquired meekly.

'I . . . I'm a friend of Bob's . . . Mr Beresford,' began Melissa, and was saddened to see an expression of anxiety flare up in Lim's lovely eyes, as she recognized a possible rival. Melissa felt burdened with an unspeakable guilt. She forced herself not to think about what had happened on the beach the other night. 'I . . . have something that belongs to Mr Beresford, perhaps you might return it to him for me.' She took her hand from her pocket and held it out, palm upwards, to reveal its contents.

'Oh, Missy, thank you! Bob Tuan will be so pleased. He has been looking everywhere for this . . .' Her voice trailed away and her eyes narrowed slightly, as she asked. 'Please Missy, where did you . . . ?'

'Mr Beresford came to dinner at my house, the other night. We found it on the floor.' The reply was too quick, too forced. There was an uncomfortable silence.

'The missy . . . would like to wait?' enquired Lim at last, and the reluctance in her voice was barely disguised.

'No, no, that's quite alright. Just give him the medallion. I'm sure he'll be glad to get it back . . .' Melissa stood hesitantly in the porch, her arms hanging awkwardly by her sides. She felt torn between the desire to get away from the place before Bob appeared on the scene and the natural compulsion to help Lim in some way. Melissa felt desperately sorry for the girl, who was no doubt hanging grimly on in the vague hope that Bob would marry her.

'When will you have your baby?' she blurted out abruptly.

Lim's eyes widened into an expression of shock. She made as if to run back into the house, but Melissa grabbed the girl's wrist and held her fast.

'How did you know?' whispered Lim fearfully.

'I have eyes,' replied Melissa simply, not wanting to mention the fact that her pregnancy was such a widely rumoured story. 'Soon, you will begin to show, so that even Tuan Beresford will notice. Then he'll be angry that you didn't tell him sooner . . .'

Lim shook her head sadly.

'I have tried to tell him, Missy. He will not hear me.'

'Then you must *make* him hear you!'

'What is the use? He will not marry me and take me to 'Stralia.'

'Perhaps not ... but at least it won't be too late to get rid of the baby.'

A look of complete misery came to Lim's face and her eyes filled with wretched tears.

'Oh Missy, it is already too late! The doctor warned me to be quick, but time has passed ...' Her voice dissolved into an indecipherable flurry of weeping. Melissa could only stand and stare helplessly at the girl, unsure of what to do.

'Here now, that won't help at all ...'

Lim nodded, sniffed, stepped back into the sanctuary of the house. It was plain that crying had become a regular occurrence for her lately.

'I am sorry, Missy. I will go now. Thank you for bringing the charm, Bob Tuan will be very pleased ...'

'Don't forget now, Lim, you must tell him everything, just as soon as he gets home. Promise me ...'

But Lim was gone, bustling into the interior of the house, alone with her tears and her sorrow. Melissa stood for a few moments gazing in through the doorway. She called Lim's name a couple of times, but received no reply. After a short while, she shrugged and walked away along the garden path. Abruptly, her own worries seemed small and insignificant compared to the problems that assailed the young *amah*. What had happened to Melissa was something transient, the memory of it would fade in time, but Lim would be forever burdened by the shame and sorrow of her affair with Bob by the very real and demanding presence of a baby. At a time when her young life should be blossoming into fruition, it was, almost certainly, ruined forever. The greatest irony of all was that the girl so obviously worshipped the man who had brought about her ruination. One thing was for certain: Bob Beresford was not the kind of man to accept his moral responsibilities. Once he found out the way things were, he would be off like a shot, perhaps leaving a little money to salve his conscience. In this country, a white man could buy his way out of anything, it seemed.

Her hatred for the self-centred Australian was now totally compounded; yet the realization that there was somebody worse off than herself had done her a great deal of good. She headed for home with a lighter step, and getting rid of the medallion trophy had served to convince her that now, once and for all, Bob Beresford was out of her life for good. She sincerely hoped that she would never set eyes on him again.

Chapter 31

In the strange hazy light, just after dawn, Haji crept slowly in from the thick scrub jungle that bordered Kampong Panjang, made reckless once again by his desperate need to eat. His injured foreleg was now so useless that it impeded him in everything he did, and the vile smell of suppurating flesh was always in his nostrils. His life was a slow, limping misery and yet he clung onto it voraciously, with every ounce of his animal instinct. How simple a matter it would have been to simply lie down in the shadowy shelter of a cave and wait for the great weakness to take him . . . and yet, whenever he felt its nearness, he redoubled his efforts in a frenzy, gulping down any foul carrion he could find while he searched for more substantial food.

The *kampong* was asleep and only the odd solitary snatch of birdsong broke the silence. Haji prowled slowly around the perimeter of the village, once, twice, three times, keeping cover every inch of the way, but coming close enough to the open to allow the sunlight to dapple his striped hide occasionally. At last, his persistence was rewarded. A slight movement in the doorway of one of the huts caused him to flatten himself down against the ground. He watched intently as an old male Upright emerged from within and came slowly down the steps, carrying a water bucket. The Upright moved off to Haji's right, heading for the nearby stream and his stooped figure was lost for a moment, as he passed behind the hut of his closest neighbour. Without a moment's hesitation, Haji slunk out from cover and followed in direct pursuit, slipping beneath the stilts of the closest building and moving from one to another as he followed his intended prey. The old Upright was not a fast mover and soon Haji was just a few yards behind him, wellplaced and confident of a quick kill. He resolved to let the old one walk on to the stream where there would be less chance of discovery.

The Upright moved out beyond the last hut and passed through an area of secondary jungle. He kept glancing about as though he was aware of the cat's presence, but Haji kept well out of sight, and after a few moments the Upright reached the water. The stream had grown fat and turbulent after the recent rains. The Upright got down onto his knees and lowered his bucket beneath the surface, watching blankly as it filled with water. He had not particularly wanted to get up early and fetch the water, but he was old and slow now and had to prove to his family that he was capable of doing *something*. He had detected an air of quiet resentment from his son lately, a resentment fuelled by the expense of providing for an infirm father. The old man was proud, and eager to show that his worsening rheumatism had not made him completely redundant. He hefted the water bucket and a dull ache rivered through his back, wrenching an involuntary grunt from him. He was about to rise, but an abrupt powerful impact struck his leg. He could feel the sharp sting as twin sets of spikes clamped deep into the thin flesh of his right shin. His immediate impression was that he had inadvertently set his leg down into a gin trap, but then there was a sudden backward jerk that was of such strength, that it pulled his other leg from under him and he flopped down, head first into the stream. He thrashed about in the water for an instant and then another wrench brought him out of the water and up onto the bank. Bewildered, the old Upright twisted around, coughing and spluttering, to see that a tiger had him by the leg. He let out a scream of pure terror and then, realizing that he still held the heavy iron bucket in his grasp, he struck out with it, bringing it across the tiger's head with a dull clang. The cat let go his hold and reeled aside with a blast of rage, his senses reeling. The Upright scrambled instinctively towards the water, dragging his useless leg behind him, but the tiger leapt forward, snatched the Upright by the nape of his neck and shook him viciously, like a terrier shaking a rat. Neck bones shattered and the Upright went limp, his hand still clenched tightly around the handle of the bucket.

Haji bore the kill unsteadily away. The blow from the bucket had temporarily affected his balance and he stumbled fitfully along, determined not to let go of the meat he had killed. The bucket kept getting caught on various obstacles and the noise of its incessant clanking was a constant aggravation. Behind him, Haji could hear the commotion of shouting voices, the pounding of feet through vegetation. With a supreme effort, he hefted the old Upright's torso as far above the ground as he could and made off with all the speed he could muster, quickly losing himself in the dense jungle that bordered the stream.

Bob was asleep and dreaming about Melissa Tremayne when the sudden commotion awakened him. There was a flurry of bangs on the front door, a child's voice shouting his name. The mattress creaked as Lim got out of bed. He peered blearily at her, but she turned her back on him as she struggled into her dressing gown. She was always being secretive with him these days. He shrugged, rubbed at his eyes as she hurried out of the room. That dream now, Melissa Tremayne. What the hell had been happening? He couldn't remember it now. Funny how that sometimes happened. They'd been on the beach again, the place where the turtles came to lay their eggs, and she'd just been telling him something . . . but what the hell had it been . . . ?

Voices from outside. A young boy talking excitedly, jabbering away. '*Harimau, harimau!*' Bob came awake in an instant. He slipped out of the bed, grabbed his clothes, and began dressing himself quickly. After a few moments, Ché burst into the room.

'Oh, Tuan . . . excuse me!'

'No bother! What's the story, kid?'

'The man-eater. He killed an old man in Kampong

Panjang, just by the stream there.'

'How long ago?'

'Maybe . . . half-hour. I borrowed a bike to get here.'

'Good boy! That gives us a real edge.'

'Yes, but Tuan, I saw him, I saw which way he went!'

'The hell you did! Okay, Ché, you'd better come along with me.' Bob snapped one hand up to trace the cool metal of his medallion. 'I feel lucky today,' he observed. 'You go and wait for me in the Land Rover. Put your bicycle in the back, I won't be a moment – ' Ché grinned with pleasure and raced out of the room. Bob put on his jungle boots and laced them up. Then he fumbled in the drawer of a nearby cabinet and began to fill his pockets with bullets. He came suddenly aware that Lim was watching him from the doorway, a look of apprehension on her face.

'Don't worry, I'll be alright.'

She nodded. 'Yes . . . but last night, you said we could talk this morning.'

Bob sighed.

'I know that, love, but I couldn't have any idea that this would happen, could I? And last night, I was too tired to do anything but sleep . . .' He gazed at her. 'What's all this about anyway? You're always wanting to have a talk these days. It's not like you . . .' He buttoned up his pockets, picked up his hat from the chair beside the bed.

'You make it so hard to speak,' murmured Lim sadly.

'Well look, I've got to go now. We can talk when I get home.'

'Then you'll be too tired!' she retorted.

'For Christ's sake, Lim, what's wrong with you?' he snapped.

'Can you not guess?' she asked him.

He shook his head in exasperation. 'Look, Lim, I haven't got time for guessing games. I've got a tiger to hunt. We'll talk about it later.' He pushed past her and took three steps towards the door.

'I'm pregnant,' she said forcefully. 'I'm going to have baby.'

Bob froze in his tracks. He turned back very slowly to face her.

324

'What did you say?' he asked weakly.

She also turned, to look him full in the face.

'I said, I am pregnant. You are the father.'

He stared at her in silence for a moment, as though unable to comprehend her words.

'Pregnant?' he echoed at last. 'But . . . you can't be . . .'

'I am. I have seen doctor.'

A few seconds of silence passed, a few seconds that seemed like an eternity. Then Bob said simply.

'Jesus Christ.' Lim had just broken his dream. Only in *that*, it had been Melissa Tremayne who was pregnant. He scratched his head, glanced over to the open front door. 'Well . . . I have to go now, Lim. We'll talk about this again, alright . . . ? Don't worry, we'll sort something out.' He headed for the door at top speed.

'But Bob Tuan, it is too late to . . . ' But he was gone, hurrying out into the bright glare of morning. Ché was waiting impatiently in the Land Rover. Bob clambered in alongside him and sat for a moment, gazing blankly at the empty street ahead.

'Something is wrong, Tuan?' enquired Ché, impatient to be off.

Bob frowned, shook his head.

'Nah – Come on kid, let's get after this stripey.' He revved the engine and accelerated wildly away from his parking spot, kicking up a thick cloud of acrid dust in his wake. His driving was even more reckless than usual and Ché was obliged to hold on tightly for fear of being thrown clear of the Land Rover, every time it bucketed over a rise in the road. It took a little over ten minutes to reach Kampong Penjang, where a crowd of noisy and very excited villagers had gathered to await the Tuan's arrival. Snatching up his rifle, Bob followed Ché in the direction of the stream, while the whole rowdy entourage trooped along in his wake. After a few minutes walk, they had reached the water and Ché was indicating the scene of the brief struggle. The ground here was fairly muddy and a clear set of drag marks led away from the blood-stained ground and off into the undergrowth.

'Right, let's get after the bastard,' whispered Bob. 'We

couldn't hope to be on the scene any quicker . . .' He took a
few steps forward and then realized that the villagers were
still following him. 'Tell this lot to stay where they are,' he
told Ché. 'They'll scare the tiger away.'

Ché translated the terse message and immediately, the
people started making loud noises of disapproval.

'They want to come along,' observed Ché.

'You just tell 'em, anybody who follows me is liable to get
a bullet through his head. Out in the jungle it's hard to tell a
man from a tiger.'

Ché announced this and the villagers quietened down
considerably. Bob and his young assistant were able to move
off unattended. They stooped to duck beneath a thick
overhang of thorn bushes. Beyond, everything was clammy
green silence. Ché peered apprehensively in and gave a
nervous cough.

'Maybe tiger will be gone when we find the body,' he
reasoned.

'Maybe, Maybe not.' Bob wished vainly he could rid his
mind of what Lim had just told him. God, but she'd chosen
a wonderful time! He frowned, shrugged, moved cautiously
from sunlight into shadow. He was terribly aware of the
eyes of the villagers on his back. He turned to face Ché for a
moment, held one finger to his lips, and gave the boy a
wink. He moved onwards, walking as silently as possible,
and Ché followed. The bushes closed around the spot where
they had been standing. To the villagers, the impression was
that the jungle had simply swallowed them whole. Realizing
that the show was over for the time being, the people began
to drift back to the *kampong* and the more usual routine of
their lives. Only the sound of gunshots would serve to bring
them running back to this place, in the desperate hope that
the man-eater had finally been destroyed. Till then, they
would have to be content to wait and hope.

The sun began its long slow climb across the empty sky.

Chapter 32

It was unusual for Pawn to be late and Harry was annoyed,
annoyed as only a man who was consistently punctual could

326

be. It was not that he was particularly hungry and required his breakfast; it was simply that a certain time had been agreed upon at the beginning of Pawn's contract and she had always managed to make an appearance within a few moments of that time, thus far. This morning, though, she was over an hour late. Harry was suffering from a mixture of irritation and anxiety. Supposing she was ill or something? Supposing she had suffered an accident on her way to the house? It was a break from routine, and at Harry's age there was nothing more upsetting.

He gave a sigh of relief when he heard the iron gate creak and he quickly settled himself into his favourite chair on the verandah, opening his copy of the *Straits Times* and pretending to be absorbed in it, in a typical show of unconcern.

Pawn came hurrying along the driveway, quite out of breath.

'Oh ... so sorry, Tuan, so sorry ...'

'Sorry?' He glanced nonchalantly up at her. 'Sorry about what, Pawn?'

'I am so late. It is unforgivable.'

He glanced at his wristwatch.

'Well, so you are! Do you know, I'd quite lost track of the time ...'

'The man-eater, Tuan, it killed another old man from the *kampong* this morning. Everywhere there was such a fuss, such a noise ...'

'Another one, eh?' Harry shook his head. 'Is that eight ... or nine? I'm beginning to lose count.'

Pawn nodded.

'Tuan Beresford was very quick coming this time,' she told him. 'The people say there is good chance shoot the striped one today ... and with Ché tracking for him, he ...'

Suddenly, Harry was up out of his chair, the newspaper lying forgotten on the table. 'What was that?' he demanded.

Pawn looked confused.

'I sorry, Tuan. What was ... ?'

'About Ché. You said he was tracking ...'

'For Tuan Beresford. Yes, that is right. He has helped before, you see.'

'Well, yes, I know that. But you say they are going right after the tiger? They're not going to build a *machan* and wait for him to return?'

Pawn shrugged.

'I cannot say, Tuan. What do I know of hunting the *tok belang*?' She climbed the steps of the verandah and made as if to go into the house.

'Where did you say it happened, Pawn? Near the village?'

'Yes, Tuan. By the stream that borders it on the west. It happened early this morning . . .'

'Yes, well thank you.' He sat down again, a look of intense worry on his face.

'The Tuan is troubled?'

'No no, I'm fine. You can get about your business now, Pawn.'

'You are hungry?'

Harry shook his head. Pawn shrugged and padded away into the house.

It was ominously quiet out in the garden. Harry felt a strong premonition of impending disaster settling around him. Something was terribly, terribly wrong. He thought of Ché, trailing along through the jungle with that irresponsible idiot Beresford and the image made the blood in his veins run cold.

'It's not done,' he muttered grimly. 'You *don't* track a cat through his own territory, you just don't.' He got up from his chair again and walked out into the garden where he paced restlessly about for several minutes, muttering darkly to himself. He could not rid himself of the conviction that something bad was going to happen, even though he rarely set any store by such feelings. He squinted up at the sky for a moment. The sun was a relentless ball of flame, searing, oppressive. He could almost smell the humid stink of the jungle undergrowth, he could almost picture the great striped cat, crouched down in shadow, awaiting the approach of the hunters. A fishing eagle sped across the great blue vastness of the sky and was gone. Harry turned to stare back at the house; and then he was hurrying towards it, his mind abruptly made up. He went on inside and made his way directly to his bedroom where he began to rummage frantically in drawers and cupboards. A few moments later, he appeared in the kitchen and handed a surprised Pawn his haversack and a water bottle.

'Put some food in here, will you? And fill this from the tap.'

'The Tuan is going somewhere?'

But he had already vanished, back in the direction of his room. Now it was Pawn's turn to mumble as she filled the haversack with whatever leftovers happened to be in the refrigerator. Had the Tuan taken leave of his senses? He hadn't used these things since he had come to live at the house. What on earth was wrong with him? A short while later, she had further case for alarm, when Harry rushed into the kitchen dressed in khaki green jungle clothing and wearing a broad-brimmed bush hat. He had his rifle slung over one shoulder and he paused only long enough to throw the haversack and water bottle across the other, before heading for the front door.

'Where is the Tuan going?' enquired Pawn meekly.

'Out!' was the simple reply.

'And . . . when will you be back?'

'How the hell should I know?' He strode away along the drive, flung open the gate and set off down the street at what could only be described as a fast march. Pawn stared thoughtfully after him. The next door's *amah*, pegging out some washing on the line, directed a questioning glance at Pawn, but the old woman could only shrug expressively and spread her hands in a gesture of bewilderment. Harry was around the corner and out of sight in a matter of moments.

Once out on the coast road, Harry strode along waving frantically at every vehicle heading in the direction of Kampong Panjang. He must have presented a curious spectacle, this lone overdressed Englishman, sweating and toiling along in the heat of the day and carrying a lethal-looking weapon over his shoulder. But the Malays being a very forgiving race, a ramshackle flatbed truck soon drew to a halt and the grinning driver was urging Harry to clamber up on the back, along with a pair of tethered goats. This would normally have been below Harry's dignity, but such was the urgency of his mission he climbed aboard and sat, straight-backed and resolute, as the old jalopy sped him bumpily to his destination.

Once at Kampong Panjang, it was a relatively simple job to find the place where the killing had taken place. As soon as he appeared, there was a whole crowd of noisy children eager to lead him to the spot. He went along with them and stooped to examine the blood-stained ground that they indicated.

'Hunter-man already go after him,' observed one of the older boys.

Harry nodded. He gazed calmly at the deep set of drag marks, where they vanished into the undergrowth. Then, with no further explanation, he stooped to pass beneath an overhang of spiky thorn bushes and set off in pursuit. The children called after him a couple of times but they received no reply and they were too nervous to follow the old Tuan into the jungle. So they retraced their steps and resumed the game they had been playing before his arrival. After a few short moments of boisterous play, they had forgotten that he had even been there.

Time passed. It was a little after midday.

'She needn't think I'm going to marry her,' thought Bob, as he moved resolutely forward. The tiger had dragged his food an incredible distance and the hunters had spent several hours creeping fruitlessly along in pursuit. The kill had to be near now, but still Bob could not keep his mind on the matter in hand. 'After all, she's got no real hold on me. Strewth, I can be well away before the baby's even born . . . of course, I'll have to leave her some money to help make ends meet. It won't be easy for her . . .'

Ché was tugging at his sleeve and indicating that they should move to the left. Bob wondered vaguely how the kid could know that. The ground here was hard and rocky . . . unless, of course, that sudden bird call had meant something . . . bloody hell, but it was hot out here! He paused for a moment to mop at his brow with his already sodden shirt-sleeves. Ché had moved instinctively ahead and was peering cautiously through the tangle of greenery ahead. The silence was unbearable.

'I'll have to tell her when I get home,' thought Bob with calm conviction. 'I'll have to show her she can't trap me in any way. Christ, you can't let one mistake ruin the rest of your bleeding life . . .'

Ché was tugging at his sleeve again. Bob glanced down in irritation, then saw that the boy was pointing directly ahead, his dark eyes flashing with excitement. Bob stared intently in the place where Ché was indicating . . . and Christ, what a stroke of luck! For there was the tiger, stretched out in a small clearing, beside a meandering jungle stream, and the bastard was still feeding on the old man's skinny carcass. It was the chance that Bob had been praying for since he began the search for the man-eater. Gently, hardly daring to breathe, Bob inched his rifle up into a firing position. He had already pushed a bullet into the breach a mile or so back, something that was generally disdained by the hunting fraternity, but Bob wasn't going to let the sound of loading rob him of his long sought-after trophy. He blinked the sweat out of his eyes and lined up a bead on the great cat's black-striped hide.

Sunlight dappled the tiger's fur, giving a false impression of movement but the cat was sprawled like a domestic fireside pussy, tearing contentedly at the feast which he held in his vast front paws.

'A neck shot,' thought Bob calmly. 'I'll go for a neck shot. Always the best chance that way . . . take my time, no need to hurry. He's not going anywhere . . .' He glanced down at the boy beside him. Ché was staring at the potential target too, holding himself absolutely still. The moment was almost at hand. The bullet would burst through the tiger's hide and smash that great old heart to pieces. Bob aligned the barrel fractionally, allowing the front sight to become as one with the tiny notch set in the backsight. For some reason, Bob had not bothered to bring the telescopic unit, but there was little need of it here. He was too close to miss. A smile of triumph curved itself over his lips and he gently squeezed the trigger.

The butt jumped against his shoulder and for an instant. Bob's smile faded. There seemed to elapse a long eternity of waiting, before the bullet actually found its target. But then abruptly, the tiger's long flank shook with the impact of a terrible blow, a blow that sent the heavy body lurching upwards through the air. It happened in eerie silence. There was no roar from the cat, no gasp of exhaled air. The striped body simply twisted sideways and crashed through the undergrowth, rolling over and over and finally vanishing from sight in the greenery beyond.

The screams of exultation that erupted from the throats of both hunters seemed to echo through the jungle. They burst into abrupt motion, leaping up, flinging their hands skywards as they yelled their triumph to the four winds.

'Tuan, you have killed him! You have killed him!'

'Did you see it, Ché? One shot, one brilliant fucking shot! He went down like a stuck pig, the son of a bitch!'

'The man-eater is dead, Tuan! Dead, dead!' And Ché was running forward, eager to examine the corpse, to measure the great man-eater, to see the size of his teeth, the curve of his great claws. Bob came strolling after him at a more leisurely pace, the rifle slung carelessly over his shoulder, a victor's smile on his sun-burned face.

And then, suddenly, horribly, everything was a nightmare. The undergrowth burst aside and the tiger came charging out from cover, straight at Ché, straight at the boy who was now no more than a few feet from those great slavering jaws. Bob screamed something, he didn't know what. He tried to fumble the heavy rifle back to his shoulder, he tried to work the heavy bolt, but his strength had evaporated and he could only look in horrified fascination at the awful slow-motion sequence that was playing out before his very eyes; the huge bristling form of the tiger, leaping up now at the screaming boy, with pain-maddened eyes blazing fire, while the great open jaws roared thunder and vengeance. Bob fell to his knees, struggling helplessly with the bolt. The gun was jammed, he could not make it work. And then the teeth were around Ché's neck in a single, crushing, destroying bite and the child's frail body was being shaken like a rag doll, left and right, the nerveless limbs flailing wildly.

The great formless scream of anguish that wrenched itself from Bob's throat shattered the silence, drove the tiger back into cover but it was already too late. Ché was dead, his body little more than a broken, tattered doll, discarded in the undergrowth. The victory had gone horribly, horribly awry. Sobbing, confused, Bob broke and stumbled back in the direction from which he had come, the discarded gun trailing uselessly from his left hand. He ran blindly, overcome with horror and the shame of his own recklessness. He banged headlong into a low tree branch, fell back with a groan, and lay weeping like a child, no longer knowing or caring where he was. And it was there, some minutes later, that Harry Sullivan found him.

Harry had made good time through the jungle. Less concerned with the problems of tracking a dangerous quarry, he had simply travelled at the best speed he could manage. The drag marks were well defined and needed little more than a cursory glance from time to time. But it was the recent blast of a rifle that had brought him up with Beresford. What he saw now confirmed his worst fears. He moved forward until he stood beside the sprawled hunter. He prodded the man's quivering shoulder with his boot.

Bob looked up, his tear-filled eyes staring but not seeing. Then he sat up with a groan of misery, cradling his head in his hands.

'Where's Ché?' demanded Harry tonelessly.

Bob pointed back along the track and tried to speak, but his voice failed him.

'Where is he, dammit? What happened?'

Bob gestured helplessly. His voice when it emerged was a dry emotion-filled croak of despair.

'The tiger . . . I put him down. A good clean neck shot. I was sure he was done for.' He shook his head slowly from side to side, reliving the gut-wrenching terror of the incident. 'The boy . . . ran forward. He thought . . . we both thought . . . and oh God, the cat got back up again, he came right out at the boy and . . .' Again his voice collapsed into a wheezing fugue of misery. Harry reached down, grabbed a handful of Bob's shirt material and yanked him unceremoniously to his feet.

'Show me,' he snapped. 'Take me there!'

Bob's eyes widened into a stare.

'No . . .' The voice was now a tiny whisper of dread. 'I can't . . . the tiger, he's still there . . . it's too late to do anything for the boy, you see, it's too late!'

He broke off as the flat of Harry's hand lashed across his face with a loud crack, knocking him backwards a step. Harry's expression was one of barely controlled rage.

'Goddamn you,' he said through gritted teeth. 'Goddamn you to hell, you insolent dog. There's a lot we can do for the boy. We can take him home to his family and tell them that the Great White Hunter didn't even bother to check the tiger was dead, before he let somebody approach it. Haven't you ever heard of throwing stones at a tiger to check that he's not shamming? Didn't you have that written down in any of your goddamned books!' Harry's whole body was shaking with anger, and it was all he could do to refrain from striking the younger man again. 'Now you listen to me, Beresford, and you hear me well. You're going to take me back to the place where it happened or I swear I'll take my rifle and I'll put a bullet through your stupid head myself. Now move!' He prodded the Australian sharply with the tip of his rifle barrel and Bob began to move, stumbling helplessly along, his head bowed, his spirit completely broken. It did not take very long to reach the place where Ché's body lay. Bob hung back, unable to even look at the child, but Harry went straight up to the corpse and stood staring at it in silence for a moment.

The boy's face was calm in death, the black intelligent eyes staring upwards at the sky in an expression of surprise. Harry kneeled reverently beside the body, and reaching out a hand he closed the eyes with a little pressure from his fingertips. He had dearly loved those eyes, and he could not bear to see them now. They made him think of another time, when he had held out a bright shiny watch and the eyes had gazed up at him, glittering with excitement . . . and Harry had made the boy say the word 'tiger' to prove to him that it was superstitious nonsense to believe that he could bring down the beast's wrath on his own head. A glint of sunlight on silver made him look down, and there was the watch, dangling from its fob at the child's waist. Harry could see that the second hand was still ticking urgently

334

around; but for Ché life was stilled forever.

Harry hunched forward and his shoulders shuddered involuntarily, a dryness tore at his throat, his eyes blurred with hot tears. He wondered if it was possible for him to go on living with such sorrow, with such horrible injustice.

He glanced up at Bob once and said coldly. 'It should have been you.'

The Australian looked away. He could not meet the old man's accusing eyes.

After a little while, Harry managed to calm himself. He wiped at his eyes with his sleeve and then, reaching down, he lifted the child's torn body up in his arms. He moved quickly over to Bob and made as if to pass the burden over to him. The Australian recoiled in horror.

'I can't . . .' he gasped.

'You *will*,' retorted Harry simply. He thrust Ché's body against Bob's chest so that the man had to take it in his arms. 'Now, take him back to the village, you hear me? Take him back to his family and tell them what you've done.'

'And you . . .'

Harry turned and gazed resolutely off into the disturbed undergrowth.

'I'll go and finish the job,' he said quietly.

'No . . .' A glimmer of bravado reappeared in the Australian's eyes. 'He's *mine!* I've done all the hard work, and now you just want to step in and pick him off . . .'

Harry stared at Bob in silence for a moment. He had never felt so much contempt for another human being in his entire life.

'My God, you *are* despicable,' he murmured. 'Look where your lust for glory has got you, and you still cling on to the belief that some higher power ordains that the tiger belongs to you. That cat is a miserable man-killer, but for all that he's worth ten of you, Beresford. *You're* the animal! D'you hear me? *You're* the animal!' Harry stooped and snatched up his rifle. He brought the muzzle up and pointed it squarely between the Australian's eyes. 'Now you start walking back towards that village, or by God I swear I'll blow your head all over this clearing.'

Bob took a step forward, tried to speak, but Harry simply lifted the gun forward in a gesture of warning. Bob's head dropped forward again. All the fight had been driven out of him. Slowly, hampered by the burden of the boy's limp form, he turned and began to stumble away through the trees, weaving left and right to find a path through the undergrowth. Harry watched until the man's figure was hidden from view. Then turning, he picked up his haversack, slung it over his shoulder and approached the thick tangle of grass and bushes into which the tiger had vanished. He stood for a moment, staring straight ahead, flaring his nostrils to smell the wind.

'It's madness,' he murmured to himself. 'You don't follow a tiger across his own ground. You simply don't.' But it was a personal matter now. And the old beast would be in such pain, such terrible pain.

Slowly, cautiously, and with infinite precision. Harry took his first step into the bushes. The cat was out there somewhere, wounded, desperate. Harry would keep searching until their paths crossed.

Chapter 33

The trail led deeper and deeper into the heart of the jungle. Harry followed at a slow and cautious pace, stooping down occasionally to examine a pugmark or an overturned stone. There were frequent splashes of fresh blood on either side of the tracks, which suggested that Beresford's bullet had gone clean through its target; but the blood did not have the light frothy consistency that would have suggested a lung wound. The tiger clearly possessed a charmed life.

The ground over the last mile or so had declined gradually into a deep marshy valley, overrun with tangles of swamp grass, bamboo thickets, and thick rotan creepers covered with fishhooklike thorns that continually snagged the khaki material of Harry's shirt. The Malays called the creepers *nanti sikit*, which literally means 'wait a while.' It was mid-afternoon now and Harry was tiring rapidly. He was obliged to stop and rest every so often, for he was finding it difficult to keep his breathing regular. But the tiger showed no signs of pausing at the moment. He was moving straight and true along well-worn cattle trails, as if heading instinctively for some refuge.

At one point the trail led through a thigh deep swamp and Harry was obliged to wade through, an exhausting proposition, as his boots kept slipping and sliding in the deep deposits of clinging mud beneath the stagnant water. When he emerged on the other side, he found several leeches clinging to the bare skin of his calves, around the top of his tightly laced boots. He sat down on a rock, and taking a cigar from his pocket he lit up, and then applied the hot end of the cigar to each of the pale grey creatures in turn. He watched with satisfaction as they curled up, wriggled briefly and dropped to the ground. After this, he quickly extinguished the cigar, not wanting to make his presence too well advertised. After a brief respite, he plodded on his way again, sweltering in his thick khaki clothing. But he knew that if he had to spend a night out in the jungle, he would be more than glad of it.

Now the ground began to incline upwards, to a distant granite mountain, the slopes of which were shrouded with coconut palms and thick stretches of rain forest. Directly ahead lay a wide, almost impenetrable bamboo thicket, the thick stems of which were perilously close together. Harry hesitated a moment. Some sixth sense deep inside warned him that the tiger was near. He thought he could feel the hot stare of yellow eyes peering at him from cover. He began to move slowly towards the bamboo. Somewhere, off to the east, a troop of monkeys chattered a nervous warning. Yes, he was in there alright! Lying up in cover, waiting for the hunter to come in nearer. Harry licked his lips. They were as dry as a bone, the rasp of his tongue over the parched flesh sounding incredibly loud in the silence. He glanced critically at the thicket into which he was walking. It would be almost impossible for him to move with his rifle held out ahead of him in firing position. He would simply have to move with it pointing upright and hope that he could lower it sufficiently to fire when the opportunity presented itself. He moved into cover, setting down each footstep with painful precision, aware that the cat would hear every rustle of a leaf, every snap of a twig. Meanwhile, he willed the tiger to make a move. . .

Haji lay crouched on his belly, behind the rotting stump of a fallen tree. The pain in his chest kept coming and going in jolting spasms, but for all that he suffered the agony in silence. Meanwhile he kept his gaze fixed firmly on the old Upright who was moving gradually towards him. Haji did not know this Upright, but he could see the glint of light on a black stick and he was afraid and wary and burning with the dark rage of the hunted. The old Upright was also wary. He came forward with inexorable speed, stopping every few moments to gaze intently around in each direction. It was clear that he suspected Haji's presence, but, as yet, he had not spotted the hiding place. From the high tree-tops a magpie robin shrieked an abrupt warning and the Upright reacted immediately, swinging about to stare straight in Haji's direction; but then he came onward again, the black stick held tight up against him as he pushed his way through the narrow openings presented by the thick stems of bamboo. It was plain that the Upright was finding the going difficult here, hampered as he was by the clumsy pack on his shoulders. Haji could hear the hoarse shallow sound of his laboured breathing as he drew nearer. Soon, the hunter was near enough for Haji to see the thick film of sweat on his grizzled face, the dark stains of perspiration on the fabric of his khaki shirt. The magpie robin shrieked again and the Upright stopped in his tracks, resumed his careful scrutiny of the surroundings. Then he did an inexplicable thing. He sat down on the forest floor and waited. He had clearly decided not to come any closer.

Haji growled, a low rumbling sound deep in his throat, too quiet to be audible to the Upright's poorly developed hearing. It was to be a waiting game then . . . Haji inclined his head very slightly to one side, to allow him to lap at the gaping wound above his right shoulder where the bullet had emerged. Blood was still flowing sluggishly from the orifice and the rasp of Haji's tongue sent fresh spasms of pain rippling through his body.

Time passed. The magpie robin gave a last despairing cry and fluttered away above the tree tops. A silence settled on the clearing, a silence so complete that the slightest sound would have constituted a rude interruption. They settled down to wait, the hunter and the hunted, each waiting for the other to make the next move.

Harry sighed. His legs, crossed awkwardly beneath him in the confined space, were beginning to ache terribly. It seemed hours that he had been sitting here but a quick glance at his wristwatch informed him that, in fact, it was a little over twenty minutes. He frowned, glanced around again. The cat was here somewhere, that was for sure; but there were any number of places where he could be lying up. Behind that tangle of scrub there, perhaps . . . or concealed in those great green giant ferns off to his left . . . stretched out behind that fallen tree trunk directly ahead . . .

Harry froze with a gasp of shock. A head had slid up into view from behind the rotting wood; a great tawny-red, black-scarred face, with two blazing yellow eyes and jaws, wide open, bellowing hatred. The tiger leapt across the decaying surface of the wood in one terrible leap that made Harry's heart skip a beat and then it powered forward through the thicket, swift and terrible, an engine of pure destruction. For a moment, Harry was hypnotized by the cat's approach. It was a simple enough task to track down a wounded tiger, but quite another to stand and face the raging beast as it came in to attack. To Harry's shocked gaze, the cat looked big as a house and the speed with which it was approaching left no time to think.

Galvanized into instinctive action, Harry attempted to struggle upright, but his legs were rubbery and unreliable, so he settled back into a kneeling position and fumbled the rifle up to his shoulder. The cat was already dangerously close, it filled his vision with a blur of black and tawny movement. In the instant before his finger tightened on the trigger, the eyes of hunter and hunted locked together for a fraction of a second. Harry gave an involuntary cry, because there was a feeling of recognition there, it was like looking into the face of a long-lost friend and the sensation was enough to stay his hand on the trigger. Then the tiger was leaping up and over him, the bulk of its body blotting out the sunshine for an instant. Harry steeled himself for the impact of teeth and claws against his flesh, but it never came. The tiger continued up and over, to race madly away on Harry's other side, into the shelter of the thicket. Harry slumped down with a gasp of surprise and disbelief. The cat had altered its course at the last instant, to leap clear across the man who had set out to kill him. Had he felt some sense of recognition too?

Harry had little time to think about it. A slow steady pain began to rise in his chest, a pain that wrenched the breath from his lungs and turned the flesh of his face deathly white. He groaned, let his forehead sink down to bump against the soft ground. A series of jolting spasms thudded in his chest and he gritted his teeth, lay still, waiting desperately for the pain to subside. After a few minutes it did, but he remained lying for the moment, while he reached weakly for his water bottle. He unscrewed the top and swallowed a little of the precious contents. The pain was now a powerful ache that throbbed relentlessly in the arid vacuum of his chest. Gradually, the ache subsided but it was some considerable time before he felt strong enough to move on again.

'Old fool,' he muttered to himself. 'Coming out after a tiger in my condition. I ought to go home . . .'

But, without a moment's hesitation, he located the pugs that the tiger had left and struck out in this new direction, massaging his chest with one hand as he went along.

Chapter 34

When the brief tropical twilight descended, Harry chose a suitable clearing where there was little surrounding cover for any hungry predator and set about building a fire. It was a simple enough task to collect bundles of dry twigs and grass and he soon had a passable blaze going, with enough fallen branches to keep it burning through the night. He sat with his back up against a tall Kapok tree with his rifle lying at hand as he rummaged in his haversack for the provisions that Pawn had packed earlier that day. It was no great surprise to him to see that she had provided for him most handsomely, considering she had been given only a few minutes to prepare things. There were little plastic pots of cold meat and savoury rices, slices of flat bread and various items of fresh fruit. Using his jackknife as an eating utensil, he began to eat, gazing thoughtfully into the fire as he did so.

He could not stop thinking about the tiger, the way it had seemingly changed its course in mid-leap to pass harmlessly over its tormenter. It was as though that single exchanged glance had spooked the cat every bit as much as it had Harry. The hunter could not have failed to miss at that range. The hunted could not have failed to kill such a vulnerable prey. And yet neither had struck the fatal blow. Not this time anyway. But the cat had to be killed one way or another. Harry had seen the maddened brute rage in its eyes as it charged, had noticed the great ugly wound in its flank. In that condition, it might survive a week or so, gradually succumbing to loss of blood or hunger, a miserable, wretched death. And besides, there was no telling how many other people it might kill in its desperate quest for food. It was ironic really. Harry had resisted for so long any attempts to get him to hunt this particular tiger; it had taken the death of Ché to make him realize that it had been his job all along. Perhaps, if he had shouldered the responsibility earlier, less people would have fallen victim to the man-eater. Perhaps Mike Kirby would still be alive. And Ché . . . ah, poor little Ché! Reminding himself of what had happened only served to rekindle his grief. He could no longer force himself to eat. Setting down the food, Harry threw some fresh branches onto the fire and poked the red ashes until the flames flared up, throwing their warmth onto his face. He felt exhausted after the long day's trek and a combination of the heat of the fire and the low rhythmic chirruping of the jungle insects, served to lull him into a shallow, restless sleep in which he was plagued by terrible nightmares about Ché's death.

He awoke abruptly with the conviction that he was no longer alone. The fire had dwindled down to a low red glow, and he was reaching forward to pick up another log when a soft movement on the other side of the clearing made him freeze. He stared intently into the shadows and thought he saw the redness of the fire reflected in two crimson sparks that seemed to hover in the darkness. Curious, he very slowly picked up the firewood and dropped it into place. The flames crackled, came alive again, and there in the increased glow of light was the tiger, stretched out on the ground some fifteen feet away and staring intently across the camp fire at Harry.

Harry took a long deep breath. The cat looked to be in a bad way. His flanks were caked with dried blood and his jaws were open, while his chest pumped spasmodically in a frantic effort to draw breath. Harry could see quite clearly the creature's worn and broken yellow teeth, the thick ruffs of grey hair that framed the still noble face. There in the front foreleg was the swollen suppurated wound that only porcupine quills could cause. There was a pleading quality in the cat's eyes, a desperate searching stare that was both saddening and terrifying.

Harry glanced sideways and down, to where the loaded rifle lay, mere inches from his right hand. Beside it lay the hardly touched pots of food that Harry had picked at earlier. Slowly, hardly daring to breathe, Harry began to move his fingers closer. The tiger gave a long, low rumbling growl of warning, but Harry continued the action. He felt both frightened and elated. The tiger had crept up close as he slept and surely could have dispatched him very easily, but for some reason it had chosen to wait, to simply lie and observe the hunter in the light of the fire. Perhaps it was simply not the right time to culminate the hunt.

Harry's hand closed, not around the stock of the hunting rifle but around the container of cold meats that was already being investigated by several soldier ants. He lifted the container slowly, keeping it in view all the time. Again, the tiger growled and there was such pent-up power in the sound, the ground seemed to vibrate with the force of it. Harry swallowed hard. What he was about to do might easily be misconstrued and it was a simple enough task for the tiger to reach him, one easy leap across the short distance that separated them. Nevertheless, Harry raised his hand suddenly and threw the meat across the clearing, straight at the cat's feet. The tiger recoiled with a roar of warning, seemed on the point of running away, but then the scent of the meat reached his nostrils and lowering his head, he sniffed at the spilled contents of the container. In an instant, he had lapped the meagre contents up with his great rasping tongue. He glanced up at Harry again, as though hopeful for something else, but Harry could only shrug.

'That's all there is, old fellow,' he murmured. 'I'm sorry.'

He watched as the tiger sniffed vainly at the empty container, lapped up a couple of spilled crumbs on the ground. It would be such an easy task now to put the creature out of his misery. . . Harry's hand strayed in the direction of the rifle, but as if realizing that this was the hunter's intention the cat wheeled about and limped away into the darkness.

Harry sighed. 'Tomorrow then,' he mused. 'We'll finish it tomorrow.'

He leaned back against the tree and closed his eyes again. He felt quite secure, convinced that the tiger would not return that night. He fell quickly back into a deep sleep, and this time there were no nightmares to trouble him.

Haji crept silently into the small cave. He had not been here since the time he had found Seti's body, but the recollection had dimmed in his mind now and he only associated the place with shelter. The various scavengers of the jungle had picked the place clean of any evidence, there was not so much as a bone left to mark the incident. Haji paced restlessly up and down for a moment in the narrow confines of the cave and then flopped down to lap at his wounds for a moment. The pain was a constant torment to him, more terrible than the misery he had endured with his leg, for this was something that clawed at his guts from deep inside, he could not even reach the source of the agony. He felt weak now and closer to death than he had ever been before, yet he would not give in to it readily. He had gone to look at the old Upright earlier with the object of making a kill, but for some reason, he had been unable to follow through. It was because the Upright had *looked* at him, had gazed deeply into his eyes and no other of these strange intelligent creatures had ever done that to Haji before. The same thing had happened when he had begun an attack in the bamboo thicket that day. At the last moment those eyes had looked into his and the look had not been that of a stricken creature about to die. It had been the look of a brother, the calm peaceful gaze that one tiger gives another upon a chance meeting. The shock had been so great that Haji had veered away in surprise, had been unable to continue the attack. The same feelings had communicated themselves tonight. It was not that the Upright wasn't afraid; the strange lonely smell of terror had been on him on both occasions . . . but that look, that calm, accepting . . . almost welcoming look . . . that was what Haji could not understand. And, like any animal, he feared that which was inexplicable to him.

He gave up the vain task of lapping at his wounds and stretched out on the reassuring hardness of the cave floor, closing his eyes and giving out a low formless moan of misery. He was exhausted and, despite his discomfort, he soon drifted into a shallow, fitful doze.

He dreamed that he was a tiny puling cub again, nestling blindly up against the great reassuring warmth of his mother, in a time when his only needs were a belly full of milk and the cruel dictates of survival had not even occurred to him. He woke once just before dawn, with the firm conviction that the strange old Upright would come after him again at first light. With a growl of annoyance, he settled down again but the dream was lost to him now and he could do nothing but lie, wide-awake and racked with pain, till the first rays of light illuminated the eastern sky.

Shivering in the first light of dawn, Harry stamped the ashes of his campfire away and resumed the hunt, casting about until he picked up the trail that the cat had left the previous night. The tiger's wounds were slowing him down, and Harry felt sure that he could not have travelled too far.

344

After a couple of miles, he found a small cave, where the cat had obviously rested for the night. There were dried bloodstains on the floor where he had stretched out to sleep. From the cave mouth, the pugs led upwards to higher, rockier ground, where tracking was difficult, but luckily the cat's exertions had set the bullet wound bleeding again. The fact that the splashes were barely congealed suggested that the quarry could not be too far ahead. Harry climbed steadily upwards, stopping occasionally to catch his breath. Soon he was able to gaze down into the lushly vegetated valley, spread out some distance below him. The hours went steadily by. A little after eight o'clock, his gaze was caught by a signal flare soaring up into the sky from down in the valley. Listening intently, he thought he could just about make out the sounds of distant shouting. Clearly a search party had been mounted on his behalf. He felt rather flattered that anyone should take such trouble on his account, but nevertheless he did not check his pace.

He moved into an area of deep granite gulleys and large strewn boulders, where there was scant vegetation, but ample opportunity for a predator to take cover. The sun was growing in strength by the minute and there was not a single streak of cloud in the sky. Harry could not have asked for a more magnificent day. He found himself thinking about what he would be doing if he were at home now. Not a great deal, he decided. Reading the paper perhaps or eating a little breakfast. He wondered how Beresford was feeling right now, with the weight of Ché's death squarely on his shoulders. For the first time, he actually found himself feeling sorry for the Australian, though he could surely never forgive him for his irresponsible actions.

'But I've been irresponsible too,' he reasoned. 'Perhaps if I'd swallowed my dislike of the man and agreed to help him earlier . . .'

The trail led into a steep gulley, the site of a dry river bed. Granite walls rose sheer on either side to obscured boulder-littered ledges. Harry advanced cautiously forward. Everything was as quiet as the grave here and he had, once again, the distinct impression that the tiger was not far away. This suspicion was amplified when he could no longer spot any traces of blood directly ahead of him. It seemed likely that the cat had climbed up one of the slopes to take up a position on one of the ledges. Harry didn't much fancy the idea of staying on the river bed where the tiger might just drop onto him at any moment, so after casting hastily around for signs of blood on the inclines with no success, he decided to follow suit and climb up to the ledge himself, hoping to get a better view of the possible hiding places. He could only hope that he wasn't heading directly for the place where the tiger was concealed.

He began to move slowly upwards, his boots slipping awkwardly on the steep granite surface. It was hard going and after a few minutes, he was bathed with sweat. He was about three quarters of the way to the ledge when he abruptly realized that his luck was out. The tiger appeared from behind a large boulder directly ahead of him and came charging down the decline with a bellow of rage. Harry fumbled the rifle from his shoulder and began to swing it up into a firing position but he was slow and badly out of balance on the steep ground. The tiger's great paws struck him before he could even fire a shot, knocking him to the ground and sending him sprawling over and over, back down to the river bed. The tiger struck ground badly too, landing squarely on his injured leg and with a howl of pain, he went spinning too, to land with a heavy crash some ten yards from the place where Harry was stretched out. For a moment, neither of them moved.

Harry gave a slight groan. He had landed awkwardly on one leg and was unable to move it. Glancing up, he saw the tiger was momentarily stunned by the impact of the fall. Harry began to look desperately around for his rifle and then he spotted it, lying on the slope, some ten yards above him. He swore beneath his breath and started dragging himself towards it, gritting his teeth at the agony this induced in his left leg, which was quite obviously broken. Behind him, a low growl suggested that the tiger was recovering his senses a little too quickly for comfort. Galvanized by fear, Harry lifted himself clear of the ground and literally threw himself across the intervening space. The shock of pain as he struck the ground nearly caused him to faint, but his hands closed around the stock of the rifle and he twisted over onto his back, to stare down at the tiger. The cat was hunched at the bottom of the gully, snarling ferociously and preparing to leap upwards. There was no time to aim. Harry simply pointed the barrel downwards, between his feet, and as the tiger launched himself, he squeezed the trigger. The tiger was in mid-leap as the bullet slammed its way right down his open jaws and into his heart, killing him instantly. The leap fell short but the tiger's great weight came crashing down on Harry's chest, pinning him to the rock. The beautiful yellow eyes stared sightlessly into his own and the great open jaws were frozen in a grimace of death, mere inches from his face. Harry's head fell back and he gave a groan of mingled pain and exhaustion. He was close to fainting. He put his hands beneath the tiger's carcass and attempted to lift the body off, but it was a crushing dead weight that simply would not be moved. Harry dropped back again, gasping for breath. His senses were reeling and the terrible pain had come back into his chest. He had gashed his head on the rock during the fall and a trickle of blood was running into his eyes.

He remembered the signal flare he had seen earlier, and with one last effort he managed to pull the rifle clear of the tiger's body. Pointing the gun into the air and working the bolt each time, he managed to fire three shots before his strength finally gave out and unconsciousness came creeping in to claim him.

The last thing he saw was the tiger's snarling face, gazing at him from the midst of a rushing roaring mist, but then the image was gone and there was a blackness that took him in, offering rest and shelter from the cruel sun that was burning into his eyes. He slept and did not hear the sounds of the rescue party as they came racing along the stone-littered dryness of the river bed.

Chapter 35

Bob Beresford gazed apprehensively at the telephone booth. He glanced at his watch. Almost time. It was early morning

347

and the sun had not reached its full strength yet. The long dusty street was completely deserted. He had not slept through the long interminable night, plagued as he was by doubts and a terrible sense of guilt. Worst of all was the knowledge that he could do nothing to make amends for Ché's death. It would be on his conscience for the rest of his life. He recalled the faces of the boy's parents back at the *kampong*, when he had brought the child's lifeless body home. At first their expressions were just masks of inarticulate grief, but as Bob had stammered his clumsy explanations, those expressions had quickly turned to stares of hateful accusation. He had sobbed his apologies and escaped as quickly as possible, driving home at a dangerous speed, realizing that there was the only person in the world who could give him any solace. Lim had stayed with him since then, attending to his every need, talking with him, insisting that he could not be expected to bear the full blame for Ché's death. She had not managed to convince him of it, but at least she had made the pain more possible to sustain.

She stood beside him now, a guardian angel that he did not rightly deserve.

The telephone rang shrilly within the glass booth. Bob glanced nervously at Lim and then moved away from her, opened the door and stepped inside. He was grateful that it was not later in the day. The small glass box would be like an oven with the sun's full strength beating down onto it. The phone continued to ring. Bob stared at it for several moments, wondering vaguely why it was only now that he had chosen to take this action. Perhaps it was simply the instinctive reaction of any boy who had suffered an unexpected fall. He picked up the receiver.

An operator's clipped tones reached his ears.

'Hello, Mr Beresford!'

'Speaking.'

'Your long-distance call to Sydney, Australia.'

'Thank you.'

'Will you put your money in now, please? I am trying to connect you.'

He gorged the metal box with coins, pushing them one after the other into the slot, until he had reached the prearranged amount. There was a long silence, during which he visualized mile upon mile of metal cable, along which a tiny spark of electricity was speeding. He turned and gazed thoughtfully at Lim through the glass. She gave him a reassuring smile. Somewhere, a long way away, a telephone rang, a tiny metallic insect buzzing. It rang for what seemed an eternity and Bob was almost on the point of replacing the receiver when unexpectedly, someone picked up the phone.

Another silence. Then a woman's voice, cautious, unsure of herself.

'Hello?' The voice was painfully familiar and the sound of it made Bob's eyes fill with moisture. 'Hello, who's there?'

'Hello, Ma,' he said simply.

'Bob? Bob, is that you?' He could picture her astonishment. She must have given him up by now. When she spoke again, her voice was tremulous with emotion. 'Bob, where have you been? I thought you were angry with me . . . you never answered one of my letters . . .'

'I've been very busy, Ma,' he lied. 'But I'll be finishing up here in a week or so. I was thinking about coming home for a while . . .'

'Home? Oh yes, that would be wonderful . . . you . . . you know that Frank will be here, don't you?' she added cautiously.

'Sure. Where else would your husband be?'

She sounded relieved.

'Oh, he's a nice man, Bob, I'm sure you'll get on well with him, if you just give him a chance . . . oh lord, I can hardly believe I'm talking to you after all this time! It will be so good to see you again, Bob. I can't begin to tell you . . . when can I expect to see you?'

'I don't know for sure yet, Ma. I've got to make all the arrangements . . . but I'm looking forward to being home again. Things . . . didn't really work out too well for me here . . .' He glanced once again through the glass, and Lim was gazing hopefully at him. He nodded almost imperceptibly. 'One other thing, Ma,' he added. 'I won't be coming by myself. I'm . . . planning to bring a wife with me . . .' There was a long stunned silence on the other end of the line. 'Ma? Ma? Are you still there?'

The taxi screeched to a halt by the gates of the Kuala Hitam Army Hospital. Melissa thrust a five-dollar bill into the driver's hand and clambered out, not waiting for any change. As she hurried towards the hospital entrance, her father came out to greet her. He took her arm and escorted her inside.

'There's not much time,' he told her tonelessly. 'He's been asking for you repeatedly.' They moved along grey corridors that smelled of antiseptic.

'Is there no hope then?' asked Melissa in a small, anxious voice.

Dennis shook his head.

'The doctors say it's a miracle he's hung on this long. If the Gurkhas hadn't been so close behind him, he wouldn't have even survived the trip back. There isn't the equipment here to give him the attention he needs, but he wouldn't last out the flight to K.L. I've been with him this morning. He knows he's on the way out, but he's going with grace.'

'But why me? Why does he want to see me?'

Dennis shrugged.

'He didn't say. But listen, love, try to put on a brave face for him, eh?'

She shook her head.

'I just won't know what to say,' she reasoned.

'Try your best.' He came to a plain, black painted door and rapped politely with his knuckles. The door opened and a white-coated doctor came out.

'This is my daughter,' explained Dennis. 'How is he now?'

The doctor shook his head.

'We're losing him very quickly now. I'm afraid it's just a matter of time. You'd better go along in, Miss Tremayne.'

Melissa glanced helplessly at her father.

'Come in with me,' she pleaded, but he shook his head.

'It's you he wants to see now,' he said gravely.

Melissa nodded, took a deep breath. She was shaking. She had never been in such close proximity to death before and it frightened her. She stepped into the room and the door clicked quietly shut behind her. She stood where she was for

350

the moment, staring sadly at the figure in the bed.

Her first impression was of smallness. Harry's six-foot frame seemed to have dwindled to half its size; it was dwarfed by the great snowy immensity of the bed in which he was lying. Around the bed was hung the various paraphernalia of science; clear bottles hung on racks, tubes fed into arms, electrical machines that clicked and buzzed and all to no avail. Harry was dying and nothing could change the fact.

Melissa took a step forward. His eyes were closed and his chest rose and fell beneath the white sheets, almost imperceptibly.

'Uncle Harry?' she murmured, but at first there was no response.

'Uncle Harry . . . it's me. Melissa . . .'

His eyelids trembled, flicked open. He lay gazing up at her for a moment and then the faintest trace of a smile curved itself upon his lips.

'Melissa . . . so there you are . . .'

The voice too was small, a ghost of its former self. Melissa stepped forward again, to stand beside the bed. Instinctively, she reached out to clutch one of his hands in hers, and she felt the gentle pressure as he tried to squeeze it in a gesture of affection.

'How . . . how do you feel?' she asked and hated herself for such a stupid question.

'Oh . . . I feel . . . restful. Very restful. I hope I didn't drag you away from anything . . . important.'

'Don't be silly. I'm glad to be here . . .' She pulled up a chair and sat beside him, hardly knowing what to say.

'The tiger . . . is dead now. Did they tell you?'

She nodded.

'Ah, but the poor old devil,' sighed Harry. 'In such pain, such terrible pain. All he wanted was to rest, you see . . . and did they tell you about . . . poor little Ché?'

'Yes, they did. They said it was Bob Beresford's fault. How could I have ever felt anything for that . . . that megalomaniac . . . ?'

Harry shook his head.

'We mustn't be too hard on him,' he warned. 'The poor

351

devil will always have it on his conscience. In a way, I wish that he'd been able to get . . . that tiger. Then he would have been happy and Ché . . . Ché would still be . . .' His voice trailed away for a moment, and an expression of pain came over his features.

'Uncle Harry, are you alright? Shall I call for . . . ?'

'No no, I'm fine . . . just a little . . . discomfort now and then. Somebody trying to tell me I'm . . . outstaying my welcome, that's all.'

'You mustn't talk like that! I was speaking with the doctor just now and he said everybody was very hopeful . . .'

Harry gave a weak little chuckle.

'Pish, girl! You never could lie to me and get away with it. Remember when you were only little, and you broke a teacup at my house? Goodness, the elaborate stories you created . . . but all along . . . I knew it was you . . .'

Melissa bowed her head. A terrible ache was filling her chest and she could not prevent her eyes from filling with tears.

'Now, now . . . No crying now . . . you'll spoil that pretty face . . .'

'Oh Uncle Harry!' She tried to say something else, but her words collapsed into the formless misery of sorrow. It was several minutes before she could control herself enough to hear what he had to say.

'You were always my favourite, you know . . . you and Ché . . . now he's gone and you . . . you'll soon be off to start a new life in England. I just wanted to tell you . . . that you must forget about any mistakes you've made in the last few months . . . you're going to begin again . . . and you're going to reach the potential I know you're capable of.' He lifted his head with great effort and pointed to his bedside table. 'There . . . something for you . . . I want you to have it.'

Melissa turned to look where he was pointing. A silver chain lay on the table top, a silver chain, with a tiny Saint Christopher medallion on it. Melissa thought of the bullet-shaped pendant she had contrived to steal and she felt horribly ashamed.

'Oh, Uncle Harry,' she whispered. 'It's far too good for

352

me.'

'Nonsense, child. Please . . . keep it . . . wear it . . . and think of me . . .' His eyes seemed to widen a little and he seemed to be attempting to sit up, but he did not possess the necessary strength. 'Please . . . write to Marion for me . . . tell her . . . tell her that I lo – '

A shadow seemed to cross his face. The eyes, gentle in death, clouded and his head moved slowly back down to the pillow. The remainder of his sentence escaped as a long harsh exhalation of air. Melissa sat staring down in horror at the abruptness of the transformation. His hand was still clutched tightly around hers. With an effort, she prised the gaunt fingers away, and clutching the Saint Christopher tightly she walked quietly to the door. As she went out, Dennis and the doctor came hurrying towards her. Melissa stared at them through a film of tears and shook her head blankly. The doctor hurried into the room.

'I'll take you home,' murmured Dennis.

'Please . . . no. Can I – can I walk?'

'Well, do you think that's a good idea? You're not in a very good . . .'

'Let me walk!' she snapped, and hurried away along the corridor, wanting to be outside when the full grief of Harry's death hit her. For the moment, she was still stunned by the suddenness of it. She groped her way blindly along the corridors and out through the exit into the sunlight. She stood for a moment, gazing blankly around at the deserted barracks. This place too, was dead now. Impulsively, she kicked free of her shoes and ran across the parade ground, towards the main gates. Overhead, a grubby Union Jack fluttered forlornly at half mast. The sentry at the gate stared at her in surprise as she raced sobbing past him, but he made no attempt to stop her. Then she was out on the road, running hard between ranks of lush green vegetation, oblivious to the pain that the hot surface of the tarmac caused to her naked feet, aware only of the great aching void of misery that was rising, steadily rising within her. She had just witnessed the death of the finest man she had ever known and she could not rid herself of the awful conviction that in the last months of his life, she had treated him shabbily, blinded as she was by her infatuation for a younger and far less worthy man.

The misery in her chest welled into a great bitter balloon, that burst abruptly, flooding her with sorrow. She slowed to a walk, her shoulders heaving with uncontrollable emotion. She walked blindly onwards, blundering occasionally into the overhanging bushes at the edge of the road, her eyes blurred with tears, as she gradually sobbed the grief away. Harry was dead. Nothing could ever make the loss seem easier to bear.

She walked onwards, her head bowed and as she put distance behind her, so bit by bit, she gained control of herself, fell into a grim melancholic silence. She wiped her eyes on the sleeve of her blouse, smearing the white cotton with trails of black mascara. She stared impassively along the deserted road ahead. Now, more than anything else, she wanted to be away from this place, away from the humid, unrelenting heat, away from the strange dusky people and their ancient customs which she had never learned to understand. Harry had been a part of it all, he belonged somehow, but the day of the Tuan was over with now and Melissa wanted no part of it. What was it Harry had called himself that time . . . ? Oh yes – the last dinosaur in this patch of swamp. The edges of Melissa's mouth curved upwards the smallest amount as she began to remember . . .

She was approaching Kampong Panjang when she first became aware of the sounds, distant at first, but rapidly growing in volume. It was a clamour, a rhythmic cacophony, an exhaltation. She quickened her step a little, puzzled and intrigued. The noise swelled. Now she could make out the sounds of voices, making a rowdy incomprehensible chant.

Around a curve in the road came the tiger. Melissa was momentarily shocked by the sight of the dark-striped tawny body, curving and threshing in the brilliant sunlight. The body was supported on stout poles that had been impaled into chest and groin and throat and paws; beneath the heavy body, a series of men danced along, manipulating the poles, oblivious to the dark splashes of gore that rained down their half-naked bodies. The tiger was thus imbued with new life, it lurched and bobbed in a pathetic semblance of life, its great jaws gaping, its swollen tongue lolling out, surrounded by a filthy halo of buzzing flies. In the wake of the slain tiger followed a noisy jubilant host of villagers, many of them beating on drums and tin cans, all of them shouting and singing about the death of the man-eater.

Melissa stood hesitantly in the middle of the road as the procession bore down on her. She stared in horrified fascination at the great dead beast that seemed to hover, godlike, above her. The pole carriers, spotting the lone white girl, swooped forward in a sudden whooping run, shouting gleefully at her; but she could not understand them and felt only threatened by their exhortations. She began to back slowly away, but then they were up with her, they were circling around her laughing uproariously and the tiger was so close, she could smell the stink of its already decomposing flesh.

'Please . . . let me go. I – '

But now the crowd was pressing in around her, she was at the centre of a great dusky circle of jostling bodies and flashing teeth. She glanced around in a panic, as arms pulled at her, invited her to join the procession. She glanced up and the tiger swayed in a bloated dance of death, the once magnificent eyes staring sightlessly at the puny creatures gathered below.

A sensation of revulsion filled Melissa. She had but recently seen the death of one old tiger and at least he had been allowed the dignity, the sanctity of rest. For this beast, the path would not be so smooth. When the villagers tired of parading the heavy carcass around, the body would be torn up to provide keepsakes and souvenirs, medicines and charms. If by some miracle the hide was left intact, it would doubtless end up in some souvenir shop in Kuala Trengganu, being ogled by a succession of silly tourists. Whatever was left would be thrown out in the scrub, for the various other scavengers to dispose of. For all his depredations, the tiger surely deserved something better than that.

Lost in noisy chaos, Melissa found her own voice. She began to scream a vicious collection of curses as she pushed her way roughly through the crowd seeking escape. The villagers fell obediently aside, shocked and bewildered by her reaction. Some of them paused to stare at her as she burst out of the crowd and ran away along the road, but the white girl was quickly forgotten. The villagers closed ranks and moved rowdily onwards, beating their drums, chanting their chants. Above them, the tiger god danced, a tragic, jerky ballet. In life he had always gone his own way; only in death could he be made to dance to someone else's tune.

Melissa slowed to a walk again. She did not glance back at the procession as it moved on in the direction of Kuala Hitam. She wiped the last vestiges of tears from her eyes with her already sodden sleeve, and then, lifting her head, she began to move on in the direction of home, walking with a newfound spring in her step. For the first time in many long months, she felt that she really knew where she was going. She began to make plans for her return to England and so occupied was she with her thoughts, that she did not notice the approach of her father's car until it was right beside her. She turned, gazed in at Dennis.

'Better now?' he asked her cautiously.

She nodded, forcing a smile.

'Better,' she replied. 'Let's go, shall we?'

She opened the door and climbed in beside him. She could see from the redness of his eyes that he had been crying too and she was momentarily shocked by the realization that her father was capable of such a thing. They sat in the car for a few moments, neither of them saying a word, both realizing that there was very little they *could* say. Both of them felt a profound sense of *ending*, as though something very important had abruptly finished.

'Did you see the procession?' asked Dennis at last. 'The tiger . . . ?' His voice was hoarse and heavy with grief. Melissa nodded. She watched her father for a moment, seeing that he wanted to say more, but that he could not find words. She reached out and squeezed his hand gently.

'It's over,' she said simply.

'Yes.' Dennis nodded. He reached out and turned the ignition key. The engine rumbled into life.

'I wonder . . .' he murmured, 'who'll tell Marion?'

'*I* will,' replied Melissa without hesitation. 'Harry asked

356

me to tell her.'

Dennis glanced at her in surprise, noting the new look of determination in her eyes. She looked away from him and stared down at a small silver medallion she held in her hand. It had been clenched in her fist all this time, so tightly that it had left an angry red imprint on the soft flesh of her palm. 'He wanted me to have this,' she said softly.

Dennis nodded. He let out the clutch and the car accelerated away down the road. They drove home in silence.

Timah approached the cave cautiously. Instinct had brought her to this place, just as instinct told her that the time was near, that the increasing movements deep in her belly could be contained no more. She hesitated in the entrance of the cave, staring into the shadows and snuffing the air nervously. But there was no occupant. She slipped gratefully into its cool sanctuary and paced restlessly up and down in its narrow confines for several minutes. Haji had been here recently, she could still detect faint traces of his smell and this comforted her, for it was her first litter and she was anxious. After a while, she sat down in the farthest corner with her back up against the granite wall, and lifting one back leg she reached down to lick at her vulva. This stimulated pain there, but she bore it in silence, began to exert pressure on her hind quarters, pausing every so often to repeat the licking process.

After ten minutes, the head of the first cub had emerged from her body, red and unidentifiable in its fleshy sac. She increased the pressure and the protuberance slid smoothly out and dropped to the floor of the cave. Two more cubs followed at ten-minute intervals and only the last provided her with any real problems. It was lying awkwardly in her womb, and she was obliged to sit with one back leg raised, exerting powerful pressure before she could expel the sac. Only then did she set about freeing the cubs from their bloody prisons, lapping up the sacs, umbilical cords and placenta that would provide her with much needed nourishment over the next few days. She licked the cubs clean with her great rasping tongue, rejoicing at the wriggling motions they made in response. They all seemed healthy enough, blind, mewing little bundles that began to grope their way towards Timah's milk-filled teats the moment she stretched herself out.

Outside the light was failing fast as the brief twilight advanced. Tired from her exertions, Timah settled down in the shadowy sanctuary, while the cubs moved warm and impatient against her belly, their toothless little jaws seeking nourishment. The anxieties of the last few hours had gone now and a great contentment settled over her. She lowered her head to the cave floor and settled quickly into a deep dreamless slumber. She woke once, some hours later, when one of the cubs moved restlessly in his sleep and tumbled away from his two sisters. Timah raised her head for a moment and nudged him gently back to the reassuring warmth of her flank. She glanced calmly out to the mouth of the cave, but the unfathomable darkness there did not frighten her. It was an easy enough matter to find sleep again.

Glossary

amah servant
berok pig-tailed monkey
bomoh witch doctor
chit-chat gecko or house lizard
gaur wild buffalo
harimau tiger
kampong village
kris ceremonial dagger
machan a tree-platform
nanti sikit creepers (literally 'wait a while')
padi wet land in which rice is grown
parang long-bladed jungle knife
penghulu village headman
rusa deer
san fu trouser suit
seladang wild cattle
selamat petang good evening
Sepak Takraw game played with a rattan football
Si-Pudong Old Hairy Face
terima kasih thank you
tok belang tiger (literally 'striped prince')
tok landak porcupine
trishaw bicycle-driven taxi